FireLight
AND
FRØST

Haunting tales for long nights

J. T. Croft

ELMFIRE PRESS

First published by Elmfire Press 2022

Copyright ©2022 by J. T. Croft

First edition

ISBN 978-1-7397277-7-2

Cover design by Fay Lane:

www.faylane.com

Elmfire Press

Unit 35590,

PO Box 15113,

Birmingham, B2 2NJ

United Kingdom

www.jtcroft.com

CONTENTS

PREFACE

The tales within are chronologically arranged to span the traditional winter period from late November (*The Skerry Rose*) through to my own personal and long-held association with the season's end on Valentine's Day (*Entwined*). With notable, summer exceptions, such as *August Heat* by W. F. Harvey, and *The Man Who Went Too Far* by E. F. Benson, western Gothic and ghost story fiction lend themselves to dark nights and firesides.

I always come to the season of firelight and frost with a renewed creativity in my own writing and anticipation to revisit and discover classic tales emblematic of my favourite parts of the festive season. I'm with Jerome K Jerome when he writes in *Told After Supper* (1891): '*Whenever five or six English-speaking people meet around a fire on Christmas Eve, they start telling each other ghost stories.*'

The stories within this collection have grown in the telling, not only indulging my own passions (and word count) for character building but also by absorbing feedback from readers who love my own little niche of Gothic fantasy fiction: *more heart-tugging, romantic and human elements please, longer stories, flawed protagonists, all hand tied with a supernatural bow and delivered with unexpected twists and turns. Oh, and don't forget to add a pinch of 'frost'...*

No problem.

Enjoy the long nights and let in the 'frost' to share the pages beside your own firelight, because even if you don't believe in ghosts, it's okay to be moved and haunted by them.

J. T. Croft
November 2022

ACKNOWLEDGMENTS

For the lights that burn brightly throughout
our own personal winters

To my Advance Reader Team, *The Muses*:

Audrey Adamson
Siobhan Allen
Richard Brulotte
Tracey Bryant
Ali Christie
Laura Coveney
Matthew Coxall
Karen Furness
Julian Grant
Lana Kamennof-Sine
Daniel Nobles
Christine Ruiz Noriega-Hollnbuchner
Rosa Reyes
Jackie Tansky

THE SKERRY ROSE

'Are you frightened, lad?' said the pilot, urging the tiller hard to starboard against the Atlantic swell to position the prow toward the lonely isle. Seated at the bow, and clutching a salt-rusted rollick, Jack lost sight of the promontory and its granite lighthouse as the boat dived into the valley between the mountainous waves.

'No.'

The hard-working *put-put* of the outboard motor all but drowned out his reply aided by the howling wind, raucous gulls and crashing waves that threatened to turn over the small bobbing tender three miles out into Skerry Sound.

'You should be,' shouted the man, putting away his pipe now that the rip tide was upon them. Navigating the treacherous stretch of Hebridean seas took heart at the best of times, but the gales had come early and stayed late, forcing the transport vessel to brave waters unaccustomed to its design or the skill of its master. Jack glanced back as the pilot fought for mastery over the sea, his weathered, salt-stung face alert with the inner frisson of calculated risk in a seasoned sailor transporting men and provisions to this isolated spot.

Jack wondered if the question was in part to settle the older man's own nerves.

'If we make it to the cove,' continued the pilot, eyes focussed ahead to avoid the litter of jagged granite teeth bearing from the waves, 'you'll need courage, faith, and over-coming fear in abundance on Skerry Ròs. Not to mention the witch.'

'Hush, Seamus,' said the only other passenger, huddled beneath a segment of the tarpaulin amid the supply crates and carry-alls necessary to automate the lighthouse and relieve the two men already a fortnight overdue because of the November gales.

'Go easy on the lad. There's many a man with more summers than he that wouldn't have set foot into this leaking tub or to visit the isle even just for the week we are there. He's made of sterner stuff than you were at his age.'

The prow rode the steep rise of the next wave and Jack shut his eyes as the boat crested the watery arête, glad to have his back to the pilot and the relief lighthouse keeper. For a moment he could see the rocky shore clearer and closer, making out the black maw of a cave as the vessel sought for the narrow channel in which to offload the men and its cargo. Two men, seeking deliverance from their purgatory and the promise of home comforts back on shore, waved from the promontory. The boat plunged downwards, lifting the propeller of the motor into the air, spinning wild and shrill like a banshee, until the wooden gig slid to the base of the next foaming trough and the high revving rotating brass blades re-engaged with the cold, dark sea.

The pilot staggered with the sudden lurch and whistled to challenge the gale.

'What do you reckon, McConnell?' he said. 'As bad as 1912? The men on the quay said the weather will get worse before it gets better; I'm not coming out again if it stays like this.'

The old lighthouse keeper scratched at the heavy thatch on his chin. 'Maybe – that was over twenty years ago and the memory dims, even if the tales that spring from it at Macready's bar grow and grow, like your portage fees. Winston was there with me and will stand by my word that the waves reached the crest of the beacon, four floors high, blowing out the window and casting rotten storm fish and weed throughout the place. The water gushed down the stairs like a waterfall soaking everything in the blessed place.'

'Are you sure the stink wasn't him?' laughed the pilot. 'I bet he's glad he broke his leg on that charabanc step and is even now eating Cullen skink, with a dram or two, in the warm and the dry. Character building for the boy, though. Wherever did you find him?'

With the mention of food, Jack leaned over the side, no longer caring about his pride on this first journey to the Skerry. He retched, snatching glimpses of the heads of seals bobbing and heaving with the motion of the waves making his stomach worse. Laughter erupted from the direction of the tiller.

'You've brought a whelp, McConnell! There's neither hair about his chin or ink upon his arm—'

'He's left Carrigh a boy and will return a man,' interrupted the keeper. 'And I'll set the first tattoo upon his skin when we return.' An unforeseen appearance of rock close to the bow provoked a sudden veer to port. 'Look to your boat, Seamus, and weary us no more with your speech!'

The keeper lurched forward to drag Jack from the edge as the boat listed in response. 'Best stay this side, lad. If the seals don't eat you, the sea will drown you and carry you to the Americas.' He released the young man and put a hand on his chest. 'We lamplighters are creatures of the land, and we

3

are in her domain, but she will not claim either of us today while I still draw breath.'

'How far, Mr McConnell?' asked Jack wiping the bile from his mouth and pulling up the coarse woollen scarf wrapped below his waxed sou'wester.

'Not far, we've made the channel and things will go easier from here. You'll be the last wickie on Skerry Ròs and I the last keeper now that the beacon will be automated. It is a place that will never outgrow the impact it has to change a man or his perspectives; remember that. Do not be afeared, lad. You'll be home in time to celebrate St Andrew's Day with young Catriona Macready, and with a tale to tell.'

The swell eased, cut off from the Atlantic by the shielding sea shadow of the small island of Skerry Ròs. Barely a quarter mile long and wide, the ground sloped haphazardly down from the high lighthouse promontory to shingle and sand pocketed coves bounded by banded and impregnable Lewisian gneiss. The alternating light and dark layers of crystalline rock stood firm against the monstrous surf on the seaward side showering the rough grass and broken rocky splinters with seawater. The only other living things apart from the resident keeper and his assistant were a few wild sheep and goats grazing near a reeded freshwater pool, roughly central in the isle. It shone like a glassy, water-laden eye stinging from the salt-laden spray.

Two men waved from the inlet to a nearby cove like liberated convicts, directing the landing and steering the pilot to an ancient iron cast metal grille that jutted out on angled brackets that spilled rusted tears down the face of the rock. The man at the tiller cast them the rope and cut the engine, watching as the crew tugged in unison to land the craft against the makeshift metal quay. The boat rose and fell for the last time until it lay sheltered and secure against the seaweed-strewn platform. Small cliff steps led up to the static world of stone and safety and Jack wobbled to his feet, gingerly testing the give in the metalwork before landing for the first time on Skerry Ròs.

Hurried by the pilot's insistence that all normal courtesy and procedures would need to be abandoned, they set about unloading the boat of its stores, fuel and crated boxes of equipment in a five-man chain. The boatman would not spend a single night on the Witch's Isle with the weather set to deteriorate further. There was talk of storm force for many days and a November to remember according to the ancient mariners that shuddered at the sky from the safety, firelight, and whisky of Carrigh's only inn.

'Telegraph's down' shouted the retreating keeper as he handed his keys and log book to McConnell. He raced to join his companion already seated among their duffle bags, calling back with hands about his mouth. 'Mast blew out to sea two nights ago; you're on your own till this hell blows itself out. Be careful, Dougal!'

The pilot started the motor, and they cast off, pulling round with the oars to speed the turn and make their way out to the sound and the three miles home. A moan, carried on the wind like a deep and mournful bassoon, hurried their work.

McConnell rested a hand on the young man's shoulders calming the uncertainty. 'Mhairi's pipe, he said pointing to a distant stretch of the coast. Jack turned as a spout of water sprayed into the sky, several hundred metres inland, accompanied by another booming low note. 'It's only a blow hole.'

Jack nodded, relieved at the explanation while McConnell took a long look at the clouds, bracing himself against the rope balustrade suspended through iron rings on the narrow stepped ledge. Jack saw the concern mellow into a grim smile.

'They'll have a rougher time of it on the way back with less ballast,' he said stepping over the cargo-like jetsam that littered the landing at the top of the cove. 'Let's leave the crates and bags for later. It doesn't smell, sound or taste like rain just yet, but we'll freeze to death if we don't get into the warm for a bit.'

Jack shouldered his stuffed duffel, a donated, faded relic of his uncle's foray into Flanders two decades earlier. All he owned for the foreseeable future was on his back; everything he relied upon shuffled before him towards the great, smooth-skinned edifice towering some hundred yards ahead. The old, gruff keeper, a fixture as tough and enduring as the lighthouse itself, steadied himself through chisel-channelled steps out of the upper promontory rock. Jack stared at the great tower, giddy with vertigo.

All his life it had been a distant candle on the horizon from his small village just outside Carrigh; now he was a hastily arranged keeper's assistant, a wick-trimmer, lamp-lighter, clock winder, and cook because of the injury to the other, more experienced man. Jack had jumped at the chance, one week prior, when the seas were calm before the storms had arrived. He shook with cold, glad that it hid the fear of accepting the work despite the attempts by superstitious men to dissuade him. Cowardice was cheap, and Jack glanced apprehensively ahead, ready to pay the steep price of premature entry into manhood among his peers.

The whitewashed tower, stained and weathered, reached for the sky like a budding Babel. There were three floors plus the beacon, the room at just over one hundred and twenty feet housing the lamp, and a narrow catwalk gallery. A series of narrow, fixed windows speckled the smooth, mitred granite revealing the storerooms, living quarters, and winding room for the clockwork mechanism. A single ancillary block lay encrusted to the far side like a man-made barnacle housing the gas generator with piles of slaked lime – the spent slurry of the carbide gas generator, heaped alongside. It seeped and coated the rock below like guano graffiti scrawls. Jack turned toward the mainland finding only a sheet of grey where the sea and sky met shielding the coast of Lewis, and home, from his gaze.

McConnell dragged himself up the final set of rope-assisted steps to stand at the rusted door. The lighthouse would be their home for many days, and unable to find any solace or comfort from the island about him, he saw it for what it truly was to those that manned the toughest gig on Trinity House's register – a powerful and immutable sentinel whose belly offered warmth, protection, and total isolation from everything one had known.

McConnell turned to see the pensive sense of awe and followed the young man's eyes to the beacon far above. 'I feel it too, my lad. You never quite get used to her and just when you think you'll never spend another day entombed in one of Stevenson's needles, you end up counting the days back on shore till you can be standing here all over again. The old girl is not as tall or grand as Eddystone or Bishop's Rock, but she's the most beautiful.' He pointed to the tangled mass of angled metal and cable near the outbuilding. 'You must be careful, lad. That's the old telegraph, and where the mast is now, God only knows. This storm is set for the rest of the week.' He grabbed at the oilskin, pulling Jack close. 'There will be no help to come unless it be a week on Thursday if anything happens to you. Do you understand?'

Jack nodded, twisting round as the deep, resonant sound of the blow hole boomed like a fog horn. 'What's that?' he said pointing to the southern edge of the isle. The ruin of a long-deserted croft stood, partially roofless and speckled about with stunted, leafless trees within collapsed walled rings of dry stone. 'Did someone farm here?'

McConnell clutched at the rope and sighed, audible even

above the freakish gusts that threatened to lift them both from the rock.

'Yes. God rest her soul,' he said raising a finger in warning. 'Don't you go poking about down there among her house and herbs. There're poison plants as well and things buried that shouldn't be disturbed.'

Jack nodded. 'What things?' he said, uncomfortably reminded of the pilot's superstitions. Everyone knew the stories of the old woman of the isle who talked to seals, crossed the waters of the sound at Samhain riding her pet goat, and caused the wrecking of ships if children were naughty and did not eat their neeps.

'The Skerry Rose,' said the old keeper, scratching at his silver-streaked, black beard as though the very banded granite beneath him had made its way through his bones and out onto his very chin. 'The tale can wait – let's get inside, out of this devil's breeze. There's work to do, but first things first. I'll show you where we hid the whisky from the wreck in 1923 – after ten years there aren't many crates left, but I think you've earned a dram.'

The lighthouse was highly labour intensive. After several days, Jack soon discovered the beacon had to be tended and serviced constantly throughout the short hours of daylight in readiness for the long, howling night and a few blessed hours of sleep. The lenses and reflectors had to be polished, the rotating mechanism had to be kept wound and everything that moved required oiling or feeding. The aged mechanical components that made up the clockwork heart were especially temperamental and seemed eager to break down as soon as the pair left for another task.

'Automated, my arse,' swore McConnell to the empty

room above as they climbed the stairs for the umpteenth time to tend or fix the petulant device. 'Nothing but a spoiled child after its mother, aren't you?'

Jack had taken several days to get used to how the man often spoke to the lighthouse in various moods. Sometimes strict and paternally when things went ill, gentle and comforting when he thought he was alone. He mewed like one half of an old married couple that bicker and bluster, each knowing they have grown so inseparable as to make peace moments later with soft eyes and tender speech. Isolation with the sardonic keeper had been Jack's chief anxiety, but the work was so constant and consuming that all such worries vanished, replaced by the incremental assault on his young body. His burning thighs protested against the repeated ascents to the upper levels and even when he caught moments outside on the level pad of the generator house, his body was buffeted and bludgeoned like a sea-tossed schooner.

The worst parts of the day were spent within the small ancillary outhouse. The generator needed to be topped up with calcium carbide chips, dusty and smelly, and Jack, during his first instructive visit a few days after their arrival, had screwed his face with the pungent, pre-filtered impurities and the cloying heat radiating from the chemical reaction creating the gas. McConnell looked unsympathetically at his discomfort.

'Can't you smell it?' said Jack pinching his nose.

The keeper shook his head. 'Can't smell or taste anything since the bout of Spanish flu that nearly killed me in 1920, which is just as well considering the meal you cooked last night.' He took out his pipe and rapped Jack on the head with the cupped end before refilling it with moist, acrid tobacco. 'Sometimes I can recall the taste of single malt before it evaporates in my mind like ether, but my old tongue can still just make out the bitterness of black Spanish shag.' He stepped back, shielding his struck match from the gale and closing his hand so tightly around the proto ember that Jack thought the man's whole hand was alight from the smoke straining through his clasped, calloused fingers. McConnell grasped the match, putting it out in his free hand before opening it rapidly like an exploding shell, sending the charred chip of wood adrift on the wind. 'Need to be careful around acetylene, Jack. Liable to go boom if you don't have your wits about you.'

The slaked lime had to be cleaned out from beneath the water tank that supplied the controlled flow of water dripping onto the carbide. Through a filter and thence across a short, chiselled channel, the pipe entered the lighthouse, heading for the beacon high above and feeding the gas mantle of the lamp. Through the four floors, it finally met the sun valve and its glass-imprisoned black rod that cooled during the night opening the flow of gas to the permanently lit pilot flame, sparking the light as darkness fell and danger rose. As night receded and the wan, weak warmth of dawn once more affected the black body of the rod, the device expanded, closing the valve and shutting off the supply of fuel, turning the venerable lighthouse into a mere day marker.

'Whitewashed the entire village has that,' said McConnell pointing at the useful waste by-product and puffing on the lit tobacco. The glede glowed like his own portable lighthouse as Jack wheeled the barrow of cement-like slurry to the dumping ground, near to the hidden crannied crook that stored the crates of flotsam whisky.

'We hid it there because no one has a mind to walk through that sludge without cause,' said McConnell, overlooking the edge and the narrow ledge that led downwards. 'And if they do, then the thief's footprints are present for me to see. It's awful stuff to get off your boots.'

'Who knows about it?' said Jack sweating with the exertion, shivering as it chilled inside his heavy, waxed leather coat, 'and why are you telling me?'

'Only you, Winston and I; it's our investment you see. Whatever we haven't drunk over the years we aim to collect with a clever, trustworthy and fit young man who can keep his mouth shut and isn't afraid of heights or narrow places – I'm too old to keep going down there and there are a few bottles stashed in the false floor of the storeroom. I talked it through with him and we'd be offering such a man a generous commission. We've only to wait a few more weeks till the island is deserted, at least until the men come to lay the cable to electrify the old girl.'

'Isn't that smuggling?' said Jack naively, and resentful that he may have been picked for the job on other merits than simple lighthouse duties.

McConnell laughed. 'I prefer the term "moonlighting", but I am as serious as a Presbyterian about drinking on duty, most of the time. Don't get any ideas – the glass last night was medicinal.'

McConnell staggered back to the lighthouse against the westerly gale and Jack scanned the horizon for any glimpse of the mainland shore and its brilliant sands, as white as any quicklime. Infrequent snatches of hinted-at cliffs flitted between large waves and a sea-soaked sky. His spirits sank. Even from the spyglass in the beacon on the previous evening, he could barely make out the twinkling lights of home.

The deep firing of the blow hole brought him back to the gulls and gale with an adrenalin-fuelled suddenness. A movement, from the ruined croft, triggered his peripheral vision, and he turned to shield his watery eyes. For a moment he thought he caught the semblance of a figure, waving something akin to a flag or sheet as though to attract attention or deliver a warning. His heart thumped with uncertainty and a little fear at the idea of someone else, so close, being part of this banishment but nothing revealed itself apart from the sullen movements of the wild sheep and the occasional flight of sea foam bubbling from the turbulent blow hole like a salty washing tub.

Sudden numbness in his hands encouraged the laying of his palms to the warm generator and he stood for a while like an evangelist trying to raise his own personal Lazarus. A glance sideways revealed the pipe exiting the building. Jack followed it up the exterior wall, crusted, rusted and coated with lumps of ice around the rotten clasps where the heat of the virgin gas could not penetrate. He picked off a lump, bringing with it several flakes of rust. Levering off several further rotten layers reaching back onto the pipe he stopped, conscious of the finite eighth of an inch thickness, now much reduced after nearly eighty years of exposure to the elements, and his own bored playfulness. Pipework in the lighthouse, degraded by damp and steam from decades of countless boiled kettles and the sea air was in a similar condition and on every level around the ring cut into the floor through which it passed, flakes and fragments fell and lay like spent rose petals. He glanced up at the lighthouse, superficially indomitable and unchanged in its golden years, but Jack could see its internal organs were haemorrhaging, its main pipe-like artery varicose and in need of repair. Now was a good time to retreat from this place and let the ministry have its automatic station.

The sense of being watched caused him to turn once more in the croft's direction.

Nothing.

A glance out in the sheltered cove confirmed his suspicions. On the heaving surface bobbed the head of a large seal, watchful and curious with large patches of pale mottling about its rubbery skin. Jack leaned down, considering the toss of a stone before the gruff call of McConnell from high above brought him to attention.

'Leave it be, lad,' he shouted from the exterior gallery, as though aware of the intent. 'We need no more bad luck; now come inside and help me grease the chariot wheel beneath the Fresnel lens.'

———

'Could there be anyone else on the island, apart from us?' asked Jack, scrubbing at the crockery in the tepid water of the wash bucket. The unsuccessful culinary spectacular of tinned peaches, pickles, and peppermint tablet was thankfully over and the gloom of the living quarters, broken only by the two paraffin safety lamps scattering the men's shadows across the far wall, pressed close enough to quell all lightness of conversation. It was a question he had been meaning to ask all night, and the opportunity of broaching the subject had yet to appear. He was about to repeat it assuming the partially deaf keeper had not heard.

At last, McConnell peered over the top of his reading glasses and shut his log. He withdrew his feet from the rough wooden table at the centre of the circular living and sleeping chamber and scratched at his arthritic fingers.

'You all ask that question eventually. I thought you'd ask it sooner, perhaps after your first night on Skerry Ròs.'

Jack wiped his hands on a dirty rag and checked the sleeping coals of the stove, air starved to prevent any hazardous flame, or meaningful warmth. 'What I meant was, after all these years, would you know if there was someone else on the island?'

'Yes,' said the keeper sharply, 'and there isn't.' He softened his tone and held up a hand in pardon. 'If it makes you feel any better, I asked the same question on my first visit and long before you did.'

Jack dragged out a chair to sit nearer to the stove.

'It's like you are being watched,' said McConnell. 'Is that how you feel?'

'Yes. Like there's someone there just at the edge of sight, but not when you turn to look.'

The keeper stroked his beard and pocketed his glasses, perching upright, ready to talk.

'Everyone who comes here feels it, lad. Perhaps every wickie gets it wherever they watch across these isles from the Scillies to the Faroes. It's the isolation; plays tricks with the mind. Men have gone mad with it, which is one reason they lessened the time offshore. It used to be six weeks when I first started, sometimes more if they couldn't get to you. That was before the old queen died.'

'I think a fortnight would be more than enough for me,' said Jack, rubbing the warmth into his hands and glancing at the drawings and sketches pinned to the crumbling, plastered wall. 'What will you do when all is over and there is no more keeping to be done?'

McConnell puckered his lips and stared at the stains on the floorboards between his feet.

'There'll always be a need for someone to come out here, so maybe I'll do that if I can endure that fool, Seamus Monaghan, and his leaking bathtub of a boat. Winston and I will have our pensions providing we keep our noses clean in the remaining days. There's our little investment I told you about, and a lot of talking, walking and drinking to be done.' He followed the young man's gaze to the clippings and charts decorating the wall. 'There's also a lot of remembering to do.'

'You'll miss it, won't you?' added Jack.

McConnell sighed and nodded. 'And what about you, lad?

You have your whole life ahead of you – what's next for the last wickie of the Witch's Isle?'

'I thought of becoming a sailor like my father...'

'You don't sound very convinced,' said McConnell placing a hand on the rusting artery of the gas feed pipe. 'When was the last time you or your mam saw hide or hair of him? Suriname or some such place wasn't it, this time?'

Jack thought back to a cool April morning when, for a brief few days his father had returned, laden with trinkets, money and sweet talk to offset the time spent at sea and in foreign lands. A few dawns later, he was gone, leaving Jack questioning if the encounter had been nothing more than a phantom. His mother stooped and sighed as the fuel to her inner light was sealed off once more, resuming her watch on the narrow cobbles outside the house for the man's next appearance, like a keeper vigilant for a ship in distress upon the sea.

'Easter,' said Jack with a shrug.

'And what does your mam and Catriona Macready think of you following suit?'

Jack tugged at an ear and inspected the sketch of a young woman standing tall and proud with a lamb in her arms, a shawl about her shoulders and sea-blown upon an alluded to section of exposed rock near the lighthouse. The drawing was old and mottled, stained from years of lamp soot and damp air. Handsome but hardy, the woman gazed out toward Seal Rock, long the scourge of passing vessels rounding the Hebridean coast from Liverpool to Scandinavia that were too large or spendthrift to navigate the Caledonian Canal.

McConnell grunted his amusement. 'I see, they have yet to be briefed. Don't go out there assuming all of life is beyond the horizon.' He slapped the corroded pipe to gain Jack's attention, sending a shuddering harmonic throughout the tower. Flakes of rust fell to the floor and McConnell rubbed the oxide from his palms. 'You know what a sailor sees for most of his life?' he asked rhetorically, 'nothing but the sea and the sky. That's not living, lad, that's waiting whilst moving. There must be something else you're good at, a calling that inspires you?'

Jack glanced over at the shelf and the meagre spine-split stack of mouldy books. 'I'd like to write, but I don't feel I have anything yet to record, which is why I thought of travelling.'

'Write about life,' said McConnell, 'in the here and now. I dare say even I might make a few admirable paragraphs one of these days when folk grow too soft to remember days gone by. Document your experiences or things that might never come again. The world is changing, and old tales get lost...' He tapped the sketch of the young woman upon the wall.

'It's her, isn't it?' said Jack. 'The woman you call the Skerry Rose. She lived in the croft, didn't she?'

'Yes,' said McConnell digging his dirty hands into his dusty corduroys. 'Her name was Mhairi, and it was a long time ago.'

'What happened to her, and where did she come from?'

The keeper retreated to a drawer in the pitch pine dresser, removing an old leather binding incorporating many loose pages. He shuffled a chair closer to the stove and sat down, flipping through the charcoal drawings that exposed themselves at every turn. Most depicted the lighthouse from different aspects and were drawn by many hands, some of which, as McConnell pointed out, were by former keepers now deceased. Jack pointed at an illustration of the croft in bygone days, roofed and adorned with hanging nets, lobster pots, drying kelp and baskets of all manner of foodstuffs. A modest plot or garden lay to one side with small trees bearing what appeared to be hardy damson plums.

McConnell smiled wistfully. 'She died a long time ago,

long before you were born; the Skerry Rose was here before I had ever set foot upon the isle. Mhairi was getting on when I first clapped eyes on her, but that drawing on the wall was made a good many years before that and is an accurate likeness. Some great beauty, come from the sea they said – a seal wife.'

'A what?' said Jack, straining to hear the keeper's voice, hushed, and doused by the waves battering for entry to the second floor to hear the whispering tale for themselves.

'A selkie, lad, a fey creature, seal-born of the sea who came to the island in human form to marry a mortal man and have children. However, her seal mate followed her and demanded she return to the sea with him, or he would take the bairns. Mhairi refused, and so her mate killed the little ones and left her broken-hearted on the Skerry. In her grief, she turned to dark magic and became known as a witch.' The keeper blushed. 'It's just a fable, told when folk were simpler.'

'She lived by herself, alone on an island with two wickies?'

McConnell perceived the meaning. 'No man ever touched her as far as I was ever told. We are a superstitious lot and talk of her being a witch was the best thing to keep herself clean from the likes of us. A woman skilled in herb lore also knows a thing or two about poisons – many of which serve the same function – only the dose is different.'

'She kept to herself, then?'

'Pretty much. She spoke little Gaelic or anything else, and we guessed she came from foreign parts, but Mhairi was mighty proficient as a healer and saved the lives of many men over the years, be they washed up from the sea or fool enough to get injured working here.' McConnell rolled up his calico shirt to reveal a faint, hairless scar on his upper arm. 'See that? Cut myself as a youngster on that damn platform. Near bled to death and would have perished from gangrene or worse if she hadn't nursed me back to health.

She stitched up my arm as able as any gentleman's tailor in Inverness.'

Jack winced as the old man reinstated the sleeve and buttoned the cuff. 'Did it hurt?'

'Surprisingly no, not with whatever she gave me to sip an hour before. I recall the severe beating, mind, from old McGinnis when I got back to shore, him having to do all the work while I was laying idle in the croft.'

'What was it like inside?' said Jack taking the drawings and continuing through the scenes familiar and unknown.

'Mighty busy, like an apothecary's shop. Stuff hanging from the ceilings, skins, herbs, and bones of all sorts. To tell the truth, I half believed the tales at the time, but I got better, and those that she helped sent her things in gratitude.'

He dropped his head to suppress a smile.

'What's funny?' said Jack, raising an infectious turn of his lip.

'They used to send her nice things like dresses, embroidered mattress covers, and linen, but she would cut them up to make tourniquets, wrappings for the newborn lambs, or drying cloths for her seaweed as if she didn't know what to do with 'em. After that, they gifted her knitting needles and ointments, plants she craved from her depictions dispatched back with us, and lots of brown sugar tablet; she had a sweet tooth, if I recall. They once sent the minister over with us but he was so ill with the crossing, and what he found over there, that he declared some folk would be best left alone, free in the eyes of God to come to him in their own good time. He never came again, which only added to the tales of the Witch's Isle. She was a kind soul, and I had many a heated moment with folks back on the mainland who said otherwise.' He raised his hand into a fist. 'Those that know don't talk, and those that talk don't know.'

Jack glanced up into the chivalrous canker of McConnell's

face. 'So she just lived out her days with her garden and livestock?'

'Pretty much. We used to spy her from the telescope singing to the seals down on the shallow sand of the south beach. The sound of her voice used to carry and make things brighter if you catch my meaning; like a tonic taken through the ears that soothed the loneliness for a while. From the gallery, we could watch her sit and weave outside on fine days, or go bathing at the spray from the blowhole...'

The keeper blushed and turned away from the drawing and Jack's own reddening cheeks. 'I was only a young lad at the time.'

Jack reached the last of the drawings. A woman, eyes closed and hair flowing as though underwater, lay on a table enveloped by flowers, braided kelp, shells and shining beads of sea glass.

The old keeper took it gingerly. 'It's the last time we saw her. Winston drew that.'

'You brought her here to lie before taking her back to Carrigh?' said Jack trying to reconcile the likeness with the small circular table nearby or the rough workshop trestle in the service and store room below.

He shook his head. 'We hadn't seen her for days during a fair enough summer. The sheep were bleating and there seemed a commotion among the chickens and beasts that made up the croft. The seals in the cove congregated, as though waiting or listening for something, and the old sailors say they mourn their own. Then it went deathly quiet, and Winston and I went over just as the sun was setting.' He pointed at the drawing in Jack's lap. 'That's what we found, and Winston drew it so we could both be assured we hadn't been dreaming.'

'She laid herself out and then died?' asked Jack.

'Candles lit, hair combed out, and lying like a queen of old on a tomb in Stirling Castle.' McConnell cleared his throat. 'I'm telling you something I don't want repeating, but it seems fitting someone knows, though don't you go writing about it till Winston and I are in our graves, do you understand? I don't want folks thinking I'm fanciful or funny in the head.' He lowered his voice. 'There was something else, a matter we've never said ought to anyone about...'

Jack listened as the keeper paced around the edge of the room pausing to peer out of the black slit of the second-floor window toward the ruin that lay obscured by new moon darkness. He clutched at a brass locket on his chest that slipped from his low buttoned shirt, scanning as the searchlight of the rotating beacon above swept across the island hinting at the hummocks and stones of the abandoned croft.

'We determined to return the following morning with pick and shovel to give her a decent burial on the isle, but—'

Jack laid down the drawing and joined him at the window, close enough to catch the beacon's light reflecting from McConnell's dark-adapted pupils. He leaned in like a priest reassuring a penitent sinner in a confessional.

'But what?'

Lifting the locket chain above his head McConnell placed the brass trinket into his palm, clicking open the clam shell to reveal a lock of silver hair.' I trimmed a section of her curls, to remember her by and bring me luck being quite upset. Winston was snivelling even as he drew that final memorial of her, so it wasn't just me. I thought nothing of it and it has been lucky over the years. If he had done likewise, maybe he wouldn't have broken his leg on that outing to Tobermory.' McConnell snapped the halves shut and handed it to Jack, squeezing the young man's fingers over in forced endowment. 'I don't need it anymore, and I knew we wouldn't sink on the way over. Whether it brings luck, you'll have to find out, but I wouldn't show it or wear it next to any girl; bit macabre to be sporting an old woman's last bits around your neck. Perhaps that's why I never got in the family way.'

Jack lifted the locket and placed it over his head, much to the visible relief of the keeper.

'You were saying you went back in the morning?'

'We did, but there was no one to bury, not what we expected in any case.'

Jack frowned, wondering what the keeper was coming to in his own good time.

From the far reach of the island came the sound of the blow hole piping with the squall now that high tide had flooded the narrow channel. The natural bellow rose and fell as the swell advanced and retreated.

Mhairi's pipe...

'We dug a decent-sized grave in as rough a spot to be found on this rock, close to the edge of her rose bushes she was fond of. Deep purplish blue they were, like blood in a pale maiden's veins or the bright new ink of a first tattoo. So we pick and scrape away for an hour swapping stories of our encounters and remembrances before fetching her on a sealskin she was lying on, only she wasn't there.'

Jack gave him a questioning look. 'You mean someone took her?'

'No. What we found was something else. Beneath the bundle of clothes, flattened against the table was something like a skin shed from a snake, pale and long. Winston won't talk about it, and I've had only my thoughts these many years as to what it was. I only touched it once as we lifted what remained of her from the table, body and all, if body you called it. It was like cold rubber. Light as a feather it was, and we hurried to cover the thing, sealing the thin soil with an afternoon's scouring of manageable-sized lumps of rock to make a cairn of sorts.'

McConnell rubbed his hands together and looked away.

'You mustn't tell anyone lest they mess with the grave. I don't need to know anything about it.' He glanced back to Jack's hand, gripping the locket. 'I just want to remember how she was.'

He grabbed a lamp and opened the door. 'I'm going to check on the stores. You get some sleep. I'll be some time at it I imagine.'

Jack listened as the keeper's slow, metronomic steps receded to the lower floor like an undertaker fronting a funeral coach. From the stairwell, he made out the noise of the man lifting the false panel in the floor and the clink of glass bottles hidden beneath, and much later, as Jack retired to his bed, the sound of gentle sobbing came up through the floorboards.

Night after night Jack lay in his bed against the far wall, tuning in to the beats of the mechanical heart within the lighthouse, and filtering out the slumbering moans and snores of the man opposite. He calculated the intervals of time as the reassuring and rotating beam of light revealed its interval down the stairs, flooding the thin gap beneath the closed door of the first floor. The waves outside crashed like a sack of cymbals but he could still hear a high whistle from some-where about the room. On the wall space between them, the dark pipe was anchored, supplying gas from the generator in the outhouse to the great burner above, glistening with condensation. An occasional rivulet of whisky-coloured rust dribbled down its length to soak the rotten, drunken board at its base. In the winding room above, the clockwork contrap-tion clunked, the weight of the clicking chain unravelled, and the hoarse rasp of the beacon room gas mantle lulled him to light-headed sleep.

Jack awoke one morning in the darkness before dawn, a thumping ache in his head and rose, unsteady, catching the door already open and the keeper returning from his ablutions outside in the bluster and blow of the unceasing squall. A swift nod of greeting was supplanted by a laconic smile and a shake of his head forecasting the general weather prospects for the day. Jack splashed cold water on his face from the bowl, trying to soften the pain inside his skull by pressing on his temple and sighed, preparing to perform his repetitive routine once more.

McConnell regarded him. 'Three more days. Is it getting to you, lad?'

Jack looked through the mirror and shrugged. 'This storm; it's never-ending. I'll never rue silence again.'

'It's rotten,' said McConnell sawing through the last of the stale crusts and spreading dry slices with the thick tar from a tin of molasses. 'As harsh as I've ever known, but not so rough as you couldn't go abroad for a few hours later if you are careful, and after the chores are done and the sun valve is replaced. We need it in readiness for the marine engineers coming after Christmas. You must promise to stay away from the cliffs and put on the spare clothing – it's bitter outside.' Jack turned to be certain of the offer to be met by the reassuring face of the keeper.

'I think you've earned it.'

They set up the work and the glass-protected beacon room warmed up quickly as the sun rose into a cobalt winter sky among fleeces of fleeting cumulus clouds. A cold front was coming, and the respite would be all too brief, perhaps only a matter of hours. McConnell peered into the newly installed valve and pursed his lips, passing the spanner back to the young man impatient to be let out like an expectant dog long chained to a granite kennel.

McConnell rose stiffly from his knees and lifted off his

cap, wiping the sweat from his receding baldness with the oily rag from his back pocket. 'My last bit of surgery on you, old girl. I hope you'll behave yourself when those Trinity House Sassenachs arrive to inspect and make the changes.'

Jack closed the toolbox and withdrew part way down the stairs, leaving the long-serving keeper alone with his sentimentality. Just two more full days after this one and they would be away, unburdened and unbound by any force of weather or duty. As though delivering on his promise, McConnell called down after a few minutes.

'Put on Winston's extra layers and be back before three o'clock. Don't stray out of sight of the lighthouse or disturb anything you shouldn't, do you hear?'

'Understood, Mr McConnell,' said Jack leaping down the remaining stairs, two at a time. He passed the living quarter door, shut since a tea break early that morning to seal in the warmth from the dying, flameless embers of the stove. He slid round the last of the metal handhold, landing on the flagstones of the service room that doubled as the stores. From several hooks and shelves, he salvaged and put on an additional Aran sweater and over gloves before budging open the door to the outside like an alpine explorer leaving the comparative warmth of a base camp bell tent.

The frigid air bit sharply into his warm, exposed skin and he gritted his teeth, hurrying to get off the windswept promontory and into the nearby shelter of the ridge stones that led away to the centre of the island. A glance back exposed the figure in the beacon room, still and watchful for several moments, as though confirming the release of an escaped convict from long imprisonment. Jack turned to follow the spine of stones and headed for the mere in the centre of the island, face upwards, soaking in the open sky and sun-sodden freedom.

After a tedious and tufted ten-minute traverse, he reached

the boggy margins of the freshwater pool, splashing sensually among the sedges and scattering the sheep that held court around the watery round table. In the distance, he spied a clear view of the mainland and his spirits rose, as did the wind in this exposed central island belt. Downwards he strode towards the sound of the blow hole, impatient to see and feel the spray and peer into the narrow channel creating the musical spout.

High tide was some time off leaving him searching for the miniature gorge from memory, but as the grass became thinner, he reached the deep crack in the island and peered over the edge to the shallow lapping sea thirty feet below. The thin inlet, eight feet across, was topped by a land bridge near the landward end, allowing only twenty feet of open roof from which the incoming tide and storm could erupt into the sky from the cavern beneath. He knelt and peered into the abyss, edged with ledges of sea thrift and samphire. Each echoed "hoy" boomed back from the naturally resonant chasm. As his eyes adjusted to the darkness, Jack noticed large enough hand and footholds that lead down to the rock pool at the bottom. A rusted ring halfway down draped a length of coarsely braided rope the final fifteen feet down a mostly sheer wall of granite. What it had been used for, he could not surmise as an easier landing was only a matter of a few hundred yards to the south where the channel mouth widened and stepped into the sea with gradual ease. Perhaps it served for the collection of easy fish or crabs stranded in the pool between tides. He could hear the waves on the other side of the land bridge, but they did not appear to wash into the well-like cavern directly beneath him and Jack surmised there must be some ridge or rock wall damming the incoming water until it was breached at higher tides.

Leaning further over, he turned to see the underside of the land bridge, eroded and thin enough in places as to show the roots of shallow grasses. He decided against standing in such a spot, despite the thrill, lest the loose arch gave way. A sudden movement out of the corner of his eye focussed his attention, and he got to his feet to identify the source. What he thought was the waving or flapping of something linen-like akin to a flag or washing on a line proved to be nothing more than a long-haired goat standing sentry on the wall of the croft, two hundred yards inland. The animal skipped away long before Jack reached the boundary wall of deeper green and heavier soil thick with untamed and overgrown plantings. The seeded heads of many plants, some of which Jack recognised as medicinal herbs, stood shivering and rattling in the sun-soaked breeze. Stunted boles of trees, marked out the hardy orchard like those in the drawings from the previous night and he clambered over, making for the mostly intact gable end of the croft along grass-covered, hinted-at cobble-edged paths.

The ruin revealed itself in its partially roofless state, but Jack avoided the temptation to wander in through the fallen section of wall, choosing to assess the safety of entry into the house via the door, long missing but still adorned with the thin sword-like hinges now bereft of purpose. A scurry and sudden bolt of some animal shot out through the breach causing Jack to retreat out of sheer terror and it was a full minute before he attempted the tentative trespass once again.

From within, there was almost nothing that alluded to its former owner or glory. Little remained from the sketches except for the rusted hooks on rotting beams that still held roof sections of mouldy clumps of daub and thatch. The rotting stumps of what may have been the legs of a great table stuck out from the tall weeds like bad teeth. An interior wall suggested a sleeping area, but the door was blocked by all manner of debris and fallen timber. Several old gulls' nests lined the eaves, streaking their breeding morass and muck down the worked stone blocks.

Jack shuffled through the dust and detritus kicking out at something hard and round. It skittered across the floor, coming to rest against the remains of the door frame. He bent and picked up a small sea glass bead – perhaps one of the grave goods that had briefly transformed the croft into a chapel of rest, if McConnell's story was to be believed.

Candles lit, hair combed out, and lying like a queen of old...

Unbuttoning his thick coat he pulled at the locket chain letting it lie against the outer wool of the itchy, borrowed sweater. Jack opened the necklace, shielding the curl of fine silver hair bound with fishing line from the gusts that whistled in through the door and breach, and placed the dusky ornament within the simple brass housing.

'For twice the luck...' he whispered, turning with the sound of tapping against stone from without. Having reached the doorway he emerged into the garden to see a thrush breaking a late snail shell against a lump of rock acting as a white granite anvil. It was the cairn, less than fifty feet away where the two men had laid the remains of the woman they had grown to miss.

He wrapped a hand around the door, snagging his exposed left wrist on a thorny rose, climbing wild and without care from the other gable end. He winced and rubbed at the bleeding spot. It was deep and foolishly he yanked his arm away, tearing a larger wound that began to weep. He sucked at the annoyance, in between curses, seeing the late blooms of dark bluish purple springing from leaf fallen stems, protected from the prevailing wind and recent storms. As the tang of bloodied iron stung his tongue, he caught the heavy perfume from the closest flower and, placing his finger and thumb carefully between the armoured hooks to prevent a repeat injury, he plucked the stem a full six inches long.

'You owe me for that cut,' he said, momentarily leaving the saliva-slathered wrist to bury his nose into thoughts of a Persian flower market, such was the sensation and intoxication induced. After five days of sweat, boiled, bullied beef and carbide, his senses reeled. The wound blackened into an angry, weeping gash, but he proceeded towards the resting place of the woman they had called the Skerry Rose. Transferring the offering to his injured hand he crouched, just out of view of the lighthouse, sun backed and setting. The great lens was outlined against the winter sunlight, but the figure of McConnell was not standing there much to his relief. Wetness trickled into his palm, and he turned the bloodied stem of the rose before placing it upon the cairn and securing it beneath a flat stone.

The thrush flew several yards to a nearby outcrop and tipped his head, making Jack feel a little self-conscious with an audience, but he felt it was appropriate to say a few simple words.

'I'm sorry what we say about you back on Lewis. I was frightened all these years, but McConnell put me right.'

The wind rose, rustling the petals. 'It's going to be the last time that he, or any man, is at the lighthouse permanently. I don't know why, but I thought you should know.' A sudden stab on his bloodied wrist made him grimace and rise to rub at the wound. What he saw staggered him physically and emotionally. From the half-inch cut, now dry, emanated fine, flowing lines beneath his skin that disappeared beyond his cuff. Jack stumbled back, stripping off his coat and yanking at the woollen sleeve to release the layers of his shirt. The lines continued, shaping themselves into tiny vines bearing miniature blood-red flowers that entwined around his bare arm. With more skin revealed, the invisible tattooist worked, revealing images that seemed to flux and change as Jack scraped and wiped at the internally driven blood ink.

Ignoring the freezing wind he threw off his top shirt leaving only his vest, shivering as he fought for an explanation. Whatever was taking place had no sensation and disappeared when he squeezed and wiped his skin in panic, only to return once more with a new image. It reached his elbow and halted its upward travel, waxing and waning with what seemed to be the lap of the waves on the beach rather than the blood briskly pumping in his veins.

Jack stared aghast, realising nothing he could do could prevent the series of sketches and designs on his body.

Something or someone else was in control of the narrative.

The abstract windings and flowering plants receded, flushed clean and renewing with another image with each advance of the tide as a myriad of recognisable figures played out on his arm.

Heads of seals bobbed among seaweed-strewn waters, still and moonlit; a woman with a newborn lamb wrapped in an impressive garment welcomed the dawn; a dark cave surfaced with a candle, lit and surrounded by curious objects and unusual rock-clinging plants.

Jack's skin was cleansed like a sponged slate as the illustrations continued with the encroaching waves. The inked form of a woman's hands emerged from the wound on his wrist, dragging shipwrecked men further up the beach from the stormy waters. A bottle was forced beneath their noses causing them to wake from near death and vomit, coughing back into life as the woman rushed to save another soul. The picking of herbs from a small garden and collecting of sea glass from a sandy cove showed the treasured remembrances of one who knew the island well. Jack turned to the cairn, searching for answers, as his arm revealed further memories.

A larger seventh wave crashed into the narrow channel causing an almighty transforming flush on his skin. It revealed the lighthouse being built, each wave adding to the elevation like a children's flicker book until the beacon was finally fitted. Jack sensed movement from the beacon's first light shown as an absence of blood or ink, or whatever was causing the miraculous lines, passing and rotating about his forearm. He rubbed at the image, and it dispersed to be replaced by men in bandages and crutches, arms raised in thanks. One such man lay in a cot of straw reading a book and nursing a heavily bandaged arm...

McConnell?

Jack shivered, sending the moving tattoo trembling and blurring like ink dripped into water and stirred. He re-dressed, leaving the arm up to the elbow free, and looked over at the lighthouse, terrified but eager for the only help available to explain what was going on. His heart beat like a drum and he sucked at the wound, terrified of some plant-derived drug having entered his veins and now affecting his mind.

Don't you go poking about down there among her house and herbs, do you understand me? There're poison plants as well and things buried that shouldn't be disturbed...

Why hadn't he listened?

As though in response, the tattoo, imaginary or not, projected the old keeper replacing the floorboard of the store-room. A bottle of half-drunk whisky beneath sloshed as the daylight was extinguished. Jack lowered his wrist from his mouth as a throbbing pain emerged and the design focussed upon a single artery, forming itself into the likeness of the gas pipe upon the interior wall. The pipe grew with each beaching wave until it stopped and further fine markings about the vignette showed the objects within the closed living quarters. For a brief pulse, the image of Mhairi on the wall was revealed in facsimile and she turned from her gaze out to sea to look him full in the face with some urgency. The arm refreshed to show the pipe once more, at arm height, closer and more detailed. From a visible crack in the blue-black cylinder came a painful blood blister as though Jack's veins had suddenly burst from the highlighted spot. He yelped, adrenaline having no effect on the bleeding, which faded to reveal a miasma-like outline leaking and flooding the room. A faint whistling from the channel brought him to his senses, and what the image was showing.

His arm washed clean to be replaced by the drawn footsteps of McConnell climbing the steps to the closed, gas-filled room, pipe in mouth and matchbox at the ready.

'No!' cried Jack, leaping to his senses and over the discarded outer coat. With one glance downwards, he knew he wasn't seeing the past this time. The woman on his arm reappeared from the drawing in the room where even now the old keeper was headed. She opened her mouth and Jack heard it as clear as though the wind itself was amplifying the warning.

'*Run!*'

Even as he vaulted the ruined wall, he began calling, breathless with the fear of the premonition. Why had he not put the clues together? – the light-headiness, the hissing whistle, the fragments of rust and the cloying smell of carbide impurities that never seemed to dissipate from his nose long after he visited the generator house. McConnell couldn't hear it and had woken that morning with a single malt, self-inflicted headache. With no sense of smell, and about to strike a flame, the keeper was in great danger. Jack catapulted himself over the low southern ridge screaming out McConnell's name with every fourth stride and gulp of breath. Two hundred yards to run against the buffet and blow, Jack desperately hoped the keeper was on his way up to the beacon room, or that the faded image on his arm was a madness caused by isolation and whatever had infected his wrist down at the croft.

A silence fell, as though suddenly Jack was underwater. All sound seemed drowned and dulled as the wind ceased to rush in his ears. It was replaced by the sound of footsteps, the clicking of the clock chain in the winding room, and the sound of his elevated heartbeat. Even his final call out seemed dull and distant. Jack reached the promontory steps as the footsteps in his mind ceased. A silhouette in the window opposite the living quarter door was suddenly illuminated, as though someone inside had gained entry. An arm was raised momentarily before the figure turned to the window to see what the commotion was on the steps outside, striking the match even as the glass burst outwards cascading up the tower in a chain reaction and concluding with a burst of incandescent light as the beacon was engulfed with explosive flame.

Sound returned as Jack reached the door, raising his arms to shield himself from the falling glass and debris from the windows and gallery above. A deep rumble swung his attention to the generator room as he witnessed the backdraft of pressurised gas in the buckling and splitting exterior pipework. He threw himself against the shielding wall of the lighthouse as the joints in the cast iron artery surrendered and cracked, showering the pad with a release of lit acetylene. The great pipe folded over like a tossed caber, narrowly avoiding the doorway and coming to rest at a shallow angle like a Roman candle from hell. The flames erupted in a final spurt as the pressure died, and Jack hurled himself against the door and into an acrid, eye-watering stench to escape its lethal death throes.

Coughing as he called out for his companion, he felt his way up the smoke-filled staircase to trip over the limp body of McConnell blown part way back down the passage from the force of the explosion. Far above, a grinding and wheezing from the mechanics desperate for aid, but Jack ignored it and felt for the man's braces, steadily lugging him down the remaining steps and into the cleaner air of the venting store room dragging in the cold outside air. Jack rolled the body seeing McConnell was charred on one side. The flash had blistered his face and his cloth overalls smouldered with a fiery reminder. Jack shook the keeper, calling out his name among the grinding moans of the upper floors and for a moment he thought he would have to spend days and nights alone upon the isle with a dead man. The notion terrified him and he suddenly realised that being the only man on the Skerry was the most upsetting outcome he could imagine. A final shake of the man's shoulder brought him round and McConnell drew in a long, rasping breath, murmuring incoherently. A blackening bruise bled across his temple.

The keeper was badly injured, but alive.

Shuddering death throes from the generator launched the outhouse's roofing tiles, peppering slate, shrapnel and shot against the tower, snuffing out any chance of working light and killing the lighthouse. The wind outside briefly died as though in respectful silence, mourning the return of darkness the like of which it had not witnessed for nigh on a century.

———

Jack gripped the semaphore flags in both hands, waving them above his head in a scissor-like motion to attract the attention of the harbour master on the distant shore. The exposed gallery was slippery, and he braced against the soot-grimed glass on the exterior platform repeating the gesture desperate for anyone to return the signal and understand the dire predicament on Skerry Ròs. He swung the telescope through the haze to see if any receiving signals were present.

High seas and air-borne spray obscured the mainland, but Jack repeated the distress signal more in hope than in expectation. They would know soon enough that the Skerry was out of action when the last rays of afternoon sank below the horizon and the familiar light did not blink into life from daytime slumber. He placed the hand flags between his legs and blew on his hands, desperate to get some warmth into the frigid fingers, and glanced over at the croft where Winston's over mittens lay discarded next to the cairn.

The cairn…

His cut wrist itched, but he resisted the urge to scratch, trying to put out the memory of what he had seen out of his mind. The marks on his arm had been quiet since the triage of McConnell's condition, and he had haphazardly applied ointment bandages and comforting words to the pallid patient without truly having a clue what he was doing. Cutting away McConnell's clothing, washing the skin and treating the burns had given him purpose. The keeper lay on a mattress dragged from the blackened first-floor room, warmed by a small fire in a makeshift brazier fashioned from a metal wire-work crate. The gas had dissipated and there was no danger of any further explosion, so Jack had salvaged all usable items from the burnt-out chamber for the benefit of keeping them both comfortable enough until help arrived.

McConnell slept, delirious and only semi-conscious even when the acting keeper had spooned beef tea between his blistered lips. Several spilt attempts had occurred before Jack had pulled himself together from the shock and he realised he was on his own. The injured man was unresponsive to his pleas for what to do next; Jack wasn't even sure McConnell knew where he was or who either of them were. The bruise on his balding head grew ever darker and more extensive and a soft lump appeared on his temple where the main force of some immediate and violent impact, likely a sudden meeting with the stairwell wall, had taken place.

At least he's not dead...

The cold front had arrived, bringing with it a low cloud and driving rain, and his thoughts turned to the uppermost room and the devastation of the lamp from his initial reconnaissance. Fortunately, the inner lens panels had taken the brunt of the rapidly expanding combustion, cracking and preserving the outer glass of the beacon from the elements but rendering all within the former light a tangled mass of fused cable, scorched valves, and barely recognisable mechanical parts from a few hours earlier. All that remained was the great metallic dish, installed, McConnell had said, to take the mercury allowing the lens apparatus to move freely and lessen the load and frequency of winding. The liquid lubricant had been lost on transport along with a good many other things to update the beacon many years ago and had never been replaced. One of the chain weights was damaged, as was part of the geared chariot wheel, toothless from the shearing and grinding of broken parts that had landed between the cogs and gears. The squealing of the lighthouse for its master had ceased, but it would no longer function fully each hour without manual winding when the missing teeth lost their bite on the powered clock gear. It didn't matter – without a light source, what was the point of spending fifteen minutes of the night, twice an hour, ensuring the teeth once more tracked into the operating wheel?

He glimpsed a steamship on the horizon heading for the safety of the North Minch route between Cape Wrath and Butt of Lewis. The vessel was sailing south in-between the Hebrides and the mainland where the Atlantic was pacified, but danger was ever present from the archipelago of hidden, wrecking rocks. Skerry Ròs was the only light for twenty leagues offering a navigation aid to ships in need of Ullapool or Stornoway or just to escape the wrathful sea. There would not be, and could not be, any light that night or any other until many men repaired the sentinel of the Sound. Jack feared for the men onboard and then selfishly for McConnell and his pension. Would they blame events on him or perhaps Jack for being absent – wouldn't they both have been injured, or killed otherwise?

How was he going to explain he knew what was about to happen?

His anxiety rose, drying his mouth and confusing his priorities. Too many questions, and not enough answers.

You'll need courage, faith, and overcoming fear in abundance on Skerry Ròs. Not to mention the witch...

As if in support or response, his scratched and scuffed left arm began to ache, ready to share a new image, and he shook his head confused.

The bloodied sketch of a book on a supply-laden shelf in the service room on the ground floor, wrapped with faded cloths that once might have been brightly coloured in yellow and red. A man stood waving on the unfinished lighthouse fluttering two hand flags and Jack realised the markings from the invisible artist were trying to help him. The transient tattoo flushed with each wave against the promontory rock revealing a series of signals, before returning to the sketch of the book on the ledge. He had raced down to find the semaphore manual, flicking to the page describing what his arm was teaching him.

That was thirty minutes ago, and Jack retreated inside to the beacon, catching sight of the ship and its lights just as the sun was setting. It was closer and heading towards Seal Rock.

With no lantern to guide it or alert the navigator, the vessel would hug the Minch searching for a light that would never come. Men might die and wash up on the beach...

A cry from the ground floor snapped Jack back to the present, and he soothed the wounded man who had turned uncomfortably and unconsciously onto his injured side.

'I don't know what to do!' he said to the swooned keeper. 'Mr McConnell, the lamp's broken and there's a ship out wandering in the storm. I've used the flags, but I don't think they've seen them back at Carrigh. What must I do? Please wake up!'

A firm shake caused the caretaker to gain consciousness briefly, but he was incoherent. His eyes stared at the sudden patterns materialising on Jack's arm.

'I don't know what is happening,' said Jack. 'I pricked my wrist on one of Mhairi's roses and this keeps appearing. I think it's trying to tell me something; it knew you were going to be hurt.' McConnell's eyes widened and rolled into the back of his head.

'Whis—ky...' he moaned, flailing a hand toward the door.

Jack put his head in his hands and raked his fingers through his hair. A short step away, he lifted the secret floorboard and retrieved one of several bottles from the dark recess. McConnell slapped aside the uncorked bottle, moaning and trying to speak or make him understand.

'You want a glass?' he asked, even as McConnell grabbed his wrist like a man possessed, forcing Jack to see what was drawn upon the underside of his arm. The keeper released him and fell backwards into the raised pillows propped against several duffel bags, his job done.

With each wave breaking against the promontory outside, Jack watched as his veins became a new canvas of two men rolling casks and crates of shipwrecked bottled booty across the rocky grass bumping and heaving till they reached the piles of spent carbide slurry, much reduced in height and extent than the current mounds not sixty feet away. Jack saw McConnell as a younger man, coal-black-bearded, stacking the jetsam within the hidden recess. His arm twitched as the scene was replaced with both men making merry with glasses held high, until the unknown man, presumably the notorious and accident-prone Winston, tipped over a glass into the path of a flickering tea-light candle stub. A final blood-drawn appearance showed the wickies rear back in alarm as the pooled liquid burst into a pillar of blue and orange flame. The light brightened removing all trace of an image as though overexposing and returning to the pale white skin now that its message was heeded.

'Whisky!' cried Jack, grabbing a rag and matches and racing to recover the remaining bottles. He clinked his way up the steps, arms full of the flammable liquid wondering how much he would need and whether he had the fortitude and courage to retrieve more from the secret store before darkness fell. Dropping and smashing one bottle, he cursed his over-eagerness at losing the most expensive substitute lamp oil available to man. He thumped down the surviving stores and began to uncork the water of life, hoping it would live up to the name and alert the ship heading closer and unaware of the rapidly indiscernible rocks fading into the gloom.

The whisky drained into the dish, one by one, lifting the soot and rust to the surface. Jack took a swig for luck before partially emptying the final bottle and stuffing the bottle with the rag allowing it to soak into the peaty petroleum to fashion a makeshift Molotov cocktail. He leaned over the receptacle causing the locket to lift out of his sweat-stained shirt. It reflected in the small amber pool as the blow hole sounded to break him from his contemplation. There was room for plenty more and he had little time or light to get it.

With each journey to the dangerous ledge and up the stairs, he became more tired, and it grew increasingly hazardous. At two-thirds of the dish full and eight trips from the cliff face recess with a full duffel bag, he resolved it would have to be enough. Once, he had lost his footing and only been saved by a sudden grazing slide before his hand gained purchase once more upon the sea-sprayed rock. His sweat dried quickly like a frosted rime as he lumbered back through the doorway, checking that McConnell was still breathing and in repose, before lugging the heavy load up the winding eighty-seven steps to the beacon. At last, he shuffled through empty, discard bottles to punch a hole in the central glass of the cupola with the end of a broom handle to allow greater ventilation for the uncontrolled conflagration about to take place.

Outside, the navigation lights signalled the approach of the doomed ship.

Jack retreated to the uttermost step and struck a match, quivering as he lit the whisky-soaked rag. He covered his face and head with the hood of McConnell's wetted coat and tossed the flaming brand into the air above the lamp bowl as he closed and bolted the door behind him.

He was already turning and flying down the stairs as the beacon room flashed into life sending a spirit-laden shock-wave in all directions. The door bulged and rattled as though the Prometheus himself had returned to reclaim the secret of fire, once taught to man and now horribly abused. Jack paused, ensuring the roar from behind was not just a trick of the wind, and carefully slid back the bolt to marvel at the sweet-scented lamp bowl blazing like a pagan beacon of old guiding the longships to harbour. Intoxicated by the fumes and the azure and orange flicker of the burning alcohol he realised it would not last long.

Taking an axe from the stores he returned to the living room, chopping anything flammable into pieces and carrying the splintered lumber back to feed the drunken lamp. The sudden heat was intense, and he shielded his face to sidle around to the gallery door and slipped out to search for the lights of the ship. The distant sound of a bell pealed for all it was worth in alarm could be heard near to the dangerous rocks a quarter of a mile off the Skerry. A sudden change in course brought about a shift in the colour of the onboard navigation lights, and Jack knew the captain had seen the light that had flashed out of the darkness like a blazing halo. The chariot wheel ceased in its turning of the lamp and with no time to spare, Jack hastily dropped to the winding room to force and spin the operating wheel until the gears re-engaged.

With trepidation he returned to the lantern, sweating like a gig rower sent out in a heavy sea, to see the lantern resurrected with its 'characteristic', the period of rotation allowing the mariners to tell this lighthouse from any other. The whisky lamp swept dimly across the nearby Seal Rock and surrounding islets revealing the danger and the proximity of the vessel in a full starboard turn.

Jack clutched at his locket. 'Please...don't let them die...'

From his arm, he saw the wheelhouse appear in the blood ink as though projected from the steamship close at hand. Men raced about the room and deck bellowing orders and pointing at the giant candle on the Skerry, burning like a distress flare. A man put his hands to his mouth, crying out to the wheelhouse, and pointed at the silhouette of the approaching rocks as the pilot made the perilous turn to avoid certain wreck and ruin.

The ship spun and listed heavily as it narrowly avoided the granite spines and slowed to assess its position and new course. The image on Jack's skin faded leaving only the small, crusted weep hole in the middle of his wrist.

For the rest of the night he watched, delirious with lack of sleep and the tending of the fire, McConnell and the repeated winding every twenty minutes to keep the lighthouse burning and beaming before, far off, a distant glimmer of dawn heralded a fall into sweetly scented slumber.

A gull, flapping and shrieking on its gallery rail perch, woke him with a start. The grey morning was half through, and Jack got to his feet like an arthritic octogenarian after a few hours on the cold, boarded floor. He peered over the rim of the bowl to see the sticky residue of burnt whisky-covered wood ash, caramelised and scorched against the blackened rust of the metal dish. He shooed away the bird, clambering to the outside, and gazed out with sleep-blurred eyes toward Seal Rock. No ship lay there, and no men were washed upon its meagre sands, still and lifeless. A lull in the storm caused him to look round hopefully from the corner of his eye. A distant ship's smoke from the mainland became clear in the telescope and he wondered with desperate excitement if it was the old trawler bound for the Skerry. Atop its mast flew the distress flag and Jack knew they were coming.

They had seen him the previous day, or perhaps the strange incandescent witch-light had sparked men into action. A small boat, like the powered gig they had arrived in, was towed behind, but the old tug was struggling against the waves. As much as the storm had abated, the sea was rough, wilder even than the previous week. Jack's initial feeling of euphoria and salvation quickly dived into the abyss, accompanied by the laughing shriek of the returning gull.

They were turning back.

All seemed suddenly silent, and he raced down the stairs to check on McConnell fearing the worst. The keeper lay like a corpse, a cold sweat upon his pallid brow. A small shaving mirror to his lips brought a faint condensing sign of life, but he was much worse than Jack had expected. No longer conscious, McConnell lay in a fever as his body burned with the malady afflicting his head, barely able to swallow the water dripped into his mouth by the frantic young man.

'They're coming, Mr McConnell,' he said with as much optimism as he could muster. The keeper's eye twitched as though in uneasy sleep. 'Just a few more hours. I saw them out in Carrigh Bay...'

Jack squeezed at the wet rag in distress, burying his brimming eyes into the cloth to stem and soak his tears. If the men didn't make it soon, then neither would the old keeper. A desperate solidarity with the old curmudgeon overwhelmed him. Hadn't McConnell taken a chance on him, despite his misgivings at their initial meeting?

'It's not for everyone, lad, and we'll depend on each other...'

'I'll do it,' said Jack repeating his answer. 'I won't let you down.'

I won't let you down.

'He needs medicine,' he whispered to himself. A glimpse at his exposed wrist encouraged the thought. He squeezed at his wrist trying to force the patterns and swirls to reveal what to do.

'He's saved hundreds of lives manning this place, and you helped him and his kind before. I need to know what's wrong with him and what to do. He said you were a healer, and that you saved him once before.' Jack pulled back the nightshirt on McConnell's arm to reveal the scar and something else.

The veins, just below the defender's skin, began to darken and frame the ancient wound with a vine of miniature roses and Jack watched the same ghostly tattooist at work upon another man.

'Mhairi?' murmured Jack enchanted by the image of a needle sewing the old cut shut in remembrance of its once gaping split. With each pass of the needle through the scar, it left behind a faintly stitched line reliving the act of surgery and lifesaving of the man who lay oblivious and delirious upon the mattress. The needle vanished into a single vein rising like a blue-bloodied rivulet towards McConnell's shoulder, up through his neck and against the side of his temple.

'Show me what's wrong,' whispered Jack watching as the tiny fingers of a small hand, heavily skinned at the knuckles like a webbed seal's paw, caressed the ugly swelling. The keeper flinched and then relaxed as the hand turned and dissipated into a puff of cloud-like blue. The itching cut on his wrist caused Jack to glance down and see a flash of images, timed to the rushing waves outside. He witnessed many herbs, the hips of the rose, a pestle and mortar, bandages soaked in a curious paste, a flask boiling above a fireplace and a spoon administering a dark tonic to bearded lips. Throughout the herbalism and fermentation of some unknown elixir, and between each stationary image, a strange succulent type plant appeared that he had never seen before. It seemed to be important and remained a potent, vivid symbol, flushing several times, to refresh the fading lines until it vanished with an echoing note in his mind recalling the sound of the blow hole. Jack rose, ready to save the man in his care and fulfil his promise.

Wearing some of McConnell's extra clothes, Jack shouldered his duffel bag and made for the croft. He could still hear the pipe between his ears, it being past low tide but not yet high enough for the water to cause the rush of haunting sound. His confidence grew that if he could find the items on the botanical shopping list and figure out the cryptic order of grinding, boiling and applying the salve, spooning the liquor from its oily separation, and keep the patient warm and dry, then McConnell had a chance. In hope, he turned to where he calculated the mainland harbour to be, shrouded in a stormy curfew. Bonds of fellowship were strong where the land and sea were tough, but capsized men affected no rescue except their own.

Not today, but maybe tomorrow...just maybe...

Vaulting the low ruinous wall of the croft garden he scavenged among the seed heads and sorrels for the leaves and roots that he recalled from the encounter in the lighthouse. He tore at clumps of feverfew, self-sown and aromatic, its spent flowering heads bent as though in prayer for a swift return to spring. Among the denser growth lay further plants evoked from the sanguine sketches upon his skin and several times he stung himself on nettle and thorny barberry reaching for cowering selfheal and wormwood. On one occasion, his arm burned like a bee sting, forcing him to reassess his memory and discard the rattling lady's bedstraw in favour of the reminder drawn out for him by the frustrated immaterial scribe once again.

The discarded, wet pile of clothes held no further use or interest, but various shells, limpets and lichens were grabbed, much to the apparent satisfaction of the invisible scribe with a brief glimpse of her smiling face at his wrist. Hips from the rose, carefully removed lest any further unwarranted magic entered his system, were hastily plucked leaving only one thing to find. Jack scurried around the ruin searching for the succulent, tendril-flowering plant. It seemed somewhere enclosed, moist and dim, as presented by the static tattoo flushing as though desperately important. It wasn't in the croft, and he wondered if it hid in the dilapidated room, barred by chunks of heavy masonry and fallen roof.

He unbuttoned his coat, ready for a warm bout of mauling to come and was about to roll back some of the lighter stones when his locket swung clear of his shirt, clicking open and sending the contents upon the dusty floor. The sea glass bead retrieved, he snatched at the tied lock of hair even as it rose above the wall to waft upon the wintry winds. A silvered curl chase of some hundred yards ended as McConnell's *momento-mori* slipped into the blow hole out of reach. Jack dropped his bag and looked down into the breezy well at the rock pool reflecting his silhouetted head. For a moment he stood unsure, whether to investigate or return to the internal door of the croft, and then he saw it.

The lock of silver curls lay precariously upon a plant, two-thirds of the way down.

He identified it immediately as the plant marked out on his arm. As if to confirm, the lines beneath his skin congregated at the focus of the original wound bringing forth a single drop of blood to his great discomfort. The droplet splashed into the pool far below setting the water rippling.

'You have got to be kidding me,' he said, studying the narrow hand and footholds with apprehension.

The tide was on the turn, and now and again a spray of water lifted over whatever was keeping the pool from the incoming waves. There was little time before the chamber flooded and the pipe would sound once more at high tide cutting off access until the following morning. Taking a long breath, he leaned sideways into the rock face and felt for the next step and hand hold, settling the shake in his legs with a snatch of song to ward against his worry. Going down would be the hardest, he thought, as he extended his arm towards the metal ring, placing his faith in the rusted rim. One swing drew him to the lowest ledge, still out of reach of the plant and charm nestled a few feet below. With one hand on the slippery hemp of the ancient rope, he leaned down slipping his feet from the inches of a smooth sea-worn granite foothold. He skidded down the slime of the sheer face, arresting his fall and landing heavily at the side of the pool with a stinging rope burn to his left palm. Heart pounding, Jack peered up at the sky, thirty feet above. His back became drenched, and he caught his breath with the freezing sea spray from behind. Turning, he could see a series of boulders, collapsed from the roof above to leave only the precarious land bridge above. Spots of light from cavities beneath beamed down into the grotto illuminating the purpose of the rope and the reason for anyone else to come here despite the danger. In the upper side wall was a wide recess, much littered with man-made detritus such as lobster floats, fragments of nets, stopped bottles, and all manner of smaller objects sent by the sea to lie like grave goods around the base of what someone had placed there.

Embellished in cracks and crevices around the altar-like repository, and stimulated in the dim pools of light, were the plants he was searching for. Jack skirted the rock pool and, after several unsuccessful attempts at tugging the tap-rooted succulents from their secure root hold, he twisted loose the rosette crowns complete with the spear-like tendril flower heads and, removing the box of matches from his pocket, he stuffed them into his grimy, work tweed trousers. There was a candle upon the natural dais, so sagged as to appear at first like a stalagmite, but to his surprise, it took only a few strikes to light. The sudden light blinded momentarily and, between the sprays of forceful water from the incoming tide, a seal-skin-wrapped bundle became clear.

Surrounded by the remains of once flowering garlands and sea glass beads, enough that the rock table above the water line looked to be bubbling with green frost, the object was wrapped with a woollen sash, much rotted and leaving a corner of the duffel bag sized thing exposed. Jack raised himself up to squint at the two bulges, side by side hidden within. The candle flickered as another wave crashed against the rockfall dam as though in warning or deterrence. The tide was rising, and water now trickled through and over the obstruction feeding the rock pool below. There wasn't much time before the chamber would be flooded, at least to the level at which he now stood. He tugged at the flap of furred skin to find the bundle heavier than he had expected, but a final revelatory unfolding occurred on a second and final attempt to discover what lay within.

Two child-like skeletons, distinguishable only by their size and advanced decomposition lay entwined. The remains of a matted doll and several beaded necklaces suggested two girls. Faint wisps of silver hair clung to the smooth chalk of their young skulls hinting they were perhaps two or three years old at the time of death. Jack reeled with the discovery and stumbled backwards, clamouring for escape and to make sense of the burial. He yelled wildly, as though expecting someone to be on the surface. The candle blew out with the wind plunging the mausoleum into dim shadow and Jack recalled starkly that he was alone on the Witch's Isle in the belly of a blow hole surrounded by mystery, magic, and macabre.

...her mate killed the little ones and left her broken-hearted on the Skerry...

An immense feeling of heartache overwhelmed him and even as he pulled up the rope, retrieving the curls to his breast pocket, he wept. With no one to hear, he mourned for everything and everyone that had arrived, lived, or departed here.

It is a place that will never outgrow the impact it has to change a man or his perspectives; remember that. Do not be afeared, lad.

Muddied and drained, he clawed his way to the surface and gathered the duffel bag leaving behind the encounter and strode away northwards to prepare the herbs and medicine, hoping that McConnell was still alive to make use of them.

Jack rubbed at the bridge of his nose and nudged back the over large keeper's cap on his head. The candlelight tired his eyes, but he felt it his duty to record in the singed log the night's travails and weariness caring for McConnell and the burning torch above. Dawn was near at hand and his final visit to the beacon wood fire, glowing with the last of the whisky, had still not recorded a single ship struggling in the Minch. He yawned, rubbing at his aching arms, glad that the winding was done for the night.

'For a minute...I took you for old McGinnis, alive...again,' came the hoarse whisper of the keeper. Jack turned, beaming.

'And here's me covering all the work whilst you lay in your bed again, injured and idle.'

McConnell rattled a laugh, setting a weak hand to the bandage at his brow.

'You did this?'

Jack removed the cap and spun in his chair. 'Yes. You were awake earlier for a while and you asked me about what had happened, do you remember?'

The keeper frowned and nodded. 'I was thrown by the gas. You manned the light and brought me back...'

Jack raced over to assist as the old man began to lever himself up to a sitting position. 'Be careful,' he said. 'It's barely been a day since I treated you.'

McConnell sank into the propped pillow. 'Quite a resourceful young fellow you are, Jack. How ever did you manage everything alone?'

'I had help,' he said turning over his wrist to reveal the permanent tattoo on his wrist. 'I think we are both going to be alright now.' It had appeared the moment McConnell had first regained consciousness as though in farewell or closure from the supernatural guardian.

They both looked upon the small rose, blue-black in true sailor's ink, centred about the tiny, imperceptible thorn scar. McConnell's eyes widened as Jack retrieved the magnifying glass and hovered about the intricate design.

'Look closer.'

Where at first glance McConnell thought he saw simple

petals, closer examination revealed a series of seals, paisley-patterned and swimming clockwise around the central boss of stamens, themselves all individual miniatures of lighthouses. A thorny stem extended from the penny-sized bloom terminating a few inches towards the elbow in the likeness of the flowering tendril of the curious and miraculous healing herb.

'I told you that you would have a tale to tell when we get ashore, and I hold to my promise to set another upon your skin at my expense – that and much more.'

Jack filled a glass of the watery elixir from beneath the bed and handed it across.

'I don't think I'll set any other mark on me apart from this, and I've made up my mind on another thing.'

'Oh?' said McConnell handing back the empty glass.

'I'm going to be a writer, maybe take a job at the paper in Stornoway until I learn the craft.' Jack lowered the glass to the floor and rubbed his hands.

'What is it?' asked the keeper.

'Do you remember anything before you came round last night?' Jack rubbed at the white, unblemished skin.

McConnell pursed his lips. 'Not much. You'll think me foolish, but I've had a bang on the head, so I've got a right to be fanciful with what I recall.'

'Go on.'

'I thought I heard singing, faint and distant. I felt young again, hopeful, strong and—' He paused with a smile, glancing at the marvellous tattoo on Jack's wrist. 'I don't think I'll share anymore. You have your Skerry Rose, and I have mine.'

A distant horn echoed across the sound.

Jack sprung and threw open the door, returning to the keeper with a look of overwhelming joy. 'They're coming – it's the tug and gig from Carrigh!'

'Pass me my cap and shut the door, you fool,' said McConnell shivering, 'that cold will be the death of me!'

Jack tossed the final bottle, sending it arcing into the sea to join the rest of the bobbing flotilla on the journey of a thousand miles bearing the names of the living, and the dead. Behind him, the tug lay at anchor, still a mile or so offshore. Men could be made out readying the gig boat to make the final treacherous crossing to the platform.

There was still time.

The discomforting thought of sacrilege down in the bowels of the blow hole had been on his mind, and there was also a need to say goodbye to someone he knew was no longer there. He turned and raced over the four hundred yards to reach the croft, laying a hand on the gable end to recover his breath. A single rose, blood-black, bloomed against the wall, the last of the year most likely and wearing a damp mitten from the bundle of discarded clothing left several days prior, he plucked the stem and headed for the cairn.

The rocks glistened with sunlight reflecting quartz as he fumbled for the right words.

'You saved those men out on the steamer, and you saved McConnell.'

The spent sea thrift among the lower stones rattled in the brisk breeze.

'I'm sorry for your loss, and I want you to know I won't tell a soul.'

The voices of distant seamen broke him from a hastily worded prayer. Jack took one last look at the ruin and its garden and headed for the pipe to offer one last tribute. Standing at the lip of the blow hole, he cast the rose into the darkness, straining for the sound of its gentle landing into the rock pool. Even as he caught the echo the land bridge before him shifted and pieces crumbled beneath the undercutting erosion of centuries. Several large clumps of earth disappeared from its surface bringing about a final collapse of the roof-like keystone holding up the small cave wherein lay the open grave. For a moment he thought he heard a curious singing upon the breeze causing him to look round to locate the source. It seemed to come from the croft. When he glanced back, the bridge collapsed, sending great slabs of rock to the bottom of the channel and burying the infants forever.

Mhairi's pipe would never sound again, but the secrets it contained were safe forever.

McConnell's distant voice called to him from the promontory. The men in the gig were approaching the landing, and Jack leapt up the steps, passing the keeper on his way into the lighthouse.

'Smarten yourself up, lad,' said McConnell, unbandaged and looking increasing brighter, if more anxious. 'We've duties to perform and a lot of questions to answer.'

Jack, suitably tidied and hurriedly buttoned assisted the half dozen men from Carrigh. Two men in suits and inadequate raincoats, whom he did not know, staggered out of the boat, pale and ill at ease.

'Is the old dog still alive?' called the pilot, tying in the stern. Despite the camaraderie and petty dislike of the keeper, there was a look of concern on his face. Both men were tied by the sea, the small fishing town at the edge of the world, and ultimately by blood from some distant union.

'He is,' said Jack catching the slight look of relief. 'He's not well and has taken a bad knock to the head. You saw my distress signals?'

'Yes,' interrupted the senior of the two men. 'We also observed the fire. Now take me to him and let's see what is left of my lighthouse.'

The other men offloaded several boxes and replacement telegraph poles, wires, and ground anchors to the platform before following in a train of limpet-edged steps to meet the last man to hold the post of keeper on Skerry Ròs.

'I bet you're glad you aren't taking back a body, Seamus,' said one man to the boatman. 'One spook on the isle is more than enough for anyone.'

Seamus nodded, watching his feet on the worn, slippery steps. 'Too true, it's bad luck enough and I'll be glad to be away once those two inspectors have finished their duties.'

McConnell stood to greet them, leaning stoically on the cane, legs apart like an immutable tripod. His face stiffened as the two inspectors approached. The older, senior man did not remove his bowler hat in response to the raised cap of the keeper.

'Mr Hinds, sir. A pleasure to see you so far from the comforts of Inverness.'

'Mr McConnell,' the man ignoring the insincerity. He looked up at the scarred signs of damage and blackened bruises from the beacon fire. 'So you managed to stay alive after all and decommission my lighthouse single-handed?'

'Gas explosion,' said McConnell. 'Corrosion in the access pipe. We wrote to you many times—'

'Yes, yes,' said Hinds eager to get inside and avoid any conversation on the subject in front of sympathetic men. 'Let's get inside out of this weather, and my associate, Mr Timms, can make a full assessment while you and yours answer my questions.'

The men filed into the lighthouse like pupils following masters into school. Several gasps and hushed words announced their arrival when they saw the cluttered interior and hastily stacked chaos of boxes, crates, and shelving in the makeshift living room. The inspectors took to the steps and were fifteen minutes in the rooms above. Periodically, the men below could hear the incredulity in their speech and strong words as they realised the degree of damage done to the once proud beacon. When they entered the living quarters above, where the explosion had originated, there was nothing but shocked silence.

'You're in for it today, McConnell,' whispered the boatman with some satisfaction. 'On your last day before retirement, too. There's a surprise in store that you won't forget...'

The keeper raised his stick and wobbled. 'Don't think because I'm an invalid that I won't brain you with this, Monaghan. You've no idea what's been going on over here.'

'Don't I?' he said placing a foot on the false floorboard and tapping it with his left foot. 'Tut-tut.'

McConnell could not reply with the reappearance of the two inspectors, paler than they had been from the rough sea crossing if that were possible. Hinds stared at the white footprints about the place and wrinkled his nose.

'You can start at the beginning,' he said dusting off a chair and seating himself. 'Where is the log, and what is that sickly smelling tar staining the mercury basin?'

Jack retrieved the singed tome and opened the ribbon to the entry for the day of the accident. Fearing the revelation of the unconventional, twenty-year-old single malt fuel, which was conveniently absent from the pages beneath, he made up a reasonable reply.

'Old rubbing ointment from bottles in the croft,' he lied, pointing to the remains of limp and dried plants. 'The old woman who used to live there put lots of things from the garden in it. I used some of them to help Mr McConnell...'

Hinds did not look up, apparently satisfied, and continued to read. Jack supported and clarified the events as McConnell recounted the past week. The man's expressionless face barely broke into anything more than a slight raise of the eyebrow as the full impact of the past few days was fully explained. Finally, he spoke.

'Mr Timms, would you be good enough to inspect the generator house, or what remains of it, with the rest of the men? I think we can safely say our cursory examinations on the true state of things will soon be grossly under-estimated.'

He blinked and folded over the book in his lap, waiting as the men left the room leaving the three of them alone.

'You've had a lucky escape, McConnell. Sounds as though this lad has saved you and the rest of us from a calamity, two nights ago.'

'The steamer?' said Jack impatiently.

'Yes,' said Hinds. 'The *Sea Snail* made port in Stornoway yesterday morning with tales of being out of kilter, off course, and saved from wrecking by a sudden light at the last moment. The shipping company were going to raise a formal complaint and make all our lives difficult, mine included until we all realised the lighthouse was down and that you had done your duties to protect all those on the open sea.' He rubbed at his nose with a haughty smile. 'They were going to offer to pin a medal to your chest, but I told them that wasn't in your wheelhouse if you pardon my expression.'

'That's not fair,' said Jack with a start. 'Mr McConnell deserves to make that decision—'

'Quiet, boy!' interrupted McConnell turning to the inspector. 'You know me best over all these years, Mr Hinds, and I'm sure your assessment is the right one. I would like to stress that I was very much incapacitated and had little involvement in keeping the lantern alight. Without the lad's quick thinking and dedication, those men could have drowned.'

Hinds pursed his lips, glancing over at the young man. 'You did all these things, as written in here, to save your superior's life, and to keep the beacon alight with little sleep or concern for your safety?'

'Yes, sir.'

'Then I will reward you with a new role,' said Hinds, glancing at McConnell, 'out of trouble and mischief while the lightship manages the Skerry during its repairs and change over to full autonomy; there's a lighthouse on the other side of Thurso that—'

'I've got a mind to try my hand at writing, sir,' interrupted Jack. 'I mean to seek a position with the newspaper in Inverness; they have an office in nearby Ullapool. If you feel I am owed anything for the extra duty, I would only ask for a reference.'

'A writer?' said Hinds, amused. 'You certainly are very creative in your entries, but are you sure? It's not work in the sense—'

Jack nodded, appealing to the inspector's vanity. 'I thought one day I might like to write a book about the inspectors and wickies that once worked or still work the needles.'

'Very well,' said Hinds, pocketing the log and rising. 'I will look forward to contributing, as well as reading it; I am sure I will find it most interesting and illuminating.'

Outside, Hinds glimpsed the rack and ruin of the pad and outhouse. Timms shook his head as he approached.

'Nothing left, Mr Hinds. The pipe over there has ripped open down its entire length. It's a miracle they weren't both killed and then no one might have been saved the other night.'

The inspector looked about like a general overlooking a hard-won battlefield. The Carrigh men wandered the bluff, kicked at debris and carbide chips, waiting for the off. He frowned, following the white footprints tracked and painted onto the dark rock, heading to and through the valley between the slurry pile overlooking the promontory edge.

'What's down there?' he asked.

'Nothing,' said McConnell nervously swinging an arm around Jack's shoulder for support. 'Only a small cove.'

Hinds raised his nose to the air as though sniffing out the lie. 'Why would it be necessary to make so many trips through the waste and up to the beacon, especially during a time of crisis?' He glanced over at his associate. 'Go look.'

Timms looked less than enthusiastic about getting his patent leather boots filthy and picked his way, unsuccessfully, through the soft squelch of jellied paint. His tip-toed prancing caused the men to cease in their stone casting and snigger.

The inspector became angry, sending Timms slipping and sliding to the edge of the cliff and the start of the precarious steps. 'Hurry, man! We haven't got all day.'

'They lead downwards and to a cave or crevice of sorts,' he shouted, knowing that his fate was sealed with the information.

'Go and look, then,' sighed Hinds.

The man disappeared out of sight and McConnell squeezed Jack's shoulders.

'Did you remove all the crates?' he whispered.

Jack watched the inspector ten yards away as he paced back and forth. 'I think so.'

'You think so?'

'Mr Monaghan,' said Hinds after a few minutes. 'Will you ask my associate if he has found anything or is just sightseeing?'

The boatman smiled and tramped through the white morass to repeat the question to the man below.

'Nothing,' cried the timid voice beyond the edge. 'It's empty...wait – there's something on the sand below.'

Jack sensed McConnell's gaze upon him, fearing some remaining evidence of the hidden contraband that would land them both in hot water and scupper any of the old keeper's retirement plans. He studied the muddied white prints, wondering if he had truly smashed all the crates to feed the hungry lighthouse flame. It had been dark the night before and he cursed himself lest anything be found that he had missed. Clasping the charm about his neck he heard the man call up from below.

'Whisky, by the looks of things—'

Jack and McConnell held their breath.

'—or was. The blessed label is missing.'

'Anything else?' said the inspector, cupped hands about his mouth.

'No,' shouted Timms, clambering back up the cliff side path, clutching a stoppered, empty bottle. 'Unless you count what's in it. There's a message inside.'

Monaghan took hold of green glass and the arm of the man, pulling him to the white-washed summit. With clasped teeth, he uncorked and retrieved the strip of paper inside, putting his nose to the neck.

'It's old,' said the boatman, casting a quick, knowing glance at the keeper.

One of the local men broke into laughter. 'You would know, Seamus!'

The boatman suffered the amused indignity and continued his expert analysis. 'Probably come all the way from the Americas.'

In a modestly performed act of sabotage, he juggled with the wet, glassy sides as though unable to keep a hold. With a calculated, floundering clumsiness the bottle slipped through his hands and over the cliff, smashing halfway down into splintering green shards much to the relief of the keeper and his mate. The inspector studied the look of embarrassed innocence on Monaghan's face, as though trying to penetrate any ruse.

'That was careless,' he said, snatching at the fragment of paper and reading the single word.

'Who the hell is Mhairi?' he said holding it up as though announcing a raffle ticket winner. McConnell began the shaking of heads and rubbing of chins among the Carrigh men before the inspector tossed the scrap into the wind and stomped back to the lighthouse defeated, followed by his white-footed companion scraping the side of his boots against the meagre tufts of winter grass.

'I'm indebted to you, Seamus Monaghan,' said McConnell grabbing the boatman's belt as he turned to follow.

'It's not you that owes me, Dougal; it's your first mate, broken-legged and broken-hearted, waiting for you back at the inn.'

'What do you mean?' asked the keeper suspiciously.

Monaghan cleared his throat waiting for the men to return to the loading of the boat and preparations for leaving the isle. He bent down with a smug look on his face.

'You'll be needing a man with a boat,' he said nodding over to Jack, 'as well as a boy, to haul that whisky back someplace safe or did you think to make a raft of the other crates Winston hid on the opposite side of the isle in case such a thing should happen?'

McConnell's face turned from indignation to one of surprise, breaking into wide-eyed realisation.

'I used to send him down for a snifter when the nights got tough. You're telling me the scoundrel split the crates and moved them somewhere safe? He told me there wasn't much left.'

'The greater part, you old moon raking wickie. He included me to make sure the inspector wasn't overly curious. The best thing is,' he said, holding out his hand, 'we're partners.'

McConnell closed his eyes and shook the man's hand, grimacing with the joyful whistling of his departure.

'I don't think I can bear being in the debt of a man such as he.'

'I don't think you have much choice,' said Jack re-shouldering the weight of the man propped at his side as he moved off gently. 'Your pension is safe by the look of things, as is much of your little investment. If my efforts and the number of bottles I got through are any sign, there'll be enough to keep you walking, talking and remembering till the end of your days.'

McConnell paused, forcing Jack into a sudden stop. His eyes were focussed upon a seal, silver-patched, bobbing on the surface near the inlet to the channel. 'Odd that the only bottle that came back was hers, don't you think?'

Jack nodded as the animal dived beneath the waves. 'She belongs here. What about you?'

McConnell drew in a mighty breath and looked up at the gull-circled lighthouse. The men were signalling to be away, and Jack waited for the answer before helping him across the beaten path to the steps of the landing.

'I thought so once,' he replied, 'but now I'm ready to go home.'

MOONDANCE

Ashton huddled, shivering beneath his mud-splattered overcoat as the November air stole in through its seams to pickpocket his skin with piercing frosty fingers.

'Bickford Hall' mumbled the waggon driver, nodding his pipe-laden mouth towards the dark, cherry laurel-choked gateway on the right. 'You'll have to get off here because the mares won't go in.'

'Why not?'

'Because they are smarter and more sensitive to things than you or I. There's no arguing with 'em.'

The cold breached the open, buttonless coat as Ashton released his hands from deep within the threadbare silk-lined pockets.

'What "things"?' he said watching the horses skitter restlessly.

'Bad things,' he replied. 'That place has a reputation.'

Glad that the hard journey was mercifully at an end, he rose stiffly from the wooden board beside the driver and climbed down to splash in the deep, rutted track, wet with slush from the morning sleet. He slipped to the side of the open waggon to retrieve his case, dropping it into the muck of the road from the lack of feeling in his fingers. The driver sat staring down through the once grand entrance, puffing his pipe into the air like a steam locomotive. 'Staying long are you?'

Ashton slid his remaining luggage closer to the cart's side and hooked a satchel over his shoulder.

'Just till I get back on my feet again,' he said folding an oil paint-splattered easel under one arm and a large duffel bag under another. 'I'm hoping to get back to London as part of an exhibition of new artists in January after painting the house and the gardens – I hear they are both quite magnificent.'

The driver scoffed and glanced sideways at Ashton's pitiful appearance. 'I wouldn't know about that, but if that were true once upon a time, it ain't now. There's no money in pictures while folk are starving, but I hope 1920 will be better for you.' He flicked the reins, and the horses ambled up the hill and out of sight leaving the artist alone in the lonely Lincolnshire lane.

Slip-sliding toward the gloomy entrance, gateless and devoid of any identifiable signage, he tackled the dark, laurel-tunnelled driveway noticing the potholed hoggin surface was fresh and bore no sign of traffic or footfall since the squall earlier in the day.

The journey had begun at Cambridge in a warm railway carriage, and he had been eager to be away from home but excited by the possibilities of being his own man. A three-month tenancy of a small house on the estate, secured by his solicitor and the current housekeeper, had been arranged at a fair price from the meagre allowance granted by his few remaining assets. With high hopes, he rounded a tight corner, and the dilapidated manor house came into view.

His heart sank.

The trees gave way to an unclipped hedge-lined ride of four hundred yards, open to a bright blue sky bursting with the promise of glittering starlit frost to come. He half dragged his belongings past roofless stable blocks and door-less outhouses to meet the moss-covered gravel in front of the three-floored, ivy-clad Jacobean manor. Black windows, draped from within, reflected the forlorn, unkempt scene of the drive and the shoddy appearance of the new arrival. He had left quickly after the final altercation with his father, seven months earlier, and his clothes were becoming faded in marked contrast to the painful memories that kept his spirit burning, and his desire fed, to pursue his own path. He turned sideways to see the hastily borrowed workman's coat hanging from his once athletic six-foot frame, now a size too large from the weight lost through hunger, travel, and absti-nence from creamed mushrooms, cognac, and capons.

Curtain walls draped either side of the honey-bricked frontage through which a single arch was prominent on the left, revealing itself as the route to a cobbled courtyard. A rotund woman with puffing red cheeks appeared from one of the terraced doors, her shawl tied about a clean but worn apron. She called out, beckoning him towards the tradesman's entrance.

'Mr Berkeley?' she said.

'Yes,' said Ashton joining her. 'I'm here about the lodge house let.'

She smiled, relieving her furrowed brows back to smooth, supple skin, and rubbed her blackened, Brasso-stained palms through a multi-coloured rag pulled from beneath her pinafore. The housekeeper put two fingers in her mouth and whistled, summoning an eager young man, thin and spindly in sharp contrast.

'Coming Mrs White,' he called, stuffing his hands into his overly large, hand-me-down jacket to escape the cold.

'Help take the gentleman's things over to the handcart while I make up a pot of tea; I dare say he needs it after all that way from Wisbech in a carriage.'

'I wouldn't call it a carriage,' said Ashton, releasing his luggage to the helpful concierge and relieving the ache in his arms. 'The coachman wasn't quite what I expected, but he was the only one willing to bring me out so far after the recent floods and bad weather.'

She looked him over as though examining a truant child returning from a muddy adventure, fixing on the shabby outer coat and giving him a stern but motherly glance. 'Well, you're not quite what I expected either, sir, begging your pardon, but you look half-perished, so let's get inside and I'll talk you through the arrangements. We've bread and cold meat from yesterday if you're hungry but you'll have to take us as you find us as I explained in my letter to your solicitor, but Hal, here, got the water running this morning by unfreezing the pipes so there's a comfort. We can't have Lord Berkeley's only son bathing in the lake now, can we?'

Ashton gripped the warm, enamel tea mug and thawed in a threadbare easy chair by the Hall's kitchen fire as Mrs White elaborated on the arrangements. Food and hot water would be brought over to the lodge every morning with the main meal in the evening, taken in the parlour. Candles and logs for his small fireplace would be restocked by the diligent Hal for light and warmth, not provided for by any other means such as gas or electricity.

'And the owner, Miss Pendlesham?' he said. 'Will she be in residence at all over Christmas, or during my stay? I should like to thank her for the opportunity.'

Mrs White held out a plate of brittle, baked biscuits. 'It's possible, but only for short periods and she prefers her own company, so I'll ask you kindly not to press the matter. Your coming was my doing, but I have her authority, and—'

Ashton took a honey-crumbed mouthful waiting for the woman to finish her melancholic musing around the antiquated room.

'As you can see the place needs a bit of upkeep and your rent will help pay for a few much-needed necessities.'

He nodded. 'A large house calls for a lot of maintenance – is there revenue from other sources on the estate?'

Mrs White drew in a deep breath and looked out of the window. 'There's pasture on the other side of the wood which itself is tenanted out for pannage and pigs. We've got a working cider mill on the lake, but no one was willing to take it on this year on account of the poor weather and prospects — shame all those orchard apples are going to waste.'

'Has Bickford been in her family long?'

She nodded, turning to set down the plate. 'For hundreds of years, just as it is now. My mother worked for her, and her mother before that, here in this very room.'

Ashton drained the last of his mug. 'I like the idea of things slowing down, at least somewhere at the beginning of the twentieth century, with so much change. I feel that modernism has its drawbacks, but maybe that's just my father's influence speaking...'

'Try unchanged,' she added with a flash of her eyes. 'Hal will walk you to the lodge with your belongings and show you what's off limits.'

'I wasn't aware there were any restrictions?' said Ashton, rising from the seat to bid a sad and silent farewell to the open fire. 'I don't need access to the house beyond the kitchen if that is a concern.'

Mrs White rubbed at her chin. 'It's not much to ask and

truth be told I didn't want to mention it in case it affected the terms, it being in the garden.'

'What am I to avoid?'

'There's a path from the parterre that leads to the maze,' she said, avoiding his gaze. 'It's fenced off, and no one has been allowed in there since well before my grandmother's time.'

'Is there a reason?'

'No,' said Mrs White. 'On Miss Pendlesham's orders, and what's said by her is set in stone.'

'You a painter?' said Hal peering at the easel as he pushed the handcart along the southern side of the Hall.

'I'm trying to be,' said Ashton, taking in the weak sun and dramatic view over the wide, poorly kept formal gardens. Beyond, the gently rolling landscaped park was punctuated by fallen trees and avenues of unclipped topiary hedges. 'I have had some small success with portraits, but wanted to try my hand at landscape scenes.'

'How'd you end up here?'

Ashton covered his eyes to make out the peeping, glittering presence of a serpentine lake, fed by a cascading stream. 'I was looking for a place to stay for a while and an acquaintance put me in touch with Mrs White when they could not reach the owner.'

Hal changed direction to skirt and squeak the cart past the rear façade and made for a much-used path towards a wood bordering the western edge of the garden. The thin rays of the sun were lost as they plunged into the gloom of the heavy canopy, leaving the flagstone parterre that lay at the feet of warm, wisteria-wound brickwork. Hal's bright and inquisitive nature was suddenly dimmed as they meandered their way to meet a junction of paths. Ahead, a heavily chained and padlocked gate rose defensively with rusted, lofty railings stretching off for several hundred yards on either side before cornering and fading into the trees. Sharp spears topped the cast-iron spindles, over ten feet high, and beyond, a deep and bramble overgrown ditch like a dry-moated hill-fort led to a dense, raised impasse of gloomy, unclipped yew hedge.

'Lodge is this way,' said Hal turning to the left to follow the route along the barrier that led out of the wood, eager to be away from the place. Ashton strode forward and peered through the bars.

A discernible path led on for some ten yards before terminating at a block of evergreen hedge. Moving his head to the side of the gate he could just make out narrow and thicketed perpendicular paths within the enclosure. Despite nature's reclamation of the area, it had once been nurtured and tamed by man.

'What's in there?'

Hal paused and set down the handles of the cart. 'The maze. No one is supposed to go in.'

Ashton studied the two rusted padlocks weeping ruddy tears from the condensation forming in the damp air. 'I don't suppose one could get in even if they wanted to. Is there a reason it's out of bounds?'

Hal rubbed at his head considering his reply. 'Only that they say it is dangerous inside and Miss Pendlesham doesn't want anyone getting hurt.'

'She sounds a very conscientious employer?'

Hal shrugged. 'I've only met her once on account of me only being here since the spring of last year. All dressed up in black like the picture of old Queen Vic that hangs above the archway in the village hall over at Waycross though I never heard tell of her majesty wearing a veil.'

'Miss Pendlesham wears a veil?'

'Yeah – you get used to it but it's hard not seeing someone's face – makes it difficult to appreciate how they feel about you, if you know what I mean.'

'I do indeed,' said Ashton half to himself. 'Some people don't even need to wear veils for that to happen...'

'Pardon?' said Hal.

'Nothing.'

Ashton looked at the lad trying to figure things out using the contortions of his face rather than the sharpness of his mind.

'Perhaps she was in mourning for someone — a relative?'

Hal shrugged. 'Don't think she has any family, at least not anymore. I know she never married and is very old, but Mrs White doesn't like folk getting too inquisitive.'

'She must live the rest of the year elsewhere – London perhaps?' said Ashton. 'It's a big enough place for me to not have met, or heard of her.'

'Don't know,' said Hal. 'I've never been so far as Boston, myself. She never arrives like other folks, as there's never a carriage, horse, or motorcar. She just comes and goes without warning. It should put Mrs White in a fit, but the house is always ready, such as it is.'

'Miss Pendlesham's privilege I guess,' said Ashton leaving the gate behind. 'Shame about the maze, though.'

Hal rubbed at his elbows to ward off the chill. 'You ain't missing much – just overgrown paths and a funny old statue in the centre that's seen better times.' He put his hand to his mouth to prevent further talk, waiting for his brain to catch up and realise he had said too much.

'And how would you know that if you've never been inside?' said Ashton with a smile. He put a raised finger to his lips. 'Don't worry, your secret is safe with me.'

The young man fidgeted and pointed further up the track.

'There's a loose railing up near the far corner, enough for a small or thin person to squeeze through. I don't recommend it though as it's rough work getting into it from the ditch, or it was last spring when I was mucking about in there. I didn't do any harm, honest, but—'

Ashton moved closer to see him genuinely perturbed. 'But what?'

'If no one is allowed in there and there aren't any gardeners left to maintain it, how come something makes paths in there?'

'You mean you can still navigate through it?'

Hal nodded. 'It's rough going in parts, but the grass is, or was, flattened in places and there were fresh prints in the old hoggin path that I followed, like those made by heavy feet.'

A breeze from the parkland lifted the lime-tree leaves and Ashton wrinkled his nose at the scent of a wood fire. On the other side of the water, a thin trail of pale smoke rose from a wooded copse like a cigarette at rest in a hidden, sylvan ashtray.

'Gipsy,' said Hal following his gaze. 'Someone who turns up at the beginning of November with his statues and stuff for sale, but he doesn't cause much trouble, mostly rabbiting and fishing when he can give me the slip. I'm told not to meddle in his affairs as the mistress gives him leave to stay at this time of year.'

'She seems a very charitable lady – perhaps he takes liberties and makes the tracks inside the maze?'

Hal scratched his head. 'Maybe, but he don't seem the type and he's too wide to get through where I did – a big strong man he is, built like a brick-lavvy, on account of him labouring with stone no doubt.'

'Well, if you want me to keep your secret,' said Ashton lifting the handcart carrying his belongings. 'You'll have to keep mine. Not a word to anyone that I am related to the

Berkeley family, let alone the absent, discredited heir; I prefer no special treatment or reminder while I am here.'

Hal nodded, lifting the duffel bag to ease Ashton's task, following alongside until they withdrew from the wood and turned to follow a perimeter hedge-lined path towards the lake. The small two-floored lodge came into view, squat and homely. Ashton suspected the quaint thatched reminder of former fortunes had once been an overflow of the house for those desperate to escape the bustle of the Hall. He had spent his youth in such follies and summerhouses on his family's estate before everything had changed – before Gretchen, the War, and his exile.

'Pretty ain't she?' said Hal highlighting the life-size stone figure of a woman on a short plinth. 'I mean apart from her face being rubbed away by the wind and rain. Not like that one in the maze missing bits of head and arm – enough to give you nightmares.'

Enclosed by a semi-circular screen of scrubby rhododendrons, and overlooking the lake, stood a statue of such exquisite beauty and craftsmanship that Ashton dropped the cart handles in astonishment. Marred only by the weathering to one side of her expertly carved face so that the eye could barely be discerned, the woman posed mid-dance with lichen-covered arms emerging above a thin and belted gown to twist snake-like above her head. Her hair cascaded in ringlets down the worn cheek and swept to meet her narrow waist. Unclad feet, delicately hinting at finely carved nails were bent in movement, frozen in time between phrases of the dance.

'I've never seen such work,' said Ashton marvelling at the larger-than-life nymph carved in pale limestone. 'Not even in Italy. Certainly over a hundred years old, but it's not Diana or Aphrodite...'

'One of Miss Pendlesham's ancestors,' interrupted Hal.

'There's an old painting of her in the morning room. It's getting as tired as this likeness.'

Ashton forced himself away from the Mona Lisa smile and back to the wooded copse and its spreading, smoky haze. 'Maybe the gipsy could restore this fine lady, but I daresay she deserves to be put in a museum so more people can admire her beauty. Selling her could raise substantial sums to help with—'

Hal recoiled with shock. 'I wouldn't suggest it. Miss Pendlesham would have a fit! Mrs White says they've had folk over the years trying to buy it.' He tugged at a handful of spent ox-eye daisy stems from the unkempt grass below and laid them reverently at the statue's feet. 'I'm glad she stays here where she belongs.'

After a further ten minutes of twittering from Hal pointing out the best spots for impressive and picturesque locations to view the house, they reached the lodge a hundred yards beyond a small wooden bridge at the end of the lake where it cascaded over a branch strewn weir into a rushing stream on the other side. A quarter mile back along the serpentine water stood a similar-sized building with a stationary waterwheel, positioned to take advantage of a diverted channel to power the cider mill.

Aston put down the handcart as Hal nudged open the door to the clean, white-washed interior. From within the simple ground floor room, wooden steps led up to the bedroom. 'I'll bring you some logs tomorrow as it's going to be dreadful cold and clear tonight, but the fire's all set for you and there'll be plenty for now.' He remained like a faithful dog seeking confirmation of a good deed. 'I've tried to make it as comfortable as possible under the circumstances.'

Ashton smiled to the lad's relief and reached into his pockets to withdraw a few pennies. Hal shook his head.

'No need, sir, I have everything I require right here at

Bickford, and I don't want to be anywhere else.' He shuffled his feet and looked at the floor. 'But if you have a mind, maybe you'll draw me and Mrs White one of the days, and we'll stand as still as those statues out there.'

Ashton blew on his fingers to ward off the intense cold. A mist was forming about the grassy sward leading down to the lake's edge and he squinted at the pencil sketch of the statue before him. After a short appreciation of what the sparse but comfortable interior of his tenancy offered, he had unpacked, changing into drier, fresher clothes, determined to grab the dying light to revisit and capture his sense of wonderment. It had not diminished and seemed to grow with the intimacy of being alone with the figure. For over an hour he had stood, heedless of the hoar frost developing on the spider webs of the background hedge, hurriedly working with rapid glances back and forth from the page to his subject. To his surprise, he paused and removed three pennies from his pocket stacking them next to the dew-laden daisies and stared into the beautiful, marred face, whispering aloud what he thought was only in his mind.

'I wouldn't sell you either. If you were mine, I would die penniless before I let anyone take you away from me. You remind me of her...'

He twisted round to see a swooping phalanx of swans as they noisily alighted on the lake, disappearing into the creeping mist forming from the brief thawing of the sunlit afternoon. Tonight would be cold, and with some regret he turned toward the candlelight of the lodge, wrapping his precious scarf about his mouth to dampen the sharp tang of the air. Gifted by one who would now never need such comforts, Ashton flicked through the loose-leaved pages to find her, resigned and forlorn at their parting in the previous summer, the final sketch before her sailing from Southampton to Bombay, beyond his reach, and out of his life.

A wave of gentle heat welcomed him back to his studio and home. He poured himself a cup of icy water from a chipped ceramic jug and lit one of the few remaining luxury cigarettes from a silver case in his breast pocket before retiring upstairs to order his paints and materials in the warmer, fire-grated room above.

He opened a narrow leather-bound box to remove the cold brass of an extendable surveyor's telescope, moving to the round, leaded window. Rubbing at the condensation of the glass did not improve the view in the mill's direction, masked by mist. A feeling of vertigo and being above the clouds was narrowly averted by the high hedge running back into the woodland close to the house. The hall itself was partially obscured by foreground trees but he scanned across the newly familiar route that he and Hal had taken earlier. Though modestly higher from his position, the maze was revealed, obliquely and between sections of shrubbery. Had he not known that the old garden feature was a labyrinth, he would have overlooked the thinly parted lines of yew as simply a monotonous bank of evergreen plantings, long bereft of a master gardener's skilled hand.

A pale object at its centre, at odds with the dark surroundings, brought him to a stop, and he twisted the small lens to better focus on the statue, man-sized atop a short, square plinth. Putting down the spyglass he returned with his sketchbook and pencil to define it. It was, as Hal had indicated, alike in style to that of the dancing woman, and while it suggested that the sculptor was the same, the similarities ended there. With glances at the page, Ashton picked out the details of the monstrous, almost bestial figure imprisoned within the verdant hectare.

At first, he assumed it was some depiction from Greek or Roman mythology perhaps Pan or a demonic creature from antiquity. The figure arched back, legs astride to steady a roaring challenge or cry of painful anguish from its open mouth; certainly humanoid, but heavily damaged from the midpoint of the skull down to below the waist and the whole left side of its body, arm and all, was missing. The surviving hand gripped at roughly curled suggestions of finely carved hair as though in torment. Ashton lowered the scope to relieve the fatigue in his elbow.

His heart raced as he examined the hasty sketch, cleansing his thoughts with the thought of catching sight of the dancing statue, but it was blocked and overshadowed by the taller shrubs at the outer edge of the crescent within which she remained cradled. The dusk deepened to a dim damson light, and he put aside the piece in favour of sleep and forgetfulness. Blowing out the lamp, he lay down on the bed and drowsed into dark dreams.

He awoke suddenly in a floodlit beam of midnight moon, filtered through the frost on the circular glass oculus. Blinking to set the slumber free from his eyes he rose and rubbed at a leaded diamond panel to reveal an illuminated landscape, sharp and colourless. His steaming breath condensed on the window, but through the haze, he caught sight of movement on the ice-speckled sward before the lake.

A woman, bare-footed and thinly dressed for the conditions, leapt lightly upon the grass, dancing and swirling, oblivious to the freezing night. She was pale, and Ashton found it difficult to differentiate between her skin and ivory silk. Dark, lustrous hair tumbled across the side of her young and lithe face and neck, tossed and spilled by hands that writhed and revelled in some sensuous expression of awakening and joy.

He scrambled for the telescope, desperate to discern what

manner of fey creature spun and whirled with such wild abandon, but the freezing glass simply magnified the icy haze. His
fingers twisted the ice-stinging latch to swing open the hoar-
frosted portal admitting the piercing, frigid night. The
woman was no longer there and his heart struggled with the
loss even as his shivering hand sought to hold the scope
steady. To his relief she reappeared, ghostly in aspect but fully
corporeal clutching the spent flowers and peering down curiously at something cupped in her other palm.

From the wooded maze came a wailing night sound
Ashton had never heard before. It rose like the screech of a
mating dog fox but, though he could not catch them, he
knew there were words contained within the ghastly cry. He
put the scope to his eye, leaning far out of the window to get
as close as possible to see the woman turn sharply and cast
aside the brittle bouquet and the objects from her free hand.
She raised her outstretched palms towards the forested enclosure in a gesture of rejection.

The spyglass swung back and forth, Ashton half thinking
he had seen something pale and fast-moving within the
labyrinth, but his numb fingers struggled to hold on to the
freezing metal tube and it slipped from his grasp. It fell, end
over end, striking the brickwork as it tumbled and bounced
from the humble porch roof to land on the sandstone sets of
the short entrance path in a teeth-clenching clatter of
cracked glass and dented brass. He retreated into the lodge,
scraping his stomach against the sharp, rusted frame, but it
was too late. The woman turned to see him flounder into the
first-floor room and he froze unsure whether to duck and
hide or act out some ridiculous midnight farce of closing the
window now that the chamber had been sufficiently aired.
Fortunately, the decision was taken from him.

A further scuffling and clanging from the direction of the
wood regained her attention, and the woman raced away. A

single candle burned in the central first-floor window like a golden beacon against the silvered monochrome of the moonlit, frosted scene. He followed her for a few seconds more before she moved beyond the trunk of a twisted and lightning-blasted oak and out of sight. The bitter cold burgled its way in and Ashton pulled the leaded glass shut setting his sketches tumbling to the creaking floorboards.

In a beam of moonlight, not daring to light the lamp, he sketched the vision of the dancing woman frozen in a moment of time before sinking to his knees shivering with more than just the cold. Even with the window closed, a final, mournful, and whimpering cry from the wood penetrated the silence and chilled his blood.

Hal was breathless and red-cheeked from his flight to the lodge carrying the hot water and basket of provisions. He coughed and spluttered with the exertion to relay the shocking news – the statue of the dancing woman was missing. A rapid dress and march brought them to the hard-frozen spot, freshly trodden with the young man's boots. Upon the ground lay the scattered flowers, and Hal found one penny, with Ashton discovering another of the remaining two even as he imagined faint, bare footprints leading away from the empty plinth.

Whether through a wish to keep the midnight fantasy to himself, Ashton remained quiet as Hal mumbled about the same having occurred about the same time the previous year. The statue had been returned undamaged and unmolested the following month after both the gipsy's departure and that of Miss Pendlesham. The coincidence seemed bizarre.

'Why would he remove the statue for a month and then put it back?' asked Hal thoughtfully. 'It weren't in no better condition after it turned up again so he didn't take it away to fix it.'

Ashton had no answer and only a single question following the demise of his telescope. 'What about the one in the maze – is there any sign of the locks being tampered with?'

Hal shook his head. 'I hurried past just as dawn was breaking. If he or anyone else has been in there, it weren't through the gate.'

The ground about them showed no evidence of a sled or cart necessary for the removal of such a weighty object. Ashton doubted even one man could drag it far without heavy effort, and the thought of two men carrying it for long was equally unlikely.

'Did you hear anything strange last night?' he asked, wondering if it bore any relation to the disappearance. 'It sounded like an injured animal over in the wood closest to the house.'

'I sleep soundly on account of the work I'm given,' replied Hal, yawning, as though honesty was not persuasive enough. 'But you hear uncomfortable sounds if you're unfamiliar with them. There's muntjac for example. The first time I heard barking and grunting like that in the middle of the night I swear I didn't close my eyes for days till I saw the prints not far from here. Queer things for sure – escaped from some estate down south by all accounts.'

There in the early morning sun, the threat of something unseen and unimaginable had diminished and Ashton had accepted the suggestion to end the conversation. No animal had such a call, even one as strange and eerie as a Chinese deer. 'Probably nothing more than night noises in an unfamiliar place.'

Hal returned to his work and Ashton retired briefly to the lodge to collect his tools and materials before settling off on a cursory walk to sketch at various points on his way to a prime vantage point across the lake. The sun passed the low, noontide high for the day as he put down his pencil on the easel's lower rail and reached for the thermos flask. The hot tea steamed in the cup and he mused on the larger piece before him, detailing the house and major garden features. Despite the distraction of the mysterious theft, and circular reasoning in his head, the morning's work had gone well: a vignette of the plinth, bereft of purpose; a distant impression of the cider mill from the partly frozen race that fed the icicle-bearded water wheel; and now the grand view of the south aspect of the hall.

From the central first-floor window, a dark silhouette flitted between the tied-back curtains. Ashton rued the loss of his surveyor's scope as the slim figure briefly reappeared and paused, seeing him. Averting his eyes and picking up his pencil in the pretence of working at the drawing, he stole glances at the occupant. Too svelte for Mrs White, and Hal could be heard distantly corralling wayward chickens from the courtyard. The person stepped back into the shadows of the room and vanished, but Ashton had the uncomfortable sense that the eyes were still watching him from the darkness.

He drained the remnants of the tepid brew and went on for a further hour at the sketch hoping to realise the designs on canvas when his pre-arranged supplies arrived, and the weather became too inclement to be abroad. From the parterre he caught Mrs White waving to gain his attention. She waddled along the central path to join the hedged lawn calling out and beckoning him with urgency. He trudged up the garden rise to meet her, case and easel in hand.

'Mistress is here,' she puffed. 'Arrived in the small hours. I've just told Hal, but she's wanting to see you.'

'Now?' said Ashton glancing anxiously at his work tweeds

and looking up at the first-floor window. The curtains were drawn against any possibility of further voyeurism or sunlight.

Mrs White shrugged. 'You'll have to do, and I daresay you look a darn sight better than you did this time yesterday.'

'What does she want to see me about?'

'I was only told to fetch,' she said grabbing the easel, 'and carry. I'll show you to the morning room and you can pick up your things when you are done.' She halted. 'She seems intrigued because you're an artist, and a Berkeley, but Miss Pendlesham's got an audience with another in a short while, so you'll be free to go back to your painting soon.'

Leaving his case in the kitchen, Ashton followed the huffing and puffing housekeeper up the main staircase of the hall, sketchbook, and folio in hand. Candlelit sconces bobbed to illuminate the beeswax-polished linen-fold panels, directing him to a set of double doors.

'I'll leave you to it,' said Mrs White. 'If you'll excuse me, I need to make preparations for the other...gentleman.'

The housekeeper retreated down the corridor and Ashton knocked on the panelled wood.

'Come...' said a whispered voice, hoarse but clear.

The doors parted with the lightest of touches to reveal a rich, fabric-draped room lit by pale green glass oil lamps. A merry fireplace rejoiced in glowing amber to meet the opulent plum and burgundy velvets of the drapes that covered two floor-to-ceiling windows. Between them hung a great tapestry, indistinct but bearing the sparkling reflection of gold thread in the coats and tabards of medieval figures at play among the branches of a starlit wood. Ashton squinted in the fantastical setting, old, out of fashion, but vibrant and decadent. Heavy, carved Jacobean side tables and caskets, among the Georgian plush sedans and jacquard couches, were draped with lengths of white cotton, rucked as though only recently removed from their dust-protecting duties. Ashton's clinical eye saw little that belonged to any period later than the early nineteenth century, a remarkable feat for a house apparently forgotten by the Victorian and Edwardian ages.

The sense of loneliness, solitude, and quiet contemplation was broken from the shadowed corner as a veiled woman in raven black raised a sable-lined velvet glove to indicate a seat in a high-backed, cushioned chair to her right.

'Won't you sit down, Mr Berkeley?' she said, her voice croaking as she cleared her rattling throat.

'Miss Pendlesham,' replied Ashton coming over to take her hand. 'A pleasure to meet you—'

The soft gloved fingers hooked into his palm, but despite the gentile cupping, the weight seemed uncanny. She appeared frail, her speech harried and hoarse, and the thickly patterned lace of her dark veil all but obscured the face. Neatly bound hair, black and lustrous, glistened beneath the pearl-pinned embroidery of the veil's web-like hood.

She withdrew her arm and settled it beside the other in her lap and Ashton sat down, eyes adjusting to the dim surroundings.

'Welcome to Bickton. I trust Mrs White has made you comfortable and you are enjoying the landscape and gardens laid out by my fath—' she corrected herself and acknowledged a large richly framed oil painting above the fireplace, 'laid out by my forefathers.'

Ashton studied the artwork, whose age-cracked surface became clearer with each passing moment. He recognised the oblique views of the house and garden, almost as though the artist of the Regency period had shared the same vantage point that afternoon. The Hall stood proud in its red-bricked majesty, crowned about with a once fine parterre of scrolled, boxwood topiary, colourful plantings, fruit trees and sharp, geometric hedging. The edge of the lake shone in the foreground, glittering in the closeness of the flickering oil lamps on the marbled mantle below, but dominated by the hedged lawn and two figures – a young, dark-haired woman and a small white dog sitting attentively beside. Her hand held out a piece of parchment upon which could faintly be made out the design for a maze.

'She's been most accommodating, thank you. The painting – I'd recognise the gardens at once from such a fine —' He stopped to examine the pale face of the woman, the same, beautiful visage of the dancing moonlit maiden. Ashton rose, unwittingly scattering the folio and the contents of the sketchbook onto the floor, and made his way closer to confirm his suspicion. 'Remarkable,' he said studying the detail of the enigmatic woman.

'Thank you,' said Miss Pendlesham. 'It was commissioned at the opening of the works and represents both the beginning and end of Bickford's fortunes. It was a warm day even in the shade...'

Ashton turned, absorbed in the retrieval of his fallen sketches. 'Forgive me, I was professionally curious; I thought I recognised the likeness of the woman in the painting from someone I encountered yesterday.' He shuffled the pages to a pile before they were pressed by the shining black boot of Miss Pendlesham. She bent lithely to retrieve them. The dancing figure captured her attention, and Ashton, kneeling before the mysterious matriarch in mourning garb, caught the firelight reflecting the wide-eyed astonishment in the polished jet of a single pupil.

'You have talent, Mr Berkeley,' she said. 'If I didn't know better, I'd say this was drawn from the life...'

Ashton rose and rearranged his composure, and his sheets, in the seat beside her. 'I saw someone last night from the lodge, the very image of the lady in the painting – a relative staying with you perhaps?'

The woman remained transfixed on the sheet. 'It's been a

long time since anyone painted a Pendlesham at Bickford. I wonder what it portents?' She turned the page to the next drawing. 'And who is this fine lady – your wife, Lady Berkeley?'

Ashton plucked at his lip and glanced upon the remembrance of his beloved Gretchen. 'No. We were to be married, but circumstances dictated otherwise.' He held out his unsteady, ringless fingers. 'If you haven't already been told, my father and I are...estranged, so there's unlikely to be a Lady Berkeley.'

Miss Pendlesham raised her left gloved hand. No ring adorned any of the fingers. 'I sympathise,' she said. 'We appear to have something in common. My own father dictated a course for me at variance with my true feelings and wishes. He died shortly after I refused to be his chattel and marry someone to serve his purposes. It was a long time ago and I'm saddened to hear that marriage for love is still a privilege granted only to the poor.' Lowering her hand, she tilted her eyes to meet his own through the embroidered lace. 'I hope you will both find a resolution, in time.'

'You see plainly, or at least are well-informed,' said Ashton raising a half smile. I thank you for your wishes and your hospitality, but I am resigned to be my own man and not merely the instrument of my father's ambitions.'

'A noble gesture for a disinherited nobleman,' she said returning the smile, visible at the margin of the veil. On the side of the portrait's face, a smudge caught her attention.

'A pity about the stain.'

'It's part of who she was. A wine mark, a disfigurement of the skin that she ensured I kept in her portraits. She insisted it didn't matter between us in the flesh, so why in the realm of art?'

Miss Pendlesham shuffled in her chair and released the

drawing back to his outstretched hand. 'The ability to see beyond another's imperfections is a rare gift indeed.'

'My father had a better match in mind to bolster the family's ambitions, one that did not incur any racial or political ramifications, or unscientific, superstitious notions of her disfigurement despoiling the Berkeley line for generations to come.'

'She was not English?'

He shook his head. 'Her name was Gretchen, and we were about to go to war with Germany.'

'I see,' said Miss Pendlesham. 'How inconvenient.'

Ashton smiled sadly, surprised by his candidness in front of the spinster.

'She was the daughter of the Count of Bavaria.'

'What happened to her?'

'At the outbreak of the war, her family took her to India to avoid any consequences from their pacifistic objections and close ties with the British government. She died the following spring from malaria.' Ashton sighed and held out his hand for the remaining sheets. 'Forgive me, I have been so long away from society that I forget my manners—'

'I knew a Harlon Berkeley, once,' she said handing back the sketches with no sign of boredom or eagerness to change the subject. 'Tall and athletic as a young man with a dimple in his chin.' She paused, turning to stare at him from within her veil. 'Not unlike the one you bear yourself. You remind me of him...'

Ashton raised the end of his clenched palm instinctively to shield the lower half of his face. He coughed to hide his self-consciousness, and she returned to gaze at the landscape painting above the fire. In a distant corner of the grand work, small figures upon horses racing point-to-point caught her attention.

'He was an excellent horseman and due to inherit a large estate in the south—'

'My great-grandfather was called Harlon,' said Ashton, surprised with the revelation, 'and there's a painting of him in his colours that hangs in our morning room, just after he won the St Ledger Stakes back in 1816. Legend has it he paid off the jockey to take his place and impress a young lady.' He closed his eyes to recall the east-facing suite with its fragrance of Earl Grey and gladioli, the sounds of the mantelpiece clock ticking away the restless, rainy hours of a childhood spent inside jumping among cushions. The smile from the fond remembrance faded as he wondered when or if he would return.

'Green and yellow,' said Miss Pendlesham, stroking a hand across her black gown as though to smooth through the creases of the silk tabard recalled from memory. 'Did he?'

'Did he what?'

'Impress her?' she asked.

Ashton frowned. 'Possibly, but I'm not sure he ended up marrying her. Your description sounds on point, but he would have been far too old for you to have known him in his prime.' His host raised a hand to pluck at a tarnished silver locket around her silk-wrapped neck, the only bright and reflective thing about her person apart from the sparkle of her eye, untainted by cataract or time.

'Perhaps you visited my father, the present Lord Berkeley, and saw the portrait?' he said seeking to avoid any offence regarding the woman's age, or her mental capacity to grasp the passage of time.

'Perhaps,' she said after a long pause.

Ashton stole a lengthy sideways glance. Miss Pendlesham sat upright, staring into the canvas, focussed on the young woman and the small white dog at her feet. She rubbed at the back of her hand to scratch at some itch, removing the glove, unaware of being observed. He only glimpsed the smooth, pallid skin for a moment, heavily freckled and tainted by some unknown callous. It was taut, supple and not marred by age except by its complexion. An unseasoned log spat out a fiery glede and he jumped causing her to turn and see his gaze upon her. The glove was hurriedly replaced, and she expertly broke the awkward silence.

'Impress me, Mr Berkeley. Paint Bickford for me before my time passes. Be kind to the old place and look past its imperfections when you capture them.'

'I will,' said Ashton interrupted from further speech by the knocking and entrance of the curtsying housekeeper.

'Begging your pardon, ma'am. Mr Doe is here to see you, as arranged.'

Miss Pendlesham rose and creaked heavily across the rug-covered boards despite her modest height and light frame. Her black, bustle-backed gown rustled as she turned to signal the audience was over, and for a moment Ashton thought she appeared older, hunched in her shoulders as though the lightness and familiar remembrances had been replaced by a heavier, more sombre premonition of what was to come.

'If you'll forgive me, Mr Berkeley, I have an engagement with fate that cannot be avoided.'

Ashton rose and collected his folio and sketchbook, nodding his goodbye as he reached the doors. Turning to close them, he glimpsed her, gloved hands raised to stifle a shuddering sob beneath her veil. From the stairs below came the hurried voice of the housekeeper and the heavy footfall of another, climbing and thumping between the steps with what sounded like a walking stick.

As he descended to the landing, he passed the approaching, thickset man in a long burgundy corduroy coat and flecked woollen trousers that bulged to hint at the muscles bristling beneath. Red-haired and bearded, he thumped up the stairs like a Dickensian beadle bearing a chunky ebony cane, mounted with a carved granite ball. The man briefly hesitated in his climb to acknowledge him with a twitch of his green eyes and the tip of his ribbon-lined Homburg hat before continuing upward.

On the ground floor, Mrs White was poorly attempting to remain outside of eavesdropping range, and from above there came a loud thud on the double doors, answered by the strained hoarse rasp of Miss Pendlesham.

'Every year he comes just like his father before him,' said the housekeeper, half to herself. 'Bad luck to have that folk in the house, especially that one.'

'What folk do you mean, Mrs White, and why him in particular?'

She lowered to a whisper as though the mere mention would bring down the Hall about them there and then.

'Gipsies,' she said. 'He's the king of the gipsies.'

The late afternoon dimmed to dreary dusk as Ashton wound his way through the parterre knots, leaving behind his belongings in favour of a long and circuitous walk back to the lodge. The dark wooded path heralded a gloaming so deep that he blinked to reassure himself that night had not yet fallen.

'*Not far,*' he thought, '*and then out into the brighter overlook of the lake and the waterfowl settling on the water.*'

He crunched upon broken beech seed cases, pausing at the gate to the maze. A glance showed patches of dim light pooling within dark, leafy walls of yew, but the padlocks remained firm; the portal impregnable, unscalable with its bristle of sharp spearheads. Ashton walked on to meet the far corner of the cast-iron palisade. A few short strides brought him to the railings, and he stepped between tall remnants of nettles to test the legitimacy of Hal's testimony.

The braced corner railings were firm and his hands became caked with damp, rusted flakes as he tested each adjoining spindle sandwiched between horizontal bars four feet apart. About to give up and return to the promise of open ground, he pushed away on an upright to discover it bent backwards, broken at the lower perpendicular bar. With a little effort, he bent enough space to fit a shoulder through, almost touching the brambles in the ditch. It would be tight, even if he removed his coat...

With a guilty look about, he squeezed down through the makeshift triangular sliver, barely eighteen inches wide. Even with his loss of weight and the abandonment of his coat to an accommodating oak stub, he had to breathe in to rub himself unceremoniously through the bars. Crunching and weaving through the steep, moated bank, he reached the wall of the perimeter yew seeking an entry to the maze. If the statue he had seen at its centre from afar was missing, and heavy boots had recently left any prints, then he would make his host aware of his suspicions; she would surely forgive his trespass to discover the truth. He failed to understand how such a man would gain entry, let alone carry off the valuable and weighty piece. Perhaps he had a key to the gate or had secured some other railing entry, wider than that of his own inglorious ingress.

Ten yards along the ledge-like top of the bank he found a small dead section between two trunks and pushed his way through to the centre of the leafless hedge. It was wider than he imagined and took several yards of scratching subterfuge to emerge on the other side into an overgrown path that stretched in both directions as far as the eye could see. Yew branches stretched from either side like lovers desperate and divided, trying to reach the comfort of each other's arms. The hedge resisted any similar shortcuts, and he meandered through the centre line of the path whose surface was lightly muddied leaving light footprints on the surface of the clay.

Trying to recall any hint of form or solution from his cursory glances the night before, or the design upon the parchment held by the beautiful young ancestor of Miss Pendlesham, he remembered Theseus' good sense and tied a handkerchief to a branch on the perimeter path to highlight the way out. A path on the right plunged into a myriad of turns, but it became easier the closer he moved towards what he estimated was the centre. The hedge towered above him, but impassable turnings gave way to thinner, easier-accessed routes guiding him by necessity into the centre of the maze.

He caught a glimpse through a thinner patch of yew as he was about to turn back. Something ornamental and structured, man-made within a defined clearing was close and within touching distance. He staggered on, hand before his face as he abandoned any stealth and hurried along the pathways most accessible. At first, and as expected, they took him away from his objective, but after several false turns, he emerged into the open air to see the ruined, mossy remains of a small Roman temple, a folly at the heart of the maze that had not been visible from the lodge. Before the partially roofless building lay a worn kerb-edged circular pool eight yards wide, stagnant to appear a verdant lawn from afar, with a squat stone plinth devoid of any statue or ornament at its centre.

A sense of not being alone cut short any further examination. Something stirred from the other side of the labyrinth, hidden but large enough to rustle the branches and break those that had fallen into the path.

'Hello?' called Ashton, retreating to the opening from which he had emerged. He stood silent, heart pounding in his ears, but no reply came, only an increasing cadence along one

of the many paths out of view. Whatever scurried towards
him was unafraid.

He slipped around the corner, rapidly intent on getting
back to the opening and hurriedly trying to recall the passage
through the maze in reverse to bring him to his illegitimate
start. Behind, the figure let out a hoarse but agitated moan, a
wordless command to halt, perhaps, but Ashton raced on
catching sounds of crashing and lumbering from adjacent
pathways about him as his own twists and turns left him
bewildered. Breathless, he turned a corner to see a dead end
he had not expected and realised he was out of his reckoning.
Glancing down to confirm his footprints for the first time
Ashton realised he had not been here before, but something
else had.

There were large, barefooted prints impressed by an inch
into the softer, wetter parts of the clay. The right foot had a
cut-out, like a crack or a deformity that repeated itself. What
frightened him most as he turned to retreat to another junction was that they were fresh. Whatever had made them was
closing, perhaps intimately more aware of the layout of the
place. He caught a flash of man-shaped movement through
the hedge to his right accompanied by a growling whimper
like an excited hound at bay chasing a fox. He turned back to
the impasse and threw caution to the wind, pushing and
pulling himself through the far corner to clamber within the
hidden recess of the inner hedge. As he moved away into the
yew-needled cave, the foliage sprang back just in time for him
to see the thing that pursued him enter the topiary trench.

It bounded into view, grotesque and half-human. Its
deformed and partly missing skull left a single eye, lidless and
pink-rimmed like a tortured beast. Clouds of hot breath
steamed from its heaving, calloused chest, pockmarked and
stone-like with what little was left for its left shoulder and
arm were missing in a diagonal line from head to waist.

Whether through some calamity at birth or life-changing injury Ashton gave little thought, only marvelling that the crude, imitation of a man could still exist as a living being. The thing turned to test for any weakness or hole in the hedge about it and Ashton saw the cauterised callous or rough scarred growth along the entire length of its ribcage and skull.

Ashton sipped in breaths, alleviating his hypoxia, and trying to remain silent as the man-shaped thing looked about, confused in what little remained of its face where its lure or prey had vanished to. A slamming of the Hall's side door caused it to turn and lumber back to try another route.

...they say it's dangerous inside and Miss Pendlesham doesn't want anyone getting hurt.

Ashton listened to the fading steps and whooping of the creature, pushing himself out into the path behind with great effort, clammy and covered with scratches. His heart leapt as he saw his prints, all but obliterated by those of the other creature. A cry from the further reaches of the maze launched him forward to follow the heels of his previous prints conscious that the thing had now turned whatever far point it needed to return to the perimeter path.

Putting who it was or what it could be out of his mind, he resisted the urge to call out lest it signalled his location and bring the freakish horror upon him in some other dead end, or against the interior of the locked gates. Either solution provided little hope, and he briefly gave thought to how to overcome the one-armed beast should it come to it. Following his several earlier false turns he raced past an opening, coming up short as he saw the handkerchief, limply hanging from beyond a thin barrier of the hedge. He squirmed through to make the path on the other side realising he was close to the perimeter corner where he had entered. From the long pathway behind the creature emerged, now on the same track to intercept. It paused like a bull ready to paw at the ground but planted its legs apart and arched back bellowing in the statue's form he had seen the night before.

The statue that was no longer there.

It was answered by a loud cry from beyond the maze, somewhere out in the wood towards the house. Ashton heard his own rapid heart and breath in the silence of that instance, broken by the wail of the monster as it began its charge. With only a few seconds in which to escape without further deviation, Ashton dived through the overgrown path, flying with all speed into the final corner and crashing through the dead yews at the hidden entrance. A voice called out to him from the path beyond, but he had neither the time to locate its source nor its intention. He tumbled down into the ditch, snagged and torn by the bramble barbs, then regained his feet to clutch at the railings Ashton pulled himself along, testing each one with desperation until he reached the corner, and he knew that freedom lay a few yards further on. A man, large and tall in his periphery called out again even as his hands found the loose railing.

'Hurry!' cried the man Ashton had passed on the stairs. His great, burgundy-coated shoulders bent into the space, widening them to aid in his escape just as the horror from behind erupted from the yew like a cannonball, clawing the air with its single arm to tear at Ashton's upper right arm. He cried out in pain and was tugged by both arms, and for an instant, he thought he would be ripped apart. The man in the burgundy coat struck at the pale, clasping arm with his stone-tipped mace and the thing abandoned the trial but not the chance of escape. Ashton was jerked outwards by his saviour's strength and flung like a rag doll to land painfully in an uncontrolled roll some distance away. The creature emerged from its prison to face the bulk of the ginger-haired giant blocking his way who called out in a language Ashton did not recognise, holding the stone-headed staff aloft. The creature backed away, not pacified or afraid, but mollified and aware of its significance like a sudden parley before inevitable combat. It mouthed and moaned short staccato raspings in reply, short staccato raspings, and Ashton knew it was intelligent. The man lowered the sceptre-like weapon and spoke again, backing towards the injured painter who was feebly attempting to rise and clutching at the deep graze through his blood-stained shirt.

With a final whimper, the creature held out a hand toward the Hall, turning to mouth final, desperate words but the giant took off his hat in a bizarre mark of respect and shook his head, watching as the thing retreated into the woods and out of sight.

Ashton wobbled as he rose, blurry with clammy confusion and exhaustion, as the man raced towards him, catching him in his huge arms as darkness descended and his eyes went out.

'You're lucky to be alive,' said the red-haired man, binding the cleaned and resinous poultice-packed wound with a coarse but clean length of calico cloth.

Ashton glanced about the makeshift camp and the shadows flickering from the open wood fire. The traveller's Welsh cob grazed on rolled oats in a leather bucket in front of a covered wagon, not typical of a Romany home, but more akin to a mobile tradesman or tinker. Beside was struck a makeshift tent with waxed tarpaulins and a store of provisions in various small kegs and baskets. The cart itself was functional and from the rolled sides of the hoop-mounted canvas, Ashton spied several large partially sculpted stones, figures of fantasy and mythology in the process of release from their billion-year limestone captivity. Several more lay at the outer edge of the campfire like a gallery awaiting patrons to admire and purchase. It seemed a very meagre court for a man calling himself a king, even as the head of nomadic clans. A shadow stretched out from behind his great size like a train making the man appear robed, regal and worthy of respect. As though sensing Ashton's thoughts, the man lifted the stone-headed sceptre towards him.

'Yes. We have something in common, Mr Berkeley – poverty. Both of us are disinherited, but not from our responsibilities, eh? We have been made poor, but free through circumstance, and our choice in the matter is but an illusion we have created for ourselves to soften the loss.'

'How do you know my name and my business?'

'I'm trusted by the lady of the house despite my people's reputation and social standing among folk like you. Every year around the first full moon of winter, I visit Miss Pendlesham and make camp at Bickford Wood. I saw you leave – it's been a long time since she had male company; she is intrigued by you and I'm not sure that's a good thing.'

'Mr Doe?' asked Ashton shrugging off the intimation.

He nodded. 'The name's Manfri, and I advise you to drop whatever fascination you may have with her or the woman you think you saw last night, for everyone's sake. Miss Pendlesham is not who you think she is.'

'She's just a lonely, reclusive old woman in mourning, after company—'

Manfri rose and wandered over to check on the horse. He pointed the stone-mounted staff like a shaman from the other side of the fire. 'She's far older or stranger than you realise. She's lonely alright, but not in mourning.'

'Then why does she cover her face and hide from the world?' said Ashton.

'For modesty,' said Manfri receding to place a hand on the

shoulder of one of the Greek muses, 'and to hide her from our pity.' He returned to seat himself on an upturned log and stared at the glittering firelight sparkling from the speckles within the polished, granite-topped head of the staff at his side. 'How's the arm, now?'

Ashton winced as he lifted his elbow, moving it until the discomfort eased. 'Better. I owe you for saving me back there and for this.... gipsy remedy: I understand the nearest doctor is twenty miles away.'

Manfri's calloused hands tightened the slipped upper knot of the bandage as he raised his blue eyes to his patient. 'My people and I prefer the term Roma if you please, and I'm better with tin and stone than skin and bone. When you wake up tomorrow and the effects have worn off, you may wish you had walked that far.'

'Who or what was that thing in the maze?' said Ashton still shivering from the sudden wakening in the wooded copse twenty minutes prior. Dumped unceremoniously onto the bracken-strewn clearing from the man's shoulder after a quarter of a mile's distance, he had recovered from his faint to find that night had fallen alongside him and his arm was burning with an ugly, bruising graze.

'His name is Grell and long ago he was once a man of my people, a King of the Roma in this land.'

'You weren't afraid.'

Manfri lifted a stick and poked at the campfire. 'He's kin, despite what he is now. The first time you see him is the worst, and I remember feeling the same fear as you did many years ago. There's no shame in it. He still remembers the old speech, but what he has become is not something I wish to dwell upon.'

'But he's missing virtually half of his upper body, how——?'

The man raised his bushy eyebrows. 'I don't know, but pity him as I do.'

'She had him imprisoned,' said Ashton, 'and now he's escaped because of me. Shouldn't we call the police?'

'No!' said the man sharply. 'This is a private matter for her, and I don't think he will return soon now he knows I am here. There is still some honour left in that half-empty shell and he won't attack me unless he has completely lost all sense of who he once was. Do not fret for your life, or hers – it was only a matter of time before we came to this. I've seen the defences and the watch on the maze degrade over the fifteen years I have been doing the calling and my father highlighted the same lack of vigilance and repair.'

'The calling?'

'I call on her to honour a debt, long outstanding, to see if it will be repaid one way or another. Only that will put an end to Grell's misery, as well as her own.'

'Miss Pendlesham owes a debt to that—'

He nodded. 'Her father owed it before he died, but she is liable for the settlement and does not have the means to repay. The price goes up each year as her assets decrease – there is nothing of great value left in the house and not even the property can command the sum owed. The morning room you visited is the only one left with any meaningful contents; all the others are empty. I assist her, privately, to pawn and sell items to continue for as long as she can in her purgatory despite the losses of my people. I am not a monster, Mr Berkeley, despite what you think of Grell. Her father caused the chain of events that led to his condition, and hers, though it was one of our own that delivered the cursed blow, a fact I am not proud of.'

'What do you mean?'

'I believe that punishment should fit the offence and not be eternal for finite crimes, however egregious. It isn't one person who suffers, it's both parties, and that isn't right.'

'Is that why she imprisoned him, to avoid paying?'

'No. I truly believe she would pay if she could. She lives with the consequences of her father's non-payment every day, as does Grell, and there is no escaping it. Her father was unable or unwilling to pay what was owed and imprisoned him once the full knowledge of the consequence began to transpire.'

'What consequence?' asked Ashton.

Manfri lifted a large pewter tankard beside him and drank long from the small beer, wiping the light foam crescent from his beard. 'He lived long enough to see his estate and gardens built by the hands of our people over many years, but when his investments in the South China Sea were wrecked on their return to Southampton, it left his overstretched ambitions without the means to pay the final year's account. He escaped his debtors shortly after by dying, a privilege not afforded to Grell, and left her with a similar predicament.'

'You mean she was disfigured by fate or action, but to a lesser degree – is that why she is veiled?'

'In a manner of speaking,' said Manfri.

'If he is one of your own,' said Ashton, 'why not free him and take care of him?'

'He is beyond our care or willingness to listen. I have tried many times, like my fathers before me to reason with him. He seeks only the repayment of the debt by force or the promise in its stead, and that is not our way.'

'What promise?'

'When her father couldn't pay Grell was offered Miss Pendlesham's hand without her consent or knowledge as full settlement. You have seen her great beauty in the statue and in the painting that hangs within the morning room, and Grell agreed much to the clans' protestations when it was discovered.' He glanced over at the horse, kicking at the empty bucket. 'Not only were they owed a great deal of money, but we Roma also have our customs and do not inter-marry with gorgers...'

'You mean the likes of "us"?' said Ashton.

He nodded. 'He took it upon himself to overreach his station and condemn us to poverty for his own selfish gain. She refused him and still does. We are owed a fortune that will never be repaid and cast him out. I do not blame her for his folly or inability to pay; enough blood has been spilt over the matter.'

Manfri removed a silver locket from his coat pocket, the same that had adorned the neck of Miss Pendlesham only a few hours prior. 'She loved another. I'm aware people think we are all thieves and scoundrels, Mr Berkeley, but this is the endgame for her. I will not sell her prized possession to some common tinker, and I gave her the money in its stead to pay the bills hoping one day I can return it to her, debt repaid.'

'But the woman in the painting and the likeness in the statue can't be the Miss Pendlesham at the Hall – they are well over a hundred years ago – she said that herself, and so did you. It's not possible to be that old—'

'Isn't it?' he said, weighing the locket in his hand. 'It was not so long ago they burned people who were unnatural in their span of years.'

'What do you mean?' asked Ashton.

The man plucked at his beard. 'How old do you think she is?'

Ashton shrugged his shoulders. 'Eighty, perhaps; it's diffi-cult to tell. Her movement, manner, eyes, and aspects of her face seem younger, but she struggles with speech and her hands are rough as though...'

'As though they are worn, like mine?' Manfri held out the ruddy palms like a boy awaiting inspection before being allowed to eat.

'No, not like that.'

The traveller returned from the wagon with something heavy, wrapped in dirty sackcloth. The bundle was unwound to reveal the lichen and eroded stone of an upper arm and hand.

'Like this?' said Manfri, holding out the broken piece of statue. 'It's what I come to mend, and deal with every year I'm in the district of wealthy folk, as well as do the calling on Miss Pendlesham just like my grandfathers and great-grandfathers before me.'

A spark spat from the fire as Ashton shook his head. 'This is a piece of worn stone. What disease or condition causes the skin to appear so similar?'

Manfri shook his head and retrieved the hand, wrapping it reverently back into its makeshift shroud. 'It's no disease, it's a curse.'

'Don't be absurd, there's no such thing as—'

'As statues with half a face and body chasing landless gentry around at night? She is an honourable woman and knew that her family had cheated another's otherwise his fate might have been otherwise decades ago. I fully believe she intended to repay at some junction, even as she became reclusive with the years, or took pity on the Roma who she could not marry for the debts of another, who can say? Perhaps she feared some greater calamity. Old magic never dies and has a way of reinvigorating and reinventing its terms if attempts are made to alter its purpose.'

'Magic?' scoffed Ashton. 'Someone, perhaps even you or your ancestors carved that statue in mockery of the creature that attacked me. You're making up fairy tales to fill my head with nonsense, so I won't go to the police—'

'Don't be ridiculous,' said Manfri. 'That creature was once a man, and perhaps still is if he hasn't been driven mad from the years of imprisonment within that damn maze or the lightning strike that ripped his manhood apart in the greatest storm of the last century. Don't you understand? Grell and Pendlesham are the same, they don't eat, they don't sleep, and they don't age like us.' He pointed to the statues: weeping, dancing and posing in mock emotionless pretence. 'They age like them, and only wind and weather, frost or fire can change them until they fall into ruin and become as dust, which is what she intends for herself from my meeting not two hours ago.'

'You are telling me they are the statues I have seen?' said Ashton, incredulously. 'There is a statue that is missing and bears her resemblance, but it's a relative, isn't it? Just like the painting in the great hall of the Jacobean lady and her hound?'

'She's had no relatives for over a hundred years, Mr Berkeley.' He lifted his gaze into the blackness from which could be seen the dim lights of the nearby village. 'A close examination of the under-used family churchyard will show you that. They are cursed and tied to the stones that bear their semblance.'

'You said one of your own caused this,' said Ashton. 'How?'

Manfri sat back, rubbing at his bearded mouth for where to begin. 'Grell and a large part of his men were skilled in stone and masonry, not to mention other crafts that made them highly sought after in the landscaping and adornment of gardens in the early nineteenth century. Over a decade, they remodelled the house and parkland around you, as well as many statues of which the ones you have seen are the only ones that now remain – his own and that of Pendlesham's daughter. Things went well until the final year before the maze and lodge were constructed.

'He was the last to hold the kingship in more than name until Elizabeth Pendlesham refused her father's wishes and he cast them out like beggars. Hired men returning from the wars with Bonaparte, hounded them, making them homeless from the burning of their camps. They were left with only what they could carry and fended from the land as they were driven away during the great winter of 1816. Grell's mother, starving and half-frozen, clawed her way back to the spot where the cider mill now stands. She was the last of the cunning women of our folk and died cursing the very stones of the place until the debt was repaid, the marriage was honoured or lords of men from both sides of the divide, Roma and gentry, came into their own and settled their differences in some other arrangement beneficial to both.'

Ashton listened in silence, spellbound by the deep, resonant voice of the traveller.

'It wasn't until the Cold Moon in December when they both vanished for the first time, reappearing in place of the statues the following moon in November, that Grell knew what his mother had done and returned to kill many of those that had played a part in the massacre and clearance of our people. Shunned by his own people out of fear and reprisal, he transformed back to stone in the centre of the maze at the rising of the next moon, even as she did the same at the edge of the lakeside lawn. What money was left was put into securing the perimeter with the railings you see today before those that were involved died out, taking the secret with them. Each year I ask if the debt can be repaid, or if she will consent to take him as her husband, and each time I have to stand and face what is left of our mad, but rightful king and deliver the answer.'

'You spoke to him in Romany when he emerged,' said Ashton. 'What did you say?'

Manfri sighed. 'The same as every year – it is "no" on both accounts.'

'You mentioned a third way – a lord of the Roma, and of the realm sorting out their differences to each other's benefit?'

Manfri shook his head. 'That time has passed with the

99

death of Miss Pendlesham's father, and the debt would need to be paid to make it right for the rightful king. I don't see any lords from your world coming forward to honour a bad debt, or do you think your father might intercede at your bequest?'

'No,' said Ashton sharply. 'He wouldn't likely even allow me back onto the estate, let alone entertain the notion. What is the amount of the debt in today's money?'

Manfri shuffled his feet and bridged his hands beneath his chin, staring into the fire.

'As it stands,' he said. 'Forty-three thousand, two hundred and thirty pounds, twelve shillings and sixpence...'

Ashton tilted back his head in disbelief. 'You and he may as well wish for Christendom, Mr Doe. That is an extraordinary amount of money—'

'And...' continued Manfri, 'an honourable burial place for our people in land granted and sanctified by the seal of a queen.'

'Is that all?' said Ashton rolling his eyes in disbelief.

Manfri frowned and clenched his fists. 'Have you not seen the labours of my people? What you see now are shadows of its former glories and we were paid in blood. You were moved enough to come to this place because of its splendour and you drew her statue before you knew its true value or its secret.'

Ashton closed his eyes, recalling the calmness of the encounter from the previous evening with the figure and the intense wonderment of seeing her in the flesh hours later.

'I saw her dance under the moonlight like some fey creature...'

'She still performs the moondance, then? A custom around the time of the November moon, but there is no power in it nowadays to remove such hexes, and much good it will do her to try,' said Manfri raising himself on the staff and staring into the dark, moonless sky. 'She'll not change a single thing while the debt is unpaid and Grell lives, if living you call it. He was my great-great-granduncle and carved that statue of her over a century ago. The line of Roma kings and her family are long-lived, but perhaps immortality, while their statues remain, is the worst punishment of all. Between Frost Moon in November and Cold Moon in December, they contemplate the follies of both parties, unable or unwilling to effect an end to it.'

'I saw them both as statues only yesterday – are you certain someone hasn't just removed them for some purpose...'

'No,' said Manfri. 'They live as we do between the month of the last full moons of the year, in guise to the statues that bear their likeness. One month every year alone they are free to resolve the debt, and I come to honour the traditions of the calling at this time. There is no escape – no matter how far they run or sail they will return to the plinths at midnight of the following full moon. They are bound to this place, the curse, and each other.'

'Mrs White says you are the King of the Roma now?' said Ashton. The fire crackled, and he stretched out his hands slowly to test the arm, feeling the comforting warmth seep through his limbs. 'Can't you put a stop to it and declare the debt void or change its terms? Perhaps instalments?'

'It is an honorific title passed down from Grell's brother, and ultimately to me but truth be told, I am merely a steward while the old king lives. I am Roma, Mr Berkeley, honourable and proud, monarch of migrants in name only, regent of a remnant people in these isles. I know what it is like to live with something lost, like yourself.'

'You are related to Grell?' said Ashton ignoring the assertion of his own situation.

'Distantly.' The man raised the heavy staff and bound it

against his chest diagonally like a Roman emperor bearing a sceptre. 'He bore this himself before it passed to my great, great-uncle, and thence through my fathers to me. There is no crown or throne for a Romany king, and this totem is all that gives me the right to settle disputes and marriages between the clans at the gatherings. In between, I earn my living as everyone else, trying to recapture the artistry and genius of my forebears.'

'Did they carve many statues on the grounds?'

The man nodded. 'And dug the lake, planted the trees and hedges, and landscaped the whole park during the Napoleonic wars when men were scarce and—' he glanced into Ashton's eyes, '—"gipsies" weren't allowed to fight.'

Ashton withdrew from the stern gaze.

'Does the housekeeper and the lad know about this?'

'She does, but the other is new and impressionable. Miss Pendlesham means to let him go before he begins to suspect. He is overly curious, and a secret should be shared sparingly.'

'He's also overly loyal and that would be a great blow to him, and the estate. Why are you telling me, then?' asked Ashton. 'Is it to get me to keep my mouth shut?'

Manfri opened his great hand to reveal the locket, now open and bearing the inward-facing portraits of a young man and beautiful woman of the same age. He recognised them both immediately.

'It's the woman in the painting and the one I saw perform the moondance—'

'Elizabeth Anne Pendlesham,' said Manfri. 'Born 1797 and living in a single room at Bickford Hall for one month of the year until this very day. The man who promised to take care of her and marry her is alongside. Unfortunately, he did neither or was forced to do so when the financial situation of her father, Edward Pendlesham, became common knowledge and caused a run on his creditors. He left her to fate, and the curse of my people – will you do the same?'

Ashton took the locket into his shaking hands to stare at the handsome face with its dimpled cheek. 'It's my ancestor, Harlon Charles Berkeley.' He glanced up to see the Roma nod sympathetically. 'What must I do to make it right, on both accounts?'

'What must *we* do, Mr Berkeley,' he corrected. 'We need to inform her. My people don't believe in coincidences of this magnitude, and perchance your coming at this precise moment to set off a chain of events that no one can anticipate is an encouraging sign or a portent of disaster. Perhaps fate has been repaid and is trying to tell us something.'

Ashton stared at the two smiling figures, distant yet so familiar. 'Or is coming to collect with compound interest,' he said snapping the locket shut and bringing the former lovers together once more in the intimacy of timeless darkness.

'I blame myself,' said Ashton staring into the morning room fire. 'I had no right to enter the maze against your wishes; it was dishonourable and disrespectful.'

Miss Pendlesham stood in the bay window looking out at the rising moon and the shadows of her once fine estate. She raised her hands above her head and outwards to the silver beam welcoming it into the room and across her gloved hands in a private salutation. She turned and gave a short shake of her veiled head. 'Keeping him locked away was far worse. He is released along with my guilt – you have nothing to be ashamed of, Mr Berkeley. At least you had the fortitude to withstand his appearance and remain—' she moved to the fire and took the hand of his bandaged arm, '—something Harlon could, or would not do, even for me. Is he so very terrible to look upon?'

Ashton felt the gentle, velvety squeeze and looked above to the painted image of the beautiful woman, trying to process the fact that she was present in the room over one hundred and twenty years later.

'Is it true?' he said ignoring her question to avoid reminding himself of his fear. He studied any hint of age upon her plump, lower red lip and smooth chin lightly brushed with pale foundation. 'Was it you whom I saw out in the park last night and the one that was carved in stone, and painted in oil?'

Manfri shifted his weight, creaking the floorboards beneath. 'If I hadn't revealed the secret, Miss Pendlesham, he could have informed the authorities—'

She held up her hand to silence his muted apology. 'I could get used to men apologising for their failings, but now is the time for the unburdening of truths, The answer he seeks is here—' She plucked at the fingers of the glove and removed the tight, fitting velvet to reveal her bare, offered hand. Ashton took it and brushed his fingers lightly over the rough, sandy skin, pitted in places, while smooth and untarnished in others. A concentric series of orange lichens encircled her third knuckle and ring finger.

'It's like supple, living stone,' he said, turning the palm to see fine unblemished skin, unlike the back of the hand except in its grey pallor. He rubbed at the smooth, young surface and she trembled with the tickling sensation.

'Shielded from the months of wind and rain,' she said. 'A small mercy from such a vicious condition.' She withdrew the hand and held it before the fire. 'One of the few areas I feel anything, anymore.'

The skin glittered with a silvery, speckled, mica-like sheen as she twisted it toward the flames.

'I think it's beautiful,' said Ashton suddenly stammering to make sense. 'I mean it's unique, and part of you.'

Miss Pendlesham twitched, seeing the sincerity on his face. 'It is imperfect, but I had not looked at it that way before.'

'It is who you are, and I am sorry my great, great-grandfather could not say that or see beyond your predicament.'

'Love is skin-deep,' said Manfri opening the doors and admitting Mrs White bearing a tray of tea and honey-baked biscuits.

It was some time before Miss Pendlesham averted her eyes from Ashton's gentle study of her veiled face. The housekeeper, nervous of the giant beside her made ready to leave.

'Stay,' she said removing her other glove. 'Please, Mrs White. You and your family have cared for me and my secret for three generations. There are to be no more secrets in this house.'

The housekeeper set down the tray and noticed the bare hands for the first time.

'Mercy,' she whispered. 'That's a sight and no mistake. Whatever do you intend to do?'

'Accept the hand that was dealt to me by my father,' said Miss Pendlesham turning to the Roma, 'and your ancestors. Will he attack the house or my staff, do you think?'

Manfri swallowed a handful of biscuits and shook his head. 'I think not, but he may try to reach you before the Cold Moon. He is in love with you, as deranged as it sounds, and still believes that with your hand, he will be restored.'

'And is he right?' said Ashton taking a sip of the hot tea.

Manfri shrugged. 'I don't know. If not then I have the skill to repair in stone what has been damaged, but I do not have any power in me that will break old magic, or change it from its intended course. None of my people does, and meddling might make the situation worse. It would have to be done when he returns to his...other form.'

'We would be back to square one again, and I will not have him imprisoned for a further eleven months,' said Miss Pendlesham. 'It ends by the next moon, one way or another.'

'You intend to honour your father's wishes at the expense of your own?' said Manfri.

She lowered her head. 'As a last resort and to avoid the stalemate, but I see now the estate must be sold as the opening move. I was content to fade into dust, but perhaps he will accept that this is all I have and release some power within him to restore us to our former lives.'

Mrs White held up a handkerchief to her wet eyes, visibly shaken by the news of the sale. Ashton put an arm around her.

'With respect,' said Manfri. 'It may not be enough.'

'Then I suggest a parley to determine the matter if we can find a way of safely approaching him. Can it be done, Mr Doe?'

The giant lightly tapped the staff on the rug-covered floorboards. 'There are symbols carved into oaks and boundary posts that we once used to communicate with each other over great distances and passages of time. With your permission, I need to broadcast our intent by carving into stone and wood across the estate and maybe beyond. This will also bring those that remain of my people in this district to keep watch on the grounds and house in case I am wrong and he tries to gain entry by force. Even I cannot be every-where at once.'

She nodded and looked long into the painting above the mantelpiece. 'For now, it is best to keep this among ourselves, and the Romany.'

'They won't talk to any gorgers about this,' said Manfri.

'You have my word. I will keep watch tonight but must be away at first light to begin the summons.'

Miss Pendlesham removed a small purse from within her dress and moved to place her hands softly upon the clasped grip of the housekeeper's own. 'You must leave me soon, Annabelle. Take the lad and this money to get away from here and start afresh. It's too dangerous and you are far more valuable to me than any pawned gold.' She held out the small purse, but the housekeeper shook her head, caressing the hands of her mistress. 'My grandmother wouldn't go anywhere, and neither would my old mum, so I'm sorry, Miss Pendlesham, the answer is no.'

'Then the lad, at least?' she said. 'Whatever happens before the Cold Moon I need to die in the eyes of the law of the land and be forgotten by all but yourself if you intend to remain. Then to be reborn as some distant niece set to inherit – it has been ever thus to avoid suspicion.'

'If I may?' said Ashton, 'The lad is loyal and committed to Bickford, and you. You may find that he keeps your secret closer than you do yourself.'

Miss Pendlesham set down the purse. 'And what is your assessment of his character, Mr Doe?'

Manfri huffed. 'He's a rabbit that will put up a fight if cornered, as we say in our tongue. He's overly curious and talks quicker than his legs can carry him but I suspect that any unintended chatter to others is likely to be put down to moonshine and ale, though folks in these parts have long memories and mention of Bickford in anything "out of the ordinary" might prove ruinous.'

Miss Pendlesham paced between the tapestry and window, looking out onto the moonlight mirror of the lake. 'I'll leave the decision to you, Mrs White, You have kept my confidences these many years and I trust your judgement.'

'Very good, ma'am,' said the housekeeper, escorting the

Roma out of the room. He replaced his hat and nodded his farewells to them both. The doors closed behind them.

'You can't seriously be intending to marry him, even as a last resort?' said Ashton hearing the heavy footfalls of the unlikely couple recede down the stairs. 'I've seen what Grell has become, and even if his body is restored alongside your own, his mind is broken and that is something that cannot easily be repaired, if at all.'

Miss Pendlesham paused in her return to the fire to remain in front of the tapestry, framed by the glittering stars of the wooded scene. 'I am afraid, Mr Berkeley, and have been afraid for one hundred and four years, but I release you from any sentimental or chivalrous notion you feel honoured to redress for your ancestor's abandonment in my hour of need. It is noble of you, but you and your family can not help me, not this time.'

Manfri was gone for over a week and Ashton started to think he had absconded or arranged for men to arrive and enforce an arranged marriage. Curious markings, like glyphs of ancient peoples carved into stone, appeared on mature trees, walls, and posts. Alongside the symbols appeared men and women in small bands, directed by unseen waymarks to the tracks that led into Bickford Wood. By the time Manfri returned, a camp of some forty Romany people was established and able-bodied men were wandering the estate like sentries wielding heavy cudgels and accompanied by fierce-looking dogs. Nothing had been seen or heard of Grell, and Ashton began to hope that he would not return and that the gathering of his people was some earthly ploy by Manfri to take back in collateral what he could not attain by settlement.

The giant slumped in a chair by the kitchen fire, bedraggled and weather-beaten while Hal took charge of the horse and cart outside, leading the exhausted animal to shelter and oat-earned rest.

'There's been no sign of ...*him*,' said Mrs White laying a large plate of bread and cheese in his lap. He picked at it and shook his head, seemingly too weary to eat.

'If he's between here and Timbuktu, he'll have seen the signs. I haven't travelled so hard in all my days,' he said. 'Now we wait.'

'What do the signs say or mean?' asked Ashton.

'Peace, parley, and water; he'll know to come to the lake. I made sure the marks still recognise him as the elder king, and he is honour-bound to accept the summons.'

'Your people have been tireless in keeping guard,' said Mrs White. 'Miss Pendlesham has offered them rooms in the hall but they wouldn't take them,'

Manfri smiled. 'I thank her, and the gesture was worthy, but we are best to keep our distance. What do you think of us "gipsies" now?'

The housekeeper blushed and wrapped the food into brown paper to offer as a picnic. 'I say that I take folk for their actions, not for what others say about them.'

'Then that is a start,' he said, rising to thank her. 'I must return to the camp and do my best to be a king in his stead... for the moment at least.'

A further week brought heavy snow from the east and Hal, unaware of his reprieve, raced back and forth as the messenger and errand boy, stopping to relay information and recover at the lodge. The Hall was cut off from the villages, which were remote to each other, and nothing came in or out of the district except the flock of crows cawing from their roosts high above the wintry wilderness.

'I never knew there was a mad gipsy in the maze or I

wouldn't have gone in,' said Hal talking to the back of the easel on the ground floor of the lodge.

'They prefer the term "Roma" or "Romany",' said Ashton from beyond the canvas occupying himself with the infill of autumn leaves upon the almost finished painting of the Hall.

'I don't know how you remain so calm, Mr Berkeley. I'm quaking right down in my boots thinking he might come back to do Miss Pendlesham or one of us some injury.'

Ashton put down his brush and invited him to see the work in progress.

'I paint to calm my nerves, Hal, and finish this awkward character here who is causing me some distraction...'

Hal's face beamed with joy, seeing the small figure of himself, next to that of the housekeeper beside the oak tree on the front lawn. The Hall in the background was tidier and the gardens full of vigour than it truly represented. His eager finger pointed at the many statues in the foreground that lined the hedge. In between, the figure of a beautiful young woman with dark hair smiled from the foreground beneath a black umbrella. 'Be careful,' said Ashton, 'the paint is still wet.'

'You painted us both, Mr Berkeley!' he said jumping like a jack-in-the-box. 'But why put the lady from the old painting into this new one?'

'Continuity, Hal. A place should always have something of the past in any restoration or re-interpretation.'

The young man frowned, trying to comprehend the cryptic response. 'The Romany folk and Mrs White won't tell me what is behind all this; you aren't going to either, are you?'

'I will when it's all over,' said Ashton, ushering him outside to the undelivered cart of late autumn greens and vegetables from the cleared kitchen garden due for delivery to the camp. 'I don't want you getting involved until then, for your safety and to ensure nothing gets out.'

'Fat chance of that in this weather,' said Hal. 'But they say he'll come back – why would a prisoner do that?'

Ashton glanced at the mark carved into the lintel of the lodge's porch.

'To talk,' he said, closing the door. 'Nothing more I hope.'

Several weeks passed and barring a few false alarms triggered by solitary tramps, a sense of watchful calm descended about Bickford Hall. The day of the next full moon dawned crisp and heavy with the threat of snow. The main routes to the south remained impassable, and a congenial fellowship formed between the parties forged by isolation but tempered by the wisdom and selfless actions of Manfri Doe.

He kept a close eye on the watch, like a military commander, while providing for the families and repairing many of the carts and tools alongside them. Drawn at short notice from different clans, their distrust amongst themselves and the people of the hall and lodge grew less and flourished into a productive sharing of gifts, stories, food, and labour. They even began to prune dormant shrubs and plants, weeding, mending and repairing features after decades of neglect.

'It seems we have a successful arrangement in common adversity,' said Miss Pendlesham watching the flakes of snow settle thickly upon the pillowed mounds of woody shrubs in the parterre below.

'They are proud and look to restore a small part of their masterpiece. You can look, now,' said Ashton pulling off the cloth to the painting. The late afternoon was failing but cast enough sun on the autumn scene as though to mimic the trick of the light employed by the artist. She turned and caught her breath, stumbling for words to describe the accomplished piece as her eyes darted around the scene to discover the fine details and figures from beneath her veil.

'It looks just as I remember it,' she said, voice quavering. 'How—?'

'I had some help from descriptions sent to me before the snow cut off the mail – a friend of mine works at the national archives. Some books and items you have sold over the years have made it into collections and they reveal some of Bickford's earlier architectural and landscape history. Mr Doe spoke with a few of the older Romany who recall their grandparents' accounts to flesh out further details.'

Miss Pendlesham shuddered as though moved by some great sadness but she waved his attempts to offer a handkerchief or further consolation.

'I am moved beyond words, Mr Berkeley. I am transported back to a happier time...' She clutched at her neck searching for the locket that was no longer there.

'Tell me about him,' said Ashton coming to stand beside her. 'If it does not upset you.'

'You have his looks, his mannerisms, and his bearing, and share the predicament of being promised to another though he didn't have your fortitude to resist his father's commands.' She laughed as she recalled some pleasant memory and Ashton caught the ring of gentle sound before it returned to its hoarse, throaty tone. 'I was there at Doncaster when he won on *The Duchess* trying to impress me and outplay his rivals. I wiped the smile from his cocky face when he realised I had bet against him.'

Ashton chuckled and a broad smile punctuated by bright white teeth lit up the darkness of her veil.

'But he was foolhardy, prone to bouts of melancholia and ignorant in the ways to truly make a lady happy. I loved him, but now I forgive him. It was not meant to be.'

Outside the beacons, strategically placed around the gardens, were lit to ward off the chill from those on watch and provide some light to defend against any shadowed intruder.

'Tomorrow is the Cold Moon,' she whispered turning to

see the bonfires. 'Why does he not put an end to this waiting, or do you think he waits till the last to show himself?'

'Manfri thinks the latter,' he said. 'He fears some mischief at the very end that will rob us of any time to react.'

'Perhaps he fears the same from us?' she said, holding out her bare hand towards him.

Ashton put his hand in hers and squeezed gently. 'If he comes, you must not go with him; I will find a way—'

She tightened her grip momentarily. 'If there is no resolution, at midnight tomorrow when the full moon rises I will change, and in another few months, you will be gone. Take away my thanks and...admiration, for staying with me. This past few weeks in your company, outside of your tireless interactions and planning with Mr Doe, have been more than I could have wished for, or deserve. Do not return – I could not bear it...'

'What is it like?' said Ashton turning to face her. 'Do you see and hear when you—?'

She hurried to answer, saving him from the awkwardness. 'It is like a dream from which I sometimes now recall, I remember the first swallows above the lake this year, the clutched feet of red breast upon my hair bearing its beak of worms to the bush behind, and I recall the words of those few who look into my face and leave me flowers...'

'Do you remember...me?'

She nodded and withdrew her hand. 'Your words were a comfort to me in my final hours and I confess I wanted to make sure you were not some vision from the past come to torment me.'

She moved to the side of the room and unlocked a small drawer, removing a long, wrapped object from within. She placed it into his hands.

'A parting gift,' she said, 'to one who has seen the moondance...'

Aston unfurled the cloth wrapping to see the spyglass, polished and worked to remove the worst of the dents. A new lens glittered in the low rays of the sun, and he put it to his eye to spy the snow-dusted overcoats of the wardens on watch.

'Mr Doe and his associates,' she said before he had the chance to question the repair. 'The last of my secrets, Mr Berkeley.'

'I have nothing to offer except for my desire to see you safe and restored to happiness.'

She glanced at the painting and reached out her hand to touch the side of his face. 'You have already done so, and now we are on equal terms. I will miss you, Ashton...'

A horn call from outside broke them from the intimate moment and Ashton looked out of the window to see men racing from the gardens in the drive's direction, each blowing on whistles of their own to signal their solidarity.

'He is coming...' said Miss Pendlesham, placing her head in her hands.

'Stay here,' said Ashton, 'and lock the doors.'

'No!' she said. 'He comes to parley with me and I will not hide away in the dead end of a maze of my own making.'

She lifted her gown and rustled past to join him on the stairs.

Outside in front of the house, Manfri was already there alongside several armed men. A man halfway along the snow-covered drive put down the horn and signalled towards them.

'Is it him?' said Ashton peering into the gloom of the entranceway trees. Miss Pendlesham followed closely behind and stood resolutely beside him reaching for his hand.

'It's something large or heavy in outline, alone, but far up the drive and stumbling through the snow.'

Men arrived from the far side of the house heralding a rapid back and forth in the Romany tongue before several pairs broke away to position themselves about the shrubbery and hedges of the unblemished white ribbon of the drive. From the depth of the wooded gateway, a lone figure, large and bulky, shuffled towards them.

Realising he still clung to the spyglass, Ashton discerned the grey figure labouring against the cold and snow. It appeared at first to have no arms and its head was covered by a great scarf that disappeared into a great stone-grey overcoat.

'It's a man,' he blurted. 'He's wrapped against the elements and is struggling.'

The relief among the men seemed palpable.

'Snow's not that deep,' said Manfri, 'though it's been heavier over at Waycross and no carts or lorries have come through for days.

Ashton watched the man stagger and reach out with both hands to soften his fall.

'It's not Grell,' he said. 'But he's in trouble.'

With a whistle and a word of command from the Roma King, men softly ambushed the figure and helped it to its feet, half carrying the man down the rest of the drive.

'Get him inside,' said Miss Pendlesham removing herself from his hand and the peculiar looks of the Romany people who had only now set eyes upon her. 'Hurry!'

Ashton put away his telescope and rushed over even as the figure pushed aside all attempts to help. The man staggered and pulled away his scarf to show a pallid, frost-weathered face. 'Is this...Bickford?' he croaked. 'I have been many days on foot – pray God, tell me this is where I can find Lord Berkeley.'

He sank to his knees and Ashton joined him in the compacted snow. 'I am here, but I am only his son. My father, Lord Berkeley is—'

The man clutched onto his shoulders interrupting.

Ashton looked into the pallid, stubble-lined face to recognise his father's steward, far removed from the well-groomed man he remembered. The man shivered and pulled a great leather-bound book and pouch from his breast pocket from which he tipped out a golden object onto the snow. Ashton retrieved the great ruby-mounted signet ring and in that instance, he knew.

'—dead. I've been trying to reach you for days, sir; your father has been dead for nearly a week.'

'Your man is sleeping,' said Manfri, returning from his portage of the steward to the warm bed of the servant's quarter. 'Mrs White is with him and the lad has graciously given up his room to stay with us tonight; I think he may be warming to our way of life.'

Ashton rubbed at the signet ring in his fingers, staring through the golden circle at the open letter and watermarked papers at his feet. The fire crackled beside him and not even the approach of the Welsh cob outside, and the giant's heavy footfalls on the lodge stairs had shifted the numb detachment in his mind.

The giant sat on his haunches, dripping from the light dusting of melting snow. 'Lord Berkeley?'

'He died shortly after a short illness but left a letter before his heart finally gave way. I did not realise his regret at our estrangement, I thought he hated me...'

Manfri held out his hand for the ring. 'The approach of death makes a man rethink many things. He has made you his heir?'

Ashton nodded and placed the precious object into the outstretched, calloused palm.

'I should have tried harder to mend our differences by

becoming more like him, even as I now see he was becoming further like me.'

'You feel unworthy?'

'Yes.'

Manfri held out the band of precious gold and slipped it on Ashton's finger.

'Then that is the perfect place to start.'

Ashton glanced at the ancient ring and the responsibility and privilege that came with it. 'I feel ashamed that he left this world with such love and high regard for me knowing that I did not reciprocate and now it is too late. I did not hate him; I just did not want to become him.'

'He knows, I'm sure. Such a bond exists between father and son that transcends earthly squabbles. Be the man in between and walk the centre ground, neither fully you nor him, and you will find compromise in your grief and remembrance of him.'

'You speak from experience?' said Ashton studying the green eyes as the giant shuffled to his knees.

'I do, and it has served me well. What will you do now?'

Lifting the pile of papers, Ashton leafed through the documents to open a thick envelope containing several large denomination notes. Manfri whistled.

'I've not seen many of those.'

'Several hundred pounds brought by the faithful steward to assist in my transport and expenses back to the estate. I need to get back, but...'

'Bickford Hall is no longer your business, my friend. You must honour your commitments...'

'But the steward needs rest, and the snow...and Elizabeth—'

'I can take care of her, even though things will remain the same. I will ensure she does nothing rash and mend the defences at my own cost in memory of bringing my people together and the brief union of our cultures. You played a part in that as a Lord should do.'

'I have the means to pay the debt, Manfri,' he said, returning the notes to the envelope and handing it to the bemused Roma. 'It's a considerable sum, and I would need some time, but I could arrange it if this would serve as a down payment?'

'It's not your debt, Berkeley, and she has her pride.'

'If my ancestor had honoured his commitment to her, the debt could have been repaid much earlier. I am merely putting right his mistake. I could buy the estate if she won't accept charity or the reparations I feel my family owes hers.'

Manfri clasped his hand around the envelope, pushing it back. 'You feel for her, truly? And not just pity?'

Ashton sighed and nodded, removing the ring and offering it up. 'My heart is telling me not to make the same mistake again, despite a change in my circumstances. If not the money, then take this as a token of my honour to repay every penny. I will guarantee the resting place of your people on consecrated Berkeley ground in perpetuity, land granted to us by Queen Elizabeth I, herself.'

The large hand closed around the ring, and Manfri offered his other to seal the deal. 'Then I accept on those terms, providing it meets with her approval, and Grell's.'

'Fate appears to have taken and given in equal measure,' said Ashton shaking the massive hand in a silent contract. 'Two lords of men coming into their inheritance for the benefit of both.' He smiled at the giant at eye level dispute kneeling before him. 'You should get up – a king should never kneel before a Lord.'

Manfri laughed, put out a knee and rose, pocketing the ring but retrieving the silver locket. 'This belongs to her, and you. May it benefit you both, greatly.'

Ashton shot out of his seat as the giant raced to the

window. A blood-curdling bellow echoed around the lake – he had heard that terrible cry weeks before. A dreadful silence fell before the clanging of a distant alarm bell from the hall was accompanied by a cacophony of whistles, horns, and cries from the beacons and lamp-lit shadows of sentries summoned to sudden readiness.

'Grell...' said Ashton. 'I need to get to Elizabeth.'

'Hurry,' said Manfri, bounding down the stairs to the open door and studying the scene of lamp-bearing men and women flitting back and forth like fireflies in the night. 'He's still some way off, but he's coming. Take the horse and meet us by the lake; you'll need to use the command "Shav" to get him moving – Charlemagne only understands Romany.'

'Stay inside and look after Mrs White, Hal,' said Ashton, outside in the courtyard, robbing the young man of the cudgel he bore and placing it through the saddle bag of his attendant horse.

'But I want to do my bit. I was too young for the war...'

'That's very brave of you, but I need you to ensure her safety,' said the veiled Miss Pendlesham, lightly dressed but covered by a woollen shawl to give the semblance of warding off the cold that she barely felt. She sat upon the Welsh cob lightly testing her remembrance of riding with small adjustments in her weight and balance. 'Whatever happens tonight, I will remember your courage; now do as I ask – I trust no other.'

Ashton mounted and swung a lamp onto the pommel to light their way to the lake. They cornered the parterre, and he halted waiting for the cob to pull up alongside, lifting the locket from his pocket and leaning over to place it around her neck. 'I almost forgot,' he said. 'For luck and remembrance.'

She clasped at it and grabbed his hand. 'You are stubbornly resigned to wasting your money on my estate and purchasing it if anything should happen?'

'I am,' he said. 'I will restore the estate, in time, and have the greatest summer residence and pleasure gardens in England, all at the bargain price of forty-three thousand, two hundred and thirty pounds, twelve shillings and sixpence.'

'More than it is worth. Are you only concerned with the value of my inheritance?' she said hesitantly.

He glanced into the veil. 'No, Elizabeth, but my desires do not extend beyond my courtesy and I seek no further while you are beholden to fate, or the memory of another.'

'Even if I were to pour out my feelings to the same effect, you could not hope to love someone so...imperfect.'

'I could and we would be well matched, but it matters only that you are safe and I leave the matter along with my feelings, with you.'

'I think you would truly know how to make me happy, so take this...' She leaned over and lightly raised her veil far enough to plant a light, supple kiss upon his cheek. She grabbed the lamp, swinging it to her saddle and spurred the horse with the command in Romany. 'Hurry, if you have lost none of the horsemanship of your great-great-grandfather.'

They rounded the house to see a swathe of flickering torches forming a defensive line in front of the darkness of the lakeside lawn. The snow had stopped and broken clouds billowed in the moonless sky.

'There is little time,' said Miss Pendlesham. 'Midnight is not far off and we need to make haste — why has he left it so late?'

'If he's not come to talk,' said Ashton, 'then we have a problem...'

They parted an honour guard of Romany, protecting the access through the central hedge and Ashton dismounted leading the Welsh cob through the crowd to meet Manfri standing forward of the front line, staff in hand and peering into the gloom ahead.

Silence fell as Ashton's eyes became accustomed to the darkness. He scanned the shadows for any sign. 'Where is he?'

A sliver of rising moon broke from a low bank of clouds above the wood bringing the distant lake and trees into relief. Backlit in sharp silhouette stood a figure, statue-like in its stillness. A grotesque mockery of a man, pitiful in what remained, rather than what was missing. From behind there came a murmur of unease and several of his folk took a step back.

'Stand!' said Manfri turning to encourage them. 'We deal with the past tonight so that your children's children sleep soundly.' They halted and regained their step.

The figure shifted and lumbered forward to the edge of the lamplight, hesitating and staring with its unblinking eye at the bright lights until its pupil receded to a mere pinprick in the bloodshot of its pink puddle. It noticed the veiled rider and shuffled towards it. Manfri interceded with a cry in Romany and Grell halted, glancing at the giant standing like a herald of old.

'*Parley...lake*,' groaned the old king. '*Eliz...abeth...*'

She cast her head aside in shock, seeing what he had become. The shawl slipped from her shoulders revealing the beautiful silk dress. Grell whimpered like a spurned dog.

'The debt will be repaid, in full,' said Manfri holding up his hand to display the signet ring between his fingers. The ruby blazed at its centre from the sea of fire behind. 'A place of eternal rest for our people is also assured and bound by this token of gold. What say you, lord? Shall we have peace and the lifting of hex and spell?'

Grell swung his arm beneath him, swaying with uncertainty. '*How...who?*'

'By my hand,' said Ashton stepping several paces forward. Miss Pendlesham's horse followed instinctively. 'I am Lord Ashton Berkeley and I honour the debt in a full and final settlement.'

Grell stepped forward to study his face, recognising him from the encounter in the maze. '*Berkeley... Why?*'

'Because my family failed her once, and because I love her...'

Grell shook his head and rubbed at his deformed face. '*Nooo...Elizabeth. Mine. Dead Berkeley left her...long ago.*'

Miss Pendlesham shook off the shouldered coat to reveal the thin white silk of her gown, belted at its waste in the manner of her first appearance, twenty-eight days before. She held out her hands in defiance. 'Let it be ended, Grell, and let us have peace, whatever may come after.'

'The debt is settled,' repeated Manfri holding out the sceptre between them. 'As is the custom of our people, you must honour the outcome for the benefit of each lord of men. I return you the kingship of our people, now restored, and long in my and my fathers' stewardship.'

Grell inched forward writhing as he turned towards the moon to see its beam illuminate the woman in white. Beautiful and timeless she seemed to all who saw her lustrous black hair tumble from her embroidered lace cap, even though her face remained veiled.

'No,' said Grell. '*Only settle if...together. Nothing else, I choose her...over all.*'

'You will bring dishonour upon us,' said Manfri. 'Midnight approaches and I need your assent. You are the rightful king that lives and you must agree before you return to stone...and your prison. This cannot go on, lord...'

With the mention of prison, Grell called out to the horse. '*Shav!*'

The reins of the horse slipped out of Ashton's hands and darted around the giant who lunged to prevent it from reaching its caller. Miss Pendlesham bounced and leant forward to clutch at the lamp-lit pommel, unsure whether to slip away or hang on. Grell raced to meet it, swinging his single arm around the pommel and scooping himself onto the croup of its back, pinning her between. The horse buckled under the weight but recovered to twist and turn beneath the guiding legs of the monstrous horseman as Grell sort for mastery, scooting forward to meet the horse's flank. Grabbing the fallen reins, even as she fended off his mighty arm, he wrapped his elbow around Miss Pendlesham's neck in a dreadful lock forcing Ashton, Manfri, and the front line of his clan to halt.

In a diabolical act of cruelty, he tore at the embroidered cap with his teeth, ripping it from her head and revealing her face in the light of the Cold Moon.

The horse struggled against its unbalanced burden causing Miss Pendlesham's face to turn in and out of the shadows. Fearful words from behind that Ashton could not understand were joined by gasps as she sought him with a look of shame and humiliation. The right side of her head was at utter variance with the left. Heartbreaking beauty shone, pure and undefiled, mirrored by a visage on the other of utter ruin. A vague outline of an eye, without sight, was the only visible mark on an otherwise featureless face bisected down the bridge of the nose before careering off at an angle towards what once was an ear, now only a slight lump holding back the cascade of hair. Her lips were complete but twitched in such sadness with the marred revelation in front of so many, but particularly before one. Not so much a disfigurement, more akin to nothingness,

Ashton recalled the smooth weathering of her statue and knew why she had hidden behind the veil, and the solitary room. He glanced into his eyes recalling the question.

...why does she cover her face and hide from the world?

For modesty...and to hide her from our pity.

Ashton shook his head free of the shock and raced towards her, certain of his convictions. 'Elizabeth!'

'*Mine!*' roared Grell kicking the horse into the darkness behind. '*Keep money...and kingship. I want only her. No more prison or stone...live far away, as before!*'

Ashton raced ahead aware of the large strides close behind.

'He can't be reasoned with,' cried the giant, staff in hand. 'I see it now; he will never stop or accept the payment which absolves her of the need to marry him. The damn fool doesn't realise he'll change back to stone, as will she if she refuses him.'

Ashton breathed hard, sprinting towards the receding horse, weaving its whinnying way around the opposite side of the lake. 'We only have minutes to wait...and then we can... deal with him when he returns to stone.'

'It's what he will do to her...in the meantime if he doesn't...get his way,' said Manfri. 'I know what I must do tonight, hurry – he is heading for the shrubbery path to the mill and...it is overgrown and we might outrun him beyond that.'

A glance behind showed a wavefront of torch fire as the Romany raced down the lakeside lawn like a frenzied pagan horde charging into battle. Even in their fury, they could not hope to catch a mounted man, however burdened.

Ashton wept as he tired, his legs refusing to maintain the previous several hundred yards, and even Manfri began to heave and wheeze with the exertion. Out of the darkness, the horse cried in panic from a suddenly uncovered solitary blaze of light. A bobbing lamplight forced back the beleaguered beast of burden until it twisted against the sudden appearance and tipped backwards casting the two riders to the ground.

In the moonlight, Ashton made out the form of Grell rising and grabbing towards the light that darted around like a willow-the-wisp, trying to end the unseen lamp bearer's baiting. The monster turned to see the oncoming tide of flame and dragged Miss Pendlesham to her feet as the horse rode off in sweated fright towards the dim, twinkling lights of the camp. Both figures disappeared into the gloom.

A minute later, Ashton reached the spot where the dismount had occurred and the light reappeared illuminating the pale and shaking lamp of Hal.

'You damn fool!' said Ashton. 'Are you hurt?'

Hal shook his head. 'Miss Pendlesham, and the thing. I saw them...'

Manfri staggered to a halt, panting and put his hands on his knees to steady his breathing. 'That's the bravest thing I ever saw a rabbit do.'

'What?' said Hal handing Ashton the paraffin lamp.

'I'll explain later, but this time stay out of trouble and keep behind us.'

'The thing is taking her towards the cider mill,' said Hal bouncing along behind the tired men. 'It's where this path leads.'

'We'll need to make sure he doesn't get away or circle back,' said Manfri. 'I'll catch up, but I need to tell the others what to do.'

'There's a shortcut around the southern side from the lodge if they hurry.'

Disappearing back into the path Ashton and Hal ran on, hearing the labouring of Grell and the screams from Elizabeth Pendlesham as they gained ground.

'What will he do to her?' said Hal, keeping up behind the bobbing light.

'It's what I will do to him if he touches her,' said Ashton. 'Now quiet!'

A hundred yards ahead, the footprints ceased at a bridge of slippery railway sleepers that spanned the rushing lake stream. The black outline of the cider mill loomed on the other side. It was separated by the stream and beyond that a large flagstone above the diversion channel. A leaking lock gate supplied nothing more than a trickle of water in the mill race, creating a solitary artery through the snow-covered trench. A rusting, winched handle, bearded with icicles, stood in front of the idle waterwheel to release the paddle when needed and release the water needed to power the machinery inside. Above the wheel, a large black void in the brickwork hinted at a partly shuttered window on a higher floor through which nothing could be seen.

The sound of the meltwater reaching the lake entrance cascaded over a block-strewn weir smothering any sound ahead. Ashton glanced to his right to see a line of torches less than a quarter mile away and then at his watch.

'It's nearly midnight,' he said passing the lamp back to Hal. 'I haven't got time to argue, so stay here and guard the bridge. I'm going inside to check.'

Hal's protestation was silenced with a single, penetrating glance and Ashton crossed the bridge to see fresh prints in the snow on the other side leading to a door, battered from its hinges.

'Elizabeth!' he called into the milling room. His eyes adjusted to the pools of moonlight filtering in through missing slates to form a chequerboard on the grimy flagstones. A great central, wooden spindle arose centrally from a wide and deep stone apple crush to meet a perpendicular cog to the waterwheel. At the base of the spindle, a worn and cracked milling wheel stood idle in a crushing circumference around the stone apple press. It was braced and banded by iron, well beyond its useful working life, but appeared capable of supplying the oak barrel beside the lipped recess of the great stone basin with juice. The pungent smell of rotten fruit and decay lingered, and he took a glance back at Hal, peering into the darkness on the bridge, and headed inside. A creak from a gallery above was accompanied by a mouthless snuffle like one prevented from speech.

'Grell!' he called turning to catch the flight of wooden steps leading upwards. 'You don't have long. Give up your claim on Elizabeth and return to your people. You have my word you will not be harmed.'

'Ashton! Up—' she cried from somewhere above before a strangled whine cut off further attempts at speech.

Lifting a lump of fallen masonry, Ashton creaked up the first few treads to reach the cornered landing. Soft patches of rotting timber lay out the outer edge, and he skirted the cobwebbed and pigeon-nested rubble wall to approach the first floor. He hesitated before catching a glimmer of firelight approaching in haste through the large half-shuttered window he had seen from outside.

'You are surrounded.'

From the far corner among dry crates, packing straw and sackcloth stood the former Roma King, entwined with another, now facing inwards, his arm wrapped around her neck. *'Leave...us...be, gorger,'*

'Please, let her go. She doesn't want you.'

'In a moment we will be...together as one statue, and I will hold her...while winter gives way...to spring and blessed summer.' He pulled Elizabeth closer to bury her head within the remains of his chest. *'I will weather the storms...for you.'*

She fought against his arm and the prospect of being

entrapped for the next eleven months in a dreadful embrace and Ashton recalled the truth of her answer earlier in the day:

Do you see and hear when you—?

Like a dream...I remember the first swallows above the lake...those that look into my face...

Ashton raised the stone in his hand, glancing at the seconds ticking away on his watch. 'If you do not let her go, I'll make sure there is nothing left of you come Frost Moon next year except dust and memories of a fallen king.' He smashed the stone into the remaining shutter knocking it open to the light of the Cold Moon. It poured in to strike a path across the boards and the lower half of his leg.

Grell sneered from the opening that substituted his mouth and tossed Elizabeth aside setting her tumbling to the floor.

'Kill petty gorger lord...first!'

He stomped through the beam and across the rotten boards enraged but stumbled to find his legs stiff and unwilling. Behind him, Elizabeth staggered to her feet and pushed away sluggishly to the far shadows of the upper floor pursued by the silver shaft.

'It's too late!' she cried. 'We're changing...'

'Stay out of the light!' cried Ashton.

Grell swung his hip forward, throwing the transforming foot of his right leg onto the next board. It collapsed right through under the weight of newly forming stone. Where once had been pallid skin there now seeped a petrifying virulence working its way through his body, yet his arm remained free, pulling himself out from the hole in the floor. Half dragging like some golem from ancient legend he thrust himself forward to thump forward like a diver in weighted boots, poorly mobile but immensely strong. Ashton backed away from the wooden railing that was all that prevented a fall of twenty feet into the basin below.

Ashton goaded and chastised one last time, pinned to the left and right by Grell's mighty reach and hoping for what was to come. The monstrous face grimaced with the effort of movement and hatred of this living, breathing rival, bellowing as it tipped forward on unresponsive legs to reach his arm outstretched.

Ashton ducked beneath and aside the muscled limb as Grell fell forward, unable to arrest his momentum and fall through the rickety barrier. He tipped over the edge and into the air, knocking and twisting Ashton from his feet. Elizabeth screamed as Ashton slipped and grabbed single-handed at the upright post to dangle from the gallery above the stone basin glancing down to see Grell writhing in pain in the press's channel and struggling to get up. Sliding down the rotten grime of the wet wood Ashton threw his hand over to grab at the soft wooden edge which gave way.

Suddenly a hand was there, delicate, stone-like in its grip and appearance, and he looked up into the moonlit face of Elizabeth Pendlesham. For an instance, and perhaps a trick of the light he saw her face whole and unmarred heaving at his wrist.

'I'll pull you over if you don't let go,' he cried. 'There's nothing to hold on to and you don't have the strength...'

She shook her head and turned to see a lithe figure leap from the curved top of the waterwheel and through the upstairs window, racing to pull at the cuff of his shirt and drag Ashton back to the safety of the floor. He rose to see Hal apologetically dusting him down.

'I told you before,' he said. 'I don't want to be nowhere else, so just let it lie, Mr Berkeley. Mrs White said she can take care of herself, and she's mighty fierce when she means to be.'

Ashton gripped his arm and shook it in thanks. 'I'm sure she is, and I'm glad you're here.' Turning he saw Elizabeth pushing herself up the wall as though wading through water, slow and ponderous to get to her feet as the curse began to work upon her body, causing a new cycle of stone. She hid the side of her face with one hand until he gently brushed it aside clasping her around the waist as they all looked down to see the rush of bodies pour into the room below.

A great light of burning torches flooded the freshly blown snow of the ground floor with firelight and frost as Manfri charged into the room bearing the granite-headed staff. Grell lifted himself from the fall and dragged himself to his knees and Manfri strode forward, unafraid.

'By the consent of our people, I cast you from the kingship and the clan. Be as dust to us that we may tread your dishonour into the paths upon which we travel.' He thrust the staff forward and Grell caught its edge in a vice-like grip.

'*It takes more than a rod...to make a king!*'

Manfri tugged and kicked out at the hand, freeing it momentarily to swing it like a mace into the elbow. The arm flew from its stony socket, transformed and leaving splinters and fragments of limestone skittering across the floor.

'Maybe,' said Manfri, preparing to strike again. 'But it's enough to end one.'

Grell launched from his knees like a battering ram, almost knocking over the giant, he recoiled and struck out again removing a large part of his adversary's thigh. Grell was thrown back by the force of the blow and collapsed into the channel.

'Unlock the paddles to the water gate, Hal!' said Ashton quickly, shielding Elizabeth from the light of the moon. He could feel the rigidness in her body taking hold. 'Set the press in motion if it still has the power to do so!' The lad leapt away and clambered out of the window and climbed down the static wheel.

A wail of dreadful anguish heralded Grell's writhing and

unsuccessful attempt to regain his feet. Grell fell forwards, pieces littering the channel as the central mill wheel began to rock on the opposite side. Defeated but defiant, the statue writhed and raised what remained of its head.

'*I will return...while the curse remains.*'

'I don't think so,' said Manfri swinging the staff with an almighty blow and lopping off the statue's head into the path of the slowly trundling mill wheel. The loosely socketed beam within the axle lifted the wheel over the skull crushing it into meal and thumping back into the channel before pulverising pieces of carved stone into smaller and smaller pieces.

'Are you alright up there?' called Manfri from the base of the steps. He stooped to toss the loose stone arm into the channel where it joined the rest of the pieces, crushed into smaller and smaller pieces as the wheel rotated and ground down the fully petrified being.

'We're unharmed, but...' Ashton felt her bury her face in his chest breathing slowly until he glanced down fearing she had ceased altogether.

'It's not yet...lifted,' she whispered. 'Will you...wait for me?'

'Yes,' he said. 'I'll be there with you in sunshine and in rain, when the swallows return and red breast nests, I'll be there.'

She raised her arms through his loving hold and wrapped them around his neck hesitantly approaching his lips. Ashton clung to her with tightly bound tenderness and pressed his lips against hers. He closed his eyes briefly with the intoxicating and overwhelming feeling of wanting and being wanted. He felt a tear from her eyes streak down his cheek as she shifted her arms away to raise them above her head, breaking the kiss and stepping back out of his loosening embrace.

It was Hal that began to sob, long before Ashton dared to open his eyes.

'Long live the rightful King!' shouted a man from below. He was soon joined by a throng of voices from the lower floor, deep and resonant, masking the sound of stone upon stone.

'You can stop the water now, Hal,' said Manfri, allowing the young man to pass, wiping his eyes upon the sleeve of his tattered jacket. 'I need a moment with my friend.'

Ashton felt the large hand upon his shoulder, and the stoutness of the man beside him, as he opened his eyes to see her, moonlit and mid-dance, arms raised in frozen serpentine phrases, hair cascading in ringlets about her worn and weathered face.

'The moondance,' said Manfri, bowing to the static figure.

A sadness accompanied the enigmatic smile that Ashton had not recalled from the last sight of the statue. Something else was new – the relief of a locket hung at her breast, open to reveal a perfectly carved cameo of two people. Finely rendered portraits in freshly carved stone appeared within each half – a beautiful woman occupied the left turning to face that of a handsome man, eyes closed, with a dimple in his cheek.

Ashton clung to the umbrella in the rain watching the tears streak down the statue's face upon the plinth.

'I've got to go, but I'll be back as soon as I can. I need to set all things in motion here, and bury the past at home to prepare for the future; my steward is strong enough to make the journey and the mild weather has opened up the roads. What a difference a fortnight makes..' He set down a tied bunch of flowering heather.

'The Romany say it brings luck. They are moving now that their vigil is ended. Mrs White has the money I received to pay for Christmas and to make a start on the repairs and restorations. I'll be sending men here over the summer before harvest sets in to help. Hal insisted on following Manfri into the maze to check again this morning, and the plinth is still empty; I think he is gone, Elizabeth, for good.'

He turned and made his way slowly back to the courtyard. The Welsh cob shifted restlessly in his harness, ready to pull the canvassed wagon and its king along the open roads.

'My offer still stands to join me in the car that is due any moment now,' said Ashton. 'Hal can look after the horse.'

Manfri tipped his hat and tapped at the wooden casket at his side. It was bound with a ribbon of purple silk and sat upon a freshly carved stone plinth, eight inches high like a miniature catafalque atop the seat of a horse-drawn hearse.

'I need to take it slow to inter these particular ashes,' he said. 'Those that weren't here will need to see the old king along the way, as is customary. I should be with you in ten days.'

'And how do you feel now that you are now confirmed as the rightful living king?'

'Unworthy,' grinned Manfri.

'A perfect place to start,' said Ashton reaching up with his hand to shake in farewell.

'She'll return, I'm sure of it,' said the Roma. 'Once Grell is in the Queen's earth and the debt is paid, she'll be back at Frost Moon; this time for good. I can mend her—'

'No,' said Ashton. 'I will love her as she is, or not at all. Look after my ring.'

'And you look after her.' Manfri twitched the reins. '*Shav*, Charlemagne, you daft thing,.'

The sparkling black motor car kicked up the dry, drive dust, scattering the newly fallen leaves from spring-pollarded entrance trees.

'He's coming!' shouted Hal.

'Well, do something with your hair or borrow Albert's cap; he's off to get the provisions in for the master's stay.'

Hal brushed his fingers through his hair to feel the gentle elbowed jab to his ribs from the recently employed house-maid beside him. 'You'll have to smarten up if you are taking me to the pictures a week on Saturday.'

House staff emerged from the courtyard doorways to take their place in front of the newly surfaced entrance circle to the house to greet their master. The windows sparkled, beaming back the sun with the pride of newly painted frames as the car pulled up. Lord Berkeley got out raising a smile at the progress from his late summer visit, and the smartly uniformed Mrs White and company, brimming with nervous anticipation.

She curtsied and came to welcome him, sending the foot-man-in-training scurrying to collect his cases.

'Well, sir, you look every inch a Lord this time, and no mistake,' she said, clasping him warmly about the hands and approving of his pinstripe and tailored woollen coat.

'Mrs White, it's so good to see you. I barely recognise the place.'

'The room on the first floor overlooking the improve-ments has been made up—'

'I'll be happiest in the lodge,' said Ashton politely, bending over to whisper. 'While it's true I purchased the house, I feel obliged to be invited by its true owner if that can be arranged.'

The housekeeper nodded. 'Very good, sir. Do you think she—?'

'I hope,' he said. 'The debt is repaid. The rest is down to fate.'

Unable to restrain himself, Hal bounded forward. 'Mr Berkeley, sir, come and see the new hothouse!'

'I will, soon, Hal. Has my deputy head gardener from my estate been hard at work providing the flowers for Miss Pendlesham?'

'He has, sir, and he's a marvel. I've learned so much that my head is fit to bursting.'

'Then perhaps I should ask him if he is willing to stay and put up with an excitable, but dependable, apprentice?'

Hal beamed and blushed.

'Has the aviary surrounding the pool in the centre of the maze been completed?' said Ashton, mindful of the other staff nearby.

'It has, sir. I doubt anything could fly away or escape from such a well-constructed cage.' He hesitated. 'Will Mr Manfri be coming, sir?'

'Perhaps in time for Christmas, along with several others. They are invited, but he is currently finishing the engraving of a memorial on the Berkeley estate. He sends his regards.'

'We hope that all will be put right on your account, it being Frost moon tonight, and all.'

'Thank you, Hal. So do I.'

Spiralled strands of mist hovered over the lake like vaporous springs. In the darkness, the sounds of a barking fox set off distant and unseen waterfowl in a short-lived and comforting clucking.

'One year ago,' he whispered to himself as the distant chime of the newly restored courtyard clock struck the full midnight hour. He looked up through the high, all-encompassing gauze of cirrus cloud to see the moon bleached and blurred, shutting his eyes, not daring to turn round, and listening to the outgoing sigh of the soothing stream next to the lodge.

He flinched and exhaled suddenly with the feel of two hands at his waist, and he moved to clasp them. They were cool but smooth. A woman's hand without blemish or roughness.

'Elizabeth...'

He opened his eyes and turned to see her face in the dim light, partly shadowed by the shrubbery. The plinth was empty, and the Frost Moon had risen.

She lifted her head gingerly and her eyes met his. Two sparkling, perfect eyes set in a face of such radiant beauty that Ashton put his hand across his mouth momentarily in shock before lowering it to join her quivering, lightly clad body in an embrace.

'Am I not free of it?' she said sobbing into his chest with a lightness in her voice.

Ashton released her to stare tearfully into her eyes and led her to the water's edge.

'Look,' he said as the brine of his eyes spilt down his cheeks and into the stillness of the mirrored lake. Elizabeth glanced down to see her reflection, marred by the ripples of his tears. In a moment, they faded, and she held her breath to see the face she feared now returned to its fair form.

'No more veils,' he said, watching as she smoothed her face in disbelief.

'You waited, and came back,' she said. 'The swallows, the nesting birds, and your flowers—'

'Yes,' he said. 'Next year we will see them together, right here, if you'll have me.'

She retreated to swirl, barefoot upon the lawn, lithely springing and laughing through the grassy dew. 'I feel everything!' she cried with joy, pausing suddenly to rub at the sole of her foot. Reaching into the grass she retrieved a penny, much weathered and dull with patina.

'If I were to have you,' she said tossing back his lost coin, 'I would not have you penniless.'

Ashton caught it and rushed to lift her from her feet. She slid sensuously into his shoulders, and only a shiver because of the cool November air severed the meeting of her lips from his.

Elizabeth landed softly and accepted his coat to warm the skin and bone of her restored form. Taking her hand, Ashton led her to the central topiary-trimmed avenue and the view of Bickford Hall, brimming with flickering candlelight in all of its windows to welcome her home.

'Is it truly over?' she asked hesitantly, clasping the locket at her neck with her free hand.

'Yes,' he said pointing at a shooting star streaking above the dark chimneys of the sparkling lights of the house. 'Shall we begin?' He jogged forward, pulling her along until she gained his stride, laughing at the joining of hands and the freedom of those that know they have their whole life ahead of them, bound by happy circumstances, with love as enduring as stone.

THE SOUL CLOCK

I had been apprenticed to Hobson's of Worcester since the spring of 1889, and my relationship with the master clockmaker had run as smoothly and efficiently as the devices we refurbished for the past six years.

We worked alone and in contemplative contentment in the ever-present sounds of our gas-lit tinkering and the tick-tocking of the shop front clocks. My studious work held the same enthusiasm, whether working on exotic or mundane timepieces as though my childhood fascination with gears and mechanisms had never left me. Perhaps as a break for his tired eyes, Mr Hobson would appear behind me, silent and unheralded, to judge my progress on some complex coil-springed chiming device. With a nod of satisfaction, as though breaking the soothing silence was somehow sacrilegious, the old master would replace his thinly framed pince-nez and return to his tasks in the connecting room leaving me to the solitary splendours of sprockets, springs, and spindles.

I enjoyed the puzzling work, diagnosing each problem like a surgeon preparing to embark on a mechanical patient. Remedying the fault, or fabricating a new part, was distinctly satisfying before reassembling the heart of the mechanism back to ticking life in the beauty of its outer case. I liked my own company, and my tutelage under the man that had learned his trade with the renowned Thwaites & Reed of London had taught me much. The whisperings of the occasional customer entering the premises coming to collect or drop off the latest interesting marvel broke up the day, and I was content with my situation. My lodgings in the room above, overlooking the rooftops to the great sandstone patched tower of the cathedral, were ample in exchange for keeping the modest premises secure and clean. One day I would own my own business and govern my affairs. This kept me focussed as I watched, no longer envious, from the wide leaded shop window at the young men of my age walking arm in arm with smiling Sunday girls down to the riverboats on the Severn.

Worcester was a lively place, never more so than at Christmas time. Our wide-windowed spot on the Foregate afforded a fine view of passing trade when a stiff shoulder or lower back required momentary relief from the sedentary rigours of our work. The shop did well during the festive season, especially in pocket watches we acquired, modified and engraved into things of timeless beauty and precision. Despite the brisk business, Hobson always suffered a peculiar melancholy that afflicted him for several days during the festive season.

I had initially put the seasonal gloom down to a sad anniversary. When he was not forthcoming, I surmised it was the shorter days or the curious shakes that were affecting his ability to do the intricate work required. Hobson's advancing years were taking a toll on his hands and temper, and I did not repeat my sympathetic enquiry into his health following the visit of a doctor, which resulted in me being tasked with menial lubricating and spring tensioning drudgery for several days. His condition worsened, but I was generous and humble enough to accept the advanced tasks he now entrusted me with because I was ready for the challenge. He would watch and guide me, placing an unsteady hand on my shoulder as he sighed at the intricate work below that he could rarely undertake, except by long and tedious endeavour. Despite his failing constitution, I discovered it was not any of the reasons mentioned that caused the melancholia; it was a clock.

Hobson could not be cured of his mood until the service and return of a certain wall-mounted pendulum clock was complete. Each year, the clock's owner, a wealthy and unpleasant gentleman called Besham, would arrive the week before Christmas and demand to see my employer. Piccadilly-whiskered, and with an arrogance, born of affluence and entitlement, he would dismiss me. Only when I was apparently out of sight, though not out of earshot, would he hand over the plain, painted pine timepiece in its scuffed leather-bound case, into Hobson's sole keeping as though it was a priceless relic. I rarely got a peek at the rather ordinary, Roman-dialled device before it was carried into the master's workshop; it seemed an unworthy piece from the middle of the century for a clockmaker of his repute to lose literal sleep over. Several tedious and testing days of near hermit-like existence followed as he replaced or fabricated parts for the impatient and ill-tempered clock owner, always from behind his locked door.

Except for food, bodily necessity, or a few hours' rest at his nearby home, he would not come out until the annual service work was completed. This left me to man the counter and see to business alone. When Hobson emerged, he appeared haggard but relieved that the labour was complete, comforted in some sense to see the owner return on the morning of Christmas Eve for the outwardly worthless object. With some derogatory comment about confidentiality, often with an undisguised glance in my direction, Besham would offer outrageous and insulting prices for the beautiful and fairly priced clocks for sale. When Hobson refused, Besham grudgingly settled the bill, grumbling about returning the following December to dampen our festivities and cloud our happy existence.

The world turned and time moved on, just like the dialled hands of our stock. Emerald spring blushed into rosy-cheeked summer signalling the riverboats and their crew. Cuckoos and egg-sized strawberries arrived from the Evesham Vale, and hardy folk in the fields sweltered and sweated in the soil. Fortunately, the fierce August sun had little impact on the blessed cool of my windowless workroom in the far reaches of the Georgian brick building. Before long, summer mellowed into amber-leafed autumn, the nights drew in, and the sound of chimes were drowned out by the newly lit, hoarse rasping of the gas mantles. Outside in the leaf-tossed air, the sand martens left the crooks and crannies of the cathedral, circling above the splitting seed cases of the sweet chestnuts in the park. We would pause in our tinkering to hear them depart, far above the mists that crept up from the river and into our very bones.

Auction season provided a keen distraction, and we worked on our purchases in time for the approach of Christmas. I entered my own melancholia, ticking off the early days of December like a dreary advent calendar before Besham bustled once more into the shop, dragging with him the sleet from the street and the leather-bound travelling case containing the pitch-pine pendulum clock.

'One week, Hobson,' he said, scowling over at me for eavesdropping from my high desk in the workroom. 'The chime is broken again; call yourself a clockmaker?'

'With respect, Mr Besham, the mechanism is incredibly delicate and was not designed for overuse.'

'Overuse! How dare you tell me how often I may play with my own things. If you fabricated and installed the correct replacements, I would not be without my clock at this time of year. It barely keeps time, and I must have confidence in what the hands are telling me this Christmas Eve.'

Besham looked around and frowned as I returned from my eavesdropping to the cleaning of an antique escape wheel. 'You are sure the boy doesn't fix the damn thing while you dawdle at the auction room?'

'No,' said Hobson in an unusual display of confrontation and defence of the assertion, 'though he has a greater skill than I possessed myself at his age.' He held up his shaking fingers. 'One day you may need someone of his skill when I can no longer accommodate you.'

'Until then,' continued Besham, placing his hands on the counter and glancing at the case, 'I ask you to honour the agreement made when you were still a journeyman.'

'I honour the covenant made many years ago in London with Mr Reeds. It enabled me to become my own man, and I have held true these many years that I would see to your affairs, Mr Besham. If you wish to alter that understanding, then you are welcome to take the clock elsewhere and I release you from any obligation; Master Jenkins and I are very busy with more mundane timepieces.'

Besham stood back as though stung and was about to launch into a tirade of further abuse when he caught his breath and reasserted control. He reached into the breast pocket of his morning suit and retrieved a pocketbook, covertly laid several high-value notes onto the glass counter. I could tell by the raised eyebrows of my employer that this was as close to a peace offering as he was likely to get.

'Will this do, Mr Hobson?' he said meekly. 'You understand the necessity to return the clock to full working order, especially considering my guest who will be disappointed not to see it once more.' Besham leaned in close and I only just caught the whisper. 'He has acquired, at great expense, one of the remaining clocks by Ambroos. It might be a century since they were last together in any room, perhaps in the hands of the master alchemist himself!'

Hobson closed his eyes and steadied himself. 'I urge you to be very careful, Mr Besham; you know the danger.'

Besham scoffed. 'Better than any man. Have I not owned this remarkable object for nigh on thirty years? Stick with your trade and leave the pleasures of the device to your betters.'

Hobson folded his arms and shook his head, backing away from the counter. 'I make the offer my master made every year, plus interest, to buy the clock and perhaps save you and others from their fate.' He turned and scribbled a figure onto a scrap of paper, placing it on the counter to lie alongside the pile of banknotes.

Besham struggled into a stiff and unsuited smile, adding several more incentives to the pile before him like a poker player calling to see his opponent's hand.

'I see business has been good, but my response is the same as it was last year, and the thirty years before that.' He glanced around at the contents with derision. 'You could throw in the flotsam and jetsam you have here and it wouldn't make a blind bit of difference; the clock is not for sale.'

Hobson sighed, and a shadow appeared across his creased and care-worn face.

'I'm sure we will both be relieved when the clock is repaired and we can go our separate ways,' said Besham, adding a final note on the pile as though issuing a summons. 'Do your job, man. I'm sure you and the boy will both have a comfortable season at my expense.'

For a moment, I willed my employer to push aside the money and preserve the merriment we were entitled to, but he relented, driven by more than financial gain. I snapped round to avoid his glance, and as I returned to my black-brassed fingers I recalled the conflict, resignation and profound sadness in his eyes. Hobson had a noble spirit and what drove him to accept the work changed the course of both our lives and that of many others.

———

Hobson began his hermitage that afternoon, while I resigned myself to a mirthless few days in the shop. Only briefly did I catch glimpses of the dismantled wall clock, shining in its shell, when he emerged for food or an urgent errand with a customer was required. I offered my help, but it was declined, though with a good-tempered nod as he closed the door behind him. He would often call for a roll of fresh architects' paper and my curious visions through the keyhole revealed reams of scattered drawings, discarded sheets, scribbled design dead-ends, and gear ratios pinned to the large adjustable tilt table.

Late into the night he worked until retiring to his house down by the moonlit, swan-swimming Severn, leaving me alone in my room above with thoughts of the work that consumed him, until the distant cathedral bells of midnight lulled me into resonant repose.

A gentle and unfamiliar quarter-hour chime woke me, and I stared into the moonlit dark to hear soft voices from below. One of them belonged to Hobson, and his seasonal dry cough confirmed my suspicion. Who the other voice was, and at this time of night, I could not tell but it belonged to a woman. We were both bachelors by trade, though perhaps in my case, not by design, and I had never seen my employer in female company outside of business hours.

I dressed and grabbed at an iron poker, still warm from

the dying embers of the small bedroom grate. Creeping downstairs I saw light peeping beneath Hobson's workshop door and the indistinct murmur of the woman's voice. I approached, setting off the creaking of a floorboard that set off a flurry of noise from beyond. Thinking better of an embarrassing escape, now that my presence was known, I stepped back to the counter to await the opening of the door.

Hobson blinked out into the darkness to see my surprise.

'Go back to bed, Daniel,' he whispered. 'I couldn't sleep and needed to return to finish the work on the clock; it is almost complete but requires reassembling. Pass me your needle oiler before you go - mine is empty.'

I nodded, and retreated to the moonlit shadows of my workplace, feeling my hand along the wall to locate the tool.

'I heard voices,' I said, handing him the oiler and raising myself on tiptoes to peer over his shoulder. 'I thought we had burglars.'

To my surprise and great curiosity he widened the door behind him. The white-hot glow of the gas mantle cursed, suppressing any sound within the empty room, but I caught the naked workings of the clock suspended above the bench. It was littered with golden fragments, dials, and delicate new workings. The only sign of movement was the gentle swing of a recently stilled pendulum. I turned back to see him wobble as though in a faint. He looked dreadfully tired, not to mention pale and sickly.

'You mustn't overdo things, Mr Hobson,' I said, desperate for the sentiment and my concern to be taken sincerely, if not seriously, at that ungodly hour. Behind him, the brass bob at the end of the rod ceased, and he rubbed at his eyes and closed the door, locking it behind him.

'Soon,' he said from the other side. 'I have so little time each year to make progress.'

Returning to my room, I tossed and turned in my

attempts at sleep, but the sense that Hobson was not alone did not recede. Whether he thought me asleep after an hour or through his compulsion to test the hammers once more, the second quarter chimed from the curious clock below the floorboards of my room. Despite the words being inaudible, I could tell from the murmurings that it was a woman, though not the same as before. It was older, richer and gentler, as though time had softened the musicality and tone of her voice. All too soon it was over and Hobson left the building, with a gentle click of the door among the ticking of the sleepless sentinels of the shop.

He did not appear in the morning, and I assumed Hobson had overslept until the district gossip, who served as housemaid and laundress, came into the shop to inform me that my employer was not well. Fever, exhaustion and deteriorating health had resulted in a visit from the doctor. Despite several failed attempts to rise and dismiss the medic and his prescriptions, Hobson had resigned to spending the 23rd of December in a mild delirium tucked up in bed with a copy of the latest H. G. Wells.

She held out a written note wrapped around the key to his workroom. 'Mr Hobson said to give you this, and told you to be mindful of what it says, particularly the last line.'

I read the instructions, directing me to complete the work he had laboured upon for three days. Several rudimentary sketches showing the positions of gears, and their three-dimensional arrangement within an unusual design, accompanied the text urging me to complete the assembly in time for Besham's return on the following morning. I turned over the second page to see the final instruction, incised by the weight of the fountain pen as though the written word itself was not enough to relay the urgency of the directive:

Do not wind the clock, interfere with or omit any of the spurious components; they are necessary.

Follow my instructions and leave both hands resting at twelve.

Do not interfere with 'it'. Under NO circumstances, engage the chimes.

'Tell him, I will do as he asks,' I said lowering the sheets and glancing towards the workshop door. Apart from spring cleaning, I had rarely been in the hallowed room alone and never to work. The woman nodded and left the shop as I weighed the key in my hand and acquainted myself with the strange mechanism sketched out before me. I unlocked the door and entered the cloistered cell of the master clockmaker to begin.

The room was in uncharacteristic disarray, mostly derived from the soiled cups and plates, many of which had remnants of food I recalled preparing several days ago. Paper lay strewn across most of the work surfaces, as well as pinned across large areas of the plastered wall. All had some design or mathematical scrawl, hastily written as though Da Vinci himself had returned in a feverish fervour to begin on some unknown and bizarre horological device. Stacks of journals showing similar recordings, findings, and embellishments were removed from their customary place on the shelf to tower on each side of the main work table. The naked clock hung from a suspended ceiling rod, high enough for the brass-bobbed pendulum to swing without catching the table or the litany of tools and fragments laid out like a jumbled jigsaw beneath. I peered at the plain pitch-pine case, stained in mockery of more expensive mahogany and it stared back from the hook on the wall like a lifeless Cyclops awaiting the return of its solitary eye.

With a glance at the empty shop, I placed the assembly instructions among the curious and spurious components necessary to complete the clock. Some were fabricated, and I marvelled at their intricacy and the skill of my employer to achieve such fine work in his infirmity. The parts were so thin for me to wonder whether they were indeed metal and not card; this was not a clock designed for longevity.

Or so I thought.

I was many minutes into the ordering of the parts within the partially assembled silvered mechanism case when I saw 'it'. A wafer-thin pair of joined, heart-shaped golden leaves were engraved with a scrolling signature of a woman's name: 'Lenora'. From the gleaming centrepiece ran a protruding set of arterial spindles, resting upon the surface as though designed to operate from a vibratory touch rather than mechanical means. One spindle anchored a rod leading to a bobbled metal roller upon which six cams connected to exquisite chiming hammers. The thin, tubular chiming bars rose like radiator fins and I flicked the hammer to strike a resonant note. Whatever the strange and inaccessible heart's function, as well as several other bizarre components, the beauty of the true clock lay hidden for the vast majority of the year within the beast of its outer case.

'The mechanism is hiding in plain sight, so as not to attract attention,' I thought, spinning the plain case over to see a paltry sum of money pencilled into the underside.

This was not the original case, though I could not date the mechanism. It was old, intricate, advanced, and unique. Turning the silvered frame over, I saw that the curious heart-shaped centrepiece could be accessed from an ornate hole. It was engraved to appear as though framing a window or valuable portrait. The heart appeared to be removable with a gentle rocking motion, but I recoiled my agile fingers as though an electric current or painful static was in play. The heart snapped back as I rubbed at my forefinger, and like any irrational human being, I extended the middle finger of my other hand to try again, this time only to dab its lustrous surface. Rather than the sting of the earlier attempt, there did indeed appear to be a gentle inaudible hum or buzz, as though a vibration had been captured within. It was a marvellous object, and despite several interruptions during the morning, I completed and reinstated most of the mechanism to the pendulum and clock face.

Glad to stretch my legs, I made several local deliveries, including a carriage clock, two matching pocket watches, and a christening spoon. Joining the road south of the cathedral, I considered paying Hobson a sympathetic and surprise visit. I shook my head. Incapacitated and away from his beloved clocks, he would be in a foul mood and incensed by the notion that I considered a visit more important than an open shop the day before Christmas Eve.

I was the only one he had, outside of the guild or the auction room. For a moment, as I studied the parallel cart tracks leading to his riverside home, I felt a sadness as though my future might be constrained by the same passion and heading in the same direction. Forcing my chill hands into my coat pocket, I rubbed at the self-engraved lines of my watch and decided that devotion to time could be an adequate mistress. I was never shy around clocks, but women were altogether a different matter.

On the way back, I bought up a great garland of aromatic fir and bundles of hoar-frosted holly within a calico sack to festoon the ledges, clock cases, and windows. I planned to visit my mother and sister in Malvern, on the eve following St Stephen's Day, though whether the shop would stay open with Hobson's illness was in doubt. It was late into a rapid, amber sunset when I returned. I lit the lamps to capitalise on the last few hours of opening before stoking the fire and decorating my dusk-lit domain.

Finding myself master of the shop provided an incentive to nose about Hobson's journals. Each one, dated from over thirty years ago to the present, represented exploded diagrams, intricate measurements, and suggestions for miniaturising the clock mechanism on the stand before me. While several clock parts held no particular purpose in winding, time-keeping or balancing, what those parts accomplished was not known. On several sheets were scribbled the hurried dictation of conversation, or more precisely, questions and answers. All appeared to be in a different hand, a flowing script unlike that of my employer; it was a woman's hand, and several references to "Lenora" confirmed my suspicions that I had not been wrong about the previous night. A sudden and short-lived pang of jealousy afflicted me until it was replaced by a curiosity surrounding the mysterious woman.

I locked the shop and attempted to tidy Hobson's workshop, more out of necessity as I needed clean cutlery and plates. I returned later with a full stomach and a nip of the brandy that I knew he kept in the cuckoo clock case, hanging above the door.

Whether it was the alcohol addling my judgement or the combination of the seasonal scent of the resinous fir, the splutter of several candles, and the distant hum of the cathedral organ piping to prepare for midnight mass, I found myself in a curiously confident and congenial mood. I also found myself next to the wall clock, key in hand, eager to hear the chime and test that my work had been successful. The anxiety that my double-checking and obsessive attention to detail would leave me without the shortest of tests tipped me into spontaneous rebellion. I tilted the glass cover to the side and gave the winged key two gentle, full turns at both the mainspring and the chime and strike keyholes. The hands stood resolute at the twelve as I set off the pendulum like a guilty child.

The clock ticked into life and I made a note of the time with the mantel calibration clock to test how accurately the device kept time or whether adjustments needed to be made. The gentle, hypnotic sway of the arm lulled me and I barely heard the winding and release of the fourth-quarter chime. A resonant sound filled the room with a bell-like tinkle as the delicate silver hammers struck the precious metal bars within. The tune was unfamiliar but so deeply melancholic as to leave me quite moved. The chimes were mostly in a minor key and there appeared to be several double strikings, harmonising and explaining several of the additional components I had reassembled.

'Beautiful,' I whispered, coming closer to capture the remnants of the echo.

'Thank you – just what I said myself,' said a gentle, but unfamiliar voice from behind. 'Sixty-three years ago.'

I twisted round to see a woman, barely out of her teens standing next to the door in clothing more suited to a winter ball than the freezing fog outside. Her scarlet taffeta gown rustled as she side-stepped to avoid my sudden startled shock and I hurriedly brushed past to the relative spaciousness of the shop to catch my bearings and my breath. I turned to glance at the lustrous plait of dark hair which crowned her head like a fascinator, reflecting the candlelight which streamed from behind her. The shop door was locked, and as I rattled the handle to make sure, the silhouette stepped back, and I saw the pallor of her face as though the sun had never kissed the pale, freckled porcelain.

'We...we're closed,' I blathered, more nervous of one beautiful woman than all the burglars in the county.

'And I do not need a clock,' she said in a low, sweet voice, scarcely raising her head as she rustled around and pointed to the suspended case above the table. 'Though perhaps a little company now that you have summoned me?'

'Summoned you?' I said, still unsure whether some ruse to distract me was at play and if some accomplice did not lurk in the dark corners between the deep, slow ticking of the grandfathers in the corner.

'You caused the chimes to sound, though I can see from your startled expression that you were not expecting me.' She leaned into the room as though searching for something or someone. 'Where is Algernon?'

I shook my head, and she wrinkled her nose. 'Algernon Hobson – the clockmaker.'

I realised throughout all my years with the business, I had never thought it polite to ask about my employer's name.

'He is incapacitated,' I said, coming to my senses. 'He has been overworked recently – who are you?'

'You ought to know that, seeing and touching the heart of the clock earlier. The cell bears my name, though before me it bore no such mark and was blank. My name is Lenora Chambers — are you the apprentice who is protective and who snores in the room above? Algernon talks about you most pleasantly though I assumed you would be younger.'

I frowned, ignoring the compliment and whatever else was intended by her remarks. 'You were here last night – I heard you with Mr Hobson.'

'Yes. I am announced, but you are not – do manners and courtesy still exist in the year 1895?'

I watched as she placed her hands on her cheeks and shook her head. I confess I was bemused by the question.

'Your name, silly,' she said. 'May the Lord preserve me from the introverted shyness of solitary clockmakers.'

I placed my hands on my hips in some pretence of masculine confidence. 'Daniel Jenkins,' I said. 'Now explain how you got in here, and what you want.'

'I have been here, within the clock, since that brute brought me to the shop several days ago,' she said. 'You summoned me from the entrapment I encountered whilst sleepwalking during the midnight chimes of a Christmas Eve long ago. What I want is to be released, and in secret, several generations of the finest clockmakers have endeavoured to accomplish the feat.' She examined the drawings on the wall and let out a sad, shuddering sigh. 'It appears the puzzle continues to evade Algernon.'

I rubbed my fingers through my hair, tugging at the short locks. 'Even if I believed you, how is such a thing possible?'

Lenora looked across at the myriad of mechanical parts, diagrams and burred metal coils that coated the small lathe like glittering tinsel. 'I understand the original clockmaker, a Dutch alchemist of great infamy with no small skill as a clockmaker, fabricated the hearts that adorn the clocks he created, one of which holds me captive.'

'Why would he do such a thing?' I said.

'Do you not see?' she replied. 'Immortality is a bittersweet mistress. She takes with one hand, to give with the other.' Lenora studied the confusion on my face. 'I get the distinct impression that you have not encountered a soul clock before and that you have been rather reckless, without permission, in your testing of the clock that holds me prisoner.'

I turned to hear the rush of many feet and excitable chatter outside in the street, giving me time to hide the embarrassing flush in my cheeks. When I returned to her, she smiled and stepped back into the room. 'Don't worry – I won't tell; our secrets, I trust, are safe with each other?'

I nodded like a fool as my heart leapt with the urge to engage the beguiling young woman. My nerves prevented me and I opted for curiosity and the answering of further questions. 'You say I summoned you by starting the clock and setting off the chimes, and that you are somehow imprisoned within the curious and removable heart-shaped object in the clock?'

She nodded and lifted a sheet of paper outlining some new and strange pocket watch design based on the strange clock behind. 'You know this to be true, yet you doubt your senses. Hobson, and Reed before him, both sought to free me from the contraption, though it is rather too late; all those that knew me in Ely, six decades ago, must surely have died by now. It is too late to restore what I once had or once was, but I wish for freedom notwithstanding.'

The footfall and mingle of voices from outside became clearer, and I saw the steam of lantern-bearing carollers, equally intrigued by the silhouette of two figures within the shop. They halted, cleared their throats, and began a rendition of *God Rest Ye Merry, Gentlemen*.

I turned to see Lenora standing, eyes closed, soaking in the music and soaring voices. 'It reminds me of a Christmas, long ago. I can see and hear it now – parlour games among the candlelight, clove-studded oranges and confits on the dresser, dancing in the main hall to the fiddle with the eligible captains, and mother's disapproving eyes...' She opened her eyes as the singing ended and the chief caroller knocked on the door. 'My last, as I knew it before the new clock came from Rotterdam.'

'You are a spirit, one that has returned to haunt the clock?' I said nervously.

'I am as a spirit only when the clock is still, and I've never died, as far as I am aware. The clock itself has been repaired many times, but I linger and return to mortal form when the chimes call me so long as the heart remains intact.' As if to demonstrate, she puckered her lips and blew a kiss toward the mantelpiece candle. The flickering flame danced momentarily with the amorous breath before returning to throb with a newfound passion. 'See? I live and breathe as you do while there is time.'

Another stanza was struck from the street, and the knock

on the door was repeated. I shook my head and gathered my wits. 'This is some malady, madness, or foolery—'

Lenora lowered her head and turned away, reaching out to the pendulum. 'Is it?' she said, sharply blowing out the mantel candle and vanishing even as her gloved hand reached out to prevent the brass rod from swinging.

A determined and desperate wassail from the freezing carollers broke me from her sudden disappearance and I only half-remembered unlocking the shop door and digging into my pockets to offer what little I had on my person. I vaguely recalled the bell sounding once more as I closed the door and shuffled back to peer into the workshop. The candlewick smoked and whirled like a ghostly dervish, and the only other sign of movement was the gentle wobble of the pendulum. I checked the dial to see ten minutes had elapsed confirmed, more or less, by the calibration clock. I hovered a hand over the pendulum and turned my head to the open door to the shop as I set the remarkable clock once more into motion.

Nothing happened. I felt foolish but called out Lenora's name all the same. Even as I made my way back down the stairs to complete my check of all the rooms, I knew I had some explaining to do, not only to Hobson, but to myself.

Perhaps the air needed cleansing and maybe the gas light was burning inadequately, addling my sensibilities in combination with the effects of the strong brandy. I smiled, looking around Hobson's workshop and whispered 'humbug' even as I felt curiously comforted by the experience. Even if it was all in my head, I now felt less alone in the dark among the remembrance of a sweet perfume that cut through the pungent smell of oil and wax.

In the small meeting circle of the Foregate, a fiddle, drum, and pipe struck up a traditional winter tune, and I put away my thoughts to listen to the music, accompanied by the deep quarter-hour bell of the cathedral tower. A child's voice rose to join the song as, behind me, the pendulum clock whirred into its own mechanical rendition.

'Beautiful,' said a woman's voice, deeper and softer than before.

I whirled round to see Lenora, changed in fashion as though the years had passed. She still wore a formal gown, but it was slimmer in outline and deeply dark. She lit a taper from the gas mantle and touched the candlewick back into sputtering life. Only then did I see the midnight blue as she moved closer, her face older by more than a few years. A woman in the prime of her life, confident, assured, like the beauty of a rose fully revealed without a hint of summer's end. She understood my searching eyes and confusion.

'Yes,' she said. 'Each quarter chime advances time and not even an immortal can avoid its ageing process.'

I held forth my quivering hand. 'You are real – truly here?'

She nodded, glided forward, and softly raised my hand into her own; it was warm and soft. 'If it is of any consolation,' said Lenora, 'Algernon took four days to accept my existence, and several more to understand my predicament.'

'What can be done to release you?' I said, pleasantly surprised to see her wind her fingers through my own in a squeezing knot.

'I can only exchange places with the keeper of the clock at midnight on Christmas Eve, providing the heart is already occupied. An empty heart gives little choice in the matter, as I discovered to my cost.'

'So why doesn't Besham want to change places?'

She held out her other hand, and I readily placed my own into her keeping.

'Because he is a monster, not liable to be at the mercy of others. The mechanism is delicate, and he prefers to display me as a freakish curio to his inner circle. He is wise enough to avoid the midnight chimes on Christmas Eve, and I rue the day I understood the passage between this life and that offered by this foul alchemy and entrusted him with the information. My honesty and virtue hold me as much hostage as the magical heart.'

'Do you suffer?' I said, feeling the blood in my veins become hot and ridiculous notions of chivalry and self-sacrifice emerged from my empathic nature.

As though sensing what I might offer, she smiled, leaned forward and kissed me on the cheek. 'Only through loneliness and the occasional bidding of Besham. I know what you intend to say, and I could not allow it. Another has already made me that offer, and I refused, just the same. If you want to offer me something that will carry me through to next year, then I ask only one thing of you, Daniel Jenkins.'

'Anything,' I said unwisely.

She breathed in, closed her eyes and swayed with the sound of the music from the meeting square outside.

'Dance with me.'

An overwhelming fear of disappointing her emerged, but I made my excuses. 'I cannot...'

She lifted my left hand and placed it on the silk just below her exposed neckline. The other she raised to the side. 'Then I will teach you while there is time, in exchange for your promise to free me in the years to come; I think it will not be long now before your master passes on the care of the clock.'

I nodded and swallowed hard as she began to lead me in a simple movement of steps. I clunked and stomped in time with the tick-tock of the clocks, realising after many minutes we were already in the shop, lightly whirling to the tunes that continued to resonate from the street. A reflection from a mirrored cabinet revealed the stupid and very unappealing grin on my face before I began to say something absurdly romantic. 'I've never been so...'

I heard the cathedral bell strike for the half-hour, closely accompanied by the other clocks in our makeshift ballroom. The pendulum clock in the workshop was late and chimed last of all. I felt a quiver in her arms and looked down with some shock to see her hand, now wrinkled with age, still lightly placed in my own. Her dress had faded to a tan satin and styled perhaps more recently in time than her previous gown. Her lustrous hair was streaked with frost and she looked up with some sadness to meet my own young eyes with the cloudy sapphires of her own. She released me as she caught sight of her reflection; a woman in her fifties, perhaps, radiant and still with the memory of beauty alongside the fading scent of her once fragrant flowering.

'We have little time,' she said, sitting down, even as the tune outside faded to a gentle round of applause. 'Let us talk, but promise me you will pause the pendulum before the third-quarter; I do not wish you to see me decrepit and old.'

I assented, though the woman I had known for less than half an hour had made such an impression on me that I begged her to return.

'Do not strike the third-quarter, the full hour, or engage the chimes again. This meeting must be our last so that the mechanism survives and is not stressed. Even now, I begin to feel the strain of our meeting. Do not fear, for I will return as you first saw me in a year's time. If you truly wish to help me, then let that be your incentive, Daniel Jenkins. Remember she who once was, not who I am now, or will be if you leave the clock to run its full course. Follow your master's instructions and do not engage the chimes again for my sake.'

As joyful as our brief encounter was to be, it was little recompense for the year of waiting in order that I might share, once again, in her delightful company. I became free and honest in my replies, and in my questioning, as though the knowledge that she would soon be gone released me like a tightly wound spring. The clock ticked on to the third-quarter of the hour and she rose, stiffly, to stand before the garland wreath. Distantly, the soft cathedral bells began their sojourn into song and she begged me to hurry. I stole a kiss on her cheek and barely caught the subtle change as the strands of grey on her hair bled across the last of the lustrous brown and became white. She covered her face with her bony hands urging me to leave her and stop the pendulum.

Turning away into the workshop with the late chiming of the clock, I hesitated and called out 'I promise!', before blowing out the candle, as she had done, and stopping the pendulum. I felt behind the rear of the clock face to the small window to feel the tremble of the metal heart within before retracing my steps to find the workshop empty, amid eyes full of tears.

Hobson covered his face with his hand to shield himself from the low dawn sun and struggled to sit upright against the large bed cushion.

'So now you know,' he said. 'I would have needed to reveal this to you, though my own failure to release my beloved Lenora preyed heavily in my decision to hold off, long past the same time that Master Reed passed the burden on to me.' He hacked a great cough and waved away my sympathetic attempts to assist him.

Waiting until he regathered his strength, I continued, rubbing at the sleep-deprived soreness in my eyes. 'I have seen the drawings and studied many of them – what is it you are attempting to construct?'

'A miniature pocketed version of superior robustness,' he whispered. 'One that can lock the passage of time, as she senses it, to a particular hour of the day.'

'What hour?'

He looked away and scanned the bedroom wallpaper to avoid my gaze. A little colour bled into his cheeks and I sensed his devotion to her, suddenly realising his bachelorhood was not down to a love of many clocks, it was down to the love of one woman.

'Any of her choosing, though likely enough it will be the youthful form that we both encountered first—' he glanced over to see me stir, '—and that has affected us both in the same way; do I not guess correctly?'

It was my turn to study the flock on the wall before rising and making some pretence of prodding at the coals in the grate. 'You cannot release her through any means of mechanical intervention, then?'

His hesitancy caused me a sudden moment of hope, but it was dashed and put out like the small lick of flame that I extinguished in my enthusiasm with the poker.

'No. Ambroos allegedly built four soul cages in which to imprison himself and other notable arcane scholars of the last century. He disappeared leaving his work unfinished, or so it seemed, and the clocks were sold off to pay his debts. The devices were more than merely mechanical, and no such knowledge now exists of how to create or extinguish such a spirit from his life's work.' He glanced at the small carriage clock above the fireplace. 'Which is perhaps how it should be.'

I coaxed the fire back into life. 'You think he may have been careless, or made a trial of his invention and is now captive in one of the other three clocks?'

'It's a possibility though at least one was destroyed half a century ago when a rival clockmaker sought to understand what the heart contained by cutting through and releasing the sorcery within.'

'I overheard Besham saying a guest of his this evening will

be bringing a soul clock,' I said, hurrying to his bedside. 'You think it could be Ambroos inside?'

Hobson shrugged. 'Only by reading the name on the soul cage would you be able to determine this, if any exists. Even more dangerous would be a vacant soul clock, just like the one that trapped poor Lenora nigh on seventy years ago.' He stifled an ironic scoff and shook his head. 'An empty heart must be filled with something.'

'Then we have to get him to see reason,' I said naively. 'Ask him to allow us, or the Worshipful Company of Horologists, perhaps even the Royal Society to—'

'It's been tried, and to no avail. Before the age of enlightenment we would have had a chance, but nowadays?' He held out his hand, and I took it in an unusual and intimate show of solidarity for our shared commitment to solving the situation.

'She made you promise, didn't she?' he asked, studying my face as I struggled to avoid his gaze.

I nodded, and he squeezed my palm as though consoling me. 'Then do what I could not, and save her in the coming years. Do not engage the chimes again and reset the clock as I told you.' He released me and pointed a knowing finger. 'I will be displeased if you make a further trial to see her. She knows no more about the device than is written in all my journals, or those of Mr Reed before me.'

'The heart is removable, is it not?' I said, watching as his eyes flashed into fiery life.

'Yes, but do not think of passing the clock on to Besham without it. He is a powerful man and keeps company best left in the dark about our covert attempts to free his "plaything". Do nothing that will endanger yourself, the business, or the chance to release Lenora.'

He fixed me with such a stare that I relented and gave him my assurance. 'If only there were a way to trick the keeper of the clock into being present at the appropriate hour.'

'Indeed,' said Hobson, sipping from a glass of water to soothe his dry throat. 'We are masters of time, are we not? It is a pity that the hands of fate are not just as easily altered as the dials of our beloved instruments.' He pointed over to a brown paper-wrapped rectangle leaning against the far wall. 'Meanwhile, open your gift; a blessing or a curse depending on how you look at it.' He scanned around the room. 'More favours will follow when I have no more use for them.'

I lifted the large and heavy object, two feet wide and a little more in length. It appeared to be several inches thick and the slither of a chain from the top suggested a wooden board. I tore open the paper to reveal a painted sign:

Hobson and Jenkins
Clockmakers of Worcester

'Hang it, but wait until the morrow,' he said as I stood stunned at the meaning.

'You are making me a partner? I don't know what to—'

'Not exactly,' he said with a wink. 'You are my apprentice no longer. Consider it an inheritance and a rite of passage now that you are aware of my little secret and are prepared, I assume, to take on the responsibilities for the soul clock should Besham continue to use us. Why do you think I make the components so delicate as to be prone to breaking? Who knows how long I have got, Daniel, so I release her to your care and may you have better success than a poor old fool like me.'

I struggled back to the shop overwhelmed with Hobson's generosity and sudden openness about his feelings towards me and my work, as well as his deeply held love for a woman he could not save. I wondered whether I would have the strength of character to deal with the responsibility without resorting to some alternative means of claiming the clock. Besham was late middle-aged and would not live forever, but what guarantee could there be that I could claim or purchase the thing, never mind wait such an indeterminate length of time? I thought of dreadful things in my anguish to get hold of the clock and berated myself for them all; it was not in my nature to become someone so vile as to be akin to the very man who owned the precious object.

Besham was waiting for me as I rounded the corner and laid the sign against the window, listening to his frustrations at being held up in the collection of his property. He became suddenly quiet at reading the new board and looked up at the old sign as though to confirm his worst fear.

'Not dead?'

I unlocked the door and did not offer him the first passage. I carried in the sign and removed my jacket and comforter. 'No, but you will be dealing with me from now on,' I said though quaking partway between my feet and the knees. 'I need five more minutes to adjust the timing; she loses several seconds each hour.'

Besham frowned, unsure of the meaning behind my words as I made my way into the workshop to avoid a show of any nervousness. I added a small counterweight to the top of the pendulum and paused as he insisted he would not be kept waiting by an apprentice.

'I promise,' I whispered, placing the clock into the carrying case and returning to hand over the precious object. For a moment, and I confess I held on as he struggled to pull it from my grasp. With a tug, he released it from my grip.

'Have a care, young pup,' said Besham with a growl. 'A sole proprietor in a shop full of trinkets can be a dangerous situation, as well as a lucrative one. I trust you will cool your cocksure heels and seek the latter.'

An oil-skinned horse cabby came in, allowing Besham to leave with a quick and menacing glance. I was over an hour assisting the man to lift and carry a Bavarian grandfather clock into the street and onto his cart ready to deliver, ensuring the heavy and delicate antique met with no injury at my hands.

The rest of the day proved busy with minor, last-minute repairs and the collection of trinkets. It was not until close to six o'clock that I shut the shop and retired to a glass of tawny port, more out of tradition than the enjoyment of the tepid treacle. I toasted the health of Hobson as I brushed the top of the new sign I would attempt to hang the following morning.

Several hours into organising the drawings and tidying the shop and workrooms for a hopeful visit by my employer on the morn, there appeared a knock on the door. I ignored the summons and continued in my studies of the designs, making one or two comments in a new book of my own. The knocks went on, and I wondered if the urgency might be related to Hobson's health. I raced out and lit a candle to shed light on the woman's face from beyond. I did not recognise her, but she was insistent that she came from Besham.

'Come for the key to his blasted clock,' she said. 'He said to make a point of you not giving it to him at your meeting and was particular I collect it right away as he has a guest. The man is most put out by not seeing the thing ticking as ought. Master has sent everyone else but Elsie and me home, though not through charity it is to be expected; he's not a man of that sort, but I'm not to leave service this evening without returning the key to Henwick Grove and it's a fair way to return on foot. By the time I get back, it'll be close to midnight, then I have to come all the way back home to Cherry Orchard, which is only a mile further on from here.'

Unlocking the door, the woman continued to babble about the unfairness of being chosen for the thankless task when all but one of her colleagues were enjoying Christmas Eve and the gin-laden milk of human kindness. I returned to the workshop to confirm she was correct – the key lay like a golden butterfly on the mantelpiece.

'I can take it for you,' I lied, holding up my pocket watch. 'There is a final delivery to make across the river and it would give the chance to apologise in person. Elsie is there still, you say?'

The woman hummed and weighed up the offer. I sweetened the suggestion by digging into my trousers for some spare change. 'If you do not need to go back this evening, then I'll get a cab and drop you off first?'

She agreed, and in a short time was dropped off only a mile away. 'Take the servants' entrance at Henwick,' she said. 'He gets mighty put out by interruptions by trade at the front door.' I nodded and watched as she made off towards the public house, which streamed out welcoming fire and light into the chill fog of Christmas Eve.

My watch showed half-past ten when I tipped the cab driver from the open gate to the walled estate. I hurried down the drive, clutching my coat about me to reach the elegant white facade of the Georgian house whose windows suggested little sign of life except for faint, curtained chinks on the first floor. I hunted around the rear to descend cut stone steps leading to the trades' entrance and knocked upon the paint-peeling pine of the door.

An elderly dame looked surprised and alarmed at the swathed highwayman emerging from the fog before her, but I reassured her with a handover of the key and the understanding I had with her colleague. She refused entry despite my request that I might be allowed to apologise, not that I thought the opportunity would arise.

'No visitors this evening,' she said. 'Master was particular about it as he has Mr Drew with him and they wish to be alone. Be off with you; I'm behind my time and don't want to spend any longer than necessary with the pair of them in this house. That one has a reputation.'

She threw the door closed, and I stood there, listening to her footsteps recede on the tiles. It bounced in the frame and creaked open. Even as I pushed myself into the darkness beyond, I still had no plan. The thirty minutes drive had revealed no reason for my sudden desire to be close to the clock and attempt some ridiculous rescue; it was certainly not to apologise for my forgetfulness for the key.

After a short time, the woman returned, heavily wrapped and brushing across the walls of the narrow corridor now dressed for the cold outside and ready for the off. I retreated into a side pantry as she made her way around the corner and passed like a lumbering thief loaded with the family silver. I held my breath as the exterior door snicked shut leaving the sound of my foolish heart thumping in my head. From the floor above, nothing but the occasional guffaw or clink of glasses combined with muted conversation could be heard. Gaining the hallway I removed my jacket and scarf to an accommodating wig stand and crept up the carpeted stairs and the first-floor landing still without a clear idea of what to do.

Are we not masters of time? I thought, recalling the words of my partner and benefactor.

'I'll be doing time if they discover me,' I whispered to myself, ducking into a quiet room away from the voices on the opposite side of the cupola-supported chandelier. The electric light dazzled my eyes, and I blinked until I focussed on the wall-mounted pendulum clock. It was still but with the key inserted as though in readiness.

I examined the room to discover several tall sash windows, thickly draped with thick, bible-black satin, which offered little reflection from the roaring fireplace. A plain mantel clock sat on a side table, out of place in the opulence of the mirrored room, and I checked the rear to see the same circular opening revealing an identical silver heart. I crept over to the closest light bulb to read "Simeon" engraved and cursed myself for not asking the first name of the alchemist and creator of the soul clocks, hoping this was him. I reached in to check for any movement in the centre-piece, like the pendulum clock, and the same, sudden shock caused me to retreat my hand. For a moment, I thought I was discovered as Besham's voice called out from beyond the landing in rebuke to any remaining staff to leave. I returned the clock to its position and hid behind the curtain until the laughing and drinking resumed in the room across the way.

I resolved to remove the soul cages of both mechanisms, but this would, of course, cause great suspicion and not solve Lenora's situation.

Think, Daniel, I mused, hearing the distant bell of St Andrew's from far over the river, signalling eleven o'clock. After a few moments of a hastily considered plan, I left the seclusion of the hiding place and scanned the room, noticing several other clocks of great worth standing against or hanging upon the walls. Opening each glass case as stealthily as I could, I reached in and altered the hands back to just beyond the eleventh hour, minutes behind the actual time. With a hurried rush to each of the clocks, I adjusted them all to the same erroneous time, completing the wall-mounted clock just as two loud voices emerged onto the landing. In a flash, I raced to the closest window and hurriedly settled the swaying curtain as Besham and a thickset, bulldog of a man in garish tweed entered the room.

With my eye against a slit in the joined curtain, they refilled their crystal glasses with liquid amber and set about the checking of their clocks as though delicately setting explosives. Besham studied the other ticking faces in the room to see if the hands were in an identical orientation. He scratched his head with the coincidence, lost on the other man, and he called out for his companion to set off his own timepiece. The two men clinked their glasses in readiness for the appearance of more than just the quarter-hour chime.

There was much chatter as I leaned back against the hard sill, trying not to breathe into the narrow space and upset the curtained cloth. With my ear pressed to the glass, I waited until I caught the sound of the quarter-hour clock bells carried across the impenetrable mile across the river. There was such a bout of coarse laughter from the room beyond that I was glad to find that Besham, and the formidable man I took for Mr Drew, were unaware. I counted two minutes before I heard first the first-quarter chime of the familiar pendulum clock. It was followed by a similar, though quieter version of the same musical method. From my hiding place I saw Lenora appear, a young woman once more, dressed in the scarlet at our first meeting. My heart leapt before being restrained; this was not the privacy of the shop, and I was trespassing in the house of one of the wealthiest and most powerful men in the district. A shadow passed in front of the slit and I noticed the rear of another man walk past as though summoned by more than the chimes of his own clock.

'Your canary is far prettier than mine, old boy,' said the man in putrid plaid. 'Care to swap?'

'Not a chance, Drew,' replied Besham. 'This Simeon of yours doesn't speak any English either from what you told me. What is he – Prussian?'

Drew screwed his face at the suggestion, accurate as it might be. 'I didn't buy it for him, just for what we can exchange. What do you say I find myself a nice young lady for this time next year and we release this poor man back for a more suitable plaything as you have?' He leered and licked his lips at Lenora.

Besham raised his eyebrows. 'You are a devil, Horace, but what a splendid idea. It would make your timepiece more valuable and I would love to see how it is accomplished, though we must take care.'

'That's the beauty of the situation,' said Drew. 'We are both looking out for each other. If something ever went wrong or one of us came a cropper, then the other would know what to do.'

Besham put down his glass. 'I wouldn't trust you with my immortality, Horace. You'd as soon trade me in for a dozen whores in Paris.'

Drew clutched at his heart and made a face of mock injury before breaking into a yellow-toothed smile.

'Dance for us,' he said to Lenora. 'Dance with Simeon, and not some formal thing, we want something lively. I'm not in the mood for etiquette and manners; it is my Christmas party after all.'

Simeon protested and railed against the suggestion as well as their combined incarceration, understanding a little English but unable to converse fully. Drew and Besham circled until their backs were to me, leaving the floor wide for the entertainment to begin.

'If you don't shut up and do as we ask,' said Besham. 'I'll be forced to put you back into your box, or lay hands on my pretty doll here.' He lifted an iron poker and made some feeble, but menacing prod in Lenora's direction, driving home the point. Simeon relented and joined hands with her, beginning a polka of such vigour as to shake the very floorboards beneath me. Drew threw himself into a long, sumptuous settee, clapping and cheering as Besham tapped and slapped them with the dirty metal bar if they slowed or pranced within reach. As they sprung around the room, I saw the young man desperate to escape, knowing that his fate also lay with his clock. Lenora clung to him, uncomfortable and unused to the dance, slipping and snagging her gown. She tripped close to the curtain and was aware of me as she was lifted to her feet. I watched, as she shook her head, wide-eyed, as I threatened to emerge with some notion of grabbing both clocks and flying down the stairs with the pair of them.

They circuited the room and Lenora spun round in front of the place where I lay hidden. Simeon was turned several times before he caught my eye, at which point I saw hope develop in his face even as it disappeared from mine. This was no organised rescue, and likely enough all three of us would be prisoners in our own way by the end of the evening. Drew howled as Besham pursued them, egged on by strong drink and a determination to watch them collapse with exhaustion.

He did not have to wait long.

Lenora stumbled in front of the settee, out of view, and the polka came to a crashing, chest-heaving conclusion. In the fall, she reached out against the occasional table causing the soul clock to wobble and tilt. Drew levered his large frame out of the velvet-buttoned cushions and hurried to prevent it from tipping over.

'Careful, old boy,' he said lifting the precious object and placing it on the opposite side of the room. He ignored the tumbled folds of Lenora, heaving and panting out of my sight, as Simeon begin another hot-headed and chivalrous rebuke of his jailors. I understood little, but the ferocity and intention in his words were clear. From the chill, dark space I heard St Andrews chime for the second quarter, drowned out by the argument now ensuing between the three men.

I wondered if Simeon and I could overwhelm them. Besham was a tall man, but it was Drew that would prove the greater matter. Once my presence was known, I would become a fugitive or worse, just as fate had provided me with all but one of my heart's desires. Perhaps we could bind them until the midnight chimes, but even as I put my fingers through the curtain to risk it all, the soul clocks chimed again, and Simeon was silenced to the floor by the fist of the ferocious Mr Drew. I retreated suddenly, realising I had missed my chance seeing him rise, older, broader of build, and wiped a hand across his split lip. Besham and Drew looked in amazement at the transformation in the two figures as the chimes concluded.

Lenora rose, dark gowned, hair in tumbled tresses, pulling at her close-fitting bodice to breathe. No longer the slender youthful beauty of the first quarter, she was mature and defiant, but wise enough to let the situation play out.

'Do not touch him again,' she said nobly. 'I will comply with your requests if you honour this.'

Drew widened his eyes. 'The wine improves with age, it seems.'

Besham threw down the poker and poured himself another drink. 'Until it becomes vinegar in a short span of time.'

His companion burst out laughing, followed by Besham who downed the brandy in one burning gulp. 'Next,' he bellowed. 'I want parlour games!'

Drew leered at Lenora, and she turned away with his sickening suggestion.

'Hot cockles!' he cried. 'I'll get my arse spanked as long as

I can bury my face in that gown...'

He was cut off by the raised poker. 'No,' said Besham. 'You will not touch my caged bird, and this isn't boarding school, Horace.'

Drew pulled a face of bitter disappointment. 'What about snap-dragon?'

Besham lowered the rod and scoffed. 'All the servants are out and I'm not going down in the cellar to hunt for raisins, never mind soaking them in cognac and setting fire to them for your amusement while they try to fish them out.' He undid his bow tie and threw it at Lenora.

'Blindfold yourself.'

Lenora stood still with shock as Drew did the same, tossing it to Simeon, with a chuckle. 'A game of Moriarty?' he exclaimed, 'I haven't played this for years!' Several minutes elapsed as the area was made ready and the two unwilling players were talked through the rules.

'You understand, Lenora?' said Besham, and she nodded, indicating to her soul clock companion to copy her movements. The humiliation began as she lay, chest down on the floor, finding Simeon's left hand and clutching it tightly. Besham rolled up two old newspapers from the bureau and placed them as mock cudgels in the players' right hands. The game started, and I knew it from bawdy gatherings where gentle violence provided entertainment at the expense of the poor victims involved. Here in this space where the combatants were enslaved, it was sinister and horrific.

Besham tapped the prostrate Lenora on her bare shoulder. She flinched and called out the phrase to begin.

'Are you there, Moriarty?'

Simeon lay still until kicked into action by the boot of Horace Drew. 'You are supposed to say "yes" man.'

'Yes,' he said leaning into a roll and out of the way as Lenora reluctantly raised the newspaper and weakly brought it down in the sound's direction. The papery cudgel thumped into the rug, narrowly missing the head of the man.

Besham sniggered. 'Seems like he's played this before; I didn't know Prussians had a sense of humour.'

Drew knelt and forced his piggy lips into the poor man's ear. 'Go on – you know the phrase, or would you rather I take your turn for you?' He cracked his knuckles causing his blind-folded champion to startle.

'Are you there, Moriarty?' said Simeon to which Lenora gently replied, mere feet away and locked in one-handed combat.

'Strike out for the voice, man!' said Drew.

With eyes covered, and now on his belly, Simeon lifted his right hand and tapped ahead seeking his partner.

'Harder man – give her a good whack!'

Simeon refused, throwing aside his blindfold. Besham grabbed the makeshift weapon from Lenora's hand and joined with Besham in a thrashing of the man until rolling into a ball, Simeon covered his head. Lenora sat up and tore off her binding, trying to drag him away from the blows. She held out her hand to prevent further strikes when a wayward blow struck her across the cheek.

I launched out of my hiding place, and for a moment, had the element of surprise though not any plan save to stop the two sadists from laying hands on either of them. Racing for the poker, I found myself tripped by Besham's leg and I collapsed like a fool into the side of the hearth. My head swam as I felt thick, strong hands lift me from the ground, choking me until I relented in my flailing attempts to resist. A sideways glance showed Simeon, unable to intervene. He rolled, clutching the grey hair of his head, tended by Lenora whose tear-brimmed eyes now understood the ineptitude of their rescuer. I noticed the heavy lines on her face and realised in the melee that the chimes had sounded three-quarters while seeing the truth that she suffered. Perhaps the oblivion of the moments spent spirited within the clock were bearable compared to the abuse of the real world. She looked away and her white hair draped across the old man shivering and shaking to his knees, clutching at the deepest black gown she now wore. Simeon raised his head, and I saw the resignation on his liver-spotted face, aged and leathered like a man in the late stage of life.

I gasped for breath as Drew turned me like a mighty wrestler and locked my head in a rigid, tweed-abrasive forearm.

'Who's this rabbit?' he said, 'One of yours?'

Besham shook his head. 'No-one – especially after tonight.'

'Let them go!' I said through sips of precious air. 'I will take the man's place if you are unwilling to release Lenora.'

'You know her name, then?' said Besham catching the urgency of my glance towards her. 'I think not, Master Jenkins. I offered you a long and fruitful career if you behaved yourself and now I find you spying and prying into my personal affairs.' He tutted. 'What will sick Mr Hobson say when you are thrown into prison, or maybe I can convince my good friend the magistrate to go one neck squeeze further.' He glanced at the poker. 'You tried to murder me, after all.'

I felt Drew tighten his arm around my throat, acting out the hanging. Lenora dragged herself and clutched at Besham's legs to let me go, but he brushed her away and I realised that there would be no rescue for me or any of us. Besham did not pay any heed to the sudden change in either of their appearances and my mind reeled with some advantage, as though a mechanism in my own mind had clicked into a calibrated, clockwork conclusion. I had my wits and the knowledge that midnight would soon chime, heard or unheard, to the unsuspecting men. Delay was needed, but I needed air more than anything at that moment. I tried to speak, but my neck was slowly being crushed.

'Don't throttle the life out of him, Horace,' he said leaning in to hear my breathy plea for mercy. 'He needs fresh air and good old-fashioned county justice.' Besham gathered the poker and prodded each of the curtained windows to check for further threats before raising the nearest sash window. Drew dragged me to the high opening and pushed me to the waist into the biting chill. I gulped at the frigid fog until the burning cold in my throat and lungs protested and I spluttered. Behind me, the satin blew like a billowing black sea and I caught sight of Lenora and Simeon clutching each other as though for support.

I snapped my head back into the high, open-air and caught the faint sound of collective, crowd-like merriment, and with the first chime from the clock, I knew that midnight had arrived to save us. I made a mockery of trying to struggle against the fierce and immutable man holding me back from the precipitous fall.

'He wriggles like a fish!' said Drew, not heeding the bells. It wasn't until a clock chimed from the opposite room that I heard a shriek from Besham. I was twisted round and dragged back into the light and warmth to discover he was absent.

'What's the matter?' called Drew looking over at the hands on the dials in the room, falsely offering a little more time before the soul clocks' proverbial prison door was unlocked. 'You'll have to come back and stop them; there isn't much time. The church bell is early...'

'There isn't any time at all,' I said clasping my hands into a fist and driving my shoulders back into the bulbous belly. The tweed soaked up the sharpness of my blow better than any chain mail, but it was enough for him to be temporarily winded and I wriggled free as he sank to his knees. Besham returned, pale and wide-eyed realising that the clock in the room beyond was not early. With the final few strokes of midnight, he raced forward to scan the dials around the room before fixing his fearful face upon my own.

'You changed them all,' he said, striding towards me as I blocked his path to the pendulum clock. 'You made us think we had time—'

'It would appear so,' I said, picking up the nearby poker and fending him off. 'The hands of fate are just as easily altered as the dials, after all.'

'You fool!' said Besham dashing for the other clock. 'You'll let her out and one of us will be dragged inside.'

'Not one of us,' said Lenora, watching as he stumbled past Drew who was rising to his feet. 'Only the keepers of the clocks.'

Besham shrieked and lifted Drew's mantel clock, shaking it and struggling to stop the unfamiliar mechanism just as the four-quarter chime began to sound from within.

Drew pointed to the billowing curtains. 'Hurry, man. Throw it out of the—'

The pendulum clock began its sequence, joining its lesser companion in a harmonious tune, deep and immeasurably loud as though the room had suddenly become a belfry in the cathedral. I covered my ears and caught sight of Besham changing his mind from the thought of the open window. He retracted his arm to throw the timepiece into the wall-mounted timepiece, but at the moment of release, his wrist was grabbed from behind.

Simeon, hale and young once more now that the hour was reset, turned his wrist and the chiming clock fell harmlessly from Besham's grasp and onto the soft cushion of the settee. Both Simeon and Lenora seemed hollow and insubstantial, but his grip was very real. I raced over and recovered the tinkling treasure even as Drew began to lumber in puffing pursuit. The chimes ceased, and a dreadful shadowed silence descended as the first stroke of this new midnight, captured just in time from the echoes of the church bell out in the fog, sounded in the room like a death knell. A sharp stab of painful ice caused me to glance down at the windowed rear of the clock and my finger pressed against the heart. It no longer displayed Simeon's name and as I stepped back, I witnessed a new signature appearing, engraved by an unseen hand.

The electric lights dimmed and became obscured by some internal, all-consuming darkness, and the sable-coloured drapes suddenly blew back in the opposite direction out of the window as though desperate to escape. In unison, the two clocks chimed, and a wind erupted from the centre of the room, dragging in burning embers to swirl like a maelstrom about us. Drew altered course and tried to leave by the door, but it was thrown shut and could not be opened even by his great strength. Besham wailed about the room clutching at his chest as though suffering some sudden attack of apoplexy as I put down the mantel clock and raced for the far sash window with the absurd notion of safety behind the satin curtains. I clutched at the cloth, watching as Lenora and Simeon strode towards their respective keepers.

Drew turned and flailed at the insubstantial form of Simeon, unable to fend off his approaching hand. He struck and slashed his great arms through the spirit, disturbing the vestige as though passing a finger rapidly through candle smoke. The form re-materialised and laid hands on his face, making contact in one direction only. The deafening strokes continued, but I had lost count as I watched Drew fade even as Simeon grew more substantial in the gathering gloom.

Lenora, ghostly, shadowed the struggling stride of her keeper like a cat readying to pounce. Besham collapsed to the floor, and I saw his dreadful visage as his heart gave way under the strain even as she sought to grasp his shuddering head. Feebly, he pushed through her spirited form, disturbing little of her semblance. With a final blood-curdling wail, he went limp, and I caught her eye as she shot a glance in my direction and clutched at her mouth. Besham was dead.

I tossed back the curtain and ran towards her, catching the last of Drew's disappearing form as it entered the small mantel clock like a funnelled twist of smoke. The final stroke of the clocks sounded, and Lenora disappeared just as I threw myself into her arms, passing through and almost knocking myself out against the heavy dresser. From all about us, glass-fronted clock covers and mirrors exploded into a myriad of pieces as Simeon turned his back to shield me. The last echo of the second and profound midnight faded, and the curtain blew back as the door opened to the landing. The two of us were now alone in a room of shattered clocks and broken hearts – Besham's failed organ, robbing Lenora of her escape, and my own bereft mechanism chiming piteously within my heaving chest.

In a moment Simeon dragged me to my feet, dusting down the fragments of metal and glass with the arm of his antique coat.

'We go,' he said. 'No time.'

Through a fog of bewilderment and dripping chandelier crystals, I looked over at the still body of Besham, then over at the pendulum clock, still and silent, mangled and beyond repair. Lifting the carcass from the mechanism, I stuck my fingers into the cavity and wobbled the metallic heart free without further injury. Whether the adrenalin kept me from feeling the sharp pain that had presented itself on the earlier occasion, or if the broken mechanical surroundings had severed a vital, static connection, I could not tell. I opened my fist to reveal the wondrous soul cage and rubbed at the engraving of her name. Simeon placed a hand on my shoulder but prevented me from reaching over to the mantel clock to retrieve the other device.

'Bad man,' he said. 'Understand. He will kill you if he comes back. Time choose his fate, yes?'

At that moment, I was so bereft of any empathy towards the men who had kept Lenora from escaping with us that I relented, allowing Simeon to help me to the door and down the stairs. I collected my coat and scarf, still clutching Lenora's heart, and skirted the empty lower corridors before urging him to stop.

'Simeon – you are Simeon Ambroos?' I said feeling a curious, sensation from my hand. I released my fingers around the soul cage to discover her name was branded into my palm, reversed, as though reflecting the dichotomy in our fates, now on opposite sides of reality. 'You can make another clock, yes?'

He glanced at the device and folded my hand back over the heart.

'No. Simeon Schulte, at your service, and hers for as long as I have my breath in here.' He thumped his chest.

I raised my clenched fists to my eyes. 'What have I done?'

Simeon clutched my shoulders and shook me. 'Cry later. English redcoats come soon.'

'Soldiers?' I said, lowering my hands. 'How long have you been in the clock?'

He held up his fingers.

'Eighty-nine years?' I said as he nodded.

'And I do not want one prison more, Englishman; come.'

We left by the front door and raced between the silhouetted sentinels of the pollarded plane trees until we gained the gate and took to the fields. For the first time in my life, I lost track of time as I led my eighteenth-century companion on a circuitous route back to the bridge, avoiding all contact with passers-by until we struck the main thoroughfare and melted into the frigid fog of the Foregate. I stood on the threshold of the shop fidgeting with the key as Simeon peered in through the window, commenting and complimenting on the quality of our clocks as though familiar with the profession. Looking upwards and past the sign to the fog-thinning sky, a solitary shooting star streaked into Christmas Day and I made my wish:

That I had traded places with the woman to whom my promise was now as void and empty as the blackness between the pinholes in the immeasurable curtain of night.

It was some time before Hobson looked up from the gently vibrating soul cage in his hand, blinking into the bright morning of the closed shop. A thin layer of snow covered the Christmas Day cobbles, not yet trampled by church service-bound boots.

'What's done is done,' he said, clearing a cough in his throat. 'Don't blame yourself – you released the watchmaker, and got away with your life; I've no doubt he would have had you hanged and whatever happens, you have at least another year before this Mr Drew comes looking for us, if at all.'

Simeon wandered about the room, talking to himself in German as he reacquainted himself with the advances in clock-making since his impromptu incarceration. He had spent the night on a makeshift bed in the workshop downstairs, not that I had slept at all. I had lain huddled, replaying my stupidity and my lack of speed to reach Lenora before she had vanished and almighty hell had broken loose.

'If the constabulary asks questions,' said Hobson, 'you will tell them you came straight back after delivering the key and you spent the rest of the early hours tending to my fever.'

'But the other man,' I said, staring disconsolately at the

pulled threads in the Persian rug. 'He was a beast but doesn't deserve an infinite punishment for a finite crime, no matter what his personality flaws.'

'That may be so, but when it is discovered he is missing and Besham is found, you will have your alibi. Assuming this is the same Mr Drew, I have heard he has a fearsome reputation for violence as well as keeping unsavoury company. The police may be satisfied with the simplest explanation that a disagreement between them caused one of them to suffer a fatal injury or malady of the heart brought on by heated debate, while the other escaped to avoid arrest.'

Simeon brushed past and unashamedly entered the private workshop. I was about to call out, but Hobson raised his hand to stop me, and the tall, frock-coated man disappeared into the mechanical wonderland.

'Let him be, Daniel. He's been cooped up for close to a century and seems more than a little curious about the advances he has missed.' He held up the silvered heart in his fingers. 'Did he say how he was trapped?'

'Curiosity and late-night working – sound familiar? The soul cage wasn't occupied, which means there's at least one clock out there still that could contain Ambroos.'

Hobson sighed. 'The continent is vast and you are the only clockmaker to have seen two soul clocks in a lifetime. Simeon learned his trade under Breguet in Paris, you say?'

'Yes. Imagine an apprentice of one of the greatest horologists of all time here in our shop. He was trusted with the miniatures and highly decorative pieces from what I could get from him; he seemed to like our pocket watches but insisted on noting down how we could improve.' I scooped up the loose sheets of paper from the counter and gave a guilty glance to the cuckoo clock above his door. 'He wrote and drew these while we calmed ourselves down last night; they might be worth thinking about.'

Hobson ignored the empty brandy bottle on the display cabinet and examined the skilful amendments. 'He certainly knows how to miniaturise, but this would call for completely new tooling to accomplish and only for a modest improvement in weight and cavity saving. I'm not sure our clientele would appreciate the demand for greater sophistication in a pocket watch – maybe in London or Geneva...'

I wrung my hands, no longer able to contain the question I was desperate to ask.

'Can you build a new clock, from the study you have made over the years – to get Lenora back?'

Hobson held out his shaking hands and stuck out his bottom lip. I felt my world fall apart.

'Yes,' came the confident voice of Simeon emerging from the workshop bearing several rolls of my master's drawings. He grabbed a pencil and scribbled across the designs for the large pocket watch. I saw it for what it was – a miniaturised and mobile soul clock ready to house a magical heart that required a new mechanical body.

'You have problems in your calculations, here—' said Simeon leaning over his amended workings like a field general over the map of a battlefield, '—and here as well. Let me show you.'

I watched as the two master craftsmen interpreted each other's corrections, consumed by a desire to impart their insights to each other. On several occasions, Hobson grabbed at the pencil, adding changes of his own, passionately conversing in his pigeon German when an impasse in vocabulary threatened to halt their great work. He called for more paper and they began again with Hobson retiring to retrieve some of his journals.

I folded my arms and paced about the empty shop for over an hour until I caught the pair of them shaking hands as though a breakthrough in a time-consuming and hard-fought negotiation had occurred. Hobson leaned into his chair and exhaled deeply, as Simeon lifted the soul cage and placed it in the centre of the hastily drafted schematic like the final piece of a jigsaw puzzle.

I pulled my fingers through my hair, leaving my hands perched upon my head.

'Will it work?' I said. 'Can you bring her back?'

Hobson removed his spectacles and rubbed at his eyes. 'The cage is intact and with our combined skill, a good deal of time – it's a possibility, though no guarantee.'

I turned and kissed the glazed face of the nearest grandmother clock much to Simeon's amusement.

'Are women so rare here in *Worchester* that you kiss clocks?'

I smiled at his pronunciation and returned to the table, eager to start. 'What must I do first?'

Hobson pointed to the sign, propped up against the counter. 'I thought I told you to hang that, Master Jenkins? Do as I say from now on if you wish to remain a partner, or at least do me the courtesy of informing me before any further heroics.'

I blushed and nodded like a scolded schoolboy as he continued.

'You are going to be very busy taking my place and training a new apprentice to do your old work, while this clever chap and I spend our waking moments keeping our promises to a young lady.'

Winter passed, and true to Hobson's prediction, I was busy managing affairs and the apprentice, Tom, a local lad with quick, nimble fingers and a mind to match. I fell into a clock-work routine to deal with my hope and anxiety. Hobson became even more consumed by work and had the new cutting machinery, toolsets, and exotic deliveries sent to his house. My fears for his deteriorating health were allayed somewhat when Simeon moved into a room down at the house where they worked long into the night, testing and trialling the new device. Closing the shop, and sending my eager junior home, I would wait to hear the small gains and dead ends in the device's construction.

Mayflies began to buzz around the flowering hawthorn and summer came a calling, heralded by the return of the martens. They chirped and whirled in joy above the Foregate on the warm evenings seeking the insects, but I felt only a tenseness as several early experimental trials to engage the mechanism proved fruitless and I consoled myself by the river lock. The shadow of the setting sun cast itself upon the quiet cobbles and I got up, extending my arms to dance with my silent companion, reliving the lesson and memory of my first, intimate encounter with Lenora.

Midsummer arrived, and the tipping point of the sun's zenith passed with some progress. I could finally see the completed device before its assembly in the case, having been deliberately caught in the dark about its construction or fabrication save some occasional requests for strange fabrications that required the lathe at the workshop. Of these, I worked on slender wires I took to be the new spindles that would attach the soul cage to the chimes and the rest of the mechanism. So fine were the tolerances that it was several days, and many attempts, before the precious needles were ready to hand over to Simeon. His English, and my German, flourished, and we were both a great comfort and support to each other especially when Hobson became so ill-tempered through poor health to continue.

The grand pocket watch, thicker and as wide as my palm was magnificent. The case itself had a thick crystal glass window, allowing the densely packed mechanism around the heart to act as a vignette to the hint of wider wonders contained within. It looked bulletproof. The naked workings were so densely packed as to be impossible to decipher without the use of a magnifier. He shook his head. 'Algernon said you are not to understand how this works, for your safety, and others. The work should be never repeated.'

'But it will require maintenance?' I said, finding the heart among the arteries of wire, and organs of miraculously minia-turised components.

'No. We agreed that once set within the case, it will be sealed and filled with oil. It may not require work of any kind for centuries and if you or anyone attempted it, the clock would disintegrate and the secret of its construction would be lost along with the drawings we plan to destroy once it is proven successful.' Simeon pointed to a hitherto unseen spring-loaded rod that projected from the side of the clock. 'No one else will touch her, Daniel – we have made sure of that.'

'What about the winding, and the hand adjustments?' I said searching for the control rod. 'Won't the access arms release the oil or require attention?'

'There are no externally accessed knobs,' he said. 'It's wound by kinetic movement and is unique. The vibration and occasional exercise of the one that bears it will cause the clock to run for many hours, if not days. The dials will return to midnight to reset the time if it is left untended for any reason by a stored charge in a crystal; it is the only way to adjust the hands once the case is sealed.'

'That's impossible,' I said even as he took back the device and pointed to several fine ball bearings linked in a race that tipped side to side with a gentle rocking motion setting off minute magnets of exquisite craftsmanship. He sighed, taking the workings and placing them within their eternal resting case. 'So is a man, and a woman trapped inside a clock, no? It is a pity that my groundbreaking ideas will never see the light of day, but no man can say we have not created a marvel to rival Ambroos' alchemy.'

'If she comes back—'

'*When she comes back*, Daniel,' he said, 'we have allowed for the passage of time. She will live as she was at the quarter-hour unless the clock is spun on its chain - there is a centrifugal component that advances the time by one minute per year to account for natural ageing if she so chooses. Perhaps she would like to live out a life naturally, alongside one that ages as nature intended.' He winked, and I blushed. 'There are no audible chimes, and she will remain as we are until the clock loses charge and requires movement once more.'

'Then she can carry it with her and be free, in a sense?'

'Yes. Though the magic within the soul cage is still governed by whatever Ambroos placed inside the heart; we cannot affect it. The clock remains a doorway to immortality, but we have made some modifications though...'

'What modifications?'

Simeon shook his head and laid a cloth over the device. 'I say too much. You'll see.'

'I've already decided that this Christmas Eve I will change places with her, do you understand?'

Simeon glanced down at the covered clock and then to the room above where Hobson was taking an extended nap. 'We thought as much, hence our great debate and amendments to the initial design.' He turned to me and fixed me with such a profound look of sadness. 'He is very ill, Daniel, so you must forgive him – he has held the burden of responsibility for so long.'

'Forgive him for what?'

'You can ask him tomorrow when he is well again. Go now

and return, but not before seven o'clock – this is his final instruction.'

He closed the front door behind me, and I distantly heard the first cuckoo of summer from the trees surrounding the new cricket ground even as I struggled to understand his cryptic words.

The following day ticked by incessantly slowly and I was left busy doing nothing. Tom was out with the covered hand cart, collecting the outdoor railway station clock that required a resolution to its rusted, rigour-mortised hands, and did not return until early into the humid haze of the late June evening. Bidding his eager but flush-tired face goodnight, I nervously changed into what counted as my finest smart casual, not being one for Sunday best, church or social occasions.

I locked the shop and in the resonant jingle of the door-bell, I jumped to set the sign swinging for good luck and strode down to the side streets towards the river. Early for our planned meeting, I paused to tease a tabby tortoiseshell that weaved its way through the iron railings belonging to the waterside cottages until a mastiff, taking its owner for a pulling, strenuous walk, broke our moment on the sunny siding and it slunk off to safety and the shade of a Mulberry Tree.

From the direction of Hobson's house, I heard exploding glass nearby, and the dog began to bark in alarm. Fearing some calamity had happened, my feet took over and in a short space of time, I turned the corner to the solitary building to find the street littered with debris. I put my hands to shield my eyes as the sudden wind washed down the roadway like a wave of heat, pushing me back with the force of the Severn bore on a neap tide. As I swung my back, I recognised the whip and crack of the maelstrom and squinted at the house enveloped within its own whirlwind. Curtains in the upper rooms streamed out like pageantry pennants as I raced over to bang upon the front door fearing that something had gone terribly wrong. I glanced down at my pocket watch to see the hour approaching seven.

After several further knocks, I shielded my head from the remnants of raining glass as Simeon, pale but in full control of his faculties leaned out onto the upstairs sill.

I called out to let me in, and he disappeared back inside. The wind died as suddenly as it had appeared and the curtains returned to drape the frames of the broken windows. In a moment, he opened the door and ushered me in across the crunching shards of glass.

'Are you alright, and Hobson—?'

'Yes, all is well, or I should say changed.'

I was about to ask him what he meant when I caught movement at the top of the stairs. On the landing rustled the gowned young woman I had fallen in love with, at first and second sight, and throughout all her time-worn appearances. She thumped her hands into the side of the scarlet taffeta and reached out to me. In several loping bounds, I gained the floor, and we flew into each other's arms. She was real, tangible and shaking.

'I'm so sorry for what I did or didn't do back on Christmas Eve,' I mumbled. 'Where is Hobson and is the clock alright?'

'You...you did it...you both did it...' she said, sobbing into my shoulder. 'You kept your promises.'

'What do you mean,' I said brushing back a loose strand of her lustrous hair. 'You are still trapped, albeit on a longer leash—'

'Not anymore,' said Simeon coming up behind me and

putting his arms around us both. 'We made...modifications. The clock has a new, and willing, occupant.'

The door opposite creaked open to reveal Hobson's room in utter disarray. I thought the devastation in Besham's mirrored chamber and him lying, contorted and gripped by the sudden terrifying and agonising final moment of his life. I feared the worst and ran in calling out 'Algernon!'.

'In here,' I heard him say as I turned to a small toilet closet. 'It's the only mirror left undamaged by the opening of the soul cage...'

'Are you hurt?' I said surveying the swaying ceiling light and wall mantles, naked and devoid of glass.

'On the contrary,' he said emerging from behind the door, with the soul clock perched in his hand. I backed away, unsure of the young, dark-haired man before me. He sounded like Hobson, dressed like Hobson, and as I saw him comically cast aside the empty frames of his spectacles, I realised it was Hobson.

'You changed places,' I said staring into the bright eyes of my master, now the same age as Lenora and I. My two companions entered the room but I could not remove my gaze from his unlined face. 'You took my place—'

'Technically, my offer made thirty-odd years ago takes precedence,' he said, coming forward and turning over the clock to see the new name engraved upon the silver heart. 'Remarkable. I barely notice any difference being contained though I feel more alive than ever before.' He stretched out his fingers, and they did not waver. 'Forgive me, Daniel, but the closeness of death and the prospect of eternity without my work was too much to bear. Besides—' he took Lenora's hand, kissed it, and placed it into my own. '—I think she deserves someone with more courage and impulsiveness than I.'

Lenora blushed but did not release my hand. 'What will you do now that you have your youth back, forever?'

'Seek for the other clocks, if they still exist,' he said, winking at Simeon. 'And free the persons within; even Drew with certain stringent conditions and long after you have departed.' He wandered over to a bureau, lifted a wax-sealed document and extended it towards me. 'Perhaps I will explore the business opportunities of kinetic and crystal-driven devices though not as Algernon Hobson.'

'What is it?' I said, leaving Lenora's hand and taking the legal paperwork.

'My estate.' He smiled as he looked around the chaos of the room. 'Or what is left of it. Quite an experience I have to say...'

'You are leaving me the house – why?'

'A young man without a history or record suddenly inheriting his lost, and missing uncle's things will cause suspicion. No, it is for the best if you move in here and I step back to the shop. I have allowed for my disappearance — the old me always wanted to visit Australia and the housekeeper will spread the news of my permanent holiday far and wide. You and I are still partners, but now a young and distant relation of Algernon Hobson will fulfil and live up to the great man's name on the sign.'

'You've thought of everything,' I said, 'but I can't accept it – I have nothing but my admiration and respect to offer in return.'

Hobson grinned and blushed for the first time that I had known him. 'Then I am still in your debt. You can always monitor the soul clock if anything untoward should arise, while you live out your natural life. Let me work in the shop with my mistress and I will be content.'

'What mistress?' I said, certain that his release of Lenora's affection had been because of another mystery woman.

'Time, my dear boy.
'Time.'

Simeon left with our heartfelt thanks, a new perspective on the approaching three centuries he had walked or been trapped on this earth, and a hefty endowment to begin again in his native country. He continued to write, for as long as Lenora and I both lived, though mostly he conversed with Ambrose, often keeping tabs on potential leads in the hunt for the remaining soul clocks.

Hobson had taken the new name, which I learned was from the Latin for "immortal", shortly after Lenora and I became wed that October. Christmas passed without incident, much to my relief, and every other festive season after that until I retired with a heavy, but happy heart. I placed my own shaking hands in his before walking my beloved home via the Severn path to feed the swans.

Hobson spun the clock every few years to give the semblance of ageing and prevent tongues from wagging, though he ticked with the same youthful passion for clockwork, kinetic and the new battery-powered devices until I can recount no more to you. Whether he lives still or found the master clockmaker and his soul clocks, this tale does not tell.

All I can say is that not once in my lifetime did the heart of the soul clock miss a beat or require mechanical intervention.

It may not require work of any kind for centuries...

He carried it with him, always, and I have no doubt still does, following the ticks and tocks of time down the years like clockwork; the only constant cog in the centuries of continual change.

MISRULE

'Will he follow the traditions of this house without complaint?' said the Master as I lowered my eyes to the flagstones, struggling to keep quiet my empty stomach in the Great Hall.

'He will, sir,' replied Old Cotton at my side. 'His father was of good stock and died for the King at Naseby.'

'As did many a good man of this shire,' declared the Master. 'What is your name, boy?'

'John Dunn, sir,' I murmured, clutching at my hat and bowing as low as I had practised for days.

'Your father will be at rest knowing that the Restoration of our beloved King Charles is yet still in its springtime. Work hard, Master Dunn, and follow the instruction of the man beside you – to the very word, mind you. I will know of it if you do not.'

'Yes, sir,' I replied, barely able to contain my relief at the prospect of employment, lodgings within the carriage barn, and food.

The Master stared into his prayer book, closing it with a sharp snap. 'Send in the new cook, Nathaniel, and take the boy with you; would that my wife was still living to deal with such matters...'

I had been three years in service when the events of that winter took place. Fortunate as I was to secure the position of apprentice to Old Cotton, my duties ranged far and wide, as did my feet, so that I fell into my cot each night taking to sleep like a drunken dormouse.

The long summer of 1661 passed, and I grew into full manhood, fed and clothed to support the water-carrying, log-splitting, horse-handling muscles required of a manor house serving man. I did it all, and more, as Old Cotton became visibly weaker and older.

'I'll soon be leaving you, John, now that there is little to teach,' he said, nursing his aching back in the open barn doorway.

'You've many a year left in you, Nathaniel,' I lied. My mentor, beyond pensionable age, was like a surrogate father and I returned to cold forge the metal ring of the cartwheel before me.

'There's one duty I'd ask of you before I retire to my sister's house in the village.'

'Name it,' I said.

With some hesitation, he pointed to the boarded first-floor attic space, accessed by the tall, fixed ladder which I had recently repaired.

'Keep watch, particularly over that locked chest up there, and let me know if something or someone turns up to claim it, especially around Christmas.'

I put down my hammer and followed his gaze to the barrels, boxes, and bags that were stored above. 'Like what?'

'Just keep an eye out and promise me you'll leave food, should anything or anyone make its home within.'

'Cook won't permit that,' I said. 'She hates animals unless it's preparing them for the pot. The only thing that frightens her more than that cat who wanders in here are the rats it keeps at bay.'

'Be careful of her,' he said, rising a solitary finger. 'She enjoys the Master's favour besides being wicked. She has ideas above her station, and contempt for those she deems below it.'

'Is it not strange to have a woman cook?' I asked.

'Indeed,' said the old man. 'Many things are altered since the war and there is nothing so constant as change. She holds court in the house now on account of her skill, if not her temperament, but the Master has little time to manage a house and so he relents. Keep your head down and your nose clean, and you may outlive her usefulness. Pride oft comes before a fall, they say.'

I nodded, testing the recently sharpened edge of the plane with my calloused finger. 'What's in the old chest up there?'

'Best not to know,' he said, turning to face the fragrant breeze blowing across from the small apothecary garden, 'and I hope you never have cause to find out because it will bring nothing but bad luck if you meddle. Promise me you won't open it, John; it belongs to someone who may return for it.'

'How will I learn if the right person comes to claim it?'

'You'll know,' said Nathaniel widening his eyes. 'You come and tell me if they do.'

Not being overly curious by nature I agreed, and he shook my hand, instilling the gravity of the verbal contract.

'It'll be around the turning of the year, if at all,' he said. 'Remember, beast or man, put food out and then leave well alone.'

Old Cotton left before the harvest, and I was without company in my quiet hours save for the farm cat who dozed upon the casks until dusk when the rats returned to scurry about the barn. I named him Nathaniel, and he tolerated my talk knowing that some tidbit stolen from the kitchen would repay his suffrage. I did not know I was observed and was fortunate not to lose my situation, let alone my hand when Cook, brimming with fierceness and strength scarce less that of a seasoned blacksmith, dragged me like a child before the Master and I was forced to reveal that the theft of a chicken leg was not for my belly, but another's.

Whatever favour I had accrued with my Lord was spent in an instant on the foolish charity and he barked at length within the Hall to set an example among all those timid faces present, downward gazing, silently thanking God it wasn't them. Two days with nothing but bread and water was hard with so much toil, not least for the cat that mewed from the post of my cot until it realised the situation, mocking me by bringing its own stiff, long-tailed offerings in sympathy during the cold first week of December.

My punishment was lighter and less cruel than those metered out to the rest of the household by the powerful kitchen devil, out of sight or hearing of the Master, for she delighted in causing misery. Following confrontation and abuse, many spoke of leaving before cooling their heads in the water trough and shuffling back to the wicked bosom and hand that fed them. Times were tough and livelihoods were scarce; she held sway in numerous things, was good at her craft, herbs, and medicines, and slipped into greater privileges usually reserved for the mistress of the house. Often out of the district on matters of regional importance, my Lord relinquished the insufferable distractions of the household without complaint as the dishes served to his guests at his table on his return became ever grander, while ours became meeker and leaner.

My association with Nathaniel, the Master's favourite, had caused a rift I could not repair or pacify no matter how hard I endeavoured, so I stopped trying. When necessity brought her to the barn, she would shriek and despatch the cat by stick or stone until it was out of sight before enacting whatever odious work or harsh words she had in mind for me. The discovery of a half-eaten mouse within the scullery, and an open window muddied about with paw prints heralded the final cruelty to us both.

Wet footprints from the morning rain greeted my arrival into the shelter of the barn, and I found the poor animal lying still with the remains of a chicken wing in its foaming mouth. I cast aside the spoiled meat and lifted my poisoned ginger companion, limp and lifeless into my arms and, grabbing a spade, strode into the deluge of the midwinter storm to bury him. The lights in the kitchen's window betrayed the smirk of satisfaction from the cook, at work feathering a goose for the festivities. All the season's joy was drowned out by grief at the callous act and the knowledge that such evil could exist within one person. The rats would become bolder – revenge enough if they tormented her with their scratchings and scurrying late at night when she was alone in the dark.

I buried him in a pretty spot by the stone wall that adjoined the road, where he had been accustomed to bask in the springtime sun, surrounded by the scent of primrose and sweet cicely. I toiled for ten minutes letting the anger seep from my arms and into the handle of the spade until I had a large enough grave in the stony ground. The sweat-mingled rain dripped from my brow as I stood upright to see a black cat, furred and soaking wet not twenty yards distance on the wall, watching me intently whilst ignoring the inclemency of the weather. I had never known such an animal to endure the rain. Its green eyes watched, emotionless, as I laid the body of its kind upon some of the refilled earth in the hole. After the grave was filled, I looked about but it was gone, replaced by something that shuffled away, manlike beneath a dark and travel-stained cloak. The figure disappeared out of sight through the torrent, head bowed, intent on its journey towards the Manor.

Returning an hour later after checking on the rabbit snares, the house was a hive of chatter and industry. A wandering minstrel had arrived seeking shelter and a short display of wizardry with flute, sleight of hand, and acrobatics had so enchanted the Master that he was proclaimed 'Lord of Misrule' on the spot and tasked with the entertainments of his guests in the coming days.

'What sort of man is he?' I asked.

'He don't speak,' said the maid, 'but you know exactly what he wants or is trying to say. Master's given him leave to stay over Yuletide as long as he performs each night. That hasn't gone down well with *her*. Masked, he is, as though hiding some affliction, but his cloak was of fair cloth or was once upon a time. Cook started to work on him and put him in place, but he fixed her with such a glance, and she just froze. You'll be able to find out more yourself; he'll be sharing the barn with you.'

Handing over the dangling rabbits, I returned to the outbuilding to warm my hands in front of the brazier I used for metalworking. A noise of something shifting through the hay stooks above caused me to reach for the poker and I called out, wondering if the newly appointed Lord of Misrule had taken up his residence already, or if more than rats was at play. The unmistakable sound of a click and the opening of a creaking lid ceased and slammed shut as the latter notion scurried from my mind.

I gingerly climbed the ladder calling out my intentions to defend myself and the Master against vagrants and ruffians. What materialised as I pulled myself up into the dust and gloom of the attic space was not the visage of a man, but the face of the cat I had seen, peeking between a bushel of rush-light candles. Its green eyes, ringed with grey suggested great age but it was dominantly black except for splashes of white hinted at beneath its belly. It seemed larger, fuller, as though the dry barn and rising heat from the brazier had teased every tangle from its luxuriant fur.

'I'd advise against staying here permanently if you want to go on living,' I said, tossing aside the poker with a clatter and sighing with relief. 'I'm in no mood to bury another so soon. Did you come with Misrule?'

The animal tilted its head, listening to the unintelligible babble.

'I saw you moments before him, out in the lane to Wood-haven. Perhaps you followed him?'

The cat chirruped as though in agreement.

Beyond the crates in the corner, I caught sight of the chest, not fully closed with something akin to a damp rag or dripping cloak trapped at its edge, preventing the lid from sealing shut. I had never known the ancient, roughly carved oak casket to be open, but moving closer caused the cat to leap upon the top, arch its back and hiss in a defensive act of warning.

'Charming,' I said. 'Whatever's in there can't be of much use or value, even to him, but I'm not happy about anyone prowling about up here with someone's things, especially when I was told—'

I suddenly recalled Nathaniel's words and request to honour with meat or buttered milk what beast or man should take up in this space. Certain the minstrel had visited the spot before his impromptu, introductory performance, I looked about to see signs of hurried habitation and the hasty making of a camp from anything that could be slept or sat upon. From within the chest's lock, a silver key was half-turned.

'Nathaniel said someone would be back for it, but I never thought it would be a wanderer.'

The animal growled indignantly in its throat and relaxed with my retreat, washing itself but keeping one green eye upon me as I returned to the floor to put on my great coat and slip through the archway of the outbuildings to the buttery.

'I'm not sure who's the softer fool,' I said, pushing the dish of milk and butter toward the cat on my return. 'Nathaniel or I, but you are welcome in place of one I now miss.' The creature flinched and then settled as I stretched out my fingers to bury them in the thick fur of its shoulders even as it lapped hungrily at the greasy meal.

I did not see Misrule but gathered that it must be he that inhabited the space above and not just the cat. Furtive investigations at night when neither was present revealed little but the cloak, much less a bag or pack. Its leather was dull and much stained, but its lining rippled with a rainbow of silken strips that took my breath away. The chest remained locked, and the key was absent.

A maid relayed accounts each morning of Misrule's marvellous mimicry, miming and magic from the evening before, setting the serving men and women's mood soaring above the menial misery of Cook who, despite having outdone herself with pie and pudding, was not the centre of attention upon the feast of Christmas Eve. At church the following morn, I heard others describe how the masked impresario had moved people to tears with his flute, caused bouts of breathlessness with his candlelit shadow puppetry, and left them in a flash of powder at the end of the performance, banging on the tables for an encore.

'The one you told me to watch for is here,' I said, walking in the lane beside Nathaniel after the service.

He stopped short, waiting for the remaining villagers to pass out of earshot.

'Are you certain?'

'A wanderer, and a player with some skill by all accounts that has been with us several days. The chest was unlocked with a silver key when—'

The old man gripped my arm. 'Describe him to me.'

'I've only caught glimpses of him, but I hear him turning in the night above me in the attic. Tall, dark, lean with a cloak of many colours.'

'Masked?' said Nathaniel, his eyes probing my lips for certainty.

'Yes. The maid thinks it's some affliction or complaint of the skin, perhaps even leprosy. They have taken to calling him 'Misrule' but he doesn't speak.'

'Is he accompanied by a beast, in likeness and colouring, but never at the same time?'

'A black cat with white markings,' I said supporting his sudden faintness. 'Are you alright, Nathaniel?'

The colour drained from his face and shook his head. 'I have been unwell, but don't mind that now. I need to know if you have done as I ask and fed the animal.'

'With butter and milk each day, as you asked. What is it that troubles you about the man – is he a danger?'

'Yes, but not in the way you think. The man and the cat are the same, John. They have returned to test the virtue of mankind and punish the wicked.'

'You are not yourself,' I said, wondering if he had lost his mind. His face was resolute and while I did not believe the superstition, Nathaniel clearly did.

We walked a little further as he continued. 'They are rarely seen these days and they are few, but the black one is perhaps the most feared. What they are none can tell, but at least one of their kind turns up a few times each century to do the rounds and test the compassion, charity, and willingness of mortals to sacrifice, like our dear Lord.' He pointed back to the church. 'But they are far older, maybe even older than pagan times, and the season draws them closer to us; they do not forgive or forget.'

'He's just a minstrel that makes coins disappear—'

'Nay, lad. Trust me on this.' His voice quietened to a whisper. 'In my youth, I heard tell of the red wanderer from my grandfather's day that turned up in the guise of a fox; and the time before that it was the turn of the white, a barn owl that transformed into a maiden with a voice so pure it broke the hearts of those that listened right until it took a child as payment or punishment.'

'For what?'

'Not passing the test. They come to see if those virtues I spoke of still exists within mankind, perhaps even within one man. Failure isn't just confined to the district, it reaches far and wide across the country.'

'How can one act have such consequences, if what you say is true?'

He leaned into my face. 'War, John. Plague, poor harvests, and perhaps the death of Kings. They don't stay long, so you need to remain out of the way lest they take an interest in you. Just carry on feeding whatever lies behind the mask, as man or beast, and keep it alive and sated until Twelfth Night or calamity will strike a member of the household and possibly the region.'

'And what do they do if we are found worthy?' I asked, humouring my ailing friend.

'They let us be,' he said. 'Until the next time...'

'If Misrule has a key for the chest, then that means he's been here before.'

Nathaniel's cloudy grey eyes widened. 'Yes, a long time ago, before I was apprenticed, and that was when Queen Bess still reigned. He turned up, but not as a cat, but that of a raven, black as the hair on his head when he changed to our form, hooded like a hangman and clever with his tricks and juggling. He beguiled us all.'

'It might not have been the same man or thing?'

He shrugged. 'Who knows if they stay the same or age and die as we do, but that spring never fully arrived. Folks starved, John, and took to eating rats when the summer baked the ground hard as flint and the harvest failed; just as we failed that Yuletide before.'

Nathaniel hacked a great cough that took a long while to settle. 'Do everything within your power to keep it fed and quiet till it makes its mind up and moves on.'

'And then what?' I said unnerved at the idea though I did not fully believe it.

'Say your prayers, John,' he said leaning on his stick and wandering ahead, leaving me in the lane. 'Say your prayers.'

I did as I was told, but with some trepidation despite being someone not prone to believing in fairy stories. Each day that followed I fed the cat from the great jug in the buttery and watched with some apprehension at its hungry, yammering tongue lapping the buttered milk. No amount of fussing or cajoling would entreat it to let me pass to investigate the makeshift sackcloth and straw bed, or the chest that I knew to be sometimes unlocked. Whoever came and went did so silently, and I slept lightly and ill at ease among the increasing sounds of squeak and scurry.

Sucking on a deep, clawing scratch from too close an inspection of the furry squatter, the maid warned me that my thefts had been noticed and that Cook was aware of the cat in the barn, and missing dairy.

'He comes with Misrule,' I said defensively, anxious that a repeat offence brought to the Master's attention might be disastrous.

'Then let the beggar feed him,' she said. 'He don't eat

from our table or what's left out for him, so he must have a store of it somewhere.'

The evening before Twelfth Night, I waited until the minstrel was at work in the Hall and crept up to the first-floor to see if sustenance was hidden that might explain Misrule's abstinence. I noted the cat was not there and confess I was more interested in putting my mind at ease than the discovery of food, as I raised the rushlight candle above my head and lifted the lid of the unlocked chest.

No crumb lay within, only a jumbled assortment of mouldy and mouse-eaten costumes, props, and disguises. Split, white feathers and a matted fox's tail attached to a belt lay to one side. Something glittered in the dim but focused light of the candle and I moved aside the grotesque raven-beaked mask to marvel at a pair of crimson silk slippers, threadbare and worn but once of fine make and beauty. The inside of the lid revealed something even more remarkable, and macabre.

Richly carved ancient symbols and runes framed an incised series of miniature mills, castles, houses, and villages with dates in Latin, alongside which small crosses were lined like a tally stick. Next to a small number of them, a circle was marked instead of a cross, and as I studied the seemingly random positions, I realised it was a map. Fine, straight lines indicated drovers roads around the district and beyond, whilst sinuous meanderings suggested rivers. It was very much like the chart of southern England that hung in the Great Hall.

My eyes hurried to the location of the Manor that lay at the centre of the county, miniaturised in exquisite detail, and the dates beside, all but one incised with a cross set slightly apart from the roman numerals.

'Twelve-hundred and fifty-three, and after that, fourteen-hundred and ninety,' I whispered, translating the last but one.

'Fifteen-hundred and eighty-eight, in the reign of Queen Bess.'

With unease, I glanced at the final date, recently carved, sharp and fresh, as yet without a cross or circle.

'Sixteen-hundred and sixty-one...'

I staggered back letting the lid slam shut and all but upset the dish of buttered cream placed earlier that day. It was strange to see it still mostly uneaten, for the cat was ravenous each morning, but a closer inspection showed something amiss with the odour as I lifted it to my nose. A putrid vein of green swirled at its edge, separating the dairy into unappetising curds and I knew that poison had been added or mixed to the small and isolated slab of butter I had stolen that day.

Whether it was rage or fear, I know not, but I found myself at the edge of sight within the Great Hall even as the performance and feasting were in full vigour. My first sight of the minstrel was profound and unexpected. He was clothed in a patchwork suit of black and white diamonds, a harlequin whose belt and shoes rang with tiny bells sewn into the cloth. His mask, cat-like and made of some dark leather or skin, fit tightly about his sallow and pitted face. I breathed a sigh of relief until I caught the eye of the murderous matriarch commanding her army of runarounds from the serving table and knew from her smug, sanctimonious expression that things would rapidly come to a head. She turned with a look of innocence towards the Master, and then back to me, mouthing the words *tomorrow...*

I had little time to think up some defiant reply because the troubadour, impersonating a large, marauding beast to the delight of all suddenly staggered and fell over clutching at his side. He glanced over, searching among the crowd until he caught my eye and I knew he was overcome with some sudden and debilitating pain. He writhed on the floor in agony while the guests roared with laughter at the strange but animated jest. I rushed over, lifting him over my back and pranced around the tapestried walls several times as though in the pretence of some audience-contrived partnership for the greater amusement of the Master before rushing through the cries and banging of hands upon the tables, desperate for more. I staggered into the barn, throwing the barely conscious minstrel upon my cot.

He regarded me briefly before rolling his green, pupil-dilated eyes into the back of his head. Writhing and mewing in a heavy sweat, I tried to remove his mask to discover it was a part of his skin and I recoiled, clutching at my hair, not knowing what to do. Misrule lay gently twitching as whatever poison had been ingested worked its course. He took rapid small sips of breath and I thought of the only person to whom I could turn.

A full twenty minutes later, exhausted by the icy, dark miles to the village I banged on the door and was admitted by Nathaniel's sister.

'I need...help. Nathaniel—'

'He's very sick,' she whispered, letting me in, but concerned about her brother lying on the cushioned floor beside the fire. 'It's his lungs and I fear for him.'

He stirred, beckoning me closer.

'The black wanderer,' I said kneeling and grabbing his limp hand for both our comforts. 'Cook has poisoned the butter and now he lies dying.'

I felt his grip tighten. 'Don't let it happen, John, the others might come and we will be damned!'

'I don't know what to do,' I cried. 'He needs a purge or medicine or—'

He waved me away, pawing for a balsam of herbs within a clay pot beside him, much to the remonstrations of the elderly dame.

'My sacrifice,' he said. 'To save its life, hoping it will leave us in peace, and count towards the tally of man's virtues.' He forced the salve into my hands. 'Give this as a watered-down paste to slow the effects, but he needs the remedy to survive and you need to find out what she used.'

'But she'll not tell me; she's going to tell the Master tomorrow about the milk and butter, and I'll be out on my ear.'

Nathaniel sat upright, pulling me towards him. 'Then you come here but listen, John. For evil to exist in this world, good men must do nothing. Folk once spoke of a cure-all, if the poison is not known.'

'What is it?' I said, uncertain of my skill with plants or potions.

'A weed that grows upon the grave of one killed by the same, but how you tell that I do not know.'

'The ginger cat,' I said, clasping the pot to my chest and rising. 'She poisoned another a few weeks ago.'

'Then hurry,' said Nathaniel, slipping back onto the makeshift bed. 'While there is still time, and if the old stories are true.'

My legs burned with the notion that I might have that time, running half-mad with the pain in my lungs from the exertion. Reaching the wall in the dark, I scoured the spot for the grave, grown over in short order with weed and newly sprouting grass from the chopped turves of the backfill. An unfamiliar plant caught my eye, red-leaved and pungent like purslane populated the tiny mound, and I hurriedly harvested the herb before returning to the barn.

The minstrel was not there, but in its place lay the black cat, chest imperceptibly rising and falling, close to death. Hastily crushing the herbs and mixing the greasy balsam into a cold watery paste I dabbed the end of my spare shirt, lifted the limp creature onto my lap and squeezed the linen to release the liquid into the tongue-lolling cavity of its mouth. It spluttered and woke, too weak to resist being in my arms, as I continued to drip the makeshift medicine into its maw.

'Don't you die,' I said, 'or take old Nathaniel when you find us wanting.' A tear, unforeseen but heartfelt splashed onto the creature's nose and it inhaled like a newborn kitten dragging in the powerful scents ever deeper to combat the poison. I smoothed and stroked its soft belly marking the white diamonds that speckled the black fur.

'You can take me, instead.'

The cat mewed weakly and swallowed more of the remedy that dripped like gentle rain into its body until I became too tired to think and sleep overtook me.

I woke, stiff and sore in the dim light of the dawn to find the cat no longer about the barn with no sign of its human form.

I was chastised for my tomfoolery in the Hall as I set about laying the fires and sweeping the spent rushes to my cart. Cook was ever-present chastising and reminding me that the Master would hear of my misdemeanour on his return from hunting.

'Enjoy your last meals, she said tossing a meagre portion of yesterday's meat upon the floor beside me. 'Or perhaps you'd rather not in case it's poisoned?'

'You've damned us all,' I said sweeping up the rabbit's leg. 'Pray Misrule doesn't take you over me if he still lives.'

She wrinkled her nose and bit at her thumb to chastise me. 'I'm not afeared of a fop.'

'You should be,' I said brushing past her and lifting my cart.

'Until tonight,' she said from behind.

'As your cold heart pleases,' I replied, leaving the room.

There was much work to do for the Twelfth Night feast, and truth be told Cook was in such a good mood with my impending dismissal that the serving men and women felt ill at ease by the change. I felt something, too. A tenseness that seemed to be all about the Manor from restless birds in the trees to the cows flighty and troublesome in the shed at milking time. It began to snow, and big flurried flakes built up over the frosted fields and fens. There was no sign of man or beast in the barn as darkness fell and the Master returned with his guests looking forward to an entertaining dinner. Fearing the cat had crept off to die, I gave up my search and headed inside to face my fate.

The Great Hall teamed with people, grand and small, merrily sharing the merriment, company, and vittles of the evening as was the custom. Garlands of pine, juniper, and fir hung in the candlelit trusses, and glistening holly berried the bowers around the main table. The Master, arrayed like a Norse God in his olive-green raiment toasted all those present asking if anyone had grievance upon such a merry night, in purely rhetorical custom.

Cook stood forward and was about to speak when the candles dimmed as though the tenseness of the very air cramped and squeezed at their bobbing flames. The sound of bells jingled with heavy footfalls from outside the great oak doors sealed against the snow and cold. A muted mumbling silence prevailed, and several of the younger guests quailed and began to cry.

The bells ceased, and the doors opened, letting in a draught of such ferocity as to extinguish all but a very few of the candles and plunging the stately room into dim expectation. Misrule staggered in, clothed in his black and white diamonds, cloak turned outwards to show its coloured ribbons. Serving men closed the door fast, and he passed me on his way to the centre of the room, glancing at me with his green eyes, the cat-like slits reverting to dilating pupils in the darkness. His brow was clammy and held beads of sweat as one newly released from fever, and I bowed my head as he took out his flute and played a melancholy tune that ever after could not be wholly recalled though its sentiment seemed clear at the time to all present. The music mourned for seasons and years past and wept in its high notes for the former innocence and kindness of mankind. The music came to a gentle end, rising to disappear into the rafters as silence once more descended.

With tears in his eyes, the Master took out a small purse and tossed it onto the floor.

'You have given my house such pleasures and qualities this Christmas time that my hospitality alone will not suffice. Come now, give us something merry, something we have never seen before.'

The minstrel leaned over with some effort to pocket the jingling leather bag and took out a pair of crimson slippers, bright and new, as though tailored that very day. Of exact likeness they were to those I had seen in the chest but changed somehow if they were not truly a different pair. Waving his hands above them they began to move, dance and pivot as though in time with his own jingling feet.

The guests clapped in time with the cantering steps watching his hands move upon unseen strings to form the twirling movements that animated the silk-slippered puppets. He spun past, and I studied his hands, trying to see the trick of the invisible lady shown only by the movement of her feet. I tell you it was nothing that man could contrive. He came to a sudden stop, and the slippers skidded to a halt with the removal of his hands at the feet of the Cook.

She stood bemused, eyeing the fine shoes with under-standable envy.

'Come, mistress,' said the Master. 'I'll be bound he means to offer you some recompense for your worthy pastries, puddings, and pies. Wear them and give us some of your finest steps.'

Cook hesitated but gazed at the beautiful objects.

'If you will not dance alone for slippers, then I will grant whatever boon you sought before our marvellous minstrel appeared to honour our hall, providing it is in my power to grant.'

She took one glance toward me and rushed at the crimson felt-lined cradles, tying them swiftly with the ribbons that streamed about the heel. She lifted her skirt and, accompanied by the Lord of Misrule, entered the floor and began a coarse, hurried jig to the amusement of all but myself. The minstrel took out his flute and began to play, the tempo increasing with each passing moment, his bells about him beating out the time until they became a continuous, tinkling peal.

Cook began to tire, but each time she tried to remove herself from the ring her feet turned, guided by the commands and music of the capering figure at its centre. Reddened and struggling to keep going, the slippers sprang away until it seemed her legs had a mind of their own, carrying the upper body and flailing arms in greater extremes of haphazard movement. All present thought it some grand jape conjured between them to mark the occasion with a memorable interlude. Feet banged on the wooden dais beneath the Master's table and hands clapped with increasing time until the roar of the crowd was met, full force with that of a sudden splintering opening of the doors and an inrush of snow.

The uninvited guest swirled around them both in such a fashion as to blind those close at hand, and they raised their arms to ward off the stinging beads of ice. Raising my sleeve, our eyes met, and he bowed his head. In a flash of dazzling white, the pair vanished never to be seen alive in my lifetime.

Heavy snowfall continued the next day forcing the guests to remain unsatisfied and mostly unfed by the apparent disappearance of both the cook and the minstrel. A hunting party braving the cold discovered her body over a mile away and rode to the Hall to inform the Master, the woman being well-known in the district for her talents and temperament. When I arrived, the ground was still unmarked, and she lay face down and barefoot followed by other, smaller and numerous prints. Marks on her heels suggested the ravenous gnawing of many sharp teeth, and I concluded that the absence of rats for many days had something to do with it. Whether she had died from exhaustion, exposure, or fear, I do not know. Perhaps it was all three? What most intrigued me were the footprints of pointed shoes that disappeared suddenly, replaced by paws that vanished into a drift of snow. When I looked back from the higher ground as we carried her upon a makeshift bier, I saw the wide and perfect ring of uncovered grass about the spot and wondered if we had passed the test, while she had paid with her life.

Her death brought relief to many on the estate, myself included, but I took no pleasure in it. I found the purse upon the locked chest, sharing out the silver coins amongst those most in need, and paid for a doctor to ease Nathaniel's sickness. He lived for many more years.

I thought to force the lid and see if a circle lay inscribed next to the date on its underside, but my old mentor persuaded me to abandon the idea. Perhaps the slippers still lie within, old and neglected along with the other rags and clothing waiting for their turn to be resurrected and rejuvenated in the service of one of those strange wanderers.

After a few days of leaving milk in the accustomed place with nothing taking nourishment from its richness, I knew we were safe, but that some toll had been taken. Could these beings feel revenge, or was it blessing us for passing the test?

The following summer was warm and glorious, the wheat rippled and bent with bounteous corn, men, and women near bathed in cider from the harvest, and babies were born curiously dark-haired and beautiful, growing into healthy, agile children full of play and laughter during a time of peace. I never tasted plum pudding, pigeon pie or punch as fine for the rest of my life, but the new cook was kind and competent and liked cats, especially for the keeping down of vermin.

The years pass and I hope to take on an apprentice from that blessed year of 1662. As I look out at the falling snow, I wonder if the time of testing will return in my lifetime and if the wanderer might remember me if he does. The old ways and customs seem overtaken by steam power and machines these days, but are no less potent or timely in their probing of our characters. Take care you are not found wanting in compassion, charity, or willingness to sacrifice so that the scales of virtue are forever tilted in mankind's favour.

ONE MORE DAY

Michael clicked on his dim bedside lamp and reached for the painkillers. Cold sweat soaked his shirt as he struggled to sit upright against the single headboard, a glass of water in his shaking hand. He closed his eyes, waiting for the nausea and sudden acute pain in his side to subside. Massaging the area had little effect except to confirm his non-medical diagnosis that this was perhaps something more than stitch, appendicitis or kidney stones. He was seeing the doctor in three days, a delay inevitable in between Christmas and New Year, but here, now, in the dark, he figured he would escalate that to an emergency call first thing in the morning.

'*Speaking of which*,' he thought, wiping the stinging sweat from his eyes to check the time.

1:30 am.

He put down the empty glass and cast back his head. There was no way he would spend the next seven hours before the medical centre opened waiting for the next debilitating wave to overcome him. Swinging his legs over the bedside, intending to drive to the accident and emergency department, he noticed a billowing of the light gauze curtains despite the third-floor apartment window being jammed shut for over three years. Hypnotic blinking lights from the gaudy decorations in the high rise opposite mesmerised him momentarily, and he recalled the time of year, the season, and Fliss. The curtain settled and a yowling catfight far below brought him back to the perspiring present.

Checking for air gaps in the old wooden frame would have to wait. Getting up, dressing and searching for his car keys suddenly evaporated with a surge of such severe and all-consuming pain that he fell back onto the sheets, writhing until the painful pulse subsided enough for him to conclude that walking, let alone driving, was currently out of the question.

He thought of his phone, ready now to call for an ambulance. Wasn't it in the adjoining room? It may have well been in Papua New Guinea at that very moment because it was simply out of reach of his unsteady, shaking limbs. In his delirium, he glanced over to the shadowy, alcoved recess and noticed movement from the high-backed reading chair.

'What the hell is going on?' he whispered to himself, taking long breaths to control the hyperventilating urge threatening to make him pass out.

'The end,' came a soft, slow, breathy reply.

Michael wriggled his way back to the pillow, fearful of the voice coming from the corner. His eyes scanned the humanoid shadow that shifted suddenly, as though crossing its legs from within the confines of the comfy chair.

'Who are you – how did you get in here?'

The voice from the shadows sighed. 'A friend who has always been with you, Michael, but only now can you perceive me.'

'I don't know you at all,' he said, bemused by the gentle echo that accompanied the voice. Its words dissipated into the corners of the room with the accompanying sound of a crowd of merry children mingled with the fading sobs of grief.

'A visitor, then,' said the voice. 'One with your current and long-term interests at heart.'

'Take what you want and get out, but please leave me my phone – I think I'm—'

'Dying?' completed the shadow, rising and shifting its arms as though adjusting some nebulous gown upon its slim, vaguely feminine form. 'Yes, you are.'

The profound and echoing sadness of its words filled his rational mind with the first line of defence – denial. Michael lifted the lamp to the end of the bed but found his eyes less adapted to see the figure. The shadow seemed to absorb all attempts at scrutiny, and as the electrical cord stretched, the plug behind the bedside loosened putting out the light and plunging the room into moonlit darkness and a kaleidoscope of diffuse festive lights blinking in time with the rapid pounding of his heart.

Michael retreated to the headboard. His eyes adjusted to the outline of the shadow as it emerged into the beam of waxing light filtering through the curtains. The figure became distinct, though remained insubstantial, and while his first inclination was that the shade was indeed female, the gentle appearance seemed to wax and wane in strength with the cocktail of lights that shone upon its face. Her features underwent subtle changes as though unsure which visage to alight upon, but after a few moments of flicking through various iterations, the figure beamed out a smile from a young, pale-faced woman in her early thirties. While certainly beautiful, the woman carried a gravitas that exuded motherly love, care and compassion.

'This one?' she said, as though asking for his permission. 'Will this one make things easier? I haven't worn it in a while.'

'You're a—'

'Yes,' said the shade, folding her arms beneath the semblance of a long brocaded gown. A small purse hung low around her neck. Michael flinched with a sudden, stabbing assault on his side and the shade glided over to sprinkle something unseen into the glass from a low-hanging purse around her neck.

'I need water—' The words died on his lips as Michael saw the jet black sparkles in her eyes indicating the refilled glass. Her closeness was both comforting and confusing. Michael tried to pick out the features, certain that the face was somehow familiar.

'A neat trick for the angel of death,' he said, after gulping down the water. It had a fragrant quality, as though infused with the blossoms of many flowers, evaporating on the tongue without really satiating his dry mouth. He felt better instantly and rubbed at his kidney as she retreated towards the moonbeam.

'I'm no angel, I can assure you,' she said with a wry smile, causing the giggling children in her echoed speech to drown out the sadness of the other mournful voices. 'More of a... collector. Death is but a moment in time.'

'You've come for me, then?' said Michael, comforted by the lack of pain and surety that the trespasser, undead or no, would not kill or rob him in the traditional sense. The reality of the situation struck him and he railed against the notion, even as she nodded.

'Side effects of the pills,' he said trying to appease his materialistic mindset. 'The pain and too many drugs have conjured Marley's Ghost—'

'I am no blob of mustard or undigested bit of beef,' replied the shade, familiar with the interchange between Scrooge and his "dead as a doornail" partner. She breathed against the curtains, setting them into gentle movement. She stepped in front and Michael could see the gauze passing through her gown, weaving and wafting through the shadowy taffeta. She gently swung her arms, and back-lit by the flickering natural and man-made lights, Michael imagined he was lying at the bottom of a deep pool looking up at a floating figure against an underwater, moonlit sky.

'You said I'm going to die – when?'

She closed her eyes briefly before breathing out the death knell as softly and without emotion as someone would a shopping list.

'Sunset – two days from now.'

'What from?'

She stroked her side and opened her eyes. 'Acute aortic catastrophe and complications arising from surgery. Nothing could or can be done.' A mournful echo of sobbing rose as though providing a compassionate and appropriate accompaniment. 'My sincere condolences.'

Michael dragged his hands through his damp hair and stretched out to relieve the pins and needles in his cramp-ridden legs. He glanced at his side as tears welled in his eyes.

'I do not know what that is, but it sounds bloody painful,' he said turning to see the curtains subside to their accustomed stationery hanging. The shade stretched out a hand and the chair slid across the floorboards with a squeal. She sat down, backlit by moonlight, and he caught the same gentle smile and a wink as he recognised the continued playful action from *A Christmas Carol* – one of his favourites.

'You are taking this awfully well, Michael.'

'I feel like there is nothing wrong with me,' he said, glancing at the empty glass. 'Twenty-eight years doesn't seem fair though. If I'm going to die in two days, why are you here now?'

'You have led a blemish-free life,' said the shade. 'Certain worthy individuals are granted a peculiar grace to come willingly and painlessly ahead of their appointed time.'

'Or what?'

The shade puckered her lips. 'I am not without feelings and those that cling to the remaining hours and days do so at a considerable penalty to themselves and the final memories of their loved ones.'

She turned, and the wan light illuminated a brief rivulet as a tear cascaded down her cheek. It dripped from her chin and vanished into the waiting open purse beneath. She clasped it shut and leaned back into the shadow. 'I weep for every one of them.'

'You want me to give up the next few days so you don't have to see me suffer – is that it?'

'I will return for you whatever you decide; do not choose on my account, but on yours.'

'Will I have to come now or can I call my family?'

'That depends on whether you can reach your phone – it is not in the adjoining room, it is in your motor vehicle on the ground floor. I don't think you have the strength to reach it and my attempts at pain relief are limited to this time and place.' She raised a hand and a cabinet drawer on the other side slid open. 'You could reach the notepad and leave a message – many people prefer to do so.'

'You are very persuasive and thoughtful,' said Michael. 'I hope I will have the opportunity to commend your attentiveness to your line manager.'

The shade laughed, accompanied by an echoing swell of childish glee.

'My first commendation in over two thousand years! Unfortunately, sweet-talking will get you nowhere.'

The echo subsided and Michael tested the floor with his feet, gaining confidence with the lack of pain. In the darkness he retrieved the notepad by touch and returned to the bed to write out several drafts, scrunching up the first few attempts and lobbing them toward a waste paper bin. Finally, he held out a simple and tender outpouring of his feelings for his mother and father. The shade scanned the page and nodded with approval.

'It's sad it has to happen at this time of year,' he said, turning to the blinking lights outside. 'I hope it won't ruin every Christmas for them from now on.'

'I see from the spartan seasonality of your surroundings that you don't keep the season yourself?' she said, turning to survey the shadowy room.

'No. There was someone I cared for that disappeared from my life at this time of year three years ago, and I still hold a candle for her; it puts Christmas and New Year in the shade if you'll pardon the expression.' Michael hesitantly looked back to his feet, wiggling his toes with the revelation. He had never bared his soul to anyone about Fliss, though as his spirit was about to be "collected" there came at once a calm and freeing sense of release to talk to a stranger, even one as strange and unique as the woman before him.

'I sense regret and questions without answers,' she said reaching out a hand in consolation. Michael stared at the moonlit, manicured fingers and imperceptibly stretched out his own. The lightest of touches filled him with a grace he had never known, but the memory of the young woman whom he lost remained as he lowered his hand to the mattress.

'If I agree to come with you before my allotted time and save you any discomfort, are you able to offer me a final request, like in the old films?'

'You are very particular for a mortal,' replied the shade, shutting her eyes and rising. A cloud bank obscured the moon and the room momentarily plunged into a dim disco of diffuse fairy lights from across the street.

'You have led an unblemished life,' she said rhetorically, raising her hand as though turning the pages of an invisible book before her. Michael frowned as she stifled a laugh. 'If you discount the pulling of ginger pigtails in primary school, and the scrumping of apples from the community orchard.'

'If you know everything, then tell me if the woman I spoke of, Fliss, ever turned up to meet me three years ago this very night.'

'The mortal you had courted for almost a year before she agreed to meet with you?'

'Yes. We met online. We were gamers, but it developed into something more. I could talk to her like I'm talking to you right now, and I'm not ashamed to say I fell in love.

I thought she felt the same way.'

'She didn't arrive at your meeting place?'

Michael shrugged. 'I do not know and I never heard from or been able to contact her since. She lived on the other side of the country and we were due to meet in a place called Church Stretton, at a churchyard below her favourite view-point; it's a hill—'

'Caer Caradoc...' said the shade finally opening her eyes.

He nodded. 'I was late—'

'When you arrived at the place, she was gone?'

'Yes. Assuming of course she was there at all and not just leading me on. I sat there shivering in the cold, staring at my phone, leaving countless messages till I felt drowsy and drove home. She said she had something very important to tell me and I would just like to know what it was and why she didn't want to see me anymore.' Michael blushed in the darkness and squinted his eyes as the moonlight crept across his face.

'Perhaps not knowing is sometimes better.'

'That's what people say when they know something you don't,' said Michael, shuffling into the shadow at the end of the bed and leaving the note in the moonlit path. 'I drove the two hundred miles there every 27th December for the next two years; I'm such a fool. I would probably have gone today if I hadn't felt so unwell...'

The shade settled into the armchair and pressed her ghostly chin against her pointed, clasped fingers. 'You were late because you were selfless.'

'Yes,' said Michael. 'There was a woman who got glanced by a hit and run; I was the only person around with a clear head. I made sure she was alright and waited for help to arrive so she wouldn't be alone and frightened. The nearest hospital was miles away. I should have called Fliss to let her know, but I was so flustered. It took twenty minutes for the ambulance and I was already late what with hold-ups on the motorways. To top it all off, when I got home I found the flat in a mess as though someone had broken in, and helped themselves to food and money in my savings tin that is hidden beneath the loose tile in the bathroom. It was odd because they didn't take my tablet or other valuable things, and they fed the cat I used to have.'

'Your act of charity cost you dearly on both fronts,' said the shade sympathetically. 'Carrying regret into the next life can indeed be a burden – what would be your final request, assuming I can grant anything of the sort?'

'That I can somehow make that meeting – or just to see if she was truly there.'

'And if she wasn't?'

Michael hesitated. 'Then I've been a naive fool and I wish her all the best with the next overly romantic first-person shooter boy she ensnares. Almost the last thing she said to me the day before we were due to meet was "to live each day as if it were our last" so I'm asking you now for one more day, to do just that.'

'A curious and harmless request,' said the shade. 'You know, most people ask for time though they think they can put all things in order: money, wills, settlements – they think they can do this all in one day. It can't. Human affairs are so complicated and besides, it gives the living something to focus on after their loved one's passing. It provides a productive solace from their grief. You are a rare bird, my dear mortal, to ask for this.'

'Then you'll grant me one more day, without pain, in exchange for the two I am giving up?'

'You are asking me to play the Ghost of Christmas Past and allow you to live this day again, three years ago. It's unorthodox...'

'Can it be done?' said Michael, scrambling over the clammy bedsheets to face the receptive gaze of the female phantasm. 'Haven't you ever loved someone? I will submit willingly once I have no more questions on the matter and save you a sorry sight in two days. I meant what I said about speaking to your superior.'

The shade closed her eyes as though seeking guidance or confirmation. A generous smile broadened her pale face as she blinked open and set her mirrored sparkling pupils to his.

'It appears you have an advocate,' she said. 'You will be mortal and I will, by necessity, be forced to ensure no 'interference' occurs to affect the future. Your former self will still miss his encounter and it will be up to you to ensure your arrival but take care – this is not Dickens' 'Carol' and the shades of what were will know you still. I will be waiting for you at the spinning of the steeple cock, whether or not you make your rendezvous; is that understood?'

Michael nodded as the moon receded into a bank of all-consuming cloud. The note upon the bed briefly fluttered in response to the billowing of the curtains as the shade wiggled her nose and raised her hand in command.

'Then sleep now and receive the greatest gift one can give another.'

'One more day...' said Michael, overcome with drowsiness

and watching the shade dissipate into the myriad of blinking, colourful sparkles. She shook her head and vanished leaving behind parting words echoing with the peaceful, mindful ticking of a hundred clocks.

'No, Michael. Something altogether more profound.'

It was the sound of the apartment door closing that woke him.

Michael prised apart his sleep-rimed eyes and blinked at the winter sun casting watery ripples on the ceiling. The sound of departing footsteps met the lift, partway down the hall, and the clunking mechanism met the early riser in the otherwise silent apartment block. He turned to see the condensation framing the window, and the models of fantasy characters acting out the battles from the gaming rig on the far wall.

Models that he had taken to the charity shop over eighteen months ago.

He sprung into an upright, seated position, noticing the sheets were of an older, faded type that should be lining the boot of his car. Far below, the sound of a squawk signalling the unlocking of a vehicle alerted him.

Someone was trying to steal his car.

He raced to the window to see a man similar in age with the same mop of blonde hair shouldering the bag that once belonged to his father. The man slammed down the boot and de-iced the windscreen, protecting his face from a funnelling blast of wind that unwrapped the wayward scarf about his neck. Michael caught his own distant reflection and knew it to be himself. He banged on the glass to attract his former self, but the younger man got into the car and pulled out into the road.

Michael grabbed at his side, but only the memory of pain remained. Glancing wildly about the room at posters, furniture and belongings that were familiar but long changed or discarded, he yelped as the soft, snaking fur of a tortoiseshell cat weaved and brushed against his bare calves.

Smartie had died six months ago.

He stooped to embed his hands in the familiar fur, massaging the shoulder and arching back of the purring fluff ball and a glance at the high-backed chair brought the previous evening's memory flooding back.

'I've missed you,' he said to the cat, and it mewed in reply. 'Just thought you should know that. I might not be able to save myself, but I'm giving you and your love-struck master half a chance.' The cabinet drawer revealed a fresh notebook and pencil and Michael wrote out a note, leaving it alongside a refilled bowl of cat biscuits.

Tell the vets that Smartie has a thyroid condition.

After a considerable search for his phone, which he concluded was now with his younger self, he turned to the PC for guidance and train timetables to Church Stretton. The cat joined in its own search for warming comfort on his lap, kneading his boxer shorts until it perched awkwardly across his thighs. Several password attempts later, the computer was accessed and the route was revealed. The seven-hour trip from Norwich, including platform waits, would make his rendezvous with destiny a tight run thing and he hurriedly dressed from a selection of hoodies and cargo trousers that had not been so deeply unfashionable at the time.

On the bathroom floor, he prised open the loose tile and raided the tin from the recess within, wondering whether a further note was necessary to appease his guilt.

'*I'm stealing from myself, you fool,*' he thought, dismissing the idea. '*It's your own money.*'

Accompanied by the breakfast radio, which confirmed the

date once and for all, he hastily tucked into a breakfast of waffles, peanut butter and chocolate spread like a man on death row eating his final, favourite meal. Unclipping the digital clock and timer from the cooker hood he turned, hand on the apartment door to see the cat stretching and clawing at the gauze curtains in the far bedroom. A sudden and repeated urge to rush in and prevent further damage subsided as the cat turned with a guilty but unrepentant meow.

'Live every day as if it's your last,' he said. 'Knock yourself out, you old thing. I guess I'll be seeing you, one way or the other.'

He closed the door and leapt down the stairs, enjoying the painless freedom of movement, and raced to the train station to make the first connection.

The garbled platform announcement obliterated the voice of the telephone operator.

'A reverse charge call to Marjorie Copes,' repeated Michael from within the ineffective soundproofing of the booth. '18 Houseman Avenue, Diss.'

Several prior attempts to call home had been unsuccessful following his parents' move in the spring, and the machine hungrily worked its way through his remaining change without remorse as he struggled to recall the previous number. The transfer at Birmingham New Street had afforded a brief opportunity to make one last contact with family, besides the note he had written, though several wrong numbers had left him thin on coins.

'One moment please,' said the faint voice on the line. 'Putting you through now.'

'Hello, Michael – are you all right?' came the comforting voice of his mother.

'Mum, I'm alright, I'm in between trains but I needed to call you.' At that moment, his rehearsed monologue vanished, and he opted for brevity and sincerity.

'I'm just calling to say I'll miss you and that I love you both.'

'What are you talking about?' replied Marjorie. 'We're seeing you on Sunday, aren't we? I'm looking forward to hearing all about this new girl of yours, isn't that where—'

The platform announcer revealed his approaching train and Michael cupped his ear.

'Mum, I haven't time. I just wanted to say I hope you won't be sad for me in a couple of years' time.'

'What are you going on about? You aren't eloping to Australia or something daft like that are you? – hang on, I'll get your father – he's down in the garage messing with his motorcycles—'

'No time,' said Michael, straining to hear her voice over the rattle of the tracks heralding the 14:03 to Shrewsbury. 'Just tell him I love him, and I'll see him on Sunday, okay?'

'You sound upset or nervous,' she said. 'Is it because of this girl?'

The train pulled alongside the platform. 'Yes, in a manner of speaking. I've got to go...'

'See you Sunday, but text me when you get back, okay?' Her parting words vanished with the sounding of the opening doors and the releasing hiss of breaking air as the metallic, sinuous snake seethed and readied itself for departure. Michael replaced the handset and rushed through the closing doors of a carriage and made his way, weeping and overcome into his final, indulgent, first-class seat.

The familiar streets of the Shropshire town were blanketed in fresh snow as Michael hastily crunched through the memorised route to the church. A glance at the kitchen timer clock revealed he was short on time, just as he had been three years prior. Out of breath but desperate to reach the appointed meeting place, he raced into the high street, almost colliding with someone with the same intent.

The identical intent.

The man rushed past and Michael caught sight of his Father's old leather bag, slung across the shoulders of his former self. Up ahead, the busy crossroads loomed and a jaywalker in a dark red pashmina and gown stepped out into the road, misjudging the distance between the traffic. Michael called out, too late, and watched with an eerie deja-vu as the colliding car sounded the horn and swerved, glancing the woman and sending her sprawling toward the opposite pavement. Michael rushed ahead even as his former self knelt in the slush at the side of the road to administer first aid for what would turn out to be a sprained hip and fractured wrist.

He heard himself offering words of comfort that he could not recall and milled at the outer edge of several bystanders, impotent and unsure how to offer assistance. The younger man reached for his phone and examined her wrist even as the woman raised her head, sudden grimaced, furrowed brow replaced by the composed and gentle countenance of the shade from the night before.

Michael suddenly recognised her, and she flashed her eyes warning him not to get involved. Lying on the floor amongst the crushed snow, her red dress and wrap billowed in the turbulent, traffic-side air in a likeness of her shadowy gown and gauze curtain accessory from the night of three years hence. She twitched her nose and jerked her head toward the distant church before resuming a contorted face, ridden by shock and pain.

Not wasting another moment, or the coincidence of the encounter, he jogged on, slipping and sliding his way to the churchyard.

'Be here, be here...' he said breathlessly as he flung open the creaking gate and followed the single line of footprints around the squat sandstone tower.

Brightly coloured houses lined the opposite side of the yard, but it was the bright pink of a cat-eared bobble hat on the figure huddled on the bench, sheltering from the chilly breeze, that answered his first question. Fliss looked up, a look of melancholia suddenly replaced by an overwhelmingly joyful, red-cheeked smile.

'You made it,' she said rising and shyly lowering her head to hug his heavily out-of-breath chest. 'I was just about to go...'

'You...you're really...here,' he panted, squeezing her. 'You came.'

She disentangled herself and stuck out her pierced tongue in a playful lie. 'None of the other guys I invited could be bothered.'

He stared into her bright blue eyes, lashes blinking rapidly with a connected sense of relief and nervous excitement.

'You're shorter than I imagined,' he said.

'We've only ever seen each other sitting down, you loon,' she replied, nudging into his side and inviting him to the thawed, mossy memorial bench. 'I don't have long and I need to explain.'

'Explain what?' he said, following her gaze to the tower, and its weather cock.

'I'd hoped to have more time to tell you, but I have to go away, and I just wanted to say that the past ten months with you have been the best time of my life.'

The feeling of euphoria was replaced by a sudden recollection of the shade's words:

You will be mortal and I will, by necessity, be forced to ensure no 'interference' occurs to affect the future.

'I can't change anything,' he mused.

'No,' she said, misunderstanding his reply and reaching out her mitten'd hand to clasp at his own. 'I wanted to tell you in person – my going away has nothing to do with you.'

'You're breaking up with me before we've even met?'

'I don't have any choice,' she said. 'It will take too long to explain, but you must understand that if I could stay, it would be with you.' She glanced over toward a smouldering bonfire against a low dry-stone wall. A capped and scarfed figure in a heavy black coat raked and lifted sodden leaves onto the smoking pyre.

'I've got a tale of my own to tell, but you wouldn't believe it. I just wanted to let you know that the memory of you has never once left my thoughts in the past three years.'

'Don't be silly,' she said leaning over to kiss his cheek. 'We've only known each other for less than a year.'

'Can't I come with you?' he said, blushing. 'Wherever or whatever it is, I'd just want to be with you.'

She retreated her hand to wipe her sodden eyes. 'I knew you'd say that, which is all I wanted to hear before I go.'

A distant clock tower chimed for five o'clock and she dragged him hurriedly to a field stile overlooking the rolling fields to a low range of hills crowned with wintry snow. The sun sneaked behind the tallest, boulder-strewn peak leaving a ribbon of pink and amber streaked across the canvas of approaching night.

'I have to go, but promise me you'll go up to Caradoc when I'm gone, remember me as I am now and try to live each day as though it were your last...'

She vaulted the stile, turned and grabbed his hooded top,

pulling him against her lips. The echo of the distant bell receded, and she released him, racing ahead through the virgin snow. Even as he gripped the sodden post to swing his leg across, she called back to the churchwarden from across the lower slope and vanished, leaving no further prints.

'I have my answer and I thank you for one more day...'

Michael scanned the ground, calling out and retracing his steps in an anxious search. A sudden breeze set the weather cock spinning, and he looked up with the sound of stiff metal joints squealing out against the cold and need for lubricating grease.

'She has her answer, and so do you,' said the church-warden coming to stand by his side, wood smoke sweetly cloying against the flowering sweet box and floral arrange-ments of the graves nearby.

A black-gloved hand held out a bunch of dried flowers, not neatly arranged but spent from several years of gentle fading. 'I kept these for you.'

Michael turned to look upon the face of the shade, all but hidden behind a black woollen muffler.

'How considerate, given the circumstances,' he said, taking them. 'I need more time. I don't have the answer to why she left.'

The shade lifted her hand, pointing with the rake in the leaf pile's direction. 'Follow and then you will be content.'

Michael followed the indicated and footprint-free path that led to recent internments. One, in particular, was freshly decorated, and he caught the words on the card even before he looked up at the engraving on the headstone.

My beautiful Fliss, how we miss you. Three years today, but forever in our thoughts. Mum and Dad.

Michael's mind reeled.

'She asked you for the same thing, one more day...'

The shade nodded. 'She wanted a single answer, and you put her mind at rest before she left; at least this time around. Do not worry for her sake, she led an unblemished life and this is a loose end I have found ponderous to bear these past three years.'

Michael lay down the flowers and spent a moment in all-consuming grief.

'I don't know whether you were right all along,' he said rising to his feet and wiping his eyes. 'About not knowing, I mean. I'm not stalling, but I have so many questions like what was it that—'

'And you will have an eternity of answers,' said the shade wrapping an arm around his shoulder. A gentle warmth permeated his body and lightened the approaching and inevitable question.

'Is it time to go?'

'Yes,' replied the shade, now transformed into a black, bejewelled and brocaded gown. 'All has been arranged in this time and in the time that is to come. We must hurry otherwise you will bump into your former self and that will be awkward.'

Michael nodded and followed the shade back to the bench.

'I'm ready, but you said that I would receive the greatest gift from this experience. If not more time or eternal life then what?'

'A new perspective,' said the shade, cupping her arm into his elbow and raising a tasselled ebony framed umbrella. 'A confirmation that you were right about certain things and wrong about others.'

Michael smiled. 'That trumps both of my suggestions, I guess.' He glanced down at the richly dressed chaperone.

'Nice frock for the occasion, by the way.'

The shade returned a joyful and bashful smile. 'A compliment to go with my first commendation – don't forget when you get across, will you?'

Michael patted and released her hand before mounting the stile.

'Crossing over from this life into the next via a gate,' he mused. 'How very prosaic.' In the field beyond, a distant figure with its back turned caught his attention.

'I hope you aren't going to leave my body out here so that walker will find me,' he said, straddling the wooden rail and taking a lingering look at the twinkling lights of the quaint little town.

'It's no walker,' replied the shade, fading as she removed her gloves. 'Not in the conventional sense. You should see the summit of Caer Caradoc on a clear winter's eve, it's truly stunning. Hurry now, your advocate is waiting.' She raised both little fingers to her mouth and blew a mighty wolf whistle to alert the woman in the field wearing a pink, cat-eared bobble hat.

'I told you I wasn't an angel,' said the shade with a wink. 'But I do love a happy ending.'

Fliss twisted round and raised a waving hand, beckoning him onward.

Michael's heart and feet leapt from the stile, into the field and eternity, leaving the late evening walkers that followed a brief moment later at a loss to explain the sudden disappearance of footprints that ceased halfway across the lower slope of the hill.

FLASH POWDER

My frost-bitten fingers flinched above the ruby glass shade of the oil lamp, absorbing the painful pin-pricking sensation of heat. The darkroom was the smallest space within our modest photographic studio in unfashionable Camden Town, and the January frost emanated from the cracks in the suspended floorboards like judgement day souls seeking the sympathy of heaven. The cold negated all notion of warmth and summer as I squinted at the developing series of figures taken against our painted background screen of Brighton Pier in the adjoining salon.

I stamped my feet, blowing on my hands, as the lone red safety lamp cast its flickering glow across the chemical bottles and hanging lines of drying collodion papers, fixing their human subjects in stinking camphor and silver-nitrate salts for eternity.

My head ached with the biting chill, but the job was done. Twelve photographic prints, from plate negatives taken that morning, revealed two melancholic Victorians, in mourning from a lifetime spent unhappily together, as well as the recent death of Queen Victoria. Claude had disappeared almost immediately upon their arrival, as he always did when there was real work to be done, and I could not single-handedly change the screen to a more sombre backdrop to match the misery of the elderly couple, intent on marking the occasion as though doing penance. He had made some pretence of popping out to photograph the demonstrations against the distant war with the Boers, hoping to sell the pictures that I would have to develop that evening, wasting our precious supplies for very little return. He lived for adventure, risk, and the vain hope the newspapers would acquire them at midnight to include in the morning editions over those of their own in-house photographers.

It was an expensive gamble, and it rarely paid off.

I rubbed my hands and refitted my scarf within my thick overcoat, designed for outdoor use. There was little money for even the most basic of necessities anymore, and barely enough to pay the debt collector that following day. Heating was so far down the list of priorities and comforts we could afford that it was almost dreamlike in its remembrance. It had become so bad with the cold that I resigned myself to another evening of toil versus the extreme likelihood of sharing bed and body heat again, upstairs with my snoring partner, just to escape freezing to death. One of us had to remain vigilant to thaw the pipes during the night with the oil lamp otherwise we would have no water in the morning. Not that washing in it was very appealing, but at least you could drink it and make the meagre tea and Bovril ration we allowed ourselves to survive on in between our erratic income.

What we wanted was trade and paying customers – what Camden Town needed was a miracle. The once lucrative business we had taken on a few years before had evaporated following the labour strikes and the sharp decline in disposable income, despite our skill and enterprise. Our portrait studio was now a luxury in a market of closing shops and hurried relocations by the middle-classes that we relied upon.

'Cheer up, Harry,' said Claude when I had brought up the subject that very morning. 'You worry too much. It's just a temporary slump. Wait till the spring – it'll pick up. We can snap the boaters on the Serpentine or down at Hampton Court lock and make a day of it, eh?'

Several springs and summers, snapping all manner of tourist launches and Thames' camping skiffs, had come and gone while the area slid further into dereliction and decay. Even the ridiculously predatory offer for the premises and our apartment upstairs, six months prior, seemed a tantalising once-in-a-lifetime offer to sell up and get out before we both lost everything. With winter's icy grip choking the profitability of the most essential business, I knew that even that opportunity was now out of reach; we were stuck with the studio, our predicament, and each other.

I blew out the lamp, and the room plunged into an all-consuming void, acrid with acetic acid. Pushing aside the heavy curtain, a precaution should anyone barge in unannounced and over-expose the valuable plates and papers within, I opened the door and entered the main salon, still set with images of the sunny seaside from the morning's sitting.

The bitter chill in the larger room numbed my fingers once more, and I caught sight of the rime on the inside of the glass now that the zenith of the sun's horizon-hugging travel was past. I could almost see the veil of ice emerging from the leaded frame edges like the imperfections in the tintype images that once were so popular with holidaymakers. The sun's wan morning gesture of meagre warmth would soon set behind the tall warehouse opposite, plunging the bay window display into deep shade. Not that it mattered; few souls walked abroad, choosing instead the comfort of their fellow man, or woman, and the fanned flames of fierce war protest in nearby Regent's Park. The only sounds outside came from the children and strays barking and skating along the frozen canal, oblivious and joyful in London's icy grip.

I opened the order book, put on my mittens to stop my fingertips from tingling, and scanned down the work-shy columns. The list held many outstanding debts to collect from premises I knew to be empty; a good number of cabinet cards for the penny-pinching postmaster whose portrait would adorn the visual print mounted on card stock; this morning's commission for six shillings; and several follow-up appointments for a widow intent on immortalising her beloved Pekingese until the dog remained still enough for the right picture to be taken, when she would then settle the escalating bill.

Claude and I had not followed our passion for photography and left our careers in journalism for this.

I snapped shut the book and watched my breath steam out through my muzzled scarf, desperate for a cigarette that neither of us could afford, so I breathed out in imitation, reliving the experience, and imagining the taste of the bitter tar as a condiment to the blandness of the fluid beef drink we would brew later on the small stove.

The painted backdrop of the sunny pier caught my attention. I had never been to Brighton, but I closed my eyes, desperate to imagine the sounds of the seagulls, beach hawkers, pipe organs and the warm sea lapping across the biscuit-brown sands.

The door to the studio flew open, setting the bell to dance like a dervish. I turned to see my current bedfellow and photographic cell mate cast aside our tripod and camera cases and unwrap the frost-rimmed comforter that mummified his pallid but hopeful face. I barely noticed the variation in temperature between the street and the inside of the shop as he kicked the door shut behind him.

'Big, angry protest in the park today, Harry,' he said, stamping his feet and sending out great clouds of visible breath from the exertion of the last snow-trampled mile.

'Did Lloyd George turn up?' I asked, hopeful that I might have a photograph of the politician to develop later. The newspapers would clamour for shots of the eloquent Welsh Wizard in the animated act of delivering an impassioned speech.

Claude shook his head. 'No sign. Probably the cold or he's been warned about setting things alight in the capital.' He slumped down into the cracked leather sitting chair, swathed in his overcoat. 'It's getting heated out there, and it won't be long before something sets them all off. Plenty of good orators egging the crowd on and there was a standoff with the police at one stage. It's going to turn nasty, and they're threatening to protest every Sunday until the government pulls the troops back from South Africa.'

'That's not likely to happen,' I said, looking down at the frost-speckled case. 'Did you get anything worthwhile – something we can sell?'

Claude shrugged. 'Got a few of the protesters trying to storm the barricades around the monument. It was a scrum, so there will be several spoiled plates, but there will be more chances to catch someone famous every week from now on.'

I winced at the idea of losing the valuable coated glass, and Claude spun the chair around to avoid the expression of injury on my face. He settled his hands behind his head, as though lounging in a striped deckchair, and basked in the imagined warmth of the seaside scene. 'Once picked a girl up in Brighton,' he said, closing his eyes and smiling mischievously, recalling some conquest in happier days. 'How was the sitting with the happy couple this morning?'

'Mr and Mrs Hawkings were as dull and awkward as always. The prints are drying up now,' I said, emptying the

case containing the wrapped glass plates, coated with collodion and sensitive to light. I had not imagined that anything
else could be colder than my fingers at that point and I
hurried over to the wall-mounted dresser lest they freeze
onto my wool-wrapped hands. 'Did you drum up any
business?'

Claude rose and returned to the present from his reverie
on the south coast. 'No,' he said despondently. 'It wasn't the
time or place.' He raised a hand to stifle my indignation and
growing anxiety. 'But I got these—'

He unbuttoned the top of his heavy coat and hunted for a
waxed brown paper bag evidently containing something
edible. I could smell the sweetness wafting from within and
my mouth began to water with the expectation of anything
solid that did not taste of beef extract. He retrieved his arm
and tossed me the bag.

I parted the creased paper and gazed into a treasure trove
of stale glazed buns.

'I traded a pretty baker's girl, and the remains of her
basket, for a photo on six by nine-inch card – she'll be picking
it up tomorrow. Not my type, but definitely yours.'

I stared into the prospect of a full stomach for the first
time in weeks while my head reviled the cost of the trade,
and my time, for a single image of a working girl. 'What do
you mean by that?' I said, closing the bag and returning his
impish grin with a raised eyebrow of my own.

'Cerebral, deep, educated – that sort of thing. Asked all
sorts of questions about photography; sounds like a keen
amateur.'

'And you gathered that just by taking her picture and
haggling over buns?' I said as Claude's grey face bloomed into
a bashful blush of colour. 'What you mean, Claude, is that
you asked her out, and she refused. That makes her my type?'

He plucked at his rakish moustache and winked. The

rogue had been rebuffed, and I took delight in the situation as one would when witnessing a rare eclipse of the sun. At that moment, I laughed, despite our hardships. Claude always knew how to charm an audience, me included, and I forgot our predicament and grabbed his shoulders. As he stood before me in the haphazard assortment of clothes, with necessity dominating over fashion, I spoke from the heart.

'You are incorrigible, but I don't know what I'd do without you,' I said, and to my surprise, he glanced around the spartan room, stared into my eyes without a hint of frippery, and answered in like kind.

'I'll get us out of this slump, Harry. I promise.'

I nodded, and we parted like magnets, poles apart, lest our bonhomie descended into greater unmanly shows of emotion and overwhelm us.

A child dragging a makeshift pallet sledge raced in front of the window, breaking the awkward silence, and I headed over to the stove, eager to light the dwindling supply of wood to boil water for the tea and Bovril. I twisted to watch Claude take off several layers of clothing, revealing his slender frame beneath his Sunday best, baggier than it once was. He bit into a suffocating mouthful of sugared bun.

'There's an auction tomorrow,' he mumbled, struggling to impart the information while fulfilling his appetite's desire for haste. 'Down at The Rooms; I might pop in and see what's afoot as well as gauge the mood. Some of those new-fangled Kodak Brownie cameras should be in, and I understand there are some American consignments in the catalogue, mostly vintage items. Some even from Mumler.'

I closed the cast-iron door, staring at the embryonic flame shivering into life through the murky glass of the stove. 'William Mumler?' I said. 'I thought he was jailed for fraud – phantom photography, wasn't it?'

'Acquitted,' said Claude. 'The prosecution couldn't prove

beyond doubt he'd fabricated the plates showing the images of spirits behind the subjects in his portraits.'

'His shot of Abraham Lincoln's widow with her old man's ghost behind caused quite a stir, didn't it?' I said, collecting the chipped cups and saucers, eager to become acquainted with the buns for myself.

Claude nodded, swallowing a final mouthful. He wiped his hands down the overcoat sprawled over the back of the sitting chair.

'The fraud made a lot of money tapping into the zeitgeist and spiritualism resulting from the civil war before he had his hand slapped by some sceptical journalist. He always protested his innocence, blaming something in the flash powder he'd bought from a magician in Cairo, but he never recovered his reputation afterwards. Odd that only us in the industry would have heard of him outside of the Americas.'

'Dangerous business, that,' I said. 'Messing with the unknown and people's grief during a time of war. I'm glad it never caught on over here. Come to think of it, I can't recall anyone being foolish enough to try it.'

I reached into the bag and retrieved a handful of sticky dough. 'Anyway, it's a moot point. We can't afford auctions, so why waste your time going?'

After a short while, the cast-iron kettle began to sing, and we huddled around the stove, eager to soak in the warmth soon to be extinguished.

Claude stared at the boiling kettle and studied the condensing cloud of steam rising to settle on the ceiling. 'It's a shame we don't have the money; Mumler's equipment was high quality by all accounts, if a little antiquated. Pity to see it sold for a song.'

We divided the remaining buns and blew onto our boiling cups of broth overlooking the backdrop screen of Brighton Pier. Claude spoke seldom, and I wondered at his unusually thoughtful face until we lit the few lamps in the studio and put on our coats for the oncoming bitter night.

After an hour of reading a penny dreadful that Claude had found on a park bench, I retired to the darkroom and lit the Bishop and Sons ruby lamp once more, hearing my companion clomp his way up the stairs to our frigid living room and uninviting beds.

Removing the dried prints from the line, I warmed the trays of laden salts and began the chemical process to bring images from Claude's plates to life. I fixed the negative and shone the filtered light through onto our dwindling supply of treated papers, waiting for the images to be transferred.

There was always a rush of excitement during the magical transformation about to take place, since my first encounter as a child obsessed with the secrets and scents of what lay beyond the curtains of a darkroom. I knew then that my life would revolve around the world of print and pictures, even if Claude was much the better photographer. He had no aptitude in chemistry or desire to learn, and so our roles developed, just like our images, with each one complimenting the other.

I stacked several spoiled and blurred dry gelatine plates against a library of similar spent glass until crowd-filled scenes, uninteresting but well-composed, depicted in vision what Claude had earlier recounted of the protests in the park. I yawned and rubbed my eyes as I reached over to uncover the final plate from its dark wooden slide.

Within the developing tray appeared the negative outline of a young woman carrying a large basket between the folds of her fine dress. Long-sleeved and accented with a sash, the hourglass silhouette could not be disguised even by the heavy woollen shawl that covered much of her shoulders. Against a backdrop of policemen and placards, her skirt brushed the pamphlet-strewn pavement, dusted with snow, while her neckline was supported by a high-boned collar. I watched and waited for the face to be revealed, always the last to be realised.

The self-assured smile appeared first, warm against the bitter cold, and in stark contrast to the dour expressions of the mournful Mr and Mrs Hawkings suspended on the line nearby. Her bright hair, arranged with many pins, showed skill and patience, as though dressing for a significant event. She was beautiful, that was certain, but not what I had expected from a baker's girl at a protest march. I was very glad that she was not Claude's type, for her sake.

It was the loss of feeling in my fingers that tore me from the long and happy gaze and hastened the rest of my work for the following hour. I bid goodnight to the young woman, now positively developed, as I blew out the lamp and fumbled my way up the stairs to the deathly dark of my damp room and a fitful night's sleep, back to back with my bundled and foetal-positioned companion.

Monday dawned with the false pinkish promise of warmth. A heavy fist thumped against the door to the street, and I turned to catch the hulk of the debt collector silhouetted against the vaguest hint of sunrise. I put away the lamp and my attempts to warm up the water pipe and admitted the man. Never was such an individual more suited to his trade. Heavily whiskered and striking the bell above the door with his dark felt-capped head, he lumbered in clasping a large pommel-headed cane. I had never known Mr Sym to limp, struggle or move in need of support, and he did not strike me as a man with any fancies towards fashion. My thoughts shifted to those who could not pay and the damage to property and bone that such an appliance might inflict. A massively built hound, well-fed but scarred and showing signs of abuse, urinated against the door frame and strutted in alongside his brutish master.

'Eight pounds, six shillings,' said Sym, snorting back the vestiges of influenza – possibly the only thing that could lay the man down – and reached inside his breast pocket for a thick pocketbook and pencil stub. 'Or goods up to the value.' He scanned the room pessimistically.

I nodded and unlocked the door to the darkroom while he rudely slumped into the sitting chair and kicked out at the dog, which was eager to join him. My heart raced as I clattered and rattled my way around the jars on the shelf, looking for the rusted tin of Cadbury's cocoa essence in the gloom. Prising open the lid, I stuck my nose into the empty memory of hot chocolate to calm my nerves, allowing myself only the briefest of remembrances before the caustic-smelling compounds brought me back to the task at hand. I emptied the notes and coins into my shaking palm.

We were short.

I counted several times, dropping some coins, and trembled with the realisation that a pound note and eight shillings were missing. A thump on the floorboards above suggested Claude was awake, as were my suspicions about a late return home the previous week from my philandering counterpart.

'Are you coming out,' said Sym, above the low growl of the dog, 'or am I coming in?'

I slammed down the tin and reversed into the studio, tipping the notes and coins into his outstretched and calloused palm. He knew instinctively there was a complication, whether by the weight or from the anxious look on my face. Only the dog appeared optimistic about the situation, and I wondered if it was not only the cane that could be employed as an encouragement to settle a debt.

'How much outstanding?' he said, staring poker-faced at the Brighton scene.

'One pound, eight shillings,' I said, listening above for any sign of support. The floorboards above remained quiet, and I silently cursed the coward lurking above. 'I can pay after Thursday's—'

Sym rose swiftly for such a large man, encumbered by many clothes, and snatched at my timing stopwatch that draped over the focussing knob of the studio camera.

'What's this worth?' he said, roughly winding the dial to check its operation.

'It's worth more than what we owe, but I need it to time the exposures, especially in this dim light—'

He pocketed the watch to my alarm, and I foolishly grabbed his arm. The dog growled, baring its yellow teeth as Sym held up his cane in warning.

'You can buy it back on Thursday,' he whispered. 'If you have the remaining money, plus interest.'

I panicked. 'Could I take your photo instead – perhaps you and your good lady?' Part of me died with the thought of it and the ridiculous notion that a man such as Sym would agree to such a trade.

'She's dead,' he muttered, with only the faintest hint of emotion rippling through his creased forehead. He shifted, and I caught the slightest glimpse of a leather chain around his collar as he held up his hand to finger the tiny wooden crucifix attached to it.

My survival instincts overwhelmed the rational sensibilities of my thinking, and I grabbed a faded photograph of old Mrs Partridge and the Pekingese from the display in the window. 'Perhaps you and the dog, then?'

This time it was Sym that growled while the dog looked insulted by the suggestion and the comparison with the pampered pet in the portrait. His large hands thrust out the pencil and pocketbook and stabbed a finger where to sign.

'Thursday then,' I replied, as he snatched back the tools of his trade and yanked at the door. The dog sniffed at the base of my trousers while I remained rigid in the frigid blast of street air; I froze at the prospect of what it might do if I startled it. A gruff call from the street saved me from whatever it had been planning, and the creature raced out to continue its rough work alongside his brutal master.

'You can come down, now,' I called to the ceiling, trying to take long calming breaths to curb the panic in my chest. 'He's gone, and you have some explaining to do.'

Claude squeaked across the floor above and descended the stairs in a rough state of dress.

'I hope you told him where to go—'

'He took the timing watch,' I said. 'We can't accurately time the exposures in this godforsaken light now, you fool.'

Claude avoided any mention of the missing expenses arrears and tried to put a positive spin on matters as he always did when backed into a corner.

'We don't really need it,' he said, rubbing his hands up and down his arms to generate warmth. 'I can count pretty accurately—'

He spun around and raced back up the stairs to safety as a shadow appeared through the frosted glass of the studio door and tried several times to budge open the swollen wood. I turned, fearing some return visit from Sym, but it was the young woman from the photograph who fell through, setting off the bell once again in a wildly protesting peal.

'Sorry to call so early,' she said, composing herself from the exertion of entry, 'but I saw the light on, and I was passing on my way to work.'

I stood, recovering from the unexpected and unprepared

encounter, and opened my mouth, waiting for words to arrive from my heaving chest. Here she was, the woman from the protest, the girl in the photograph. She was dressed in more informal attire, working clothes suited for the dreadful weather, but her smile and gentle features glowed in dimensions impossible to witness from the sepia image, frozen in time and hanging in the darkroom. She clutched at a journal in one hand and pointed to the tripod and field camera stacked against the Punch and Judy tent on the backdrop of Brighton beach.

'If it's not too soon, I'd like to collect the photograph that your colleague took in the park yesterday.' She mistook my inability to speak as indignation and peered back at the open door and the empty street. 'I can come back—'

I raced over to close the door, my mind and body released back to useful purpose.

'No, not at all,' I said, welcoming her in. 'It's all ready for you, but I wondered, Miss—?'

'White.' The young woman brightened with the news.

'Miss White,' I continued, 'I wondered what frame you might require, glass mounted or—?'

'No need,' she said, twisting and looking around at the meagre studio equipment and fidgeting with the journal, as though looking for an opportunity to ask something else. My heart sank as I wondered if she had changed her mind about the coward upstairs, taking him for an honourable and wealthy suitor.

The bell settled and Claude's best flannel trousers emerged at the top of the stairs. 'I hope you told them to push off?'

I gritted my teeth as he descended and realised his faux pas. To my surprise, it was Miss White that blushed first, setting off my cheeks in chivalric response.

'Oh, please forgive me,' blathered Claude, instinctively

smoothing back his hair. 'I assumed you were the debt collector.'

I rolled my eyes at my hapless companion. Two bumbling fools in debt was just the image I had wished to promote to a potential new customer.

I tried to recover from the situation, miserably. 'Thank you for the buns, yesterday.'

She smiled and replied as I tried to rescue my wits. 'Did you like the maids of honour, too? They are one of our specialities or were till folk turned to the cheaper buns.'

I glanced over at Claude's guilty face. He fingered his mouth and moustache as though unconsciously wiping away the custard cream of the delicate pastries never destined to make it back to Camden Town yesterday.

'Won't you take a seat and I'll get your photograph,' I said to our guest, giving my companion a hurtful look. I backed towards the darkroom, and she peered over my shoulder with interest. I felt her gaze linger as I brushed past the open blackout curtain and unclipped the print from the line.

She called out to me, ignoring Claude, able to impart what she had come to the studio for now that I was not standing in front of her. 'I hope you don't mind, but I have a huge interest in photography and was wondering if you might be able to impart some of your experience. I can't pay you anything just at the moment; Father's bakery isn't doing so well in the area with all the shutdowns.'

I waited in the room, eager to have her continue, fearful that my early return might cause her nervous silence to manifest again. 'I sympathise,' I said, collecting the other images. 'We've noticed quite a slump, too. Is that why you were selling in the park yesterday?'

'Not exactly. I did want to protest, but my father's old-fashioned about single young women going out unattended in large groups, so I feigned a commercial reason to clear some of Saturday's unsold stock. I keep the books for the business, but I'm not proud or above my station when there's honest money to be made. Father doesn't share any passion for anything other than baking and doesn't share my interest in politics, or photography.'

I retreated to the studio to find Claude had lit the stove. I did not protest – how could I in front of a customer?

'What do you know already?' I said, handing her the photograph. Her eyes widened with delight as she tapped her feet on the dusty wooden floor like small mallets. She put down the print and opened her journal, sifting through several loose papers containing transcribed text, drawings, and lists.

'I'm familiar with all the chemical reactions, albumen prints, collodion processes, silvering of frames as well as aperture stops and focal ratios. With enough savings, I hope for my own rolled film camera this year; I even bought a timing watch, look—'

She hunted in her skirt pocket and held out a modest second-hand watch in evidence. Claude lowered his cup in surprise and spat out a mouthful of tepid water, heated from the warming kettle on the stove.

'You know more than Harry does, then!'

I frowned back, annoyed by his assertion but intrigued that a bookkeeping baker's daughter should remind me of my old enthusiasm and passion. 'Thank you, Claude. I'm not sure what else I could teach you, Miss White—'

'It's Evelyn, Harry,' she said, and I nodded, catching my colleague's smirk as he made the unscheduled morning tea. 'Its practical application and experience I'm looking for. There are only so many books on the subject at the library in the British Museum and Father is becoming suspicious. He doesn't believe that photography is a viable business, or suitable for a woman of my age, but I disagree.'

'So do I,' I blurted, without a plan to follow the awkward silence.

She glanced over the studio, and her eyes avoided the sparse and poor state of our furnishings in favour of the mechanical treasures and trinkets primed for taking portraits. Evelyn looked longingly at the studio camera, burgundy-bellowed and outlined in brass and mahogany. 'May I?' she said, rising.

I nodded and watched as she approached the modified, but redoubtable, Sanderson swing front camera, as though in the presence of a holy relic.

Claude nudged into my back and handed me a cup of weak, warm tea. 'Definitely your type,' he whispered.

I nudged back, observing as she gingerly inspected the lens.

'You might like our wind-up model bird,' said Claude. 'It's next to the head and armrest stands. We use it to distract younger sitters, hence the expression "watch the birdie".'

Evelyn ignored the opportunity and stood transfixed at the rear of the camera, one hand on the hood. 'In exchange for your time, I may be able to bring you some end-of-day loaves or buns, if you maintain I have no connection with you, should my father discover my little secret.'

'That would be fine,' said Claude, speaking from his stomach and not from his head. 'Harry would be delighted to teach you. Best in the business, apart from me, of course.' He smiled, and Evelyn returned one of her own.

'Yes, I know,' she said, returning to her journal and fishing out a photograph. 'Harry took a photo with my friend Annabelle down on the river at Hampton Court last summer. It's what sparked my interest.'

She handed me the familiar scene of boaters congregating, en masse, in their narrow skiffs and Sunday best, all ready to ride the rising water between the lock gates to access the upper reaches of the Thames.

Claude looked over my shoulder. 'Sure it wasn't me?' he said. 'Looks too good a shot for old Harry here.'

Evelyn held on to the photo as though it was precious in her memory. 'No, it was you,' she said, gazing up into my unprepared face. 'You were wearing a pale blue linen shirt with rolled sleeves in the heat.'

I confess I had no memory of the encounter but was very glad that she had remembered.

'And is that your friend, there?' asked Claude, pointing in hope towards the companion seated beside her in the middle of the image.

She snatched back the print and returned it to a ribbon-marked section of the journal. 'She's my chaperone and confidant, so that Father does not discover my trips to the library, or to here if you have the time and inclination. I'm free on Tuesday and Thursday afternoons?'

Evelyn turned to sift through the pile of prints.

I whispered over my shoulder to goad my friend's disappointment regarding Evelyn's companion. 'She's not your type, either.'

'Harry is the real genius behind the scenes,' said Claude, jabbing me in the back. 'The alchemist of Camden Town – isn't that what they call you?'

'I'm sure we might be able to find time,' I said, rubbing my lower spine.

'These are really rather good,' she said, turning over the prints and making comments. She stopped and wrinkled her nose at the image of the Hawkings couple, snapped the previous day. I thought, perhaps, her sudden sourness was in response to the misery emanating from their faces.

'Shame about these,' she said, handing the batch over. 'Looks like an artefact on the lens?'

Claude and I crowded round to look at the blurred mark, hovering above the woman's left shoulder. I flicked through the eleven copies, each with a similar face-like impression.

I slammed the pack onto the table and carefully examined the glass of the camera lens, looking for a thumbprint or mark to explain the spoiled photographs. The crystal shone back clear and clean, and I straightened, placing my head in my hands. 'It's on the plate, whatever it is,' I said, lifting my face to see the penny drop on Claude's. 'We just lost a day's work and any chance of getting paid by Mr and Mrs Hawkings.'

'They can't be that bad, surely?' he said, picking through each of them. 'Looks like that steam from the kettle yesterday, or maybe someone's breath in this blasted cold?'

Evelyn nodded. 'I think you're right, on both counts. It looks like a face though, doesn't it?'

I shook my head. 'I lit the lamp beneath the lens, trying to keep it warm enough from the condensation in my breath, and theirs; it must have been that.'

Evelyn gave me a consoling squeeze on the arm. 'Even the alchemist of Camden Town can't control the weather. They have a certain phantasmagorical charm, though.'

Claude puckered his lips, trying to understand or even repeat the unfamiliar word.

'Something illusionary, deceptive, an optical illusion,' I offered, and she smiled as though not expecting either of us to comprehend. 'Almost looks like a ghost.'

Claude twirled his moustache as though formulating an idea.

Evelyn collected her journal and print and made her way to the door. 'Until tomorrow afternoon, then?'

I raced over to ease the stubborn wood and nodded, watching her as she departed to the end of the empty street.

She glanced back only once, just as the corner took her out of sight.

Fully expecting an immature jibe or two about the whole affair, I was surprised to see Claude sweep up several of the spoiled prints, pocket the spare key, don his hat and best coat, and pick up the tripod and cases.

'Where are you going?' I said as he sidled out of the door and down the slippery step.

'To fulfil that promise I made to you last night,' he said, pausing before I closed the door behind him. From beyond the glass, I caught his muffled voice.

'Don't get too cosy with her just yet, she's just what we need. Don't wait up for me, I'm going to swing by my aunt's later on and might be several days.'

His shadow flitted past the bay window, leaving me speechless, but not witless. I wondered where he was heading to first and with no primed plates in the case he had taken. I returned to the stove, desperate to warm my hands, and waited for him to realise his error, hopefully after some considerable time to satisfy my need for a suitable atonement for the missing cakes and the missing money.

True to his word, he did not return that day.

Or the next.

———

True to her word, Evelyn arrived the following afternoon laden with the previous day's surplus from the bakery. I'd made a special effort trying to clean and spruce up the studio, not for any schoolboy attempts at wooing her, mark you, but more out of a desire to provide the best learning environment for someone who had shown a real interest, and who had re-ignited my memories and desires for a life behind the lens.

I had pawned the last of my personal items to provide a

few home comforts against the cold. There was fuel and food for at least a week, a small pouch of pipe tobacco, and enough paint to touch up the backdrops and fix the sliding rail to enable one person to change the desired scene. My personal favourite was a classical scene, painted decades before, that showed a distant view of sun-drenched Calabria through a tromp l'oeil trellis foregrounded by olive jars stuffed with spilling pelargoniums. The Italian scene brimmed with colour, certainly purchased from a travelling theatre troupe in the distant past, and I praised the artist for lifting my spirits in the continued absence of Claude.

I was not unduly concerned, and only briefly entertained the notion that the rogue had run off and left our partnership for the comfort of his wealthy aunt. I found it odd that he would choose to spend time with the deeply religious widow as I fathomed, from hints and riddles during our private conversations, that they were estranged. An accident or calamity was, I knew, unlikely; Claude could talk or wriggle his way out of any unpleasantness.

'Like this?' said Evelyn, swinging the ground glass focussing sheet outwards and sliding the prepared boxed plate into the back of the camera. It was already spoiled with a half-exposed image of a soldier, taken last October before he left for the war, but I could not yet afford the additional materials, or time, to prepare empty plates destined for instruction.

'Perfect,' I said, holding up a palm-sized ocular lens, 'though we sometimes use this to sharpen up the focus before we load the plates.'

'I already checked,' she said, beaming like a star pupil. 'While you were staring out into the street. You're worried about Claude, aren't you?'

I sighed, checked the plate was loaded correctly and sat back down in the portrait chair, leaning back into the headrest to position myself in the correct spot for focus. 'Yes and no,' I said, indicating for her to remove the covering slide, exposing the light-sensitive glass to the blackness of its own miniature darkroom within the camera. 'I'm more concerned about when he shows up and tries to explain the madcap scheme he's likely got us into. Once he has his mind set on something, it's impossible to divert him from it and it usually works out to be expensive.'

Evelyn smiled, and I encouraged her to ready her stop-watch and prepare for the most dangerous part of the proceedings.

Instinctively, and without fear, she grasped and held up the T-shaped flash lamp, connecting the magnesium strip lying within its zinc tray to the lead battery at the camera stand's feet.

'If you are sure about this—'

'Yes,' she said, smoothing back several wayward wisps of silver-blonde hair. 'It's just the speed at which everything happens – the lens cover, the button on the flash lamp, checking the watch, and then replacing the cap – I hope I get it in the right order.'

'You will,' I said, 'but you only have two seconds from the removal of the cap until its replacement; the clockwork shutter is broken, which is why we have to do things the old-fashioned way. Just keep the lamp away from your head and clothing.'

She nodded, and I counted down. There was barely a tremor in her outstretched hand, despite my readiness to put out any fire from the pyrotechnics that would momentarily illuminate my face, blinding me for several moments in the gloom of the late afternoon.

The count was complete, and I saw her remove the lens cover. The faintest of clicks set off the magnesium charge, and I smiled through the shock-wave of heat and brilliance until my eyes returned to see the lens cap reinstated and the developing silhouette of Evelyn, triumphant in her first professional photograph. She clapped her hands in glee, put down the smouldering bar, and made a note in her journal.

We developed a genuine bond, and the photographs, within the darkroom. Talking in hushed whispers in the rich glow of the safety lamp, I determined she was an attentive pupil, and she asked many questions, eager to discover a lifetime of my secrets. I almost rued the divulging of information, lest she learned all in a brief space of time, and never returned.

Return she did, and I was glad of the company. She even assisted with the sole customer of the day, and I anxiously allowed her to take the lead once I had double-checked everything was in order. Mrs Partridge returned with the heavily breathless Horace, a Pekingese whose advanced years were only being supported by the suffrage of the elderly spinster. They sat for another attempt at a perfect image, and I reminded the woman that her bill urgently needed settlement.

'Once I have the perfect photograph that you promised,' she said, lifting the wheezing animal onto the footstool. I snapped the order book shut in a defiant and ultimately fruitless attempt at displaying my indignation. It had been Claude that had offered the no-quibble guarantee. I could only see one way to keep the dog, and its incessant lolling tongue, from moving during the exposure and it included a trip to the taxidermist.

Following a focus check, Evelyn opened the paper bag containing some of the sweet baked treats brought to offset the costs of her clandestine education. She scooped out the central innards from one of the maids of honour cakes and passed it briefly beneath the dog's flattened nose. The dog ceased its movement, paralysed by the potential for custard.

How Evelyn took the shot while maintaining the integrity of the sticky forefinger I could not fathom. The flash triggered, and the dog remained stationary, whining for payment.

The picture was perfect, and Mrs Partridge – who insisted on waiting while we developed the sharp and steady photograph, and paid the outstanding debt of three pounds and six shillings – allowed me the opportunity to be bold.

'I was going to scout a few of Claude's haunts on Sunday,' I said over my shoulder, opening the door for Mrs Partridge and the arm-clutched Horace. I turned the closed sign to the chilly street. 'Perhaps I might meet you in the park later?'

Evelyn looked naively back. 'Didn't you say Claude took the field camera?'

I teetered on the edge of retreat, gambling on several half-crowns in my hand, skimmed from the transaction and in compensation for a lifetime of Claude's misdemeanours.

'Actually, I thought I might buy the contents of your basket, in advance, allowing you the freedom to join me and watch the speakers. We could give them away to some of the less fortunate?'

Her face softened as I offered the coins in my unsteady hand, and I watched nervously for the penny to drop regarding my intentions. She hesitated, pinching her brow, and looked into my reddening cheeks before accepting the money. Her gaze relaxed and turned to the floor.

'We could give them out while we search for Claude, on Sunday morning after church?' she said, fidgeting with the pleats of her dress. 'I'd have to bring Annabelle along in the afternoon, just to avoid any suspicion—'

I nodded like a child eagerly agreeing to a game of chase with the promise of a bagful of chocolate buttons to follow.

She collected her coat and belongings, and I escorted her to the end of the street and into the care of her confidant. I watched as they disappeared in the freezing fog, whispering and teasing with talk of Sunday and an interesting male escort for the day.

I felt a pang of guilt, tempered by the rush of romantic excitement, as I closed the door behind me. For a moment, I had prayed Claude would not return prior to my walking out with Evelyn.

In this, my wish was granted by the slimmest of margins.

Sunday appeared sullen, sleet-squalled, and sodden. We strolled, sometimes arm in arm, when the slippery pavement demanded it, scouting for signs or news of my errant partner. I handed out the left-over bread and buns to a makeshift army hostel, close to the home of Claude's occasional amoureuse, Constance, but the woman had not set eyes or hands on him for over two weeks.

Several informationally unprofitable acquaintances later, we paused and warmed ourselves around a brazier, shelling chestnuts from an agreeable vendor in Regent's Park, waiting for Annabelle to arrive. The seller purchased the basket and traded the sweet treats, leaving both my hands free to settle into my snack-heated pockets. To my delight, I encountered one of Evelyn's already within, playfully tickling my numb fingers before she stole a cracked, fragrant nut, and protested with a feigned expression of injustice; she had munched through her own generous supply.

It was past noon when the crowds began to swell, bringing with them our chaperone and one other. Annabelle had obviously seized the opportunity for her own subterfuge and introduced the shy, young, blonde-haired man imprisoned in her locked arm. We watched the skaters on the boating lake and revelled in each other's company for over an hour before substantial numbers of protesters, police, and guards from the nearby garrison headed across Prince Albert Road to the slopes of Primrose Hill.

A swell of expectant humanity, at either end of the polit- ical and moral spectrum, migrated towards the speakers, looking for answers, and insights, while some of them were thirsty for trouble. Evelyn stood and listened as I kept guard among the shoving and pushing of those impatient to reach the front for the glimpse or words of an important figure. Several notable and erudite orators stepped forth to rally one crowd and enrage another before a minor scuffle broke out and the mounted soldiers charged the two sides apart. I urged my companions back following the loud retort of a firework, set off dangerously close to the horses. The animals reared as the men fought to control the beasts, leaving the vacant space for the police to rush in and occupy the makeshift no man's land.

The mood was ripe for ignition. Tempers, tinder-dry and tense, turned and my male companion and I hurried the ladies down towards the park and into the outstretched hand of a young boy, eager to press the leaflet from the stack under his armpit into my surprised free palm. I grabbed at it, and he made off, followed by several others, to distribute their propaganda.

Or so I thought.

I peered down onto the designed and flowing text, catching my surname, and Claude's, prominently at the top of an advertisement.

'What is it?' asked Evelyn as she turned, confused by my sudden halt.

I passed her the pamphlet, wide-eyed and unable to speak.

Spirit Photography

Dunnett and Fielding of Camden Bridge

Startling wonders and mysterious movements are produced by invisible agencies caught on film from the ether and fixed for eternity by the alchemist of Camden Town

A loved one, child or missing person returned and encapsulated from the inexplicable dark using equipment and reactive processes handed down from ages past

Commune and capture (with frame) ... £1 18s 6d

Standard portrait (with frame & absence of spiritual interference) ... 18s 4d

Cartes de Visite (portrait & ten cards) ... 8s

A visitation or apport is not guaranteed, but who knows what might develop?

Endorsed by the Pembridge and Stafferton Spiritual Society

Patron Mrs Esther Buchanan-Fielding, President of the aforementioned

Grand opening Monday 20th January.

'I don't understand,' said Evelyn, handing back the leaflet. 'What does it mean?'

I shook my head and stared down at the district wherein lay my ruin. 'It means Claude's back, and he's lost his mind.'

We bid a swift goodbye to Annabelle and her new beau and hurried the mile to the studio to find it a hive of activity, workmen, and transformation. The sign above the bay window now declared our surnames in flourishing style, rather than the preceding and practical 'Portraiture and Photography' that I had bid farewell to that morning. The door glistened with fresh gloss paint as I forced my way past errand boys carrying boxes in and out of the reconstructed studio.

How Claude had created such a change of the interior, in such a limited space of time, was miraculous and I panicked with the numbers of people engaged in the final preparations, and the ruinous cost of their recruitment. Barely anything familiar remained, save the backdrop and the camera, and from behind the mountain of boxes I saw the new dark leather sitting chairs glinting in the late-afternoon light from the incandescent mantles of the gas lamps, faced with elegant hand-blown turquoise glass. Newly installed luxuriant drapes ran on a circular rail to encompass and create a private area, leaving a row of velvet cushioned seats next to the fireplace, now roaring with purpose and seasoned oak.

I had left behind a photographic studio and returned to an opium den.

I turned and confronted a broad counter, obscuring the stove and stairs, that took several capable men to budge and nudge into position. Claude emerged from behind the black polished ebony of a sloping accountant's desk and directed the ultimate positioning of the furniture and fittings like a crazed and flamboyant ringmaster.

'Hello! Finally turned up now we've practically finished, eh? Told you I'd be back.'

Claude ushered the surviving workmen and errand boys from the shop, handing out several five-pound notes to the foreman to administer at the Wheatsheaf pub to his entourage of thirsty comrades. He gently closed the door, now much corrected by recent carpentry, with a reassuring click.

'What have you done?' I said, running my fingers through my clammy hair to feel the sweat from the blazing fire and the sickness swelling inside my stomach. 'We'll end up in jail or—'

Claude held up his hands to prevent my concern. 'I made a promise to you, Harry, and I intend to keep it. Sit down, both of you, and I'll explain.'

I strode over to the darkroom, fearing the only private space I had in the world had been defiled. I drew the curtain to see everything in its place, apart from several boxes; it seemed sacrilege had been fortunately interrupted by our arrival.

'I have touched nothing,' he said, offering to take Evelyn's coat. 'Will you calm down and let me explain.'

'Where have you been? Harry and I have been worried about you.'

'I've been to see my aunt, as well as a few customers connected with the spiritual church she frequents. Did you realise the Hawkings are members?' Claude opened a box and withdrew a bottle of brandy and several crystal glasses. 'I was saving this for tomorrow's opening, but it would appear you might need some of it now.'

I removed my coat, holding up the pamphlet illustrating Claude's hare-brained scheme. 'Is this what you plan to do?' I asked, on the verge of striking him or breaking down into a fearful state. 'Messing with nonsense and turning us into fools.'

'Rich fools,' he said, handing me a glass and retrieving a new accounts book. I opened the page detailing the days ahead and saw a mostly full order list with names, times, and estimation of costs. Flipping through the pages I saw column after column of orders for portraits and cards, occasionally with a note describing an individual. Against these particular customers was circled the higher price of one pound, eight shillings and sixpence.

'What are these?' asked Evelyn over my shoulder, curious from a professional point of view.

'Those are the patrons I've been able to research,' he said, winking. 'Members of Aunt's spiritual church who've lost wives, husbands or children. It's those we will target first, spread the word etcetera, etcetera. Not too many to arouse suspicion, just the occasional one to spark sufficient interest.' He followed my gaze around the transformed salon. 'Needed to spruce up the place a bit, some of these church folks are particular, not to mention well off. I needed to act quickly – I hope you don't mind?'

I passed the book to Evelyn who flicked through the calendared pages until the columns and rows within became broken with empty spaces. She tapped a finger against the date at the top of a distant page. 'Looks like someone has been busy – you've got work until the middle of March, if that is what you call it.'

'Where did you get the money?' I asked, looking down into the amber liquid in the glass, fearing to drink from something we could never afford.

'Aunt Esther is not a well woman and has agreed, once she examined the picture of the Hawkings and the mysterious miasma above their heads, to advance my inheritance.'

'But that was steam,' I said. 'She's not stupid.'

Claude emptied his glass and searched in his pocket for several coins. 'No, she's still quite bright, but she knows she isn't long for this world and spiritualism offers its followers hope. She's prominent in several churches and has influence far above our station. The Hawkings coughed up instantly when they saw the prints. When word got out, I kind of got carried away.'

Claude handed me the shillings with a repentant look. 'It's all there, Harry. There was a meeting of their spiritual society, and I had my back to the wall trying to remain vague about the whole thing, pretending I hadn't a clue what they were suggesting it could be.'

'People see what they want to see. It's not right, Claude, not to mention illegal.'

'Ah, that's where you're wrong,' he said, stacking the coins on the bureau and returning to the pamphlet. 'Aunt Esther's solicitor has been over the wording to ensure there is no liability or misinformation; we don't say they are ghosts, merely that there may be something inexplicable in the images taken with Mumler's equipment.' He pointed to several larger boxes.

'You went to that auction?'

Claude strode over and lifted out an antique camera and several smaller items. 'Come and look at the quality of this – there's a Petzval lens with its own clockwork shutter—'

'What about the field camera and slide case?' said Evelyn, looking into the other boxes with interest.

'Had to sell it at the auction to get this stuff. I didn't see my benefactor until that evening.' His face softened, and he stuck his hands into his pockets. 'You can relax, Harry. I haven't borrowed the money from Sym or anyone else; the risk is all mine, but I want you to be part of it – both of you. I'll do the spirit portraits if it makes you feel uncomfortable, but I need the alchemist of Camden Town to process the plates.'

'Everyone can see through the double-exposure ruse,' I said, shaking my head. 'Even the most fervent religious nut.'

'I've thought about that,' he replied. 'We superimpose one of your plates in front of the true slide so it is shooting through a pre-existing image; there's more than enough room without changing the focus point. That way, if some idiot journalist or sceptic gives us a plate of their own, it will return with the photograph captured within it. All you have to do is a slight bit of blurring or tinkering for the customers I have circled in the book, and everyone's happy. You've got a score of plates showing men, women, children, not to mention that bloody dog.' He leaned forwards as though worried that someone would overhear.

'You've also got soldiers and sailors.'

'You want me to be a party to someone's grief, especially in this uncertain time when men are getting killed in distant lands,' I said, looking over at Evelyn's sympathetic face.

'I want you to be part of their comfort, their consolation, and their desire to move on. They already speak to them in seances, and you don't believe in that tripe, do you? I figure we ask Evelyn here to join us; we need a model for some preliminary trials and prints for the window as well as coping with the demand. We can't deal with everything if I am taking the images, and you are in the darkroom. Besides, we'll require a bookkeeper, too.'

Evelyn looked over in confusion, but with some expression of interest in joining the absurd enterprise. I knew he was playing with both our affections.

'Who is Mumler?' asked Evelyn, lifting out several powder-filled jars, a flash pan and a stack of mouldy journals.

'A spirit photographer from America who narrowly avoided prison for fraud,' I said, taking the lid off the white, salt-laden jar she handed me. The dust had an unusually sweet smell for flash powder, almost as though some exotic and fragrant ingredient had been incorporated. It was like nothing I had encountered before.

'And that's his magic element, allegedly,' replied Claude, raising his arms in mock phantom pretence over the form of my female companion. 'The mysterious Egyptian compound from which all the spookiness derives.'

'We aren't going back to flash powder,' I said, looking over at Evelyn's reassuring face. 'It's too dangerous. We continue to use the strips and the battery.' I put down the jar and folded my arms.

'So, you'll be part of this?' answered Claude, coming round

and grabbing my shoulders. 'Just the odd photo to please the fuddy-duddies and to boost sales of our regular portraits. It won't be forever, just until we turn a decent profit, then we can ease off; maybe even sell the place and go abroad?' I followed his gaze to the image of the Calabrian coast on the backdrop.

For a time, my thoughts drifted to the faraway olive groves, heady with aromatic herbs and the tinkling sound of distant goat bells and chirruping crickets. I looked back for support with the decision I was about to make and my refusal to be part of this sham but found Evelyn imperceptibly nodding her head as though subconsciously attempting to change her mind, and my own.

'I need time to think about it,' I whispered, staring at the flash powder jar next to the bottle of opened brandy to avoid either of their gazes. 'But we must tidy the place up before tomorrow, and I want another drink.'

I slept uneasily, despite being warm in my bed and not having to rise to thaw the water pipes. The small box room with its round window admitted the light of the moon and I watched the blur of the clouds cross my woollen bed sheets like a camera obscura. I briefly fell into a nightmare, feeling as though I was captured inside a camera, powerless to escape the exposure and manifestation of hints and shadows developing before me in the perfume of the strange and intoxicating flash powder. I dashed to the rear of the camera hood, hopelessly seeking to find my way out before the phantoms took form and smothered me, but I only found myself suddenly awake, sweating, and wrestling with the bedclothes.

Claude woke early, lit the fire and prepared the salon, which was highly unusual. His enthusiasm at the start of ventures lapsed after some days, and I did not hurry down-stairs until the doorbell began to ring constantly. I leaned over to the poor pine wall clock and rubbed my eyes to discover it was past nine.

I washed and dressed before sneaking down the stairs to find several seated customers who I did not recognise, fortu-nate to be inside on another bitterly cold morning.

Claude came over, out of breath. 'I've got three in already, but I need your help to sort out the others – I'm not asking you to do anything, just take their names before we lose the walk-up custom.'

I frowned, not understanding, and still partly asleep. He spun me round to face the window, and I saw the line of couples, some holding familiar printed pamphlets, queuing halfway down the narrow street.

I blathered something incomprehensible and Claude shook me into the present, grinning with fervent amazement. 'Don't panic,' he said, panicking. 'Isn't it incredible? I'm just shooting through one of your blurred steam plates to test things out, nothing specific; just a hint of stuff to come.'

He rushed back to the camera and drew the circular curtain around himself and a single woman in her fifties, holding up a locket that contained the image of a young man. 'It's my Albert,' she said, sobbing. 'He's with me, I'm sure of it.' Claude gave me a sober glance as he turned and disap-peared within, jerking his head to the street and the growing line of customers. I heard him consoling the woman and instructing her on the need for stillness and patience while he checked the focus. He whispered gentle comforts and sincere condolences and if he hadn't been trying to extort money from the scheme, I would have said he was the most compas-sionate man I had ever heard. Several seconds later, I witnessed the flash go off above the curtain rail, causing a mild moment of alarm among the seated customers.

I opened the door, admitting the next batch of cold customers into the warmth of the studio, taking down names and filling up the diary until I was forced to apologise for a wait of several days before any portrait could be taken. More people joined the queue than I could process, and I was glad to see Evelyn barge through with some protest from the people behind.

'It's all right,' she said politely, 'I work here and need to assist my colleague.'

I glanced over to see the curtain withdraw and the customer rise to receive their remittance slip. Claude emerged and raced off to the darkroom to fetch a stack of prepared plates in readiness for the onslaught of photographic subjects now standing for lack of seats. The woman came over and handed me the slip with her name and address plus the deposit required to secure her portrait. A circle was marked in the corner, and I looked up to see Claude nod with silent purpose.

Evelyn understood and reeled off an improvised set of terms and conditions, offering a discount from the one pound eight shillings to the standard portrait price should 'invisible forces' not be present in the photograph to be collected on Wednesday.

'What are you doing here?' I whispered, between taking down the details of the never-ending snake of humanity desperate for solace or proof of the afterlife.

'Father's sick and I had to open up the bakery early,' she replied. 'They don't need me in as my uncle has stepped in to marshal the troops; he thinks I've gone home to administer soup and medicine to the old fool – it's only sciatica.' She hastily arranged a series of frames from a box I had yet to encounter, purchased with optimistic foresight by my snap-happy colleague beyond the black velvet drapes. 'Did you know they've been queuing since six-thirty this morning?'

'No, I mean what are you doing here, right now?'

Evelyn jotted down the woman's preference for mounting the picture yet to be developed and the woman left the shop, blowing into her lace handkerchief.

'I came to see if you had made your decision – I can see you have.'

The curtain retreated and out walked an elderly gentleman, bright and eager, like a newborn from the draped ward beyond.

'I don't appear to have much choice,' I said, beckoning the man over.

Evelyn took over the collection of the slip and the deposit, efficiently processing the transaction. He tipped his hat and winked at her blushing face. 'You remind me of her, my dear, a real beauty; Abigail was her name – I wonder if she'll appear young or old, like me.'

Evelyn squeezed his arm. 'No guarantees, Mr Cartwright, but even if she isn't in your photograph, I'm sure she's looking down on you.' The man nodded and turned to leave the shop, ringing the never fully at rest bell on his exit before another entered, eager to be captured on camera alongside the possibility of someone else dear to them.

'That was nicely done,' I said. 'You should have been a nurse or a nun.'

She cocked an eyebrow as she took down the particulars of the next client. 'Or a professional liar.' She pointed to the blank corner of the slip. 'Abigail won't be showing up without the magic powder on this occasion.'

I recoiled at the suggestion and the remembrance of the nightmare. 'That flash is going down the drain,' I said. 'Things that I don't understand make me uncomfortable.'

She looked across; a fleeting moment of concern crossed her beautiful face before it readied itself for wry humour.

'Like women?' she said, pretending her nudge to my ribs was accidental.

My reply was cut short by the appearance of Mr Sym towering before me, suited and bearing no cane. I wondered suddenly what I could owe the man and flushed with unusual cold in case Claude had fabricated a dreadful lie about his inheritance.

He slammed down the pamphlet, together with my timing watch, and looked around in amazement at the transformed space.

'Come to see the wife,' he said haltingly, 'if you know what I mean.' His hand returned to the wooden cross about his starched collar. 'I'll have my picture taken for the cost of this if you understand me. Dog's outside, so I can't be long.'

I looked down the full list for the day.

'I'm uncertain we can accommodate—'

Evelyn circled a piece of paper in front of me and cleared her throat. 'I'm sure that will be fine, Mr Sym. I can see you are a busy man and I'll just have a word with Mr Fielding if you'd like to follow me?' Sym's face softened, and I caught sight of her free hand jabbing a finger towards the darkroom as she led the giant to the curtains, now opening to reveal a departing customer and Claude's alarmed face. I raced over to the curtained room and clattered through several plates until a particularly blurred image of a middle-aged woman that could pass as anyone's wife appeared. I paused, realising I was now part of something with its own destiny and out of my control for the time being. I exhaled deeply and retreated to the salon, handing the slide to Claude, who had been prepped for the second and impromptu spirit summoning of the morning.

There was no protestation from the huddle of waiting customers, fortunate to be inside at all, and we returned to our posts to deal with the next clients. We continued, late into the afternoon, before Claude ran out of prepared plates. He caught me developing the morning's images in the dark-room during a quiet interlude.

'Thank you,' he said, avoiding my eyes and looking along the line of hanging prints.

I sighed and gave him a short nod. 'It's Evelyn that you need to thank, she's done most of the work today. It was her quick thinking that got us that extra shot of Sym and a few others; I thought you were going to have kittens when you pulled back that curtain.'

Claude snorted with the memory. 'Yes, she's doing the takings and entries as we speak. It's over fifty pounds, Harry.' He toyed with the line, as though examining his morning work. 'Which ones have the spooks?'

'I'm putting them all on the left so I can see if I need to do any more tinkering to avoid making them too obvious.'

Claude side-stepped behind me and studied the first few prints. 'This one of Sym is a cracker,' he said. 'Not enough to call a ghost but just enough to hint at a woman's outline.'

'Not enough for a court to convict us either,' I replied. 'That's my main concern. I don't want Evelyn or me to be dragged into this any longer than is necessary. Do you understand?'

I held out my hand, and he shook it.

'Just till we get healthy and repeat trade for regular work back,' he said. 'We can put aside this spook business at that time, all right?'

He was about to leave when he chuckled.

'You will not believe me, but that spoiled brat of a dog died of a heart attack yesterday.'

'Mrs Partridge's?' I said, watching him clench his face in mirth. 'What's so funny?'

He placed a hand on the blackout curtain, wiping his eyes. 'One customer has encouraged her to come and see if the damn thing can be coaxed from the ether. With all those blurred plates of poor Horace, we are spoiled for choice which one to use first.'

I shook my head, unable to avoid the sense of amusement. 'That's awful. We can't go through with it, it's dreadfully unethical.'

'I know,' said Claude, 'but look at how long she kept us dangling. She could be coming back for weeks before we run out of ideas. I call it fate and I'll follow it where it leads.'

It led to several more intense months of work and increasing amounts of spirit circles attached to names in the order book. The weather outside warmed in contrast to the cooling in our partnership. I became more uneasy by the day and broached the recurring subject of our contention one Saturday as Claude readied himself, and the field equipment, for a private sitting in the country. He was purposefully vague until I pressed him.

'It's Lady Asquith,' he said defensively. 'I don't need your permission to photograph a client, do I?'

His tone was unusually curt, and I risked another encounter with his obsession by reminding him we had plenty of standard portrait work coming in.

'Isn't she the recluse who is big into spiritualism? It could be risky to get too deeply involved,' said Evelyn. 'A member of the upper class could be trouble, and you know her reputation as an eccentric who keeps a library of the occult.'

He frowned. 'You've been reading the society papers again, haven't you? She could also be the gateway to others in her social elite. Are you coming or not? The cab outside is waiting.'

I'd been unaware that she had been asked, while I had

been purposely left in the dark, and it irked me. She hesitated before seeking my permission, if not my approval. Her work finery and the time-consuming setting of her beautiful hair now made sense.

'I don't agree with what you have planned, Claude,' said Evelyn, 'and I'm only coming to carry the cases and take a look at the beautiful things in the mansion.'

'Go then,' I said, childishly folding my arms. I glanced over at Claude. 'But you can develop your own plates when you get back – I don't want anything to do with it. You know my feelings on the increasing numbers of—'

'Yes, yes,' he spluttered. 'Here we go again, just like a stuck gramophone. She's offering fifty pounds for a few hours' work.' He gave me a patronising glance. 'Sometimes I think you lack ambition.'

I was about to confront the slur with one of my own when Evelyn interrupted and dragged Claude and the cases into the street. I watched with a scowl, practised for such an occasion, as he pushed Evelyn into the cramped seat and signalled for the driver to make off.

They returned in a sombre mood later that evening. For a while, I thought our earlier row had provoked the gloom that settled like a melancholic mist. Despite the warming weather outside, the place now seemed chilly. Claude dumped the cases and tripod and sat in the sitting chair, staring at the Parisian street scene featured on the backdrop. Evelyn put a palm on his shoulder and gave me a forlorn glance.

'What's the matter?' I asked, fearing some dispute or threat of litigation against us.

'Lady Asquith is in torment, Harry,' she said. 'Pictures, portraits, tapestries and engravings of her missing son are everywhere – on the walls and the dressers. She's even scratched his name into the glass of the mirrors. I think it's the only thing that's keeping her going, the uncertainty of not knowing what has happened to him.'

'Where is he?'

'He was an officer in the rear-guard following the rout in Tweebosch,' said Claude. 'Her secretary informed me he's been missing in action since March.'

'Tweebosch? My God, the poor man.' I bowed my head instinctively. 'You think he's still alive after that slaughter, captured possibly?'

Claude shrugged. 'Not likely, is it, after the reports of what the guerrillas did to us.'

'You didn't go through with it, then? Tell me you used clean slides – for a standard portrait.'

He rubbed at his bloodshot eyes. 'No. I went through with it, despite Miss White's mute but animated protestations. Asquith's the gateway to bigger things if we pull this off.' His legs tremored, and he fidgeted with his fingers. 'I didn't like it any more than you did, Evelyn.'

'She was black and veiled; we never saw her face...' she whispered. 'It was like being in the presence of a ghost—'

'Don't say that!' said Claude, rising and heading for the dresser to pour himself a large measure of brandy.

'This has gone too far, Claude,' I said. 'Look at what this obsession is doing to you, not to mention other people.'

'You're right, Harry.' He took out a cheque from his top pocket and threw it onto the counter behind. 'Too far, but I'm powerless to do anything about Lady Asquith. I shot all the plates through those blurred army officer slides from last year. I can't tell her that every one of them was ruined, think of what it would do to our reputation.'

I picked up the folded cheque. 'Three hundred pounds?' I exclaimed. 'I thought it was fifty?'

Evelyn broke the silence. 'She's desperate to know and crying out for news, or closure—'

Claude slammed the crystal tumbler down on the dresser and poured himself another drink with his shaking hand. 'Three hundred pounds for a delivery, in person, by tomorrow afternoon.'

'You are kidding me?' I said, reaching round to put my palm on the stopper of the bottle. 'Look at what this is doing to you and us. Let it be, man. I'll call her secretary in the morning to say the camera was damaged from the journey. You've fulfilled your promise to our partnership, with interest.'

Evelyn put her arm around him. 'He's right. We don't need three hundred pounds, or fifty for that matter.'

Claude stared at the display of portraits arranged on the shelf above, some exhibiting the fraudulent effects of our trickery. 'I keep seeing his face and what I could make out of hers, as though they're burned into my mind like a developing slide. He was everywhere...'

'It's time to let all of this go and you need a break,' I said, putting away the brandy. 'Go upstairs and get some rest.'

He relaxed and let out a sigh like a boiler letting out steam. 'Perhaps you're right, both of you. Maybe it is time to get out while the going is good.'

He turned and stared at the cheque on the counter. In hindsight, I wished I had torn it in two, but I thought Claude had relented in his pursuit of fame, glory, wealth or whatever drove him on deeper and further down the rabbit hole. I lingered until he climbed the stairs, slow and steady like the tolling of a tenor bell, before walking my beloved home.

We spent a pleasant hour with the family, and her mother yearned for news of what lay inside the reclusive noble-woman's country house. Evelyn dutifully regaled her with all the details she could recall, leaving out the mentally unstable Lady Asquith and her obsession with her son. It was late when I returned, and the studio was in comforting and all-consuming silence.

After an hour of light sleep, I woke to sounds of movement downstairs. I listened, unsure whether my imagination or the remnants of an unremembered dream were to blame. Stealthy footsteps followed the opening of the darkroom door, and I knew there was someone in the house. I was about to rise and wake my partner in the adjoining room when I heard, whoever it was, stumble into something and stifle a curse. It was Claude, and he struck a match before continuing to clatter his way around the trays and jars of my sacred space.

I was paralysed. He had lost the battle in his mind to let the damn thing go and was now engaged in developing the cursed photographs through some innate characteristic within him not to quit. I felt close to tears throughout the following hours, unable to change his course with talk, and never by force or threat.

He blew out the lamp, gently drawing the curtains back, and crept up the stairs, pausing outside my room. For an instant, I could sense his desperate struggle, urging him to open the door and ask for help. I got ready to rise, hopeful he would overcome the addiction to this new line of work, but he carried on and creaked back into his iron bedstead, knowing he had lost the battle, if not the war, within himself.

In the morning, he was gone, and so was the cheque.

I had knocked on his door to convince myself, and hearing no reply, I entered the dishevelled room stacked with slides like prayer books, the only meticulously organised objects in the room. The sweet and cloying smell of the flash powder mingled with the stale and unventilated air. I saw the opened jar on the window ledge and wrinkled my nose at the pungent potpourri; he had prevented me from throwing the flammable salts away with an unhealthy insistence.

I closed the door and wandered downstairs.

There was a note on the counter, which tore at my heart, revealing he was out for the day with Constance and would not return until the evening. Unknown to Claude, I knew she had moved on, fed up with waiting for the man to decide about their future. He no longer visited because of the new mistress that had replaced her: his obsession with his work. There would be further lies when he returned, and as I wept, Evelyn arrived and unlocked the studio door before rushing over to embrace and console me.

I listened to his attempts to disguise his whereabouts when he returned, interrupting him after I had heard enough lies.

'I'm going to start afresh, Claude,' I said hesitantly. 'With Evelyn, someplace where we won't conflict, business-wise.'

He froze as though the man I once knew was struggling to escape and reach me. I would have rescinded my intentions if only he would have given me some sign of regret or even anguish at the possibility of our partnership ending. Instead, he turned his back, and I knew it was over.

'How long?' he murmured.

'A few weeks; the end of July,' I said, stiffening with the inevitability and pain of our severance. 'Just until we finalise new premises. If I can take the field camera, we are going to start with the boating crowd down at—'

'I can use the upstairs room for storage,' he said without a hint of emotion.

'Claude—'

He collected the bottle of brandy and drew the curtain around the empty sitting area, creaking into the leather armchair in a rejection of my company and any attempt to interfere in his life ever again.

The following weeks were awful. Evelyn and I counted down the days until the new lease would be ready on a small shop and studio of our own. Claude had not shirked on the terms of our original agreement – fifty-fifty – and while he retained the premises and the fittings, he did not contest a sizeable payout for us to start over. We would be comfortable in our new enterprise, though we had purchased a large stock of the new click and wind film cameras we hoped would sell to the growing affluent classes keen to begin their own photographic journeys.

It was towards the end of the week that we heard of the suicide of Lady Asquith.

She was found lying on her bed, eyes wide open in agony, tongue blackened by the arsenic she had ingested. Reports said she still clutched the framed print of her sitting against the backdrop of her drawing-room, the faint and ghostly apparition of an army officer looking down from behind in fond remembrance.

I kept the news from Evelyn, but she discovered it from clients, morbidly curious about the last image, asking if copies of the photograph could be purchased. I lost my temper and threw them out, locking the door, until I could calm her to the state where I could investigate if Claude required some modicum of companionship with the momentous news.

He stared at the obituary page in the preceding day's newspaper and would say nothing except that it was 'too late'.

Several days later, Evelyn's father took ill and required constant supervision to overcome a suspected case of pleurisy. It was fortunate that she was not in the studio when the scarred face of the uniformed army captain arrived.

'I'm not in your book,' he said as I scanned down the order list. 'But you are most certainly in mine.'

Claude emerged from the darkroom, caught sight of the

captain, and dropped the stack of glass plates to the floor, startling the woman in the sitting chair as well as myself. He backed across the wall, hands outstretched with a look of abject horror, head shaking from side to side.

'You...'

Before I could calm him down, he shrieked and retreated up the stairs, followed by the stern glance of the battle-worn officer until he was out of sight. The woman across the room gathered her things among the broken shards, crossed herself, and left the shop without a word, leaving me in the dreadful gaze of the soldier in front of the counter.

'The name is Captain Jonathan Merriman Asquith; Lord Asquith, because of your childish and insensitive actions,' he whispered, one eye quivering with pent emotion. He opened his leather side-satchel and threw the print down on the counter. 'Returned from death, it would seem, to discover my mother has traded places with her beloved son.'

I stared at the black-laced figure in the photograph and realised the missing son from the battle of Tweebosch stood before me.

'You are Fielding?' he continued, watching as the penny dropped deeper and deeper into the well of my fathoming comprehension.

'Dunnett...' I replied. He looked up at the stairs, placing a hand on his revolver case strapped to his side. I wondered for a moment if he would ascend the stairs and commit murder.

He replaced the hand on his webbing belt. 'And will you run when your time comes?'

I shook my head, visibly unsure of what he meant. He took it as a sign of intent.

'Then there is still some courage and steel in the softness of England's youth.'

He drew out a knife, and I fumbled my way back to the wall, fearing the worst. Asquith thrust the weapon blade downwards and into the photograph, burying the blade deep into the counter's wood. I glanced down at the point of contact to see, whether by chance or skill, the knife embedded in the ghostly form of the unknown soldier.

'I tried to stop him. I'm sorry for your loss—' I began, but he had already turned to go. He paused and glanced back at the stairs, chilling me to the bone.

'As I shall be, for yours...'

We closed the shop for two days as a mark of respect, turning persistent door knockers away with news that we would only be open for standard portraits in the future. In Claude's absence, I took charge. I burned the pamphlets and cancelled the order for more. Evelyn cleared the spirit selection in the window and on the dresser, making certain all evidence of the former enterprise was exorcised from the premises.

We left food outside Claude's locked door and sat every so often on the floor trying to engage him in conversation or cajole him out into the bright sunlit days. He would only echo the phrase '*Too late*', before turning over on his side on the creaking bed and murmuring as he drifted into a fitful sleep.

Our new tenancy was fast approaching, and I was repeatedly absent attending to the minutiae and setup of the shop, all the while feeling I was forsaking my old friend in his greatest time of need. I resolved to wait an extra week and employed the services of a respected doctor to gain a professional assessment and prognosis of Claude's condition. I feared suicide, but I dreaded mentioning this to anyone, even to Evelyn.

Pills and potions were prescribed to treat the extreme melancholia and shock deriving from a severe case of mental fatigue coupled with depression. Claude took neither.

We reopened so that we might cross-promote our next endeavour. Similarly, a large sign in the window of our almost furnished and stocked studio in St John's Wood displayed the details of where we could temporarily be found. We encountered many eager hobbyists enquiring about the possibility of purchasing the new film roll cameras, so much so that we transferred several crates to Camden lest we lose the trade.

We were buoyant, especially on weekends when those that could afford the home cameras came in to purchase them for the Regent's Park demonstrations, which now attracted crowds in the tens of thousands. The local garrison was swelled with men sent to manage the mob and break any breach of the peace. The soldiers were able-bodied, though still rehabilitating following their return from South Africa. Men, intent on trouble, trod carefully around them for fear of awakening traumatic memories of the campaign, and the triggering of uncontrolled battle trauma and gunfire.

Sunday dawned, promising tense and sweltering heat in every sense of the word. The anvils of several thunderclouds threatened the horizon and the afternoon, though the steady stream of eager customers made it difficult to shut up as early as I had intended.

Evelyn arrived, radiant in her summer dress and newly purchased hat, tapping at her pocket watch to remind me I was late in closing.

'You need to get washed and ready,' she said. 'We'll be late to enjoy a safe spot overlooking the speakers if you don't hurry.'

I gave her a look of desperation, indicating the men toying with the demonstration model and wiping their cropped beards in anticipation of placing several orders.

'I can't throw them out,' I whispered. 'They've come from St John's – the one on the right works for the Royal Society and wants to buy some of the Kodaks for an expedition.'

'We've worked all week,' she said, 'and I can't go alone—'

'She's waiting,' said a voice from the top of the stairs. We turned to see Claude, clean-shaven and wearing his best summer suit and boater. His moustache was newly waxed, and I marvelled at his sudden recovery. He stumped down the remaining stairs as though unsure of his feet, and as he passed me, I saw his eyes, vacant and wide, as one resigned to follow on some predetermined course and having no power or authority to amend it.

Evelyn was overjoyed but appeared only to see the pleasing outer shell like that of a stuffed tropical bird from which all life had departed.

'Are you all right, Claude?' I said.

He offered his arm, and Evelyn took it, wrinkling her brow at my uncertainty.

'Of course he is,' she said, tapping her gloved hand on his, and readying her sunshade. 'Fresh air is just what he needs, isn't that right?'

'I have to go,' he said, struggling to open the door before Evelyn helped his unsteady free hand to grasp the handle.

At that moment, the large frame of the undersecretary blotted out my view from behind the counter. 'I'll take twenty to begin with, but under guarantees of mechanical workmanship, with replacements being issued within forty days. Another thirty following our trials at altitude in the Pyrenees.'

He took out a contract and insisted on my full attention. I signed without even being conscious of where I had put my signature, hurrying the transaction to the point where he moved away to examine several wide-angle prototype lenses I had bought from an optics genius in Bath. I rushed to the open door and lurched out into the street, now busy with a flow of people in the park's direction, searching for Evelyn and Claude. As they turned the corner, I caught sight of

Claude, unmoved by the chatter of my beloved on his arm. He walked slowly and steadily as though in front of a hearse, as one trying to slow down an inevitable meeting with fate. A call from the shop caused me to turn, and I replied I was coming back presently. My gaze returned to the corner, but they were gone.

I was pensive for the next few hours, attempting to convince myself that I was being overprotective or absurd. I ultimately put it down to jealously, and as I cashed up the very healthy takings for the day, I stared into the till wondering if some infection was even now causing me to become obsessed with my new venture at the expense of other healthier pursuits.

The passers-by on the street outside slowed to a trickle as the park drew its opposites like a giant magnet to the fray just over a mile away. I checked the stock for want of other diversions, listening to the occasional and incomprehensible sound of a megaphone or a firecracker exploding in the melee's direction, now in full swing. The sun dipped behind a dark patch of cloud as I hunted for magnesium strips for the flash. I refilled the supply cupboard with the heavy rods, almost jumping out of my skin, and my meditations, when the bell rang.

A young couple, preferring the privacy of each other's company, were passing and wondered if a portrait was available for a collection at a later date. I suddenly felt very alone and the sight of the two of them, not so very much younger than Evelyn and me, encouraged me to suggest they take a seat.

We settled on Paris as a background, and I offered them lemonade while they sat and sweltered for the focus at a slight angle to one another. Beneath the black cloth, I itched and sweated, blinking away the stinging beads while I swung the focussing plate inwards and used the hand lens to fine-tune their positions.

I emerged from the darkroom with a prepared slide, fishing out one of the magnesium rods and unsettling the old flash pan, lodged to one side. It clattered to the floor as I returned to load the plate and check the battery terminals. Holding up the flashgun I primed the clockwork aperture that would automatically open and close the shutter, leaving me to guard the pan above my head. I counted down the image as the smiling couple braced themselves for the momentary brilliance of a thousand suns. My fingers felt for the switch on the handle and depressed the button, completing the electrical circuit.

Nothing happened.

I tried again and checked the wiring circuit was complete. The battery was flat, and I apologised for the inconvenience. Perhaps they would like to return on Tuesday?

'Isn't there anything you can do?' said the young woman. 'We wanted to capture the day we became engaged.'

I apologised, looking at the available light and estimating the longer exposure. At that moment, the sun disappeared behind a dark thundercloud, gurgling and heavy with the threat of thunder and rain. The room became dim, and my calculations proved beyond the limit at which the aperture could be kept open and the subjects still enough to avoid a blurred photograph. I retreated to look out of the window, tripping and kicking the flash pan halfway across the room.

'What is that unusual smell?' asked the young man, wrinkling his nose and trying to identify its source. I had gotten so used to the faint odour from upstairs that it was all but unnoticeable to my senses.

'It's flash powder; my partner must have left his room open—'

'Oh, good!' said the woman. 'You'll be able to take our picture after all.'

'Excuse me?' I said, still peering at the blackening sky.

'The flash pan, silly. Can't you use that instead?'

Something sharp and sudden urged me to check, and to hope, that nothing or little of Mumler's salts remained. I dug my hands into my pockets with the thought, and danger, of the proposal while being able to purge us of the sickly stench that had so accompanied Claude's decline. The couple relaxed when they saw me nod, bidding them wait in position for me while I investigated the prospect. I was eager to rid the place of it now that Claude was out; he had fiercely defended its keeping, like an addict being forced to renounce a cache of hidden opium. His room was invariably locked following our final and angry confrontation on the subject; the thought that I would rob him of anything by stealth still upset me.

Until now.

I climbed the stairs to find the door to his room partially open. I crept in, with no necessity, and observed a haphazard interior in stark contrast to Claude's earlier appearance. The slides were exposed and scattered against the skirting board, and the tattered ribbons of many newspapers lay torn or clipped on the well-worn rug. The lidless jar sat on the windowsill, shrine-like between several stacked lenses. There was sufficient for two or three charges, though I determined to use it only once. The danger of injury and to property had to be considered, and I was alone in the studio except for the young couple.

It had been many years since I had last handled the outdated explosive compounds, a constituent more commonly used thereafter in fireworks rather than photography. I had never seen or used this variant. Glancing into the jar, I saw dark flecks of contaminant mixed within the sea-salt-sized grains of ashen crystal. I withdrew tiny, trimmed paper snippets of the words *waiting* and *she's* meticulously cut from each instance of their occurrence from the shredded pages of *The Times*. A loud battery of fireworks or gunfire from the distant demonstrations coincided with his bedside carriage clock chiming for a quarter past three. I retreated from the unsettling space and returned to the studio via the darkroom to solicit a short fuse and a pre-emptive bucket of water.

'This is going to be exciting!' said the young woman, glad at last to be in the final moments before being captured in the flowering of her youth and happiness.

For me, too, I thought, shuffling the powder into the pan and over the firing line beneath. I lit a taper, along with several of the oil lamps, and primed the clockwork lens.

'Ready?' I said, more to myself than to the couple. They nodded calmly, through readied smiles, and I lit the fuse, raising the pan above my head. I triggered the lens and closed my eyes, listening to the whirring of the mechanism in front and the spitting of the fuse above. My timing was perfect, and the camera aperture clicked, and the powder ignited, setting off a transient cascade of silver sparks, and sending burnt paper pieces fluttering like wedding confetti over the startled sitters. The negative images of figures remained for an instant as I opened my eyes. I blinked, trying to rid myself of the bizarre sensation that there were two additional standing forms between the couple. I dumped the pan hissing into the bucket and stamped out several embers on the rug and the foot of the curtain before the illusion vanished, leaving only the couple dusting off specks of unburnt powder and soot.

They were glad to be on their way, following the details of their deposit and address, to be in each other's company and the fresh air. The young woman looked faint with the charred, unwholesome, and sickly smell that pervaded the room.

'It's like one of those temples in Cairo,' said the man, steadying his intended. 'The Zoroastrians cremate their dead outside of them, you know. I suppose that's a benefit of modernity, not having to use that awful powder anymore; I can understand your reticence now.'

They left, taking a deep breath on the step before disappearing down the street. I screwed the lid back on the jar and hurried to open the door and vent the stinking, cloying air that seemed to thicken in the sitting area behind me.

The sound of traffic and the rush of people grew outside as I tidied the room and retrieved the slide from the camera. Even from within the darkroom I could tell something was wrong. The clock above the cold fireplace struck for four o'clock.

Pedestrians hurried past the window, animated in chatter, or dabbing their eyes with handkerchiefs, desperate to escape from some obvious calamity in the opposite direction. I stood on the step, watching the wave of worried women and men go by.

'What's happened?' I said, grabbing a young man, wide-eyed and witness to whatever woe had befallen.

'Some folk been hurt or worse in the park,' he said. 'Some idiot set off a flash charge, firework or flare and it panicked the horses. They charged wildly into them, dismounting most of the soldiers in the suddenness of it all. It was all I could do to get away from being crushed. Those poor people...'

'What people? How many?' I asked, fear rising in my voice.

'Dunno,' he said, trying to shake himself free. 'At least one I heard tell of, maybe more when all said and done; there's a lot of them lying on the ground and the soldiers and ambulances are still up there.'

I relented my grip, and he dashed away, eager to be rid of the recounting and put further distance between him and the park. I desperately tried to catch the attention of others and garner further news, but there was little to add. The sickness in my stomach spurred me into action and I locked the studio door and raced towards Regent's Park with a dryness in my mouth in contrast to the sudden onset of heavy rain from the breaking clouds above.

I struggled against the tide, feverishly hunting for signs of Claude and Evelyn until the mass of distraught humanity began to thin and I saw Primrose Hill for the first time from across the park. The mound was littered with scattered clothing and belongings, while people milled in shock near the approaching and departing ambulances. Some were sitting, aided by strangers, while others lay unmoving and alone. Several horses ran wildly against the attempted corralling from soldiers and policemen on foot.

The storm above spilt stair-rods of soaking rain. I slipped up the grassy knoll, searching the faces of those lying or sitting for signs of my companions to find only strangers, or those offering urgent medical attention in the absence of medics. I called out wildly, joining the wailing chorus of others until my dry throat burned with the exertion. I closed on the summit and epicentre from which all sorrow had rippled out.

Men rushed to deal with the crisis and ignored my pleas and descriptions, carrying the wounded away instead. I raged at the sky, opening my mouth to the onslaught of wind and rain, and cried out for Evelyn.

I saw someone rushing towards me through my bleary eyes, calling out my name. I prayed that the vision of the woman I loved was truly before me, and not some phantom image conjured from my delirious mind. She fell into my outstretched arms, and I felt her soaked, trembling body tell me everything I needed to know.

She buried her head into my chest and wept between fragments of uttermost grief.

'Too close... Claude kept walking... horses... too many people.'

'Where is he?' I whispered, but she continued, reliving the moments that I dreaded were his last.

'Something set the horses off, soldiers lost control, I got separated...'

'Tell me where he is now, Evelyn.'

She struggled to lift an arm and point in the ambulance's direction, and as the bearers retreated, I saw a body lying shrouded beneath a sheet. A trampled and muddied boater lay abreast my friend like a funeral corn dolly corsage.

I looked only once before the doors swung shut and drove away, leaving the stationary figure of a dishevelled and bloodied officer blankly staring at the space between us. He glanced up as though aware of me and we both saw each other for the first time since the incident in the studio. Asquith remained vacant and unaware of even the junior lieutenant attempting to pull him from the horror of the skirmish, the coincidence, and the memory of Tweebosch.

I turned and found Evelyn looking up, hair strewn and plastered against her alabaster face. She held out Claude's pocket watch, cracked and dented by some heavy impact showing the final moments of its life, and that of Claude.

'Ten minutes past three,' I murmured.

She nodded, regaining control now that I was close. 'I held his hand telling him it would be all right, but he just looked over, terrified, into that space over there where the horses first reared for no apparent reason.'

'Someone set off a flare by all accounts.'

'No,' she said. 'The bang came after the horses had already

bolted. Whoever set them off did so to warn everyone to get clear. I didn't know what to say to him, Harry. He was terrified before he spoke for the last time.'

I wiped away the hair from her face and dared to ask, knowing the answer.

'What did he say, Evelyn?'

A sudden stillness overcame her, and she fixed me in her mournful gaze.

'She's waiting.'

I rearranged the jars in the darkroom, trying to occupy my mind while maintaining a vigil on Evelyn, reading in the sitting chair.

She looked up kindly, and a faint smile returned to her pale face. 'I'm all right, Harry,' she said. 'It's been three days now; we should think about opening back up.'

'We should think about going to Calabria,' I said, staring at my favourite backdrop. 'Perhaps for the winter.'

'What about the business and the new shop?'

'Perhaps we could take it with us, start afresh and leave all of this behind, just for a few months?'

'Italy?' she said, with more than a hint of interest. 'An unmarried couple abroad selling cameras and taking pictures for tourists?'

I realised the trap that had been expertly laid for me.

'Perhaps not unmarried?'

She returned to her book with a barely concealed countenance of utter joy. 'Perhaps.'

I wrung my hands, unsure of the next move in the end game of the courting process.

'Well, if you are going to be my wife,' I said, holding up the undeveloped slide from Sunday's impromptu sitting. 'You can start by helping me fix this plate; the young gentleman will be picking it up later today.'

She put down the book and beckoned me over. I shuffled forwards like a schoolboy being summoned to the front of the class, unknowing whether I was to be given a toffee apple for good behaviour, or the cane for the opposite.

She reached up and grasped my cheeks, kissing me as I knelt in the closest gesture I could muster to ask for her hand in marriage. She took the slide from my hand, rose, and disappeared behind the blackout curtain.

'I accept,' she called out from the darkroom.

My face beamed in the afternoon sunlight, grateful for the few moments of grace when I had put aside thoughts of Claude. They returned, but with a gentle sadness that I could never tell him of my engagement. I looked past the 'closed until further notice' board out in the street at the couples ambling by in contentment with their own cares.

I must have stood for five minutes, losing track of time in my stillness, until I heard her scream.

I twisted, racing over to the curtain, fearing some sudden injury from a chemical or glass cut. In the few seconds it took me to enter the virtual blackout, I feared fire most of all.

I tore into the space lit only by the ruby lamp to see Evelyn backed into the corner, fingers splayed to cover her face. With mouth wide open, she shook, unable to breathe, like one suffering the contortions of apoplexy.

'What is it?' I cried, my eyes adjusting to the darkness and the shock of sudden danger.

Her head juddered as though in the throes of a fit, and she flicked her eyes for the briefest of glances at the glass plate in the developing tray. I spun around and stared at the sharpening image of the negative of the young couple, their faces fully realised with the two other figures between them.

Against the backdrop of Paris stood the hazy form of a

woman, heavily veiled in black, clawing at the shoulders and neck of another – a man desperate to escape the clutches but unable to rid himself of the agony.

It was the horrific, open-mouthed visage of my closest friend in the act of a desperate scream to which no aid would ever come. The jaw appeared dislocated or stretched, but whether this had anything to do with his mortal injury or some effect of the image, I could not tell. His eyes bulged with torment and his hands stretched out, as though imploring me for comfort and absolution. It may have been my imagination, but the faint smell of the flash powder, possibly some residue on the slide casing, caused me to gag as the pieces of Mumler's folly, and our own, fell into place.

I looked back at Evelyn's face; the beautiful features now transformed by the grotesque mask of her broken mind. She outstretched her hands to ward off the perceived horror and panted through her open mouth, unaware of my attempts to reach her with soothing speech. I returned to the plate once more to confirm the phantoms were there and ripped down the curtain to allow purifying light to cleanse the room of shadow and spirit.

Even as the image bleached and faded from view, it burned and fixed in my mind forever without hope of deliverance from its life- and afterlife-shattering consequences.

I dragged her from the chamber, mute and flailing in lunacy. I cried out without knowing why or to whom.

'I'm sorry!'

I pinned Evelyn to the counter, trying to stop her from raking her fingernails across her face. I glanced down next to the spot where I pushed her hand to the polished wood. The wounded curved slit of the table where the dagger had been embedded smiled back and I recalled Asquith's voice:

'*As I will be, for yours.*'

I adjusted the sunshade above the easel, trying to block out the intense brilliance of the Italian sun. Evelyn dabbed at the canvas, painting the Calabrian coastal scene with methodical precision.

Her landscapes drew many to our small village studio during the summer, off the usual tourist track, but it was the winter I looked forward to the most when the coast became quiet and reflective with its pleasant sunrise and sunsets across the cobalt sea a few miles away. We would have the place to ourselves once more with time to work on her rehabilitation.

Five years of care and patience had brought her back to the point where I knew she was well enough to cope with most things. I was apprehensive about our move abroad the preceding summer, and the relocation of the business I now ran alone. Evelyn's paintings generated as many sales as the portable cameras, and we returned to the fragrant pastures and olive groves overlooking the sea every Sunday for her to work, and me to rest.

She turned and smiled, as though reading my thoughts, trying to convey in gestures what she could or would not do in speech. It was enough that she loved me unconditionally, and I now believed, even if it had taken me several years to admit it, that she was happy, if not wholly recovered. I clung to her, hoping to hear her bright voice call my name one unexpected morning.

'Time to go,' I said. 'Marco is bringing baby Mariana to see you later; he's got pomegranates and sugared almonds for you.'

Evelyn put down her brush and placed her hands on her lap, allowing me to pack away the accoutrements of my artist-in-residence. She reached out a hand, and I squeezed it as she maintained her gaze towards the faraway cliffs and glittering surf.

I let go reluctantly and loaded the handcart. She removed her parasol from the stand, joining me in silence on the dusty track back to the white-walled cool of the house and the promise of lemon blossom water to slake our thirst before our guests arrived. Love needed no words, and I was content.

Back at the studio, I took off her boots, tickling her toes to elicit the excitable sound that now posed as laughter. She wandered into the bedroom, closely followed by my attempts to spoon a sweet vitamin tonic into her pursed lips. A highlight of my day, if not hers, as I got to kiss the sticky sweetness of her lips, and in those moments, she always held me as though recalling our days before the incident.

'You need to change into the linen yellow dress, all right?' I said, watching as she fumbled through her wardrobe. 'It's the only one I've had time to press.'

I closed the door, took off my shoes and slip-slapped across the cold tile floor, enjoying the coolness against my sweaty soles as I made my way to the chest to replace the bottle. I unlocked the padlock and returned the vessel to its wooden slot alongside other medicines and chemicals I still possessed for very occasional photography. From within the bottom right-hand corner, I clicked the spring-loaded false bottom downwards to release the catch. The lid sprung open revealing the white jar, sealed around its lid with impenetrable wax to eliminate any odour. I heard Evelyn humming something obtuse and unfamiliar, indicating her mind was occupied with washing and dressing, and I lifted the flash powder to stare at it with its scraps of newspaper still within.

My secret was safe, the daily ritual of checking and confronting the past, which I could not let go of, passed for another day. I exhaled as the compulsion to check the jar receded. My evening would be free of my anxiety and my guilt at not destroying the cursed salts.

I blocked the impulse to recall the final image, choosing instead to remember Claude fooling about at Hampton Lock when he once offered the prettiest girls a kiss for each photograph in exchange. A bargain you would think unless you knew full well that no plates were present in the camera.

I replaced the flash powder in its secret reliquary, and it clinked against the small vial of dark digitalin. One day, I knew the powder would be used again. If Evelyn passed on before me, I would have to know, to make certain that she was free from any taint associated with Claude's decision on that fateful day in Surrey. She had protested, had she not? I reaffirmed my decision that if there was an appearance by her or other agencies, to suggest this was the case, I would end my life, with the heart-stopping poison, to be by her side.

There would be no eternal punishment for a finite crime, and hell would freeze over before I would allow Lady Asquith to torment my love. I would remain by her side, to fend off the vagaries of life, and the fiends of death if it came to it.

THE ORDER OF THE CANDLE

Casual visitors to Compton Brierley are drawn to the redoubtable Norman church of St Margaret, which rises from the wooded coombe nestled between a fold of mist-hugging moor. Across the valley, a remote, upland crag is crowned by the crenulated ruins of a feudal castle whose Cromwell-slighted keep now impotently defends the sleepy settlement and sanctuary below. Modern-day, summer pilgrims in Gore-Tex and gaiters descend from the viewpoint, if time and tired legs allow, via overgrown footpaths flanking the eastern Pennines, to explore the squat ironstone tower steepled with sixteenth-century slates and circling swifts.

A place of worship for nigh on nine centuries (and every first Sunday of the month), the church lies empty for much of the year and is toured by those satisfied by quiet, reflective places. Those who harbour antiquarian interests will be handsomely rewarded by the six medieval tombs that lie at the intersection of the nave and north-south transepts. Arranged around a pivotal and more ornate stone sarcophagus, five recumbent fifteenth-century knights lie in effigy above plain-sided tomb monuments, three of which show hands clasped about age-worn candles carved at their breast like bladeless pommels. The two most southerly knights bear shields covering their forearms upon which the device of a candle "flammant" is emblazoned below a raised heraldic chevron band, signifying spirituality, devotion, and the extinct d'Aubernon family's monumental achievements. Pitted swords lie by the sides of each candle knight, blades etched with years of Sunday school scrawl by boys long dead and now in perpetual sleep of their own below meagre headstones among the hemlock and herb-Robert outside.

Unusual, and unique, carved circular sockets of three inches in diameter and similar depth lie centrally and marginally beyond the chiselled features of their part-plated, chain mail boots. Waxy deposits moulded into imperfections within the black stone recesses reveal their original use as candle holders for high feast days, but outside of Pentecost and Candlemass, they are filled with floral dry blocks and dusty, desiccated flowers.

The central monument does not bear any such repository or tribute. Richly decorated with cylindrical candled carvings at the corners of the catafalque, there lingers the memory of paint within its weathered panels. A much-polished brass plate, neatly affixed on the lipped lid by a Victorian benefactor, reveals the interred earthly remains of Lady Catherine d'Aubernon, the childless wife of the last hereditary Baron. Her face is all but obscured from the acts of Reformation vandals and eroded by many inquisitive caresses from the preceding five hundred years since her death. Worn, white marble roses bloom eternally at her feet forever unspoiled by spot or rust, still deathly defiant in support for the House of York during the Wars of the Roses, an on-off civil war between the main ruling families and factions of the late medieval period.

Beyond the sleeping knights and their noble charge, there

are notable carvings and fragments of ancient stained glass to admire that survived a nearby ordnance explosion following the Second World War, and the repairs to the roof, chancel mullions, and a few of the less auspicious memorials that line the partly plastered, rubble-stone walls are easy to spot. A conspicuous, and later 1950s restoration disfigures the western corner of Lady Catherine's tomb, along with several unskilled, render-filled cracks that fork into the scratched flagstones of the nave suggesting some prior blow from above, or sudden subsidence from below.

What visitors are unlikely to notice from a flying visit is the inconsistency in the dark and difficult-to-read ecclesiastical honours board – a break in the line of parish rectors between the years of John Adamson 1827-1841 and that of his successor, William Benson, 1842-67. A gap of a single year you may think unremarkable and a cursory twenty-minute examination of births, deaths, and marriages records will reveal one, Henry Bickerstaff, was in place during the aforementioned interlude.

I suggest you take my word for it and delve no deeper, for truth, as they say, is often stranger than fiction. This tale derives chiefly because of this inconsequential omission but has left me with a profound and lasting unease whenever I think back on the church and my old friend whose dying request involved me in the whole affair.

A man not prone to exaggeration, Professor Merriman Simmons, a notable historian and Fellow of the Society of Antiquaries, recounted to me in his final days much of what I now record and relates to the missing timeline. He believed that divulging the crux of this tale and what he witnessed would unburden his soul even as it shortly afterwards departed his body. Entrusting me as his executor with a post-mortem pilgrimage to the church to seek its incumbent minister was the fulfilment of his wishes, and I dutifully released considerable funds from his estate, in perpetuity, for future prayers, masses, and necessary votives to the memory of Lady Catherine d'Aubernon. My obligations ceased at that point, but the experience has never fully left me, in much the same way it affected my dear friend. He had the benefit of my confidence; I, on the other hand, have only your attention.

A promise can be a burden if the full truth, and horror, of its commitment is not comprehensively understood at the time of its pledge. Perhaps in sharing, I will uncover some hitherto rational explanation and calm my nerves at the risk of unsettling yours. I am a man of forty years standing a Member of Parliament and spent most of my life under oath of one sort or another but should you wish to test the validity of my story, or my honesty, and visit the church of St Margaret, you will find all as I describe. If you discover the socket-mounted tomb candles unlit on the feast of Candlemass, I ask only that you pause your scorn and humour me, resolving to draw the matter urgently to the verger's attention before removing yourself as far away from the place as is possible before dusk descends into that dreadful darkness.

It was in late 1945 that the Ashmolean Museum despatched Professor Simmons during his collegiate winter recess to scout out the place and see what needed recovering or repairing following a freakish accident. An unplanned detonation of unused ordnance stored nearby had killed a national serviceman and the shrapnel-studded shockwave had swept across a section of the original and dilapidated chancel roof, making an awful mess within and necessitating the removal of the remaining medieval stained glass panels that had survived the concussive blast. Fortunately, little damage to the central tombs was evident after the removal of several intersectional roof beams and lime-plastered laths. I say little, for Simmons recorded a crack to Lady Catherine's tomb, approximately three jagged feet in length that traced like an electrocardiogram from the tip of its southern corner to the polished flagstones that paved the perimeter. Caused by a glancing blow from one of the fallen, heavier beams, the hairline scar was deemed too costly to repair and not structurally essential for the long-term preservation of the monument.

Records were thin before Pevsner's Magnus opus and the learned bachelor found himself excited by the prospect of documenting and cataloguing the contents of the gloomy and chilly interior. A medieval revivalist by nature, and a Victorian by birth, Christmas came twice that year for the esteemed and enthusiastic scholar.

Simmons returned revitalised from his break in Oxford to find the removal of rubble and the covering of the roof with a temporary tarpaulin had been accomplished with the mustering of the villagers and several of the soldiers from the nearby depot. The vicar was not similarly refreshed from an unexpectedly chaotic and busy advent, fervently insistent that the church be made ready by the feast of Candlemass in early February.

My friend described the man as 'put out', eager to uphold a tradition that revolved around the d'Aubernon family and a legacy laid out by several benefactors over the centuries. Candles specifically crafted at not inconsiderable cost needed to burn for two days and nights before the holy day or some unrevealed and dire consequence would befall. The work would be costly to repair in such a short amount of time and a substantial sum of the surviving beneficiary funds were spent fixing the glass and the roof to prepare for the mass and lighting of candles, much to the relief of the wider village who shared the cleric's stubbornness and single-mindedness for getting the job done. As the last slate was positioned, a great, brooding cloud seemed to lift from all involved. On cue, the heavens opened, and the hastily forged lead downspout began its duty of diverting the rainwater of the late January squall away from the roof and into the adjacent shingled soakaway. Exhausted but dry, the workmen retired for the evening after an hour of examining the chancel floor for spits and spots from unforeseen imperfections in their hasty but ardent work.

Simmons took a keen interest in the remaining interior works, overseeing the minor refurbishments during an agreed week's sabbatical. His calming, confident influence I recall with great fondness, eased the priest's apprehension of future misfortune should the mass and candle vigil for the six notable interments not take place the following week. The source of the tension finally outed itself from repeated, exasperated curiosity from the professor and the rehanging of the ecclesiastical honours board to its accustomed position beside the pulpit. Simmons noted the break in the timeline and revealed his modest discovery from a short sojourn in the Parish record books; a name that was already well-known to the vicar.

Henry Bickerstaff: 1841-42

Perhaps there was a precedent and the missing rector had not fully served a year to entitle a position in gold-lettered ink. With a look of profound surprise and ringing of hands, the cleric revealed that his anxiety stemmed from the man which history had chosen not to record but whose actions and disappearance still cast a deep and uneasy shadow on all who held the office thereafter.

Bickerstaff had arrived swiftly after the demise of the previous and much-loved rector, Adamson. His rapid removal from a large and wealthy parish in the county's southeast to the quiet and career-stifling Compton Brierley was suspicious from the start. It was widely rumoured to have been an act of enforced re-location arranged by an indebted Bishop attempting to snuff out accusations of financial irregularity and hedonism by the ill-tempered, and ill-suited third son of a titled Lord. Whether these improprieties occurred or crimes were committed will never be known, but after a probationary period, it appeared Bickerstaff began to live up and return to his 'old ways'.

Money for the poor was diverted to fund 'necessary' enhancements to the rectory, and 'economies' were enforced despite increased collections weaselled and beguiled from gentle parishioners and naive landowners. Sermons were 'persuasive' and lurid enough to widen purses as well as mouths, reinforced, ironically, by the threat of fire and brimstone in the hereafter on those who coveted wealth in the here and now. There was much unease which went unheeded by higher authorities and boiled over during a harsh encounter with a parishioner, an 'innocent' and kindly spirit who had long trimmed the candles, polished the brass and dug the graves.

Cob was a poor young man devoid of intellect and strong mental faculty but rich in heart, who made a paltry existence bird-scaring in the spring and labouring during the harvest. For much of the year, he acted as an unpaid caretaker, bell-ringer, and key-holder in exchange for a cot within a nearby outhouse doubling as a gardener's shed, whilst living off the land, his meagre salary, and the charity of the villagers. His loyalty was long-served but soon to be cut short as the impatient rector set about removing any unnecessary expense or undesirables.

As Candlemass approached, Bickerstaff was at odds over the purchase and cost of custom-made candles and the inconvenience of saying of mass to a long-dead noblewoman. There were also the funds set aside for the task that he was eager to put to better, and more personal uses. Cob was dismissed following repeated attempts to light the candles despite the contrary orders of the new rector. No protestations or warnings of impending disaster from the poor man or the villagers could persuade the rector to reverse his decision.

On a chilly Candlemass Eve, devoid of ceremony or mass to the memory of Lady d'Aubernon, Cob was removed from the only station and sacred responsibility he had ever held and was ordered to surrender the key and remove himself from the boundaries of the church forthwith. Miserable and sobbing through a litany of tears and frantic pleas for second chances, he was forced out of the porch into the frosty air. Even as the door was locked from the inside, he begged the rector not to remain within while the candles upon the five tombs were unlit. Bickerstaff scoffed at the muffled voice and superstitious meanderings that emanated from beyond the medieval studded oak. He had heard such nonsense before from madmen and simpletons, and was unimpressed and unmoved, even in the eerie and dimly lit, isolated church. He put out the hanging oil lamp and the old tales from his mind as his eyes became accustomed to the flickering shadows of the recumbent, marbled dead. He momentarily wavered, hand ready to readmit the man who beat upon the door, desperate for the rector's wellbeing.

Tradition held that the knight protectors had belonged to the 'Order of the Candle' and were chosen for their prowess and loyalty, left behind to secure the last Baron's interests, and his noble wife, during his absence fighting the French. The five men, whose names are lost to history, swore oaths to defend the noble's beautiful and influential wife and her affairs in life, and death if need be. The estate covered much of the Lower Riding at the time and he was a powerful man with many enemies, not least the Lancastrians. He died abroad or was murdered in a scheme to remove him and his family's influence back home, and the lands ultimately passed to one of their supporters gathered in northern England in late 1460 after the murder of the Duke of York outside his castle near Wakefield. An uprising following this pretender's untimely and mysterious demise led to the reinstatement and reburial of the noblewoman and her men-at-arms with all due honour and ceremony by a Yorkist sympathiser during a period of relative peace.

Whether Bickerstaff was in full possession of the facts and fiction is unknown but what is not commonly revealed to 'outsiders' is that Lady Catherine, born in the Holy Land was reputedly skilled in forbidden and gnostic practices. Besieged following her husband's death, she took to the church with her knights in a final stand against forced marriage to the newly endowed pretender seeking legitimacy. Surrounded and outnumbered, her honour guard slew many men until, wounded and exhausted, they retreated, back to back, to closet their mistress in an oubliette of bloodied, bodied steel. As they fell during the decisive encircling assault like wheat scythed at a harvest, Lady d'Aubernon withdrew a silver-handled dagger from her belt, crying aloud a dreadful oath to seek revenge on all those present or any that defiled the sanctity of her domain. Recounting words in an ancient and foreign tongue, she swiftly drew the keen blade across her long, olive-skinned neck until the incantation was cut short. The blood that seeped from the vicious, spurting wound soaked into her ivory gown meeting the rising tide of scarlet from the spent candle knights at her feet. The soldiers quailed and stepped back in sudden fear as she teetered, arms flailing to upset an oil lamp within arm's reach upon her failing body.

A penitent soldier, from whom this vivid account likely derives, made the pilgrimage to Jerusalem shortly after to atone for his part in the massacre and did much to begin the tradition of holding vigil, masses, and prayers to her memory and those of her brave men. It was said he hoped to extinguish those final moments from his conscience of her blood-streaked arms raised high forming a flickering human torch before she collapsed to the floor in silence.

Such tales are less commonly believed than they once were, but a grain of sand lies at the heart of every lustrous pearl. It seems likely that some misfortune fell upon the young noblewoman concurrently with the five martial guardians because of the simultaneous instalment of all six tombs, but whether they died by an act of cruelty, politics, or plague, one cannot be certain. Bickerstaff made no further conjectures as he removed his hand from the key.

Cob's insistent beatings upon the door grew weaker and stopped altogether. The sound of the man's footsteps crunched along the perimeter cinder path rich with early rime, and the rector hurried to the vestry exit to ensure it too was locked. Grabbing an iron snuffer, he extinguished the outer sconces in preparation for his recreations back at the rectory once the unhappy fellow outside had given up and returned to his hut. There would be time in the morning to evict the man to some other location and tear down the shanty in readiness for a summerhouse he had planned to erect from the memorial funds. He would prove the villager's superstitions to be mere phantoms from a less civilised, but not more chivalrous, age.

The small vestry door was locked, and there was no sound from the path outside. A noise, as though from a heavy object scraping against stone jerked him back to wariness and the chancel. The tall candles on the five tombs burned once more in defiance and the cold, hard edge of the snuffer's handle bit into his palm as he feared Cob had somehow unlocked the door with a spare key or gained entrance by some unknown means to chastise him. The sound of grating stone continued and was joined by similar sounds nearby, but he saw the heavy oak door shut fast, locked and unmoving.

He placed a hand on the central tomb, listening to the scraping that seemed to come from all around him. The moon broke out from a gauze of high cloud, clear and radiant, setting the floor of the nave and transept junction ablaze with glittering mica bejewelled with projected coloured shards from the surrounding stained glass. The sound intensified, like a millstone released to its daily grind, and Bickerstaff saw the wobble of the candle on the nearest tomb, its bobbing flame and turbulent smoke set in gentle motion by the sliding of the heavy slab of one of the recumbent knights. It swung, inch by inch, to one side revealing a dark opening, from which a boney hand emerged.

All other lights in the church were suddenly extinguished, plunging the walls into darkness leaving only the five candles on the tombs to illuminate a pool of pale light. He twisted like a cornered animal to see the feet and sword tips of each of the encircling effigies turn to face him knowing that Cob, or any man living, was not present to aid him. The grinding ceased and the silence that followed rooted him to the spot, but the reprieve was temporary and replaced by the scraping of metal against coarse stone, and the tinkling, as of many steel rings, echoing from within the sarcophagi. Gripping onto the tomb of Lady Catherine with his free hand he trembled, momentarily distracted from the fleshless, armour-rusted arms and skulls lank with wisps of colourless hair, that emerged about him.

A moonlit shadow from the northern window beat against the glass. The outline of Cob ceased in its attempts to break the rector from his paralysis, and he crossed himself before becoming a mere observer of the events that unfolded. Bickerstaff trembled as he backed away from the skeletal guardians, fully wakened from their undead slumber and oath, chain mail steel shivering with animated readiness. Eyes that once beheld the light were long decayed and nothing but emotionless empty sockets stared back. The remains of tattered leather jerkins hung torn and mouldy beneath rivulets of rusting rings that loosened and fell with every boot scraping footfall towards him.

Swinging round, Bickerstaff's snuffer swung into the tarnished shield of a revenant knight, smiting the steel like a medieval mace. Its companion joined him to block any escape back to the vestry. As the clang of battle resounded once more within the sacred place, the three shambling knights before him advanced, swords part raised to cut off the way forward. The five candles flared like a firework fountain, receding in rapid retirement to their sockets having expended their energy from the wax in moments that would have sustained them for many days. Bickerstaff struck blindly outwards with the snuffer as the light intensified and consumed him.

Cob shielded his eyes and fell from the exterior window ledge onto the leaned barrow beneath before racing off to spend days wandering upon the moor, sleeping rough. Finally, through extreme hunger, he was cajoled back to the village to face questions over the missing rector. All he would say, until his final confession to an antecedent of the present vicar, was that the candle knights had spirited him away.

That the rector was gone was greeted with genuine relief, but the authorities were duty bound to discover whether this was because of some mischief, so they conducted a short enquiry that ended in the fantastical and unreliable. What remained unexplained was how the church, whose battered vestry door was undergoing repair from the forced entry, could be locked from the inside without persons within being present, dead or alive. The mystery of several rusted iron rings and newly gouged scratches upon the flagstones was uncomfortably dismissed as agricultural in origin and probably caused by sharp metal implements carelessly dragged across the floor. It was agreed that the rector's name and memory of his disappearance would not be mentioned further, or despoil the honours board within the church. One thing remembered by those now ancient in years, but young at the time of his death was that Cob never set foot inside again and was housed in the comfortable barn of a childless farming couple to scare rooks and tie stooks for the rest of his days.

My learned friend left a respectful pause at the close of the present vicar's tale. The notion that Bickerstaff had been 'spirited away' for his misdeeds was absurd, but that a cover-up had occurred and foul-play by local men had led to the unpopular rector's demise was a distinct possibility. Perhaps the cleric's anxiety was a response to the fear of murderous parishioners? While this did not appear to account for the villagers' unease, Simmons consoled his companion, knowing that he was well-liked and much admired.

Correspondence continued between the two men over many years until the dry summer of 1955 brought them once more into each other's company. The intense drought heralded a letter and accompanying photograph from the vicar describing subsidence in the central nave further widening the historic crack in Lady Catherine's tomb. Given the delicate feeling that still existed within the village toward the d'Aubernons and the concern that unchecked, the damage could become extensive, Simmons returned to Compton Brierley to revisit his nervous friend.

The church appeared to be in decline and the vicar apologetically, through no fault of his own, described the reduction in the village's size. Holiday homes were becoming a vacant and popular addition, services were monthly because of a lack of attendance, and the funds used to make the earlier repairs had strangled the golden goose that had once laid its eggs. Income now trickled in as costs poured out. What was much in evidence was a musty, mouldy smell Simmons was well-accustomed to from his formative years spent knee-deep in archaeological layers.

The subsidence in the floor of the d'Aubernon tomb had cleanly separated a modest triangular corner from the main edifice following the line of the post-war crack. A clear half-inch scar wounded the side panels affected that widened towards the lightly suspended lid. Simmons commended the vicar for the stacks of pennies pressed into place to prevent the heavy slab from snapping under its great weight. Both men noted the fine line that had run along the surface of the sleeping figure, crossing her forearm, her shoulder, and finally across her exposed neck like a sharp cut. They glanced at each other but spoke of it no further.

The vicar had not dared to illuminate the interior and had only recently that afternoon removed an altar cloth to dissuade the overly curious from peering within. He did consent to hold a powerful torch while Simmons made a cursory examination of the void with one eye pressed against the widest portion of the crack. The light was knocked from the cleric's hand as my professionally curious friend recoiled like a tightly wound spring, falling onto his back and paddling with his arms and legs as though to get away from the shock of what he had observed. I say shock, for the professor was a man used to archaeological and human remains and was hardened against what I, or you, may describe as 'fright'. Helped to his feet, Simmons dusted off his jacket and corduroys with an embarrassed blush. What he had seen would soon become apparent, but for the moment all he revealed was that he had looked into the eye-socketed remains of a skull, upright and not laid out as expected. There was also something else.

It was not the skin-starved face of a medieval noble-woman; it was a modern man.

Unable to be dissuaded by the vicar, the professor set about the modification of a series of small, lock pick-like tools he carried for the cleaning of artefacts. In a few minutes, a broken, mirrored fragment found within the vestry was gummed to an extendable rod, bent to perform in the manner of a dentist's mirror. He returned to the tomb, opened the page of his notebook, and sharpened his pencil. The vicar warily switched on the beam for a second time.

Simmons was a supremely talented artist, and his sketches recording the finds within the ash layers at Stabiae are worthy of a gallery of their own. Scribbling and scratching with constant attention for the best part of an hour, the torch bearer witnessed the emergence of the interior of the tomb. Silence accompanied the work until he laid down his pencil and rose stiffly from the crochet-stitched prayer kneeler to stare and analyse the detailed drawing in its entirety for the first time.

I have the faded and much-creased sheet on my lap as part of his belongings bequeathed to me. It shows not one, but two interments. Huddled against the corner lie the partially decomposed skeletal remains of a middle-aged man, knees drawn to his chest and arms pressed against the interior wall, somewhat reminiscent of a Bronze Age beaker burial. His grave goods are few but telling. A clutched and rusted rod-like object, hooded at its terminus, suggests its original purpose as a candle-snuffer. Following confirmation from the vicar, his tattered black cassock and notched collar infer we are witnessing the missing rector. If that were not shocking enough, scratches in the stone beside the hunched figure suggest an attempt to escape, possibly by the use of the snuffer as a makeshift chisel or prizing bar. The conclusions are obvious and horrific.

He was not entombed in death.

The two men who first considered the evidence twenty years ago in that cool church chamber arrived at the same conclusion that I did – the vicar's apprehension for his position, and his very life was historically well-founded for a man buried alive and those responsible must have had many skilled and tooled masons to raise the lid without significant damage. The marks on the floor, still present if one knows what to look for, may explain something of the enquiry's agricultural explanation as to their origin, and Cob's testimony could have been arranged, altered or his memory of the events tainted by suggestion and reinforcement by the perpetrators. For all the circular reasoning that arises, one question remains, and I put it to my dear friend before his final revelation:

Why would the villagers, sympathetic to the church, and the d'Aubernon's (if not the rector) commit such sacrilege and go to so much effort? The moors that surround Compton Brierley are extensive and a simple kidnap, murder, and burial at some lonely and desolate bog would have been a swift and less callous affair than the air-sealed, slow suffocation that secured Bickerstaff's fate.

The answer, most disturbingly, arises from the observation that the man was buried alive, but not alone, and a closer examination of the drawing so skilfully rendered by my talented friend. Indeed, he pointed out, as I do now, his interpretation of the arrangement of the other body that shared the tomb, most surely that of Lady Catherine d'Aubernon.

An older, mostly recumbent skeleton is partially obscured by the wood-wormed sawdust of a medieval coffin that once housed the remains. The bones are somewhat scattered from below the pelvis, evidence of some possible ingress by mice from the compacted clay below, but the upper torso and part of the skull remain partly bound in a waxed cerecloth. The wrapped humerus and lower forearms are no longer at the side of the body but outstretched towards the remnants of the rector, their knuckled, claw-like fingers erupting from the mouldy burial cloth to drape, or clutch, at the man's neck.

I wonder now if slow suffocation, mercifully, did not claim Henry Bickerstaff, but something far more terrifying and ancient.

There was little discussion on the matter when I invested Simmons' legacy to the vicar though we both took comfort that nothing had occurred following the hasty rendering of the crack by the practical professor who could turn his hand to most things. That the secret should remain so had long been established to avoid unnecessary disturbance or curiosity, and prayers were said, in private, for the soul of the unfortunate man.

I hope that my friend, and other agencies, find rest as I continue to ruminate and reflect on the matter. How quickly fancy can turn into unease and uncertainty, one's worldview tested by the merest glance at a piece of paper.

One thing upon which the present vicar and I agree wholeheartedly is that the name of Bickerstaff, and all it represents, should remain absent and forgotten, to die out and join the ghosts of the place if you will pardon the expression. I am agnostic about supernatural malevolence or otherworldly matters, but that does not mean I am wholly unaffected by them. Even now, years afterwards, a bright candle on a winter's eve sparks the memory and I stare deeper into the bobbing flame for longer than is natural. I have never returned to Compton Brierley to check that the charity of Professor Simmons is still doing its work but unkept traditions, like candlelight, often burn out.

I only hope that those in remote and forgotten places such as this will stay kept and lit for eternity.

ENTWINED

Toby puffed into the bright midday sunshine, breath steaming from the energetic incline of the wide pedestrian track of The Gallop. The tributary path of the great avenue of Windsor Great Park was quiet, even for a weekday in February, but the green ground was busy with the business of spring's awakening. The distant drone of traffic circumnavigating the major towns was suddenly drowned out by an early bumblebee, bustling and buzzing among the snowdrops and aconites that clothed the wooded margins, the remnants of the once formidable and extensive Saxon hunting grounds.

A stag bolted from the spinney to his left and thundered away, setting off the rooks in the ancient champions, trees whose mighty age afforded titles once given out to such men that hunted and conquered nearby, nigh on three hundred thousand noontides past.

The rooks raucously returned to roost as he crossed the Battle Bourne on its short trickling route to Russel's pond, knowing that the opening in the plantation, formed by years of secret and superstitious incursion, was close by.

With a glance at the weather-worn sign prohibiting access

and all manner of activities within, he brushed past the encroaching shrub to reach the natural archway and on to a wide, dimly lit clearing wherein sat a great tree, surrounded by a precious moat of leaf mould, spring bulbs and silence. It had once been two mighty ash trees and whether by design or careless forestry, they had grown into each other centuries ago, locked into an ever-growing and consuming embrace. The remains of an old bench sat, mossy and blackened by smuts, rusts and honeydew from beneath the ancient canopy, listing at one corner as though being devoured by several sinuous buttress roots and feeding the silver barked ash tree behind. It had once allowed a fine view of the ride, before rewilding, preservation orders of the great champion tree, and a need to marshal the public and keep order like the feudal lords who once prevailed here had been implemented decades earlier. It also afforded a slippery step up to the lower branches.

Toby tested the time-worn teak with his booted foot, noting that even here against the back of the bench were scoured and incised the names of mortals, doomed to die, scratching out in crude homage to the grand age of the great trees to leave their own piece of immortality. There was little space remaining on the lower reaches of the tree, accessible to all but those determined climbers to reach higher where the bark was softer and easier to cut into with a knife or screwdriver. The vast lower girth was a litany of calloused and cracked, indecipherable scrawls dating back centuries, and an occasional pair of names could be discerned left by those long dead in memoriam of past love, or by those hoping to find it.

Confident that the rotting slat would take his weight for at least one more year, Toby padded the metal object in his back pocket and reached up to grab at the smooth and slippery branch. Struggling momentarily to gain a foothold against a great gall on the trunk, he pulled closer to the trunk, straining to see his marks carved seven years prior above a contorted crook in the lower scaffold-supported branch. Several lactic acid-burning seconds elapsed as he hunted among the alphabets and amorous words of others before he caught his own younger hand.

Toby & Pip '02

Struggling to reach a hand closer to brush against the letters, his fingers dragged across the weeping freshness of the cuts, as though recently carved, or somehow unable to be healed. A glance before his grip began to weaken showed a few other inscriptions, yet there were others more recent in date to his own, already calloused and roughened by a shorter passage of time.

Satisfied that his pilgrimage to the past was complete, he scanned the several feet to safety beneath his feet, stretching downwards to gingerly touch toe to the tilted bench back below. A call from beyond scuppered all attempts at a graceful dismount and he fell backwards, narrowly missing the seat, and onto the soft, composted bed of the forest floor. Fearing a ranger or forester eager to fulfil the threats of the sign on the perimeter, he rose quickly and dusted off his walking trousers and fleece, reorientating himself with the exit for an undignified retreat to the open sky and wide paths of the park.

What he rose to encounter was no ranger.

The man before him leaned upon a polished, silver-barked staff barely shorter than the six and a half feet of its owner. A scarred, pale-skinned hand gripped the smooth wood, difficult to discern where one began and the other ended. His right hand stroked a large grey beard that covered most of the creased and weather-stained face, its wiry thicket tinged at the fringe with encroaching green as though a long time spent outdoors had blurred the line between man and plant. Dark eyes, like the occupied pits of watchful burrows, looked out with a youthful vigour that seemed at odds with his age. Long unkempt dreadlocks, ringed in places with ornately worked copper rings, draped his chiselled face and hung about his chest, open shirted with coarse calico to show a fibrous necklace of winged ash seeds, acorns, and galls. A worn and weary waistcoat, that might have once been dark tweed was threadbare at its margins and curtained by a long leather coat, patched and peeling from long use. Two long legs dressed by the shine of polished and brace-worn mole-skin trousers ended at a pair of supple gaiters, mud-splattered and flared like buttresses in the same material as the coat. The toecaps of black, brogue-like boots, long devoid of shine, peeped like tattooed moles from the depressions in the soft earth caused by the man's great bulk. Shifting a coarsely knitted hold-all to his side, he put a hand to his hip, thumb resting on the inside of a chain-like belt of wooden rings.

Toby stepped back, unsure of the tramp-like, outlandish figure, searching for others that might be lurking in the wood to rob him. London was a stone's throw away, he thought, but those less fortunate than to have a home must make do. The man laid his staff against the tree and sat down on the edge of the bench, causing the sunken end to rise like a rusting revenant from a grave of mouldy leaves and mulch. He sucked at his lips, curiously eyeing him. Flexing his fingers he blew into his fist, and from above a breeze shifted the great trees into a gentle sway, setting the loose woodland debris at his feet astir.

'I thought you were a ranger, but...'

'But what?' said the man in a deep, resonant voice.

Toby avoided the possible indignation and the use of the word tramp, searching for the politically correct term to no avail. He changed tack.

'I don't have any money or anything...'

The giant of a man appeared amused rather than insulted.

'Neither do I; I'm rich in other ways. Are you going to sit down, or have you seen what you came to see, Tobias?'

'You know my name?' said Toby, startled by the use of his formal first name. 'Only my grandmother calls me that.'

With a creak of his thickly set neck against the leather of his lapels, the man glanced up to the lower branch. 'Isn't it plain for all to see up there?'

'There are loads of names up there,' said Toby realising too late that he had already admitted the fact. 'How did you know it was me or which one I was looking for?'

'They all come back, eventually.' His eyes looked Toby up and down, measuring and confirming some hidden suspicion. 'You're a regular; you come back every year.'

Toby folded his arms in front of his fleece feeling suddenly naked in the man's gaze. 'I only come back to remember someone, that's not a crime is it?'

'No. Memory is the currency of life, and you are free to spend it how you please. I've lived here for a very long time and have quite an exchequer.'

'You live in the woods?'

'Yes, for more years than I can count.' Through a patch of thinning coppice, he raised his hand, pointing to the broken view of Windsor Castle and the visitor booth with pop-up coffee caravans in front. 'I was here before that pretty little house over there was built, though it wasn't pretty at the time – great hosts fought to get inside.'

Toby screwed his eyes to discern the specks of coat-clad tourists before the ticket hut. 'I know how it can be on bank holidays.'

The man returned to stroke the tangles from his knotted chin and shook his head in confusion. Considering his reply for a moment, the face relaxed as though graciously abandoning any further explanation or correction.

'What do you do when you aren't visiting sacred groves?'

he said, surveying a discarded drinks bottle nearby with a sad pucker of his lips.

'I'm a historian,' said Toby. 'I teach at the university – I'm a medievalist.'

Suddenly amused, the man's mouth creased into a wide grin, and he patted the seat beside him in invitation. 'A recent branch of study but full of surprises.'

Toby sat down, calmed by the man's gentle nature. His recent lecture the preceding day gave rise to an image from the fourteenth-century chivalric romance. He was glad the green knight before him carried only a staff, and not a great axe.

'No, it's been a serious study for quite some time – since the mid-nineteenth century if you discount *Henry Hallam's 1818 View of the State of Europe*—'

'I meant the medieval period is quite recent,' said the man, not wishing to encourage the enthusiastic academic. 'If you take this ancient landscape, for instance.'

'I suppose so, when you put it like that,' said Toby watching the man rise and place several pieces of faded litter into his woven bag, fibrous like a deep bird's nest.

The sound of an approaching vehicle caused Toby to start, but the man simply raised his head to ponder the two fleece-bound rangers in an ATV driving down The Gallop, oblivious to the trespassers at hand.

'Pinning medals on trees,' scoffed the man, returning to sit down.

'Excuse me?'

He turned and lifted his staff to point at a silver disc identifying the tree behind with a number. 'These two trees deserve a medal, but they were right to give it just one. They cannot be separated except by the calamitous will of nature and not even I, stout and ancient, can change that. People are the same, but they don't realise the importance of a soulmate.'

Toby dug his hands in his pockets, listening to the receding sound of the small 4x4. 'You sound like a marriage guidance counsellor.'

'I've been many things, to many people, mostly like yourself.' The man lifted a whip of a branch, discarded from the tree above, and began to fashion something delicate with his supple fingers. 'Always listening to give those that need a little nudge.'

'Towards what?' Toby watched as the woven heart began to take shape. The man scouted the floor and snipped a single golden aconite with his long, grubby nails from a crushed stem trampled by the young man's fall. He imprisoned the flower within the crafted totem and handed over the completed craftwork to Toby's astonishment.

'Togetherness, mostly.'

Toby turned over the intricate three-dimensional lattice, reaching into his pockets for some change before realising he had already told that lie.

As though being caught red-handed, or red-faced, was enough, the man smiled and waved away his offer.

'Give your heart to the next woman you meet,' he said.

Toby put the wicker object into his breast pocket. 'That's likely to get me arrested, though whoever she is, might make an exception on Valentine's Day.'

'Is that why you returned today?'

'Yes,' he said, grateful and at ease with the talk. 'It's silly I know, but the old story about this being a lovers' tree or wishing tree—it doesn't have to be true to make people happy or be a focal place to remember those that were once here beside me.'

'People still believe, do they?' said the man. 'That's comforting, it's an incredibly old legend. Part of me is very glad we haven't lost all touch with humanity. It's only here, of course, people don't carve their names into that old split oak that's propped up further in the forest, do they? I'm not as mobile as I once was.'

'King Offa's Oak?' said Toby shaking his head. 'That's thirteen hundred years old with bark as thick as the castle's wall. I doubt a chainsaw could carve into that.'

The man winced and tensed momentarily from the suggestion. 'There was once a tree far greater than that and it sired many a bright sapling. It was called Herne's Oak upon a time, and he would ride out on his wild hunt when all the fields about and man's incessant ordering and tidying of nature to suit his own ends was a mere thought. Now that was what I call a forest, all the way to Virgin's water.'

'Virginia water,' corrected Toby watching a squirrel dart among the canopy and bark to mark his territory.

'I prefer its original title when it was a mere stream. A beautiful place, fitting for the first queen of Albion to bear the name Elizabeth.'

'Albion?' said Toby, familiar with the ancient name for Great Britain. 'I take it back; you sound like a Dark Age or classical scholar. Perhaps you should consider a career as a storyteller? My students, not to mention the foreign tourists away at the castle would—'

'I never leave the wood,' he replied. 'There used to be many people to talk to and tell the old stories, but they dwindle as things become...'

Toby waited for the man to finish but seeing his pursed lip and distant gaze he offered a concluding suggestion.

'Forgotten?'

The man brightened and nodded. 'That's the word. We need those that listen and there are precious few of those about. So tell me your story, or at least hers. It's why you came back, isn't it? To see if what you once felt and carved into the tupping tree still exists?'

Toby looked up into the overlapping latticework of branch and twig. 'That old fairy-tale. A mark on the tree will keep true love alive between those whose names are carved into the bark. I scratched Toby and Pip into it because she insisted.'

The man slapped his wide palm against Toby's back. 'Good man, always listen to the female of the species, but you strike me as someone that would have done so with little persuasion.'

'Well, the legend didn't work, did it? I lost touch with her and that's the way life goes.' He dug into his interior pocket and removed his phone. The screen came to life, and he swiped through several screens, aware of the man's fidgeting and disapproving face reflected in the glass.

'Why does man talk into little boxes instead of face to face?'

Toby shrugged. 'We can't always be together, some people on here I've never even met.'

'Therein lies the root of the problem. Man entwines himself with memories of those not present and the intangibility of talk over touch.' The man leaned back and raised his head to bask in a brief beam of sunlight from above. He closed his eyes and lowered to a whisper.

'Patience man, there are names on here that have older claims than yours. They all get settled in time, but it takes like minds to honour the register here.'

'That's very prosaic,' said Toby nudging the man into waking and turning the phone to display his selfie of the younger man, pressed tightly against a smiling girl in what might have been the precursor to a kiss. 'Not to mention difficult when you don't know where someone is. This was one of the last pics I took from a few years ago before we lost touch.'

'Pretty young girl,' said the man. 'Grey eyes – always a good sign. What happened?'

Toby pinched to enlarge her face, caressing the rosy cheek with the side of his thumb. 'Funny, I don't remember the drifting apart, just the beginning and the way I felt about her, and—'

'Still do?' said the man, returning the offer to complete the sentence.

'Yes. I've been back a few times, if I'm being honest, just to see, it was a ridiculous notion if she might be here or had left a message.'

'Perhaps she has and has stubbornly thought the same?'

Toby shook his head and shut down the screen, ready to slide the device back into his shiny, padded outer pocket.

Imperceptibly, the man wiggled his fingers, disguising the motion with a stretch and flexing of his now joined hands.

The phone slid past the pocket flap, silently slipping onto the soft earth through the gaps in the bench. Toby blew on his hands for warmth and got up to look at the crook above.

'Cold for Valentine's Day,' he said, fidgeting with something in his back pocket. He retrieved his hand to reveal a penknife.

'You were going to leave another message, weren't you?'

'Yes.'

'There's no need to. Once carved, never parted – do people still remember that?'

'Some of the older ones do,' said Toby. 'But in my case I think I'm done, time to move on and make new memories. Wherever she is, I'm sure she found someone and is happy. I'm comfortable now knowing that Pip probably hasn't been here since. I need to get going.'

'You'll be back,' said the man, rising to take his staff with a nod of farewell. 'They always come back.'

Toby turned with a brief raise of his hand and followed the makeshift rut to the worn opening in the coppiced hazel.

With a swift movement, the man lifted the phone, bringing it back to life. For a moment, he considered placing it into his bag, but raised himself to a great height to balance the device among the upper branches. Watching Toby disappear back into the sunlight, he bent back his head to see the image of two former lovers shine, fading to black as the lock screen timer barred further enjoyment like a mechanical chaperone. He patted the tree to his left and swung a wide, embracing arm around the lowest branch of its conjoined twin.

Putting his mouth to a hollow in the trunk, ringed like silvery enveloping lips, he whispered, quivering the branches above.

'*Over to you, my dear.*'

Pippa left the lower slopes of Snow Hill and the great mounted statue behind. Few others travelled cross-country, preferring to stick to the grand tree-lined avenue of The Long Walk. For many, the statue of King George III astride his bronze horse at its southern end afforded the finest view back to the standard bearing Windsor Castle over two and a half miles distant. The view from either terminus provided the highlight of a grand walk, but she continued on, drawn to her annual pilgrimage by an absurd romantic sensibility and pausing for a moment of reflection before finding solace in a slice of strawberry shortcake in a Bishopsgate coffee shop.

'*He won't be there, you fool,*' said the humdrum, unromantic voice in her head.

'I know,' she whispered. 'But I need to make certain so I can move on. I won't come again.'

'You said that last year...' mused the voice, receding in scorn.

Leaving the tussocks of the wilder parkland behind, she leapt across the out-flowing stream of the Prince of Wales Pond and followed the minor track to reach the silent, reflecting mere. The afternoon sun made an appearance from beyond a tuft of cumulus, arcing from its high point towards its rest against the western horizon of Cranbourne Chase. Pippa took a final eye-shielding glance at the distant ant-like trail of walkers approaching the monument and backed into the encroaching scrub of the wood beyond.

With warm hands momentarily leaving the comfort of her jacket, she parted several whips and weaved her way through the naturalised plantings, avoiding the early spring flowering bulbs until the sun on her back lost its potency and she emerged into the dusk of the open clearing and the true objective of her walk.

Rejoicing to be suddenly alone and undisturbed she approached the scarred silver melding of the ancient trees and checked around its substantial, shared girth to the bench with its faded plaque to some long-forgotten forester. It looked just as it had done the previous spring, nothing unusual or added to infer he had, or had ever, been.

'Told you...' rose the pedantic, realistic voice.

'I had to know.'

Looking up into the crook above the lowest branch she tested the willingness of the wooden bench to support her weight and leapt for the limb, pulling her lithe frame closer to see if the engraving was still there. Scrabbling with her feet for a foothold she glanced down to see a recent muddy scuff atop a gall and secured her walking shoe upon it to release one arm. She took out her phone and zoomed in on the letters to take a picture, surprised by the freshness of the six-year-old graffiti. Pippa dismounted, kicking away from the trunk to land on two feet and one hand for giggles, superhero style, among the soft leaf litter and leucojum flowers.

'I wish I was that supple, these days,' said a kindly voice, accompanied by an old woman emerging from the rear of the trees, stunted and leaning on a polished stick. Warted hands, one upon another, gripped the rounded ball of the handle, polished smooth like the bony joint of a wooden shoulder. A jovial softness in her scarred, weather-beaten face shone and shifted into a broad, friendly smile and she twitched her protruding, skin-tag-laden nose like a shrew as Pippa rose to her feet. Black knotted balls, like mistletoe-d burrs, nested in her shaggy, silver hair with the memory of youthful colour and long-abandoned combing. At first sight, she appeared grubby, but this was deceiving as little in the way of muck or mud attached itself to either her letter-tattooed forearms, face or clothing. A long, intricately embroidered cloth under-garment, which might once have passed for a cotton dress, was obscured by a distressed leather apron pinned here and there with coarse ornamental items such as flakes of bark, chain rings, and sections of bracket fungi that had been so cleverly fixed to appear to be part of the material itself. Curiously, and above a cinched ribbon waist belt of faded hessian, the apron progressively gave way to smoother, silvery silk, etched with blackened, streaked lines like the lenticels of the tree behind.

'It's still there my little acrobat,' she said, wriggling her fingers on the top of the stick and shuffling forward to sit on the edge of the bench. Pippa recovered from the sudden startle and made ready to go, annoyed that the sacred space, her inner sanctum to memories of a happier time had somehow been defiled by another. She turned to go, berating herself for foolishness and eager to avoid any embarrassing conversation with the odd-looking woman, but only found herself returned to the bench where she sat down, engaging the woman as though bidden.

'What is?' she asked.

'The memory of something or someone dear to you.' Unseen, the woman tapped the end of her stick into the earth setting the nodding heads of the nearby snowdrops ringing for her amusement. Pippa felt slight pins and needles in her feet and stamped her shoes to relieve the sensation, likely, she thought, caused by her flamboyant dismount.

Pippa scoffed. 'I wouldn't go that far.' She held out her phone, snatching a glance of the recent image before burying the device in her dark green parka.

The woman shuffled across, invading her space and Pippa shifted away eager to avoid any bad breath or body odour of a seemingly unwashed person but finding only an earthy, wholesome smell, slightly sweet as though a scent of fading flowers still lingered about a bright spring day.

'So who is he?' said the woman, turning to look fully into her face for the first time with ferrety eyes, 'this boy whose name lies next to yours but who is no longer dear to you?'

Pippa caught herself staring at the curious bunions, scars and callouses on the woman's ruddy cheeks before blinking away to avoid any embarrassment. She looked down at her shoes as though weighing up the option to take flight but was suddenly aware of the bare feet to her left, toes playfully clenching with joy into the black earth. What at first appeared to be dirt and moss upon the tops of her scabby, calloused feet proved to be curious tattoos of aconites and small forget-me-nots wreathing her ankles and disappearing beneath the lichen-encrusted hem of her dress.

'I didn't say he wasn't' said Pippa, suddenly aware of the sudden and intimate interest in her affairs. She considered getting up and running away, fearful of what – a woman in the woods? Pippa had as much right to be there as anyone else, or for as long as the woman did not press or ask for anything.

'Nothing to be frightened of,' said the woman, reading her thoughts, and pointing to her bare feet. 'I wouldn't hurt a flower.'

'Why are you interested in what may or may not be carved into the lovers' tree?'

The woman smiled, creasing the sides of her mouth into radiating lines. 'Is that what they call the tupping tree these days?' She slapped her thighs and answered Pippa's question.

'Because they all come back eventually.'

'Who do?'

'People like you and your soul mate above the first branch. Once carved, never parted...'

Pippa shook her head. 'What are you – some kind of homeless agony aunt?'

'I've been many things in my time, but never rude, and never homeless.'

'Sorry,' said Pippa, reddening from the suddenness of her outburst. 'It's just that I like to spend time on my own in places like this, especially at this time of year on a day like today.'

'The feast of Lupercalia and the coming of spring,' said the woman, flashing her eyes and gently shuffling sideways to nudge into Pippa's arm. 'Always gets the sap rising.'

'No, Valentine's Day,' she replied. 'I'm not into the tat and tack that surrounds it, but I like to think there's a good and honest reason for making a day devoted to something very few of us really experience for long enough.'

The woman drew a heart on the ground with the tip of her stick. 'So you come here to rekindle a memory on a day whose meaning still resonates despite the passage of time?'

'That's one way to put it, though you could just say I come here after every failed relationship, just to remind myself of someone who I felt different about. My misadventures in love happen so regularly that I think I might get myself a plaque made for this bench here.'

The woman creaked in her leather apron as she leaned back onto the bench. 'I wouldn't do that,' she said. 'At least, not yet. Tell me about him if you think you want to?'

Pippa leaned forward and rubbed her hands together. 'His name was Toby, and we met at a friend's party. We got on really well and we came here to carve our names into the lovers' tree.' She glanced up to see the woman's head cocked slightly to one side, listening intently.

'It's a legend that is supposed to mean you stick with each other,' said Pippa. 'I thought I'd found 'the one' until we both took jobs a little distance from each other. He had to go away for a year and when he got back, I'd moved further away, and the distance became an issue – neither of us had a car or much money.'

'You drifted apart?' said the woman, using her stick to drag a long, lithe ash stem to her feet. She lifted the thin branch and tested its suppleness with her calloused fingers.

'I don't remember the end, like finishing a chocolate bar or coming home from a holiday – you only remember the best parts at the beginning or in the middle.'

The woman frowned and shook her head as though missing the allegory. She began to bend the whippy growth into a rough ball, spitting down the green, sappy growth with her brown, chisel-like nails to pair and split the twig.

'Anyway, I assumed he'd found someone else and—'

Pippa watched as the woman worked the little weave back and forth.

'Pass me one of those anemone flowers, just over there, dear,' said the woman. 'But please continue.'

Pippa shrugged and wandered toward the spot that the

bony, twig-like finger was pointing to, unsure which flower to concentrate on among the colourful spring carpet.

'The blue one dear – just a single flower.'

Passing the flower across, Pippa continued, watching as the woman worked the bloom into the ball leaving a broad flat tail of woven excess to form the shape of an ash seed.

'There isn't much more to tell. We both gradually saw each other less and less until I sat by the phone refusing to pick it up first, waiting to see if he still wanted me in his life.'

The woman lightly grabbed her wrist and turned over the palm placing the small woven samara into Pippa's keeping. 'You realise how stubborn men are? He was probably daring you to do the same.'

The finely worked seed-shaped basket containing the bright blue flower reminded Pippa of a happy memory, and she smiled with a snort. 'I hadn't thought of that. He used to bring me flowers but always yellow once he found out it was my favourite colour. But that's all in the past now – "you don't know what you've got till it's gone" and all that.' She handed back the beautiful seed lattice, but the woman held up a hand.

'Give it to the next man you meet,' she said. 'They are always difficult to find a gift for, aren't they?'

Pippa smiled and got out a pack of cigarettes. 'I've no cash on me otherwise I'd buy it for myself, not for some worthless fella. It's so pretty, thank you.' She offered the open packet across.

The woman visibly flinched. 'Not for me dear, I've what you might call a phobia around fire.'

'I was giving up anyway,' said Pippa putting them away. 'Perhaps I should do the same with men.'

The woman sighed and tapped Pippa innocently on the knee. 'I'm fortunate never to have had my heart broken, though I had to keep a tight grip on the beggar until both of us grew so old as to be inseparable.'

'You're still married, then?'

The woman smirked and winked. 'More, entwined with each other than anything formal.'

'Like the trees?' said Pippa, twisting round. 'Is that why you've come here as well, to remember?'

'In part but I'm here now mostly to do a little nudging.'

Pippa instinctively shuffled away wondering if the meaning meant something more than a push against her ribs with the woman's bare and knotted elbow. It was scaly with a depression as though a ripping cut or tear had healed over, long ago.

The woman laughed, understanding the look of concern on Pippa's face. 'I'm too old for that,' she said. 'Our children were once plentiful, though few will ever reach our age again in this world of men.'

Pippa looked curiously at her face raised suddenly to bathe in a late low sunbeam. 'Are you alright?' she said.

'Yes, thank you. I'm just waiting.'

'For what?'

'The best part.' She smiled into the sunlight and up into the canopy of the carved tree. 'Bringing people back together – it's his turn, but he knows how much I adore seeing the endings...'

Pippa was about to ask a further question when the ring tone of a phone began its tuneful timbre from somewhere above, breaking the stillness.

'What the—' said Pippa, narrowing the search to a brightly lit screen suspended between several interlaced lower branches. Rising, she jumped to dislodge the phone, catching it and raising it to her ear as it connected. 'Hello?'

'Hello, Toby? – sorry, do I have the wrong number, who is this?'

'My name's Pippa, but this isn't my—'

'Pippa!' exclaimed the woman's voice on the other end of the line. 'Toby didn't tell me you were back together. I'm so pleased and I'm just so glad he finally picked up the courage to get back in touch. I do so miss our little chats; Derek will be thrilled—'

'Mrs Hurst?' said Pippa, 'Is that you?'

'Well, of course. I was calling to see how Toby was feeling about today, being as he used to be so down about breaking up with you that he saw no one seriously again, he blamed himself—'

Pippa put a hand to her other ear to drown out the sound of a plane on final approach to Heathrow. She got up and wandered around the tree. 'Mrs Hurst, I don't think you realise—'

'Oh, and his sister will be so pleased,' continued the rush of exuberance from the phone. 'You got on so well together.'

Pippa completed her circumnavigation of the great bole of the tree to find the woman gone, the only sign of her presence a single series of marks made by her stick. They appeared to follow her route around the tree.

'Are you still there, Pippa? Let me speak to Toby...'

She rushed around the tree, anti-clockwise but not a soul, other than herself stood in the clearing.

Even as she answered the quick-fire questions coming from a woman last spoken to years earlier, she looked up to see the figure of a familiar man racing through the wood via a natural opening in the far margins of the trees.

'He's here...I can't believe... he's actually here...'

Her heartbeat rose, studying the features of the man she knew to be her former friend and lover. She disconnected the call and lowered the phone, glimpsing a happy smiling couple on the screen she knew all too well.

Toby halted, out of breath, eyes wide with the realisation of who stood before him, his lost phone in her hand.

'Pippa, is it really you?' he asked. 'How—'

'I... I just came for a walk and your phone went off and...' She held out the device, still showing them both clutching each other tightly. Fewer lines were upon their happy faces, perhaps, but they were still instantly recognisable. 'That's sweet,' she said walking over to hand the phone into his gloved hand.

'Sorry, you probably think it's a bit creepy,' he said avoiding the sudden awkwardness but snatching glimpses of her face as he blushed away his embarrassment. 'You grew your hair – it suits you.'

'And you cut yours, she said getting out her mobile and swiping to the home screen to display the same photo. 'I'm a bit creepy, too.'

Toby laughed. 'I never believed that coming back here like a right wally all these years—'

'Would eventually pay off?' she said, pointing to the trees behind and putting away her phone. 'To tell you the truth, I'd kind of given up hope of ever seeing you again.'

'Hope?' Toby's phone began to ring. 'It's my mother,' he said rolling his eyeballs. 'Wanting to wish me Happy Valentine's Day in the absence of anyone else doing it.' He took off his gloves and was about to answer when he was interrupted by her open palm containing the woven ash seed.

'Happy Valentine's Day?' said Pippa.

Toby silenced the call and reached into his pocket to retrieve the heart, placing it in his own.

'Happy Valentine's Day, Pip.'

They glanced at both items and the flowers within.

'You remembered I like yellow,' she said. 'Or at least the woman that made it did; don't even pretend you made this.'

'It wasn't a woman; it was a man I met here earlier.

Strange fellow, broad as a house, like someone dressed up as the Ghost of Christmas Present or Little John or—'

'Dressed like they were ready for A Midsummer Night's Dream? I had the same experience, but it was a woman; she was here only a moment before you arrived.'

Toby nodded. 'Maybe there's a theatre production somewhere?'

Pippa screwed her lips, turning over the heart in her hands. 'I'm not so sure. Were you told to give this to the first woman you met?'

'Yes,' he said, 'but I never believed it would be you.' He stepped closer. 'I owe you an apology all those years ago and I can't understand why I let things slip between us, but I want you to know that whatever coincidence has allowed me to say this to you right now, I want you to know that I have never stopped thinking about you.'

He blushed and retreated his hands to his pockets, watching as her startled face melded back into a broad smile.

'*Now, what do you say?*' she said to the naysayer in her head. There came no answer, so she offered the man before her one instead as well as her ringless hand.

'I might have thought about you too,' she said. 'Once or twice, I mean.'

'Want to grab a coffee, just to catch up?' he said. 'I've got a car and can drop you off anywhere later if you have plans?'

Pippa grabbed at the lure and unspoken question.

'I'm not with anyone, so I accept. There's a great place in Bishopsgate that does this amazing shortcake—'

A sudden sound like the clicking of a lock caused her to twist around. The last light of the sun shone upon the exact spot of the tree wherein was incised their original tryst, and with the dying of the last sunbeam of Lupercalia, fiery letters appeared outlining their names. Cauterised by a hidden hand and sealed with sudden gold, the letters faded after a short moment. Even from the short distance, Pippa could see the fresh weeping cuts had healed and calloused over as though they have been there for many years, joining the others to whom the tree had fulfilled its bargain.

Pippa looked into the astonished eyes of her long-lost love, finding that whether subconsciously or by some other bidding, their hands were now clasped firmly together. Toby glanced down and smiled as though realising the same significance.

'I think I have some explaining to do,' he said. 'At least you might be able to make sense of what happened to me two hours ago and what we have just seen.'

'Same,' whispered Pippa, raising a hand in farewell to the trees. 'Let's leave them be. I think they have earned some privacy.'

She squeezed his hand, and he led her through the natural arch until the trees were almost out of sight.

A final creak caused them to turn revealing the two ash champions framed by an honour guard of younger trees. Stunted and twisted by age, their great branches entwined around each other as though in a leaning embrace, one thousand years in the making.

The End

GET EXCLUSIVE CONTENT

Thank you for reading *Firelight and Frost*.

Building a relationship with my readers is the very best thing about writing. I send monthly newsletters with details on new releases, special offers and other news relating to my books.

Sign up to my readers' group at www.jtcroft.com or by scanning the QR code below, and I'll send you further stories in my collection, *Free Spirits,* exclusive to my reader's group– you can't get this anywhere else.

ABOUT THE TALES

The Skerry Rose

Inspired by Kopakonan (The Seal Wife) by Hans Pauli Olsen, this nine-foot-tall bronze and stainless steel statue depicts a selkie emerging from the waters of Mikladalur Harbour on Kalsoy, one of the Faroe Islands. Seeking to breathe new life into old legends, I took inspiration from the isolated rocks upon which she walks, shedding her sea form to seek a human mate, and merged her with another passion of mine – difficult-to-reach and atmospheric, lonely places with stories of their own.

The wild and treacherous Hebridean seas, from experience, was an obvious choice, but placing a lighthouse as a central character comes from my love of Stevenson's "candles", designed and built across the north-west of Scotland three generations before the most famous, Robert Louis, wrote the best-known island tale of all. Trying to avoid obvious tropes of missing keepers or 'lights' coming on in abandoned places, I indulged my fantasy for stories within places that have the power to affect the present by the blending of half-remembered myth and fact, distant enough in time to be unclear, but not so distant as to remove all trace of truth within it. Unfinished business is common in supernatural tales, but my sentimental twist, I hope, resolves a tale that leaves a salty but satisfying taste in the mouth. If not, you can always wash it out with the finest shipwrecked whisky...

Moondance

An unabashed attempt at a 'statue' story – a grown-up version of *Moondial* without time-slippage but not without time-consequence. I return to flirt with immortality, the consequence of destiny, and the grey area between good and evil to suggest that the best 'monsters' are those that we feel some sympathy towards, those that but for a change in circumstance or the honouring of a debt, may have trodden a different path.

I enjoyed the notion of two disenchanted and disinherited 'noble' men who ultimately regain their standing by combined actions that address the faults of the past, with each having lost something pertinent and personal, connected but each at opposites within society. Perhaps when the odds are against us, all it takes to tip the scales in our favour is someone else on our side with as much to lose, or with as little to gain.

The Soul Clock

Written as a Christmas love letter to my beloved Worcester, this damsel in distress tale allowed me the indulgence to pepper the story with locations and imagery from this most historic and beautiful of places. If you visit, look out for the corner antique shop next to the Cathedral that has many fine old clocks in the window...

Originally an idea from the nearby market town where I live, there is a 'shop' that presumably acts as storage and an excuse for one retired man's obsession with old clocks. A number is attached to the window to call and arrange a viewing of anything of interest within, though whether the owner would part with any of his timepieces is another matter. We Englishmen are a nation of collectors, so I suspect not.

Unashamedly a romantic, adventurous winter 'ghost' story, it ticks all my 'tocks' and that is enough.

Misrule

A dark fairytale with a pinch of pied piper, where the small and caring actions of a seemingly insignificant person rules the fate of many. The Lord of Misrule was generally a working man or minor official appointed to be in charge of Christmas revelries, which often included drunkenness and wild partying. Part master of ceremonies, organiser of the diversions and dancing, and showman, he was 'crowned' and given temporary leave to entertain the real lords before him.

This tale sparked into life during a visit to a Jacobean manor house, traditionally decorated for Christmas, where I learned of the custom and of the hospitality afforded to strangers and wanderers abroad at that season. I ask you the question that arose in my mind as I gazed into the fragrant applewood fire of the great hall:

Could there be someone or 'something' out there, still,

that tests and judges the fellowship and charity of mankind from time to time, blessing or damning according to the spirit of the season?

Or more to the point, should there be?

One More Day

Caer Caradoc is the steep, volcanic rock-crowned sentinel that broods over Church Stretton and the surrounding Shropshire hills. A popular walking area in the otherwise underpopulated county that straddles England and Wales, it has a 'wildwood' feel to the landscape and the ruinous castles, standing stones, myths and legends, many of which are Arthurian or from the Welsh Mabinogion (a Dark age saga).

When I was younger, I made the trip to the gently sloping southern flank for a moonlit, snowy sojourn to listen to the calling tawny owls. In a field, just before the path steepens to the summit I was following a single set of booted prints, neatly defined by the recent snowfall. I trod within the prints to save myself some effort and halfway across the field, the prints stopped suddenly, and I walked on before I realised I was alone and the first to cross since the snow had fallen. I headed back, avoiding the prints when I re-encountered them to check if the walker had not turned around and followed their steps back to the stile. They had not.

The prints were one-directional, until those that I had marred, so I turned once more to find the last set made by the previous man (the prints were booted, deep and quite large.) Apart from my own, there was no sign or altering of his course. They simply stopped.

My impressionable teenage mind ranged between alien abduction (obviously) and the ghosts of Roman legionaries that supposedly haunt the hills (probably). I've always wondered what happened to the owner of those prints, and this tale offers one explanation.

Flash Powder

Taking something too far knowing that it is wrong, especially for financial gain is bound to lead to unforeseen consequences and this story of the breaking of friendship, with a twist that bites as keenly as the cold that permeates it is no exception. From the beginning, I knew it would not turn out well, and I wanted to use cold as an allegory as well as an outside influence. As the temperature warms up outside, the true chill begins, and the relationship cools markedly.

The fiery, defiant words that burn in the closing remarks were written very early and originally opened the tale, but I prefer the ending of the main tale as it is, sudden and shocking and the ultimate fate of the otherwise happy pair, uncertain – as it should be in a cautionary tale about knowingly benefitting from others' grief.

The Order of the Candle

I am a consummate daydreamer. Ideas and fantasies play out like small scenes that occasionally make it onto the page begging for a plot or reason to exist. There is a constant clamour of ideas locked away in some vast, noisy archive in my head, each one with variations on 'Me, next!' Sometimes several of these whimsies get stitched together, fitting like jigsaws into a cohesive story.

During a visit to a church whose name I cannot recall, I came across an honours board missing the name of one its former rectors, and at Rame, at the end of Whitsand Bay in Cornwall, there are large, pillared candles that stand within another pretty church interior. They are spiralled with red ribbon, and I imagined them sparking to life trying to tell me something and rapidly burning away while time stood still. The circular arrangement of tombs in the story is likely influenced by the Temple in London, where crusader knights lie within a central, circular church.

Perhaps the most traditional 'ghost' story of this collection, it has, unashamedly, an M. R. James vibe combined with elements from my favourite writer of the genre, E. Nesbit, in particular *Man-Size in Marble*. I hope you found the ending as surprising and unsettling as I did because I did not expect it either.

Entwined

A closing tale should be a happy and poignant one. It began with an image of two trees entwined and the words "*a thousand-year embrace*", a noble pursuit if one only had the time.

I have a romantic association with places and return to spots which hold the positive memory of some emotion once experienced or a person once known. I wonder if others do the same and if they only just miss each other by an hour. Perhaps all they need is a little nudge and bizarre company to bring them back together?

J. T. Croft
November 2022

ALSO BY J. T. CROFT

Maiden Point

A House of Bells

Midnight's Treasury

High Spirits

"Dead Brilliant"

⭐⭐⭐⭐⭐

"Well written. Fascinating and original"

⭐⭐⭐⭐⭐

"Beautifully dark and bittersweet"

⭐⭐⭐⭐⭐

ABOUT THE AUTHOR

J. T. Croft is the author of bittersweet and sentimental
Gothic fiction, supernatural mystery and ghostly tales. He
doesn't believe in spirits, but that doesn't mean they don't
believe in him.
For more information:
www.jtcroft.com

I hope you enjoyed reading this book as much as I loved
writing it. If you did, I'd really appreciate you leaving me a
quick review on whichever platform you prefer. Reviews are
extremely helpful for any author, and even just a line or two
can make a big difference. I'm independently published, so I
rely on good folks like you spreading the word!

facebook.com/jtcroftauthor
twitter.com/jtcroftauthor
instagram.com/jtcroftauthor

Made in the USA
Columbia, SC
22 December 2022